Unafraid

Books by Michael Griffo

UNNATURAL

UNWELCOME

UNAFRAID

Published by Kensington Publishing Corp.

Unafraid

AN ARCHANGEL ACADEMY NOVEL

michael griffo

KENSINGTON PUBLISHING CORP.

www.kensingtonbooks.com

K TEEN BOOKS are published by

Kensington Publishing Corp.
119 West 40th Street
New York, NY 10018

ISBN-13: 978-0-7582-5340-8
ISBN-10: 0-7582-5340-0

First Kensington Trade Paperback Printing: March 2012
10 9 8 7 6 5 4 3 2 1

Printed in the United States of America

Thanks to my entire family—
from Aunt Marie to Shawna C.
And especially Aunt Ann, who has emerged
to become my biggest fan.

one drop
two drops
three drops
four

nothing is like
it was before

lives have been shattered
secrets revealed

will the world be destroyed?
or will it be healed?

prologue

Outside, the earth was asleep.

All of Archangel Academy was under a spell. No creature, human or otherwise, stirred, and the only sounds that penetrated the darkness were gentle, calm, and soothing. The sighs of the midsummer breeze, the whispers of the leaves and the tall blades of grass as they swayed in the faint wind, and the collective breath of the students who were sleeping in their beds, the few who resided here before the official start of the school semester, were all that could be heard. It was a melody that became even more beautiful when it started to rain.

As the first drops fell from the sky, Michael stirred in his sleep. He didn't wake up, not completely, but he was roused by the arrival of the familiar sound and the fresh, invigorating scent. Drop after drop after drop of water fell against the windowpane, creating a lazy rhythm, a lullaby that seeped into Michael's dream, making him feel comforted, protected, loved.

Underneath the cotton sheets his hand instinctively reached out for Ronan's, not stopping until it touched warm flesh and their fingers intertwined. Even while sleeping the boys knew their destiny, knew that their bodies, like their souls, were meant to be joined together, interwoven, one. They had no idea that it was a belief that would soon be put to a test.

A roar of thunder erupted from the sky, disrupting the peace that had cradled the campus. The rumbling continued, growing louder, louder, louder as it spread out, invading building after building until it reached St. Florian's. When another wave of thunder exploded, Michael woke, startled, unsure of where he was, unsure of what had created the noise, unsure as to why he had been ripped from the serenity of his dream. He looked over and was surprised to see that Ronan was still sleeping, completely unaffected by the harsh intrusion. Michael wished he could be so lucky.

He waited a few moments until his breathing returned to normal and then quietly got out of bed, flinching when his feet touched the floor. Even though it was the end of June the floor was cold, and as he stood before the window he shivered. He crossed his arms against his bare chest and felt chilled air pierce through the thin material of his pajama pants and swirl up and around his legs. He didn't have to look out the window to know something wasn't right, but when he did he saw that his fears were confirmed. As far as his eyes could see, the only thing they saw was water.

Racing to the other window in the room, Michael looked out, and the view was the same, water, water, water, nothing more. "Ronan," Michael cried out, trying to make his voice sound less frightened than he was feeling. "Ronan, wake up!"

His boyfriend didn't stir, his eyes didn't flutter, his breathing didn't quicken, he remained exactly the same. Ronan slept as if the world was simply resting in preparation for a new day. To Michael, the world looked as if it had come to an end.

Bolts of lightning lit up the night sky like electric eels in a black sea, thunderclaps continued to howl like banshees, and the rain, the rain that Michael loved so much pummeled the windows with such fury it was as if the sole purpose of each drop was to shatter the glass. Hoping to prevent such a result, Michael threw open the window and was instantly battered by the freezing rain that felt more like shards of ice than water. He stepped to the side to hide behind the wall and protect his body and was surprised to find that he wasn't bleeding from the attack. Shielding his eyes with his forearm, he glanced out the window and saw that nothing had changed. He couldn't tell if his room was still connected to the building; all he knew was that it was somehow floating in the middle of the ocean. And the sea was no longer calm.

Whether because of the storm or because the sea was not thrilled to have a huge, foreign substance floating on its surface, the waves were cresting higher and higher with each passing second. Even with his preternatural agility, Michael had to hold onto the window frame to keep his balance. He was gripping the floor so tightly with his feet that he thought his toes were going to break through the wooden slats. And all the while Michael was trying to stay upright, Ronan was sleeping deeply in their bed.

Something flew past the moon and caught Michael's eye. He thought at first it might just be another streak of lightning, but it was too small and not as bright. Crouching under the window, Michael rose slowly, his hands positioned in front of his face in a continued attempt to protect it from the onslaught of rain. He squinted and realized with a surge of delight that it was the lark flying in the glow of the moon. His heart swelled at the sight of his old friend, and he watched him dip and curve and weave between and above the glut of raindrops, his wings outstretched to their maximum potential. Michael thought he had never looked so magnificent. He wished that the lark would fly closer so he could hear his song, hear again his signature tune, *da-da-DAH-da, da-da-da,* but the lark stayed away from the eye of the storm. Michael couldn't blame him, but he wished he were closer so he could tell him how wonderful his life had become, how worthwhile the journey had been, how incredible and amazing every day had been since he came to Double A from Nebraska. But suddenly the lark flew even farther away.

Michael watched, fascinated, awestruck as a giant wave, directly in front of the window, slowly split in two and parted. Looking down into the abyss created by the parting of the wave, Michael couldn't see ground, he couldn't see a bottom of any kind, just infinite space. The room hung in the air, suspended, as if the millions of raindrops that continued to shower onto the roof were actually strings being controlled by an unseen puppeteer, a mastermind hiding within the clouds whose only purpose was to keep the room airborne. Until the room fell.

The abrupt descent thrust Michael upward, and he slammed into the ceiling. The accelerated speed kept him glued there until the room shifted and Michael was sent smashing to the floor. Dazed, he tried to get his bearings during the free fall, and if it weren't for his enhanced vision he would not have seen the bed speed toward him. He jumped up without a moment to spare and heard, but didn't see, the bed hurtle into the wall behind him; he was too busy looking around the room to make sure another inanimate object didn't suddenly come alive and hurtle in his direction.

"What the hell is going on?" Michael mumbled to himself.

Before he could find an answer the room tilted again to the other side and Michael flew headfirst into the wall at the far end of the room, barely missing the window. Kneeling on the floor, he reached up and held onto the windowsill. He looked over to his bed and was terrified to see that it was now empty. Ronan was no longer sleeping quietly under the covers, he was floating two feet above the bed, and yet still sound asleep.

"Ronan!" Michael shouted. He knew that it was probably dangerous to startle Ronan and force him to wake up, but he was unable to control his voice. He was no longer interested in and curious about what was happening all around him, he was scared. "Ronan! Wake up!"

Ronan's only response was physical, and it had nothing to do with the urgent tone of Michael's voice, and everything to do with the shifting of the room. As it plummeted deeper, deeper, deeper into the hole in the ocean, the room sloped sideways, causing Ronan's body to bounce into the wall. His right hand that had been resting on his chest fell and dangled at his side, swaying slightly. It was the only visible movement he made.

On his hands and knees Michael started to crawl toward Ronan, desperate to reach him before whatever magic that allowed him to float in midair died out or before they crashed into the bottom of the ocean floor. The latter thought filled him with dread as he realized the room couldn't fall forever; at some point it had to hit land, and at the speed they were falling he knew that such a landing could be deadly even for them.

"Ronan! Can you hear me?" Michael cried out, but again his words fell against sleeping ears.

From halfway across the room, Michael felt cold water spray over him, making his skin grow even colder and soaking his pants until they were dripping wet. He thought it was the rain whipping against his body, but he was wrong; the ocean water was gushing in through the open window at breakneck speed. They hadn't landed; Michael could still feel the room descending. It looked, however, as if the waves had reconnected and the room was now submerged under the hostile ocean. One of the bedside tables slid across the room, stopping only when it got wedged between the bed and a bookshelf, stopping right next to Michael. Using the solid piece of furniture as leverage, Michael pulled himself into an upright position as the water kept rushing into the room. Pouring, pouring, pouring into the room so quickly that in seconds Michael was knee-deep in ice-cold water.

Standing in the middle of his plummeting room, Ronan floating in the air just out of his grasp, Michael couldn't understand why he was filled with a crippling fear. This was only water, there was nothing to be afraid of. *I'm a child of Atlantis,* Michael reminded himself. *The ocean is home to me, sanctuary, there's no reason to be frightened.* And yet he was, he was absolutely terrified.

The room started to shake even more violently and his terror grew, because even though the room was rocking back and forth, pitching up, then falling at an even faster speed, he no longer moved. The water had turned to ice and had locked him into place. He tried to move his legs, break free from the icy grip, but not even his vampire strength could shatter the ice. Despite the freezing temperature, Michael felt beads of sweat race down the sides of his face, down the insides of his arms. For some reason the ocean, the water, maybe even The Well itself were all rebelling against him.

"Don't you know that I'm one of you?!" Michael screamed.

The ice started to rise and lock itself around Michael's legs, then his waist. He looked out the window, desperate to find a way out, anything, anyone who could come to their rescue. In the distance he saw the meadowlark, watching, staring, not coming closer, not offering any help. A cloud of smoke erupted behind the lark and raced toward the room. Michael almost cried out in joy when he realized the cloud was fog and he knew that Phaedra must have returned to save him, to fulfill the pledge that she had made to his mother when she died. But he was wrong, the fog was nothing more than fog. It didn't evaporate and reveal a supernatural being; it didn't offer his salvation; it was simply the result of the cold air rising from the ocean. There was nothing left for Michael to do except to try and reach his boyfriend. Ronan had the same idea.

"Michael," Ronan said calmly; his right arm that had been dangling was now outstretched, his hand, his fingers aching to be held. "You must protect me."

Reaching his hand out toward Ronan, Michael stretched his body as much as possible, but there were still several inches of empty air between them. "I don't know what to do," Michael said. "I don't know how!"

"You will," Ronan said. His smile was warm, his expression in stark contrast to Michael's mask of fear. "When the time comes, love, you'll know what to do."

But Michael had no idea what to do. He had no idea how to save Ronan or himself or stop the ice from rising up past his neck where it now rested or make Ronan stop floating in the air, so he did the only thing he could think of, he prayed. He begged The Well to make the nightmare end. He begged for their room to return to campus and for the water to recede and for the ocean to disappear. When he opened his eyes he wasn't sure if The Well had consented to his plea or if he had just been dreaming.

He was back in bed lying next to Ronan who was still asleep, but now safely under the covers. The rain had stopped, the room wasn't covered in ice, and Michael could see out the windows that they were back on Archangel ground, back where they belonged. Stunned but grateful, Michael turned to face Ronan. He placed his arm over his chest and shivered not because of the cold this time, but because of the beautiful warmth that emanated from Ronan's body. For a few seconds all he could do was stare at Ronan's face, christened by the shadows of the night, until he knew exactly what he needed to say. "Don't be afraid," Michael whispered. "I'll always be here to protect you."

Ronan clutched Michael's hand and smiled in his sleep. Michael felt the breath escape his lips; he knew that Ronan heard him, he knew that he believed him. And Michael finally understood his purpose.

chapter 1

A New Beginning

Happy birthday to me.

Those were the first words Michael spoke when he woke up. He whispered them to himself just as he had every morning on his birthday for as long as he could remember. Unexpectedly, he felt sadness sneak into his heart as he recalled that his birthdays had always started with promise and always ended in disappointment. When he turned and saw Ronan sleeping beside him, the sadness retreated; he knew this birthday would be vastly different.

He dressed quickly, one eye on Ronan, wondering if he should wake him. The urge to fulfill tradition, however, was too strong. Even though this birthday would bear no resemblance to any other that had come before it, he still felt the need to start the day the same way he had for so many years—alone.

As he passed by the window, he paused to remember his dream. He was greatly relieved to find that the land was dry and they weren't floating in the middle of the ocean. It had been just a dream, nothing more. Catching his reflection in the windowpane, Michael scowled. *Could've been a premonition,* he thought. *You've had a few of those before.* No, he wasn't going to believe that, he wasn't going to believe that his dream could be yet another vision of the future, a vision that contained danger and turmoil. Today was a day for celebration.

Standing outside St. Florian's, solitude felt different. Back home in Weeping Water he had begun every birthday by himself. The custom had started out of necessity—he didn't have any friends—but it soon became preference. Instead of vainly anticipating a day filled with parties, good wishes, gifts from someone other than his mother and grandparents, he would start the day with a quiet stroll, contemplating the year that had passed and wondering what the future would hold. Now, his annual ritual would merely be a prelude to a day filled with fun, laughter, and, best of all, company.

Walking across the Archangel Academy campus at dawn, Michael gazed upon the collection of stone buildings that at this uninhabited hour looked like the remnants of an abandoned village, not the revered educational institution that it was, and he couldn't believe such a picturesque setting was his home. The flat, hostile landscape of Weeping Water might have been where he grew up, but this was his home, and no matter where he traveled to, no matter where he and Ronan chose to live after they graduated, Michael would always return here. Because he considered Double A to be the place where his life began.

In front of Archangel Cathedral, Michael looked up, exhilarated as he always was by the burst of light that radiated from the large round window. He closed his eyes, accepted the church's offering, felt his face glow, and made his annual wish. This year he didn't wish for a future away from Weeping Water; he didn't wish to be rescued and taken somewhere else, he no longer had to. He also didn't ask that his future only be filled with happiness, that it be spared tragedy and pain, for he knew that would be foolish. He simply wished that no matter what surprises and challenges he encountered this year and for all the years to come that he face them directly and not be weakened by fear.

Suddenly, an odd sensation filled Michael's body; he felt warm and wet at the same time. He opened his eyes and saw that the cathedral's stained-glass window was gone, and in its place was The Well. Looking into it from this new angle was disconcerting at first, but Michael soon saw the familiar, silvery water ripple slightly and then emerging from it a thin, white light that only stopped when it touched his heart. Overjoyed, he knew his wish had been granted. His heart and his soul were connected to The Well, and no matter how difficult the year ahead was, no matter how challenging his future might be, he wouldn't have to be afraid.

And what a wonderful change that would be after the tumultuous year he had had, a year filled with events that were still almost incomprehensible. Losing his mother, the horror of learning she had died at his father's hand, the death of his friend Penry, the disappearances of Imogene and Alistair, the attack on Saoirse's life and her unexplained survival, the revelation that David longed for the annihilation of the water vampires. He knew it would be a struggle to face each new obstacle with a fearless heart, but knowing The Well supported him, knowing The Well was an ally, would make it easier for Michael to find his own courage.

He continued to walk across campus and proudly surveyed his domain. When he came across the white roses that sprouted from the ground in front of St. Joshua's he laughed out loud. No matter how strong and how gifted he might be, he still couldn't decipher their mystery; their truth was just beyond his grasp. Beyond everyone's grasp for that matter. No one understood why they were always present, always in full bloom season after season, century after century. No one, including Michael, understood their purpose, or if they even had one other than adding beauty to the school. Michael bent down to caress a milk-white petal that was incredibly smooth and thick, and he felt like a child and an adult at the same time. He was filled with wonder by this baffling creation and the knowledge that mystery was merely a part of life. Accepting that some things could never be explained was all a part of becoming an adult. So too was understanding the need to exercise caution.

In the distance he saw the headmaster's office. It looked like all the other buildings at Double A, and yet Michael knew it was unique. It was where David presided, where he and his dutiful subjects conspired to destroy The Well and wage war against Michael's kind. He knew that David was a formidable opponent, and he wasn't naïve enough to think that he and his army wouldn't strike out against them again. However, David's plans had been thwarted once already, and David had learned that victory would not be easy or achieved without bloodshed, so they had all settled into an uneasy peace. How long that peace would continue Michael had no idea, but he didn't want to dwell on it, not on his birthday.

The past, however, was strong and tugged on his memory. In the presence of the office he thought of David's predecessor, Alistair, the headmaster who had welcomed him to Archangel Academy. He hoped that wherever he was, he was at peace. He hoped that was the case as Alistair had offered him kindness and support when he first arrived here, and Michael had never properly thanked him. Sadly, he suspected he would never get the chance.

Walking back toward the heart of campus, Michael thought

about the other adults in his life and silently remarked that they were truly a disappointing group. He didn't care if he ever saw his father again. His grandparents allowed their own limitations to prevent them from ever having a fulfilling relationship with their grandson. And then there was his mother. He understood Grace's actions and her motives now, he knew that she had fled London to get away from Vaughan in order to prevent him from turning Michael into one of Them, but it still didn't change the fact that she had kept all her secrets to herself and as a result Michael only got to know his mother after she died. They had closure, but they were never close.

Stop thinking about the past, Michael, he thought. *Stop imagining what you might do in the future and pay attention to the present.* He took his own advice and looked up to find Ronan staring down at him from their dorm room window. Michael was so overcome with a collection of emotions—joy, pride, love—that it took him several moments to feel the rain. Unlike in his dream or premonition or whatever it was, these were just a few drops falling from the summer clouds onto the earth, onto his and Ronan's faces, making them glisten the way they did the night they first met. How his life had changed so drastically, so magnificently since that night. Maybe it was time to bury all those thoughts and feelings that had plagued him; maybe it was time to let go of the past; maybe it was time to grow up.

"Happy birthday, love," Ronan said sweetly. One drop of rain fell from Ronan's lips and didn't stop falling until it landed on Michael's. "Why don't you get up here so I can give you your gift right proper?"

Half a second later the boys were tumbling onto their bed, their bodies damp with rainwater and anticipation, their quickened breaths and the fumbling of the sheets almost drowning out the sounds of the summer rain shower outside. Almost. No matter how hard Michael tried, no matter how much in love he and Ronan were, the world, for better and for worse, would always be waiting for them.

"What was that?" Michael asked, looking out the window over Ronan's bare shoulder.

"What was *what?*"

"I thought I heard a noise," Michael clarified. "Sounded like a bird flew by."

Pushing Michael's body deeper into the pillows and the mattress, Ronan laughed. "That meadowlark of yours needs to find his own boyfriend. You're taken."

"Guess he wanted to wish me a happy birthday too."

Words quickly gave way to kisses and all thoughts of the lark were forgotten.

It was good that the boys had something to keep them occupied, because if they had inspected the situation further they might have discovered that, while the noise was indeed the sound of wings flapping in the wind, it wasn't created by the lark.

It was David.

His feathered wings, black as sin, created a sinister silhouette against the pale blue sky as he soared over Double A to test out his newly acquired ability.

And, of course, to spy on the unsuspecting couple.

chapter 2

Even with his eyes closed Michael knew he was being watched. It was a glorious feeling. The sound, however, was not.

"Happy birthday to you, happy birthday to you."

Another one of Ronan's flaws revealed—he couldn't sing. His Irish brogue, so melodic when speaking, somehow lost all of its musicality when he tried to sing. Still it was touching to hear words that were so heartfelt and meant only for his ears, touching and, unfortunately, embarrassing as well. Ronan's attempt at crooning made Michael remember that he had completely forgotten Ronan's seventeenth birthday a few months ago. True to his word, Ronan didn't hold a grudge and seemed to have forgotten about the incident until Michael was compelled to bring it up again.

"Thank you," Michael said, sealing his words with a kiss. "And next year I promise I won't forget yours."

Ronan changed position so they were now lying on their sides facing each other. "I told you, love, it's not a big deal," he replied. "Birthdays don't mean much to vampires or to Atlantians for that matter."

Tugging on the curls of black hair on Ronan's chest, Michael whispered, "I know, but I still shouldn't have forgotten."

Ronan grabbed Michael's hand and pulled it away from his chest; he loved the sensation, but he just felt the need to kiss Michael's fingers. "The concept of age is kind of meaningless to us now," he explained. "I just know you still enjoy this human tradition."

His comment made Michael roll his eyes. Yes, Ronan had been a vampire for longer than Michael had, but only by a few years. And yet sometimes when he spoke he sounded downright ancient. "Well, I promise not to forget your birthday," Michael declared. "Even when we're 362."

Ronan traced his cheek with Michael's fingers. *How wonderful it will be to spend 362 years with you, Michael, but before we spend another moment together things need to change.* "I want to give you a gift."

Unable to contain his excitement, Michael sat up in bed, bouncing a little bit, delighted and hoping that Ronan's present would be better than his singing.

"I want to give you the gift of honesty," Ronan stated.

Hmm, maybe not. "Is that, um, a new cologne?" Michael asked.

Shaking his head, Ronan wrapped his leg around Michael's waist so their naked bodies were intertwined. "No, I'm talking about the actual word and everything it means."

"Oh," Michael replied warily.

Ronan held Michael's hands in his and looked him directly in the eyes. Whatever he wanted to say, he was serious, and Michael's caution turned into intrigue. "I don't want there to be any more secrets between us," Ronan said. "I didn't tell you about my past with Nakano, or about your father being a vampire, or the fact that Saoirse's different from all of us, and if only I had we could have avoided lots of turmoil, lots of unnecessary pain."

"I told you," Michael said, "I understand why you did all that. You were protecting me."

"And look how it all backfired," Ronan added. "So to bloody hell with all that. From here on out, no more secrets."

Slowly, Michael nodded his head in agreement. He was happy to hear that Ronan wanted to substitute truth for secrets, but he couldn't help wondering what else Ronan could possibly have to tell him. Secret telling, however, would have to wait a while longer, because just as Ronan was about to speak he was interrupted by a knock at their door.

"Open up! We come bearing gifts!"

The high-pitched voice was unmistakable. It belonged to Saoirse.

"Hold on!" Ronan cried.

Like two mice scampering in a field, Michael and Ronan raced around their room putting the clothes back on that they had so carelessly discarded earlier in the morning. Fully dressed, Ronan opened the door to see not just Saoirse, but Ciaran and Fritz as well, all bearing gifts. "You two were in your birthday suits, weren't you?" Saoirse asked.

"No," Ronan said emphatically.

His staunch tone was undermined when Michael said, "Kind of," at the same time.

"Aren't ya glad I told ya to knock first?" Fritz asked.

Despite the interruption to their privacy, both boys welcomed the intrusion. The camaraderie made Ronan feel like part of a family, and it reminded Michael that he now had friends who wanted to celebrate his birthday. Both were changes for the better.

Those weren't the only changes that had taken place since the end of the school year. Ciaran and Fritz had become closer, and as a result they were beginning to adopt each other's personality traits. Ciaran was continuing to break through his shell and was no longer so stuffy and reserved; he wasn't as laid back or as funny as Fritz, but he was starting to lighten up and realize there was more to life than just being a lab rat. For his part, Fritz had learned that you can't always get what you want just because you ask for it loudly. He had wanted a more intimate relationship with Phaedra and as far as he knew she had just up and switched schools without even saying good-bye. It had been a hard lesson to learn, but he had come to realize that he had obviously overestimated the depth of their relationship. As a result, he had become more pensive and reflective.

And then there was Saoirse. After surviving the attack on her life during The Carnival for the Black Sun, she had greatly matured. Unfortunately her development was more physical than emotional. Her lean tomboy's body had started to gain curves in all the right places, and she had grown about two inches in height in the past month. She had always been told that she had a beautiful face, but now she had the shape to match.

Although she was becoming a woman, she clung tightly to her girlish charms. She was still a spitfire with a firm grasp on her adventurous, mischievous spirit. As far as her puzzling heritage, the more she thought about it, the more conflicted she became about truly wanting to know why she was so special, so different. The only thing she did acknowledge was that, as a girl who was almost sixteen, she didn't want to be anything close to *different*.

Piling with his friends on the bed, Michael sat on the pillows like they were a throne. Ronan was next to him, then spread out in a circle, Saoirse, Ciaran, and Fritz, all, for the moment at least, his subjects bearing their majesty gifts and hoping to secure his royal favor. Michael tried to act mature and as if this wasn't one of the most exciting days of his life, but he couldn't; he was practically giddy at being the center of attention, and he decided to embrace it. "C'mon—don't keep me in suspense any longer!" he shouted. "Gimme my gifts!"

The kids were just as excited, and three pairs of hands thrust their gifts toward Michael at the same time. Before he could choose, Fritz made the decision for him. "Open mine first," he ordered. "Because there's no soddin' way their presents can be better."

As Michael took the gift-wrapped box from Fritz's hand, Ciaran commented, "Didn't we just have a conversation about the importance of humility?"

Shrugging his shoulders, Fritz replied, "No need to be humble when I know my gift's the bloody best."

"Maybe you should all act like gentlemen and let the lady go first?" Saoirse suggested.

Fritz only took a second to reply. "All right, Ronan start us off."

It took only another second for them to crack up laughing, Ronan loudest of all. A year ago Ronan might have sulked all day from such a comment or perhaps struck out and hit Fritz in retaliation; now he raised his hand and met Fritz's in a high five, proud to be the butt of his joke. Fritz was even prouder of his comment and laughed so hard he almost fell off the bed backward, saved only by Michael's lightning-quick reflexes.

"Thanks, Nebraska," Fritz said, still laughing. "You got a firm grip there. You hitting the weights or something?"

Just my preternatural vampire strength. "You know me," Michael replied. "I just come from good ole Midwestern stock."

Fritz was so excited about the prospect of Michael's opening up his gift he didn't notice the others glance at one another conspiratorially. "Okay, mate," he declared. "Go ahead and open it."

Like a kid much younger than seventeen, Michael tore at the red and green wrapping paper, which looked like it had been salvaged from last year's Christmas supply, to reveal a plain cardboard box underneath. Crumbling up the paper into a ball, he tossed it playfully at Ronan, who deflected it nicely with a flick of his hand, so it landed squarely in the wastebasket next to their desk.

Next, Michael removed the lid from the box and, although he was stunned by what he saw, when he inspected the gift further he couldn't hide his disappointment.

"You hate it!" Fritz cried.

"No," Michael protested. "I love it."

Shaking his head, Fritz pouted. "No you don't, mate. I can see it in your face."

"Seriously, Fritz, I love it," Michael said. "But . . ."

"I knew it!" Fritz shouted. "Nothing's ever any bloody good if you have to say 'but'!"

"I just don't think I look like this."

To get a more objective opinion Michael held up Fritz's gift to the others. It was a whole issue of his comic book, *Tales of the Double A,* that was clearly a dedication to Michael, entitled *Invasion From Nebraska.* Most of the cover was filled up with a close-up drawing of Michael's face. At least Michael thought it was supposed to be his face; he wasn't completely sure.

Taking the comic book from Michael's hands, Ronan glanced at it and nodded approvingly. "Looks just like you, love." To Fritz he added, "You really captured his eyes."

As proud as a cross-legged peacock, Fritz grinned. "Thanks, mate."

Slightly appalled, Michael grabbed the comic book back from Ronan. "I do not look like this!"

This time Ciaran grabbed the comic book out of Michael's hands so he and Saoirse could get a better look at Fritz's artistic rendering of their friend. "Oh sure you do," Ciaran confirmed. "Looks just like you."

"Especially before you put your hair gel in," Saoirse added. "And, you know, gussy yourself up."

Luckily, Michael knew when he was beaten as well as when to let go of his vanity. "Then I think it's positively perfect, Fritz!" Michael declared. "I absolutely love it."

Still beaming, Fritz conveyed a bit about the plot of the Michael-centric issue. "I called it *Invasion From Nebraska* 'cause it's all about how you came to Double A from America."

"That is brill, Fritz," Ronan shouted, truly impressed.

"Except that you're a zombie and you bring with you a tribe of Nebraskan zombies who try to kill all of us students," Fritz explained. "Well, I won't say anymore 'cause I don't want to spoil the plot."

Now that Michael had gotten over the shock of seeing himself depicted as a comic book character he was downright thrilled to be the focal point of the issue. Saoirse, however, wasn't convinced it was as great an idea as everyone else was. "Didn't you already have an issue about zombies?"

"Yes!" Fritz admitted. "But it sold out in a bloody hour! Everybody loves zombies, Seersh."

Jumping onto her knees, Saoirse bounced up and down on the bed. "I forgot to tell you all that I have a new nickname," she announced. "Henceforth and jolly-o, please address me as Seersh."

Michael smiled. He really enjoyed being in this girl's presence. She could be frustrating, annoying at times, but she never failed to make him laugh. He glanced over at Ronan, and he could see that he felt the same way. "Will do, Seersh," Michael confirmed. "Should I open your gift next?"

"No," she replied. "I've decided that I want to go last."

"Because it's a lady's prerogative to change her mind?" Ronan asked.

Smiling devilishly, she answered, "You should know, Lady Ronan."

Again the kids cracked up, and even though Ronan found the joke funny there was no way he was going to allow his sister to stick him with such a nickname. "You call me that again, Seersh," Ronan informed her, "and you'll be back at Ecoles des *Roaches* in time for the next semester."

"All right, ladies, enough, it's time for my gift," Ciaran announced, then added a bit more seriously, "I hope you like it, Michael."

Taking the package from Ciaran, Michael immediately noticed it was much heavier than Fritz's gift. "Thanks, Ciaran, I'm sure I will."

In spite of his certainty he once again found himself trying to hide his disappointment as he stared at Ciaran's gift. "Um, thanks," Michael mumbled. "I guess I can always use some more notebooks."

Ciaran wasn't upset by Michael's reaction; in fact, he had anticipated Michael wouldn't be excited at first. "No, open them up."

Michael opened up the notebook on top of the pile to find that it was already written in. He flipped through the pages and found that the handwriting continued on every page. The whole book was filled with scribbling, numbers, and diagrams. "Oh they're *used* notebooks," Michael revealed, somewhat sarcastically. "Well, you know, you can never have enough of those."

Obviously Michael wasn't getting the true nature of Ciaran's gift, so Ciaran had to explain. "They're my notebooks from advanced geometry and chemistry last year." Although Ciaran was going to be a junior like the other boys, he had been taking additional accelerated science and math classes for the past two years, so he was a year ahead of them in certain subjects. "I thought you could benefit from my, um, expertise," Ciaran said, somewhat sheepishly.

Despite his initial skepticism, it turned out to be another great gift. "This is absolutely incredible, Ciaran!" Michael shouted. "You know how I hate chem labs."

Equally surprised and impressed by his brother's generosity, Ronan couldn't find the words to respond. Saoirse didn't have that problem. "Isn't that called cheating?" she asked.

Before Ciaran could rationalize the ethics of his gift, Fritz jumped to his friend's defense. "It's what mates do for each other, Seersh," Fritz explained. "And I've been teaching Ciaran how to be a right proper mate."

"Well, you've done good, Fritz," Ronan declared, finally finding his voice.

"So based on these first two gifts," Michael started, "I guess this means that I have bad hair and I'm stupid."

"Quite," Ciaran replied dryly.

How wonderful to be insulted by your friends on your birthday, Michael thought.

The boys jabbered on for a few more minutes, the conversation flowing from how thoughtful Michael thought the gifts were to how Fritz's sense of humor was rubbing off on Ciaran to how Ronan might want to take a peek at those notebooks as well since he disliked chemistry almost as much as Michael did. The chattering continued until Saoirse couldn't take it any longer.

"Oh put a bung in it boys, will ya!" she cried. "It's time for me to give Michael my gift."

Effectively silenced, the boys willingly gave the spotlight over to Saoirse, knowing full well that it was useless trying to prevent the handoff once she had decided she was entitled to it. "I really hope you like it," she said, suddenly shy.

"If it's half as beautiful as this wrapping paper, I know I will," Michael said, taking the gift from her anxious hands. Even if the gift hadn't been wrapped so artistically, he still would have made a big deal out of it; he had become aware since her arrival that Ronan's sister had a little bit of a crush on him. "It's really gorgeous, Saoirse, I mean Seersh," Michael said. "Did you do it yourself?"

Self-conscious from Michael's praise, Saoirse hoped the boys didn't notice that her cheeks were growing a darker shade of pink. "Well, yeah, I did," she admitted. "I thought you'd, um, like the colors."

Fritz didn't understand the appropriateness of the wrapping paper's design, but to the other four the symbolism was obvious—it was an abstract depiction of the ocean. The paper's design was a series of horizontal lines in deepening shades of blue from pale to navy. Saoirse had wrapped the package with a delicate white lace ribbon and topped it off with a huge, red bow. Fritz thought he understood the significance of the colors and although he was wrong, his assumption actually made sense.

"What's all the fuss about?" Fritz asked. "It's the colors of the American flag."

Not wanting to divulge the real meaning behind the gift wrap, Michael spoke for the group when he said, "Oh my God, Fritz, it is!"

"What else could it be?" he asked rhetorically. "Now will you open the damn thing so we can see what she bought for ya!"

Michael pulled the bow off first and playfully stuck it on Ronan's head; he good-naturedly left it there. This time when Michael saw his gift he wasn't disappointed. "They're perfect, Seersh!" Leaning over, he gave his unofficial sister-in-law a hug that made her blush a bit more and then held up his gifts so the others could see. In one hand, a book of British slang, in the other, a framed picture of Saoirse and him taken under the brass apple tree sculpture the last time they had gone into Eden. It had only just started and already it was turning out to be a perfect birthday.

Grabbing the photo, Fritz compared it to his comic book. "I think I made you look more lifelike."

Yanking the picture back, Michael laughed. "Fritz, this is a photo; yours is a drawing."

"I know," Fritz replied, undeterred. "And I still think mine looks better."

"And I still can't believe a camera can capture your reflection."

Well, it had been a perfect birthday. Saoirse didn't immediately fathom the impact of her comment until she looked around the room. Fritz looked downright perplexed, Ciaran's jaw had dropped as if someone had just told him his lab had burnt to the ground, and Michael's and Ronan's eyes bulged so wide it looked like they might escape their sockets. Once she realized her gaffe, she opened her mouth to speak, but couldn't think of a thing to say that wouldn't compound the situation. Michael felt the same way, so when he spoke he did it without sound.

"This is because a vampire traditionally doesn't have a reflection," Michael said to Ronan telepathically. *"Or appear in photos, right?"*

"Yes," Ronan replied, silently. *"Or have a sister with a big mouth!"*

Inevitably, Fritz asked the question they all knew he would. "What the bloody hell is she talking about?"

Knowing that no one wanted to respond, Ronan, as the oldest, took it upon himself to take control of the situation. "Should we tell him?"

Three heads snapped in Ronan's direction, Michael, Ciaran, and Saoirse, but each remained silent and each had the same thought: Ronan couldn't possibly be suggesting that they let Fritz in on the fact that two out of the five people in the room were inhuman and one was the offspring of two vampires.

"Roooooooonan," Michael said, stretching out his boyfriend's name so it took him about ten seconds to say it.

"Well, brother," Ciaran said, "you are the oldest and therefore the wisest."

"Um, yes, brother, if you really think it's wise," Saoirse said, then added in a whisper, "You don't really think it's wise, do you?"

Ronan lay back on the mattress and swung his legs up and over Saoirse's head. He started to pace the room, but the others couldn't tell if he was doing so because he was nervous or because he was setting the stage to share their extraordinary secret. "I think it's time," Ronan announced. "I was just telling Michael this morning that there shouldn't be any more secrets."

Bug-eyed, Saoirse turned to Michael. "Did he say that, Michael? Did Ronan tell you that this morning?"

"Well, uh, yeah," Michael confirmed. "He actually did."

Tired of the suspense, Fritz wanted an answer. "C'mon, mate, just spill it!"

Michael saw Saoirse reach over and grab Ciaran's hand, and he was jealous that he had no one to hold on to. He couldn't believe Ronan was going to do this; he couldn't believe Ronan was going to tell Fritz that they were both vampires. It was insane, it was unthinkable, and yet Michael couldn't think of any way to stop him that wouldn't make the situation more tense or Fritz more suspicious.

"The reason Saoirse is surprised that Michael has a reflection," Ronan started, pausing for effect when he saw his boyfriend and his siblings hold their breath, "is because she thinks he's some sort of god and not human like the rest of us."

As Ronan's words sunk in, they all exhaled in relief. All except Saoirse.

"I never said he was a god!" the girl screamed, her face reddened not by embarrassment this time, but by anger. "I said he's really, really cute and all, but don't make me sound like I'm round the bend!"

Now that the crisis had been averted, Michael thought it

was time to have some fun. "You really, really think I'm really, really cute?"

"Oh blimey, Michael!" Saoirse exclaimed, jumping off the bed. "You know you're cute, everybody says so, even Fritz."

Once again Fritz proved that he wasn't threatened by the fact that Michael and Ronan were gay or by the concept itself and was man enough to admit that he could notice if a guy was really, really cute. Sort of. "I don't think I used those exact words, Seersh," Fritz said. "But I did mention to Phaedra once that you were a fine looking chap."

"Thanks, Fritz," Michael said, proudly accepting the compliment. "Right back at ya."

"And lucky too 'cause girls can be certifiably crackers!" Fritz added. "For a second, I thought you were going to say she didn't think you would have a reflection 'cause you're a bunch of bloody vampires!"

They were all so stunned by Fritz's comment that at first they didn't realize they were laughing. Of course they were laughing more out of shock and the absurdity of the situation than because they thought the joke was particularly funny. Fritz, however, thought his comment was hilarious. "Bollocks! I should've made you a vampire, Michael, instead of a zombie!" he exclaimed. "I could've called it 'Bloody Nebraska'!"

Desperate to steer the conversation away from anything that had to do with vampires, Ciaran noticed one more gift that hadn't been opened. It was on top of some books on the side of the desk and wrapped very simply in what looked like a brown paper bag. When he picked it up he saw that that's exactly what it was, and he knew immediately whom it must be from. "Michael, I think this is from Ronan."

Holding the gift, Michael looked over at Ronan and wore an expression as if to ask if it were okay to open his gift in public. "Go ahead, love," he said, "otherwise I think the audience may revolt."

He noticed that Ronan hadn't written "To Michael" on the paper, but "Forever Beautiful, Forever Mine." He hoped the gift was like the packaging—simple and sentimental.

It was.

"I love it, Ronan, thank you," Michael said as he showed everyone that Ronan had given him a copy of Oscar Wilde's play *An Ideal Husband*. The others might have thought it was just another book for Michael to read, but he understood the significance that Mr. Wilde's works had in their relationship. When they had first met Ronan had compared Michael to the titular character in *Dorian Gray*, then last semester Ronan had bought Michael a collection of short stories that included "The Young King," which Ronan said reminded him of Michael. Now, he had a new title to add to his growing library.

As expected, Saoirse started to giggle when she saw the name of the play, and not so expectedly Ciaran joined her. "Have we all noticed that I'm the only one who's acting like an adult and not snickering?" Fritz asked.

"Yes, Fritz, we have noticed," Ronan replied, slapping his sister in the head and his brother on the arm.

Getting up from the bed, Fritz had one more declaration. "I think Nebraska would make a right fine husband and if I'm not invited to the wedding, I'll knock both your bloody heads in."

"Fritz," Michael announced, "it wouldn't be a party without you."

The moment after their impromptu guests had left, Michael thought Ronan would continue their conversation about honesty and reveal to him the remaining secret, or God forbid, *secrets* that he was still concealing from him. But the gift giving had yet to cease. "I have something else for you," Ronan said.

Now Michael really felt uncomfortable. Not only had he

forgotten Ronan's birthday completely, but now Ronan was showering him with gifts. "You've already given me so much."

Ronan kissed Michael softly on his cheek. "And I'll never stop."

He shoved his hand into the pocket of his jeans and pulled out a ring. It was silver with a thin blue band around it that looked like the waves in the broach Edwige always wore. "It's the symbol of Atlantis," Ronan explained. "Never-ending water." Slowly, Ronan slipped it on Michael's finger, and Michael felt a flurry of emotions rise from his stomach and swirl around his chest. It was such a beautiful ring, such a heartfelt gesture. Michael had no idea that it was also a family heirloom.

"My father left it for me," Ronan explained, "along with a note that said, 'You'll know what to do with it when the time is right, when you become a man.' Well, the right time is now."

Speechless, Michael stared at the ring and then at Ronan; he just didn't know how to respond. As he started to cry he simply said, "Thank you."

"There's something else I need to tell you," Ronan began.

"No," Michael said. He couldn't take any more; he was too filled with emotion. He didn't want to listen to anything, he didn't want to hear about any more secrets, all he wanted to hear was the sound of Ronan kissing him, the sounds of the two of them making love. But just as they embraced, the door flung open.

"Ronan! Just how long did you think you were going to be able to hide this secret?!"

Neither boy knew what Saoirse was talking about. "Yeah right," she said, not believing their baffled expressions. "Well, follow me and I'll show you."

Downstairs they were as shocked as everyone else to see a car parked on the lawn in front of St. Florian's with a huge, black bow on its roof, but shocked for different reasons. Ronan because he genuinely didn't know who would leave such a gift and Michael because he couldn't believe Ronan would buy him a car on top of all the other presents he had given him. "Oh my God, Ronan!" Michael squealed. "I love it!"

In complete amazement, Michael walked around the red Mercedes Benz SUV. He had wanted a car ever since he passed his driver's test and got his license, but he never thought Ronan would be the one to fulfill his wish. He was right. "Sorry, love," Ronan said. "It's not from me."

"You're just being coy, mate," Fritz said, " 'Cause you wanted it to be a private surprise."

Even Ciaran thought Ronan was lying. "How did you ever convince Mum to spend so much money on someone other than herself?"

Michael noticed that a card was tucked under the windshield wiper. He ripped open the envelope, read the handwritten message inside the card, and every beautiful birthday memory was wiped away, every happy moment that he had just shared with Ronan and his friends was erased. He felt like he had been punched in the stomach. "To my son. Ad infinitum! Happy Birthday. Love, Dad." Michael spat out the words as if they were poison, and in his mind he was transported far from Double A to a padded room where he saw his father kill his mother, brutally and cleverly so that everyone would believe the body left behind was a suicide. The same father who now sent his love attached to a bright red car. He tore the card in two, flung the pieces into the air, and stormed upstairs with Ronan close behind him.

"Why the hell would he do such a thing?" Fritz asked.

Picking up the pieces of the torn card and placing them together so she could read the note herself, Saoirse remarked, "He's got some issues with his dad."

"So bloody what! The bloke gave him a Benz! In red! It doesn't even come in red, it had to be specially ordered!"

Ciaran understood Fritz's confusion, but he also understood Michael's pain at receiving a gift from his father, whom he had completely written off. He knew that he couldn't share their history with Fritz so he tried to channel his friend's energy and make light of the situation. "Look at it this way, Fritz," Ciaran said. "Since Michael doesn't want it, maybe he'll let you drive it."

That was all Fritz needed to hear to make him forget about Michael's fury and abrupt departure.

Unfortunately, Michael couldn't forget. He couldn't forget witnessing his parents at their defining moments: his father committing an act of unconscionable violence and his mother begging God to save her son seconds before she died. Sitting on his bed next to Ronan in thick silence, it was with an unwanted sense of maturity that he realized no matter how hard he tried to move forward he could never fully escape his past.

chapter 3

Summer was no longer the same.

Deep within The Forest, Michael sat on the bank of a stream that led somewhere, nowhere, and watched the water glide over his submerged feet. Even though it was July the water felt cool, and Michael wasn't sure if it was because the thick shade blocked out much of the sun's rays, because the weather in this part of the world didn't get too hot, or because as a vampire, temperature, like age, was an irrelevant concept. Watching the water trip over and through his toes, he had to admit it: he was confused. And it was all because of that stupid car.

Well, the car wasn't stupid—it was pretty amazing actually. It was everything Michael had ever hoped for. It was like somebody reached into his brain, picked out the car of his dreams and made it materialize. But why did that somebody have to be his father?

It couldn't have been a gift from Ronan? Or Edwige? Or even his grandfather? No, it had to come from the one person he wanted nothing to do with, the one person he wanted out of his life for good. "Oh my God!" Michael groaned out loud. "What if that'll never happen?"

Collapsing backward onto the dirt, Michael looked up at the pieces of sky he could see through the lush foliage and called out to the universe, "Thanks a lot, guys!" For the first time it hit him, no matter how long he lived, no matter how many birthdays he celebrated—100, 200, 362!—he would always be his father's son instead of his own man. Most children outlive their parents, escape them, but not Michael, no, he was lucky enough to have been given the gift of immortality, but guess what? So was his father! For as long as Michael walked the earth, somewhere on the planet his father would be walking as well. "That totally sucks," Michael moaned.

Sitting up, Michael noticed two leaves floating on the current. One was vibrant green with dark, almost black veins, the other much lighter in color, its veins, translucent. Visibly different, yet connected, the leaves touched and never separated as they rode on the water's surface. Some mornings Michael woke up and wished he and Ronan were like the leaves, that during the night they had been taken elsewhere, far from Double A, far from his father, and David, and the threats that hung over them. But when his mind cleared and he could think like the formidable creature he was and not the child he had been for so long, he realized distance was not salvation. It didn't matter where he was, the intangible ropes that connected him to his past and even to his enemies would still be tightly bound around him. What Michael needed to figure out was how to live with those ropes and not be strangled.

Michael splashed some water onto his face, and, as cool drops ran down his cheeks, onto his chin, into his hair, his mind took control of his eyes and he saw into the past. R.J.

was standing before him, as lanky and relaxed as ever, sweat dripping down the sides of his face, his cheekbones reddened and moist. R.J.'s eyes barely opened, the sun was too strong, so he had to squint, but it was enough for him to see. "Ya lookin' all grown up, Mike," he said, his lips sliding into a smile when he was done talking.

Guess not everything about the past is so bad, Michael thought. Then he wondered what R.J. was really doing right now. Sadly, he figured he was probably still leaning up against the gas pump, motionless, sweating, waiting for the next customer to drive up, waiting for the next reason to move. But where was R.J. going to go? The guy had never crossed the Nebraska state line in his entire life. At least Michael had gotten out of there. Thanks to this father. Oh not again!

Grabbing his sneakers, Michael bounded away from the stream, his feet jamming into the earth, one angry step after another. "Why can't I get him out of my head?" Michael asked, staring at the trees, a bit surprised that they didn't answer. His right foot landed squarely on a rock, but instead of wincing or losing his balance, he pressed down hard. When he lifted his foot to keep walking the rock was gone, burrowed into the ground. "I'll tell you why," Michael said, answering his own question. "Because every time I think of that car I think of him!"

And unfortunately it was hard not to think of the Benz since it occupied his world literally and figuratively. Regardless of where he went during the day—St. Joshua's, the pool, some new, unexplored area of campus, even Eden—he dreaded returning home. Now, walking back from The Forest he felt the same way. At least when he reached the clearing that led to St. Florian's he saw that the SUV wasn't waiting for him alone.

"Nice feet," Ronan said. "Looks like you stepped out of a page from *Huck Finn.*"

Michael looked down and saw that from his ankles below he was almost completely covered in mud.

"How was your walk, love?" Ronan asked.

Sighing, Michael sat on the ground next to Ronan. "You know me," he replied. "I'm just a regular country boy." Michael leaned back and pressed his body into the rough stone of the building, allowing its cold to embrace his skin. "I see that it's still here."

"Like a blighter, it just won't leave," Ronan said.

Michael knew Ronan was using one of his British slang words again, and he wished he had memorized more of the book Saoirse had given him for his birthday. "Blighter?"

Smiling, Ronan grabbed Michael's knee and played with the frayed trim of his khaki shorts. "Pest," Ronan translated. "The Benz is like a pest that just won't go away."

"Isn't there an exterminator we can call?" Michael asked. The cool stone and Ronan's warm touch almost made Michael forget how annoyed he was, almost made him feel like he was just lounging with his boyfriend on a summer afternoon. Almost, but not quite. "Or a towing company?" Michael suggested. "I'm serious, Ronan, I don't think I can go another day seeing that ... that ... thing!"

Ronan leaned back against the stone as well. He let his hand slip to hold onto the back of Michael's thigh and realized that the car really had been parked outside for quite a long time now. "You know, it's against school rules to have a car parked anywhere except for the lot by the headmaster's office," Ronan said. "Odd that David hasn't told you to move it yet."

There was nothing odd about it, at least not to Michael. His father and David were working together, in cahoots with each other, so of course David didn't care if the presence of Vaughan's gift broke school rules. The thing wasn't even a gift anyway; it was bait, a bribe to try and get Michael to forget every heinous act that Vaughan had ever committed. It wasn't going to work. "My father's one of Them," Michael seethed. "They protect each other."

Ronan wanted to remind Michael that that's what families do, they protect each other, stand by one another, but he knew that Michael didn't want to hear that. He also knew that if anyone else had given him that car Michael would be driving it up and down every road in the United Kingdom. All he had talked about was getting his driver's license and how driving to him was synonymous with freedom. He hadn't changed his mind simply because he had acquired alternative methods of transportation; it was still a dream of his to be behind the wheel of a car, and Ronan felt terrible that Michael was letting his contempt for his father stand in the way of fulfilling that dream. He had to say something that would allow Michael to see beyond his hatred. "Have to admit it's beautiful, though," Ronan said. "Betcha it's got a brilliant ride."

In one quick, brusque movement, Michael stood up. Clearly, Ronan's words had pushed him into action. Michael thrust his hand into the side pocket of his shorts and pulled out the car keys that he had been carrying with him ever since his birthday. He stared at them with such disdain it was as if he believed they would burn his flesh. Michael flicked his wrist, and the keys flew out of his hand and were caught by Ronan's. "Then take it for a test drive," Michael said. "I don't want it."

It was not exactly the action Ronan had been hoping for.

An hour later, sitting across from Ciaran in his lab, Ronan received yet another unwanted response.

"No, Ro," Ciaran said, his right eye firmly pressed into the lens of a microscope, "I haven't heard from Mum lately."

Knowing Michael needed to be alone for a few hours to sort through his feelings, Ronan had wandered around campus until he decided to go to St. Albert's lab where he knew he'd find his brother. Ciaran hadn't changed that much. Just because it was a beautiful summer day didn't mean he wouldn't be hunched over his microscope conducting some complicated experiment. An experiment that he seemed to be more interested in than their mother.

"Don't you find that a bit odd?" Ronan asked. "She used to always pop in from out of nowhere."

The oldest, Ciaran thought, *but definitely* not *the wisest.* "Into your life maybe," Ciaran stated. "But I've kind of grown accustomed to living mine without the constant appearance of our mother."

Embarrassed, Ronan gazed at the red and white blob that was squashed in between the two small, glass plates clipped onto the microscope's stage as if he knew what he was looking at, as if it held any interest. Although Edwige frequently visited Ronan and took an active part in his life, the same could not be said about how she treated Ciaran. Ronan had thought things would have gotten better after the family party he made her throw a few months ago, after she saw how all her children and even Michael needed her, but he was wrong. If anything, the party had the opposite effect, and lately, she was not only keeping her distance from Ronan's siblings, but from him as well.

"I will admit to one thing, brother," Ciaran said, tapping his notebook with the eraser end of his pencil. "It's not like her *not* to meddle in *your* affairs."

Ronan couldn't agree more, and he also couldn't push from his mind the disturbing thought that something terrible had happened to her, that wherever she was she needed her children's help. Then again Edwige didn't act like a typical mother so maybe she had just decided to spend a few months traveling and forgot to tell anyone where she was headed. "Do you think she went on holiday?" he asked.

"Possibly," Ciaran said. From the tone of his voice, Ronan knew his brother was not convinced that their mother was frolicking on a beach in the south of France or shopping in an exclusive boutique in New York; he knew instinctively just like Ronan did that she was missing. The problem was that neither boy knew how to find her. "Guess we'll just have to wait until she gets bored wherever she is and decides to come home," Ciaran advised.

The idea of not being proactive, of just letting the events unfold around him, went against Ronan's instinct, but reluctantly he had to agree. Edwige was far more powerful and cunning than anyone Ronan knew, so if she didn't want to be found, if she wanted to take a leave of absence from their lives for a while, there was nothing he could do to change that. "Guess you're right," Ronan said.

Even though he accepted fate, it didn't mean he wasn't going to try and fight it. There had to be something he could do to connect with his mother. She was often able to read his mind; it made total sense that he should be able to read hers. Maybe if he followed in his brother's footsteps and conducted more experiments to strengthen his telepathic ability he would be able to destroy whatever intangible barrier Edwige had put up to separate herself from her children. Yes, that's exactly what Ronan had to do, because the possibility still remained that Edwige had been taken by force, against her will, and the barrier that divided them could have been put up by someone else. Now that he had decided to take action, Ronan felt much better. Until Ciaran spoke.

"I haven't seen much of Saoirse lately either," he remarked. "Like mother, like daughter, I suppose."

"What are you talking about?" Ronan asked. "Saoirse's missing?!"

Startled by his brother's concern, Ciaran almost dropped the new specimen he was about to clip into place. "No, she isn't missing. I saw her this morning," he replied. "But it was the first time I have since Michael's birthday."

Relieved, Ronan forced himself to laugh so Ciaran wouldn't

think he was paranoid. "Oh good, 'cause you never know with that one."

It looked like the tactic had worked, and Ciaran resumed his study. Once again his face was practically devoured by the microscope's eyepiece as he inspected whatever germ or bacteria cell was on the glass lens. As inquisitive as Ronan could be, he couldn't imagine anything that tiny igniting that much curiosity. He admired his brother for his interest and acumen in science, but didn't understand it. "What are you looking at?" Ronan asked.

What wasn't admirable was Ciaran's lack of communication skills. "Nothing."

"Well, *nothing* seems to have you over the moon," Ronan said. "You can't take your eyes off that thing."

It was true. Despite the close proximity of his brother, despite the fact that they were having a conversation, Ciaran's eyes hardly ever strayed from his experiment. Even when he jotted something down in his notebook he kept his eyes looking into the thin, metal tube.

"Just boring science stuff," Ciaran mumbled.

It might be based in science, but it definitely wasn't boring. Ronan realized that whatever Ciaran was examining through that contraption and whatever he was writing down in his notebook were infinitely more exciting and appealing to him than any talk of his family. " 'Fess up," Ronan demanded. "What scientific breakthrough have you discovered this week?"

Without waiting for a response, Ronan spun Ciaran's notebook around so he could read it. But even with his vampire vision he couldn't make out Ciaran's handwriting—if that's even what the scribbling could be called. The opened pages were filled with a jumble of enigmatic symbols, numeric formulas, clusters of letters that didn't form words, but rather some sort of shorthand. The result was a notebook filled with spy-level code, indecipherable to anyone other than the person who created it. Ciaran, however, wasn't taking any chances.

"Leave that alone!" he barked, slamming the notebook shut.

Ronan wasn't entirely surprised by his brother's actions. He might have willingly given Michael his notebooks from classes that were part of the Double A curriculum, but when it came to his private research, he was downright territorial. Even still, Ronan felt his reaction was a bit extreme. "You don't have to get all brassed off about it!" Ronan yelled.

Stuffing the notebook into the drawer underneath the countertop, Ciaran apologized. "Sorry, you know how I get about my little projects."

The way you're reacting, it seems like this is a lot more important than one of your little projects, Ronan thought. He kept his suspicions to himself, however, knowing full well that if he accused Ciaran of doing anything more than conducting innocent experiments, his brother would respond with silence and a blank stare. "As long as you don't blow us up to smithereens," Ronan said, once again trying to make a joke despite his uneasy feeling.

"Impossible," Ciaran responded, completely missing the bait. "This is biology, not chemistry."

Shaking his head, Ronan realized he had overstayed his welcome and it was time to go. "And on that note, dear brother, I bid you adieu."

After Ronan left the room, Ciaran took out his notebook and started writing in it furiously. Line after line of symbols and formulas that ended in one word—Atlantium. Ciaran smiled triumphantly, but when he saw who was standing in front of him his smile disappeared.

"David!" Ciaran cried. "What are you doing here?"

"Is that any way to greet your headmaster?" David asked, in a voice more smooth than severe. "And your friend?"

Ciaran took a deep breath, knowing that he had to choose

his words wisely. "I'm sorry, it's just that, um, you startled me," Ciaran replied. "I was reviewing my work."

David's mouth smiled and he forced his piercing blue eyes to join in. "Then what an opportune time for a visit."

Straddling the lab stool, David sat across from Ciaran. He folded his hands, and Ciaran couldn't help noticing how strong they were, how thick and blunt his fingers looked, as if they could punch their way through concrete without tearing the skin, strangle a wild horse without effort. Bravely, Ciaran met David's gaze and thought his features had changed a bit since the last time he had seen him. His brow seemed wider, his jaw, still square, still decorated in a thin layer of red bristle, seemed stronger somehow, more powerful than before.

His entire look was softened, however, by his suit. Seersucker, white with delicate blue stripes, slightly crinkled. Underneath he wore a white cotton shirt, the top button undone, but adorned with a tie crocheted from silk yarn a shade of pink that reminded Ciaran of peppermint cream. The color should have clashed with David's red hair, but instead it complemented it beautifully. His overall appearance had been calculated to appear more casual than intimidating, and it was having its desired effect on Ciaran. Even when David spoke.

"I'm delighted to see that you haven't forgotten about our agreement," David said.

"Of course not," Ciaran replied. How could he forget? It's all he ever thought about, it's why he spent so much time in his lab. He had promised David that he would work with him to try to unlock the key to the water vamp's DNA, and in exhange he would be rewarded with prestige, honor, admiration, all the things he never received from his own family. But Ciaran hadn't expected it to be so difficult to hold up his end of the bargain. For months he had been conducting experiments on Michael's blood from samples David had given him. Ciaran never questioned how the specimens were obtained; he was merely a scientist conducting research. He didn't know that the embroidered handkerchief dotted with drops of Michael's blood was Nurse Radcliff's and had been soiled during a vicious attack. He also had no idea that the blood-stained T-shirt had once belonged to Amir Bhattarcharjee and had been used to clean up Michael's blood from the gym floor after Michael had a minor accident during swim practice. But even with Nurse Radcliff and Amir, now both destroyed, acting as unwitting assistants in Ciaran's experiments, he was still very far from a breakthrough. Ciaran had been certain that within those cells, the cells that had only recently been transformed from human into water vampire, he would find the key to their unnatural makeup and quite possibly a kind of physiological roadmap that would lead him to The Well. That had not been the case, not yet. "I think I *may* have found something that *could* be interesting," Ciaran confessed.

"Smashing!" David cried, tapping Ciaran's hand with his fingers. "Tell me, what did you find?"

"I've isolated a gene in Michael's blood that I've never found in Ronan's. It isn't human or one that's found in traditional vampire blood," Ciaran reported. "But I need to conduct further tests to find out exactly what it means."

The news wasn't entirely satisfying to David, but it was progress. And David had learned from years of manipulating the lower classes that progress deserved praise. "That's amazing," David declared. "Professor Chow was right, you really are brilliant when it comes to this scientific . . . stuff."

Ciaran felt the heat rise in his cheeks. Professor Chow and David were talking about him? Relaxing, he loosened his grip on his notebook, but kept his arm draped over the page. He was excited, but he still understood the need to keep his notes concealed from David's prying eyes. However, he hadn't yet learned to keep his thoughts from David's prying mind. "So what's this Atlantium?"

Shocked, Ciaran involuntarily glanced at his notebook. The word he had written down was being blocked by his arm, there was no way David could see it, unless he had some crazy X-ray vision. Maybe he did; Ciaran had no idea the extent of their powers. The only other alternative was that David was reading his mind. If that was true, David must have also discovered that Ciaran didn't think anyone other than a water vampire would ever be able to locate The Well.

"Oh that, it's just the . . . um, name I gave to the gene I found," Ciaran explained.

Folding his arms in front of his massive chest, David nodded. "I like the sound of it." He knew that was all the recognition Ciaran needed to make him offer a more detailed explanation. And he was right.

"It's really an anomaly, not even natural as far as I can tell," Ciaran said, fully aware that he was rambling, but fully unable to stop himself. "Like I said I'm doing some tests on it, but it's not like I can create a gene on my own. I'm good, but I'm not that good."

"Oh I wouldn't say that at all," David interrupted. "I wish I had a brain like yours. Genes, elements . . . Atlantium, it's all Greek to me."

Laughing along with David, Ciaran just couldn't keep quiet. "Plus I don't really have the resources for an experiment that advanced and unless I can do that I don't think I'll be able to find The Well."

The second the words tumbled out of his mouth, he knew they were not the words David wanted to hear. Perhaps he had said them deliberately. Ciaran knew after the incidents that had taken place during The Carnival for the Black Sun that David's main desire was to locate The Well in order to destroy it, and if he succeeded, what would that mean for his family? Could Ciaran really help David in this endeavor that had the potential to destroy an entire race? For the longest time he had tried not to think about it, he had tried to convince himself that there could be other outcomes, but the more he thought about it the more he knew there could be only one devastating consequence. Regardless of how abandoned he sometimes felt, he couldn't betray Ronan, his mother, and everyone else. Could he? Staring into David's powerful face, feeling the hypnotic pull of his eyes, he wasn't sure. The only thing he was sure of was that being in David's company felt right and he didn't want to be tossed aside and ignored yet again. "There's always Saoirse."

"Your sister?" David asked. "What exactly do you mean?"

Like Pandora after she lifted the lid, Ciaran realized there was no turning back. "Saoirse is an untapped resource," Ciaran began. "You know she's the child of two water vamps and still human."

"Yes, of course, doesn't everyone?"

Swallowing hard, Ciaran continued. "Then you must also know that she possesses incredible strength and unrealized abilities." Ciaran paused to keep his voice from shaking, but David nodded for him to carry on. "She might be human, but her blood isn't, it's scientifically impossible. Something must be preventing her from evolving into the creature she was born to be."

Resting his chin on his clenched hands, David absorbed Ciaran's information. "Yes, Chow was right, you're a regular Einstein," David commented. "Even if I could think like you can, I wouldn't know what to do with all that knowledge."

Luckily, Ciaran did.

"Let me compare Michael's blood to Saoirse's, let me conduct experiments on her as well," Ciaran suggested. "She has got to be linked to The Well even if she isn't aware of it."

"Do you think she'll go along with it?"

Ciaran didn't blink. "If I can't convince her, I'll do it without her consent."

"It looks like you have a lot of work to do." Without another word, David rose and walked to the door, turning back to face Ciaran only when he reached the archway. "Thank you," David said humbly. "I only wish I could count on everyone the way I can count on you."

Only after David was gone did Ciaran feel the sweat on his brow and his heart thump so wildly in his chest that he thought it might rip open his skin and burst through his shirt. He had no idea why he had offered his sister as a sacrifice, he had no idea why he was allowing his partnership with David to persist, but he knew it, ultimately, made him feel good. It was refreshing to have a purpose and be treated like an adult, like someone with worth and expertise. He didn't know where any of this might lead, but he knew that now his only choice was to forge ahead.

Hiding behind an expansive oak tree a few hundred yards away, Ronan felt the same way. As he watched David leave St. Albert's, one thought entered his mind: he had to confront his brother. Had Ciaran learned nothing from the recent events that plagued Double A? Why in the world would he be meeting secretly with David? What could they possibly have to talk about that wouldn't end in disaster? The only thing that stopped him from racing into the lab and dealing with his brother's duplicity head on was hearing Michael call his name.

"Ronan!" Michael cried out. "Where are you going?"

Stopping abruptly, Ronan turned around shocked to see Michael standing before him. His first instinct was to ask him why he was walking outside by himself, but he knew that would only serve to make Michael angry and was only a reaction to his just having seen David. Michael was capable of protecting himself; Ronan knew that. He also knew that Michael would understand what he had to do.

"I just saw David leave Ciaran's lab," Ronan explained. "I've got to make my brother understand he'd be insane to join his side."

But Michael didn't understand. "You'll be wasting your time."

"How can you say such a thing?" Ronan cried.

"Because it's the truth," Michael said, growing exasperated. "If Ciaran doesn't get the severity of the situation by now, there's nothing you can say or do that will change his mind."

"So what are you saying?" Ronan shouted, throwing his hands up in the air. "That I should do nothing?"

"Yes, that's exactly what I'm saying."

Ronan couldn't believe what he was hearing. Frustrated, he kicked a rock with such force that it flew about twenty feet above the highest tree before disappearing out of sight. His thoughts ricocheted in his mind: *Doesn't Michael know that David isn't going to stop trying to find The Well simply because he failed the first time? Doesn't Michael know that David's trying to coerce Ciaran into helping him defeat our kind? Doesn't Michael know that we could lose Ciaran forever?*

"Michael knows all of that, Ronan."

Stunned that Michael could telepathically hear him even though he wasn't consciously calling out to him, Ronan realized that his boyfriend was harnessing his vampire powers at an increasingly faster speed. He was impressed, but he was still concerned. "So does Michael know what Ronan should do?"

"Stay out of it," Michael said. "Whatever Ciaran decides to do is his choice."

That wasn't advice, that was an observation. "Well, yes," Ronan stuttered. "But . . ."

Michael wrapped his arms around Ronan and drew him in close. "But what? You've done everything you can for him," Michael continued. "You've been a good brother, not the best in the entire history of the world, but a lot better than when I first got here."

Their lips were so close that Ronan was finding it hard to concentrate on what Michael was saying, but he knew the words were important so he forced himself to listen. "If Ciaran can't see that and if he wants to work with Them like my father has chosen to do, well then as hard as it is to admit, you don't have the power to stop him."

Ronan had made the smart choice; it was what he needed to hear. Yes, he was a vampire and stronger than Ciaran in so many ways, but he was still his brother and because of that their relationship would always be complicated. It might serve them both best if Ronan stepped away and let Ciaran choose his own path. Ronan just prayed he didn't choose the one that would destroy him.

Pushing thoughts of his brother out of his mind, Ronan exhaled, releasing a long, slow stream of air so he could focus on the handsome boy wrapped in his arms. "Well, love, only seventeen and already such a wise, old sage."

Michael felt Ronan's lips press into his, and he started to chuckle. "Maybe Saoirse's right after all and I really am some special god."

Without letting go of Michael, Ronan knelt and laid him down on the ground. Ignoring the rough earth under them, the boys kissed and laughed and caressed each other in the shadow of the trees. "I don't know if you're a god," Ronan whispered. "But I do know that you're the ideal husband for me."

Abruptly, Michael pushed Ronan away and sat up. "Hey, wait a second."

"What's wrong?" Ronan asked, trying to get Michael to resume his horizontal position.

"You still haven't told me your secret."

Not now, now is not the time. "Tomorrow," Ronan said. "After our feeding."

Thankful that that was enough to satisfy Michael's curiosity, Ronan lay on top of him and kissed him deeply so he could satisfy his own growing desire.

The boys were so connected to one another, so lost in each other's embrace, they didn't even hear Imogene start to sing.

Had they listened to something other than the sound of their own breathing, had they reminded themselves to be aware of the world around them, they would have heard the clear, dulcet sounds of Imogene's tune. They could have followed the melody all the way to the cave where she had resided since her partial-death and uncovered her hiding place. But they were preoccupied, too engrossed in exploring each other's bodies, and for the moment weren't interested in exploring things that were just out of their reach. Imogene wouldn't have any new visitors today; she would still only have one companion—Brania. Both, however, were starting to become more aware that their constant cohabitation was losing its novelty.

"Don't stop!" Brania ordered when Imogene's singing was replaced with silence.

"I'm tired," Imogene replied, leaning her head against the soft, white satin on the inside of the coffin.

Brania understood the need for children to occasionally be disobedient, but her own child should know better and not behave like a savage human. "It's my favorite aria," Brania said, trying to find a tone that would appease Imogene.

"I don't care!" Imogene yelled. "I told you I'm tired and I don't want to sing."

Walking slowly toward the coffin, Brania felt her face contort, her hands curl into two clenched fists. She wanted to be a good parent, she wanted her daughter to know that she was loved and cherished, but she also wanted to hear her music. When she reached the side of the coffin, Imogene turned her head away from her, and Brania had to resist the urge to grab Imogene by the scruff of the neck and force her to look at her, show her the respect that she deserved as her mother, her savior. Instead, she bent her head and willed her voice to sound caring and doused with a mother's love. "Please, Imogene, do what you do best and make your mother happy."

When Imogene resumed her singing, when the cave was once again filled with the girl's sweet, lilting voice, Brania was horrified. She was no longer listening to Imogene sing; she was no longer in the cave. She had been transported back through time and was a young child, standing in a field with cornhusks almost taller than she was. In her hand was a rock, and crouched next to her was her father. He whispered into her ear the words that would entice her to commit the evil act she didn't want to perform, the words that would convince her to use the rock to strike the little boy who was running toward her, the little boy who thought she had called him over to play, not to die.

"Please, Brania, do what you do best and make your father happy."

Repulsed, Brania realized she was indeed her father's daughter.

chapter 4

For the first time in years, Michael was excited about the start of the new school year. In Weeping Water it had always filled him with contrasting emotions—he embraced his education and loved learning new things in most all of his subjects, he just hated feeling like an outsider among his classmates. It was how he had felt all through grammar school and junior high. He had thought his freshman year at Two W High School might have been a new beginning, but he had been wrong. Everything changed when he transferred to Double A. Not only was the education superior, the social aspect was immensely improved as well.

But then last semester, his first after crossing over and being transformed into a vampire, the luster had faded. He had thought that as an immortal creature education was now beneath him. Thanks, in part, to Ronan's guidance, he had quickly learned school was more important than ever before.

If he were going to live forever, it would help to acquire as much knowledge as possible. Sitting on the bed together side by side, their legs casually intertwined, Michael and Ronan reviewed their schedules to see what the new term would offer them. And of course to see if they shared any classes.

"Just two," Michael said. "British lit first thing in the morning and Advanced Geometry in the afternoon."

"Really?" Ronan asked. "My head might explode."

Michael laughed, but didn't agree. He found Father Fazio's somnolent lectures so boring he usually found himself falling asleep in class. "The only way my head's going to explode in Father Faz's class is if his voice puts me in a coma and I crack my skull on the desk."

"No, I'm talking about Brit lit," Ronan corrected. "I'll start my day with the two hottest guys on campus, you and McLaren."

This time Michael laughed even harder and had to agree; McLaren was the most handsome professor they had, complete with Hollywood tan, dazzling smile, and a worked-out body. But he whacked Ronan in the shoulder with his class schedule just the same. "Don't you get any crazy ideas about becoming teacher's pet and volunteering for extracurricular activities," Michael warned.

Grabbing Michael's wrist, Ronan gave him a tug so he fell into his lap and joked, "But think of all the extra knowledge I can acquire from private sessions."

They were laughing so hard they didn't hear the knock at the door and only became aware of David's presence when he cleared his throat. "Forgive me for interrupting playtime."

His words hurtled toward the boys like a rush of cold wind. Instinctively, their bodies separated; an intruder was present and they were on guard, prepared to defend themselves. Ronan felt Michael's heart race as if it were beating in his own chest, and he placed a hand on Michael's knee to prevent him from getting off the bed. No need to give David a reason to get violent. Ronan prevented Michael from attacking David, but not from speaking.

"It's impossible for you to enter our home without an invitation!" Michael barked.

David howled. He threw his head back and his laughter engulfed the room. He cherished moments like these, when his opponents proved themselves to be nothing more than fools. "Oh Michael, I thought you were smarter than that," David chided. "Haven't you yet discovered that conventional rules have no meaning here at Archangel Academy?"

Feeling like a jerk, Michael felt the temperature of his blood rise. David was right. Everything he knew about vampires was turning out to be antiquated folklore; the truth of the species was much different than the legends. Plus, Double A had its own set of complex rules and regulations, all of which defied logic. *Fine,* Michael thought, *score one for the redheaded beast.*

"What do you want, David?" Ronan asked.

Even though he knew Ronan had addressed him informally on purpose, the muscles in David's cheeks still flinched. He decided to ignore the breach in decorum and answer the question as directly as it was asked. "The new term is about to begin, so Michael will need to move his car from its current location," David said. "It makes a colorful lawn ornament, but it's impinging the growth of the grass. And our landscapers work so hard to keep the grounds pristine."

"How do you know the car is mine?" Michael demanded.

Sneering at the boy, David felt his body stiffen and his fury swell. If Michael were alone, he would use all his preternatural strength, all the strength endowed to him by Zachariel, to attack, destroy, and kill the disgusting creature who dared to defy him. He would rip the flesh off his bones with his own fangs and spit out the pieces of rancid meat as he watched Michael's dirty, hybrid blood pour from his ravaged body and flood the room. He would cry victoriously as he rammed a stake through Michael's heart. He would smile as Michael's body burst into flames. He would accept the ash that would spray over him as glory from his god. But Michael wasn't alone; Ronan was beside him, and David understood all too well the power of love. It wouldn't be wise to attack the boy with his lover present. David might be growing impatient, but he wasn't impulsive.

He also wasn't going to give Michael the answer that he wanted to hear: that he knew the car was his because Michael's father had told him so. "There's a big, black bow on the roof of the car, and you've recently celebrated a birthday," David said. "Whose else could it be?"

Before Michael could respond with another antagonistic remark, Ronan intervened. "Just tell us where we should move it to."

David's grin became genuine. It was heartwarming to hear even the most disobedient student speak words of compliance. "The parking lot outside the headmaster's office," David instructed.

Pressing into Michael's knee with a bit more pressure, Ronan replied, "That won't be a problem."

The boys watched David's grin morph back into a smirk, and they knew he felt as if he had won this little confrontation even before his words confirmed it. "I didn't think there would be."

Standing in the doorway, David turned to offer one last piece of instruction. "And remember, students are only allowed to drive on the weekends and only into Eden."

Although he turned his back on them to leave the room, it didn't signal the end of their conversation. Michael was determined to have the last word. "I didn't think rules had any meaning here at Double A?"

When David turned back to face them, Ronan could see the man's body vibrate, and he could tell David was fighting the urge to transform into his true, vampiric self. He knew that David wanted his fangs to descend and his eyes to blacken in order to show Michael that he wasn't dealing with a mere adult but an ancient being who possessed extraordinary power, power that was begging to be released. But David surprised them both and displayed immense restraint. He simply gripped the side of the door with his hand, but so tightly that Ronan was afraid the door would snap in two.

"As your headmaster, Michael, the only rules that have any meaning here are mine," David said, his voice as firm as concrete. "If you'd like to remain a student of this institution, I implore you to remember that."

David left as quietly as he had appeared, the door barely making a sound as it closed behind him. It took less than a second for the quiet to be disrupted.

"Are we supposed to just forget what he tried to do?!" Michael screamed, jumping off the bed. "Are we supposed to forget that he's our enemy and act like he's nothing more than our headmaster just because school's about to start up again?!"

Ronan watched Michael pace the room like Michael had watched him do so many times before, but this time there was a change. Michael wasn't moving from one end of the room to another as a result of frustration; he was moving with purpose. His strides weren't occupying time because his mind had lost control of its body; they were helping him formulate a plan. The realization made Ronan both proud and scared. He didn't want Michael to scurry away from confrontation, but he didn't want him to run headlong into it either. It was time to offer some insight. "As difficult as it might be to accept," Ronan began, "as long as we're at Double A, David is our headmaster."

"He's a piece of sh . . ."

"Who deserves our respect!" Ronan shouted over Michael's more derogatory description.

Finally, Michael stopped in his tracks and stared at Ronan as if he had never seen him before. "Are you serious?"

Ronan knelt on the bed and reached out his hand to Michael, but Michael wouldn't budge. When he realized his boyfriend wasn't going to reconsider, Ronan let his arm fall limply at his side. "Our race agreed a long time ago to coexist peacefully with David's kind," Ronan explained. "Regardless of their actions we will not provoke a war."

Michael knew the jargon, he knew the peace-comes-first philosophy of The Well and he agreed with it, but The Well didn't have to live near David. The Well didn't have to see his smug, ugly face every day and bow to him like he was some righteous ruler. It was outrageous to be expected to sit by quietly and not do anything. "So we just let them destroy us?!"

"Of course not! We defend ourselves when necessary!" Ronan said, his voice rising to match Michael's volume. "But we *do not* instigate violence, Michael. It's not who we are! We're about bloody peace for God's sake!"

There was nothing peaceful about how Ronan looked. Kneeling on the bed, his back was rigid, his fists were clenched, and one arm was raised high over his head. The only movement, in fact, came from his chest that heaved from the exertion of his declaration. Despite his words about upholding an ideology of peace, Michael thought he looked like some fanatical warrior hell-bent on leading an army into a deadly skirmish. His unbridled passion was unexpectedly comical. "Should I call the troops to war, general?"

Catching a sideways glimpse of himself in the mirror, Ronan collapsed onto his bed into fits of laughter. Once again, Michael had helped diffuse a situation that threatened to get out of hand. Once again he showed Ronan that there were more important things in life to worry about than David and his next actions. Things like grabbing Michael's hand and throwing him on their bed so they could laugh and cuddle and kiss. "Sorry, love," Ronan murmured. "I can get carried away sometimes."

Ronan's excitement didn't bother Michael at all; he welcomed his passion almost as much as he welcomed every opportunity to get lost in his kisses and his embrace. However, at the moment they had other things to do. Squirming out from under Ronan's body, Michael jumped to the side of the bed. "No can do, Ro," Michael announced. "Per the headmaster's decree I have more important things to do, like convince you to move my car."

Extending his hand to Michael, Ronan had other plans. "I have a better idea," he said. "Let's feed."

They found the body less than a minute later on the outskirts of Eden, at the bottom of a hill that was steep, but not particularly tall. Maybe thirty years old, the man was thin and dressed in shorts and a T-shirt, his knapsack still on his back and his hand still clutching a map of the area. Although Ronan and Michael both had the ability to detect when death was imminent, they didn't need those skills to know the man was seconds from dying; they simply had to look at the way his body was distorted. His legs were bent at peculiar angles, and his neck was twisted severely to one side. It was an unusual state for a body to be in, but one that was enormously appetizing.

Michael watched as Ronan's face elongated, his eyes became more like diamonds instead of circles, his sharp, white fangs appeared and rested on his plump, red lips. Michael thought Ronan had never looked more beautiful.

The man barely moved as Ronan's fangs plunged into the largest vein that protruded from his neck and Ronan sucked out the blood that would soon be wasted if it remained in its original host. The blood was refreshingly sweet; the man had obviously been healthy, and his irreversible condition the result of an unfortunate accident. Unfortunate for him, but bounty for Ronan and Michael.

As he lifted his head, drops of blood spilled down the corners of Ronan's mouth. Unable to control his hunger at the sight, Michael leaned forward and licked the blood from Ronan's chin until there wasn't a trace left. Unfulfilled and growing delirious, Michael punctured two more holes into the man's neck with his fangs and held his body close to him as he felt the man's blood gush over his tongue. A rush of energy entered his body and spread out through his limbs, caressing his organs, making him feel superhuman. Consumed with desire and vitality, Michael spontaneously kissed Ronan deeply on his bloodied lips, their fangs pressing against each other roughly. He was wild-eyed, and Michael's voice was a harsh whisper when he spoke. "Let's offer ourselves to The Well."

Naked, they dove into the ocean and plunged deep into the sea's belly until they reached an area that could never be seen by a mortal's eyes—the underwater cave that housed The Well of Atlantis. When they entered the enclave, a low hum emitted from the rock walls as if to welcome the boys. The sound was familiar and yet thicker than usual, more resonant, and it seemed to pierce through their bodies even as it floated gently over their heads. The Well was greeting them as it always did, but this time its greeting was more intense.

Kneeling before the circular stone, Michael and Ronan each cut their palms with their fangs and lifted their hands above the center of The Well so their blood could spill into the silvery water below. Even though they had witnessed this miracle many times before, they still watched in awe as their blood swirled with the holy water to create something new, something that only their eyes could behold: the mixture of their blood, their souls, and the life force of The Well.

Their voices mimicked their clasped hands, and they became one as they recited the ancient prayer:

> *"Unto The Well I give our life*
> *our bodies' blood that makes us whole.*
> *We vow to honor and protect*
> *and ask The Well to house our souls."*

Immediately the transformation began. Their hands and feet lost their human appearance and became webbed; their bodies and their limbs grew even longer. Together, they dipped their webbed hands into The Well to scoop up its silver water, and then they drank the now-familiar brew. As the cold liquid filled their bodies, a translucent light—like the one that shone from the center of The Well—emanated from their skin. They were being illuminated by their creator, in Its beloved image.

The cave was suddenly aglow with the combination of light that shone from Michael, Ronan, and The Well, and it looked as if the sun had fallen from the sky, submerged itself under the ocean, and decided to light up the sea. The rock walls of the cave twinkled as if they were covered with rows and rows of sparkling lights. The ground was hardly visible, and the boys looked like they were standing on a floor of white electricity. It was obvious: The Well was truly grateful for their offering, and in turn the boys felt truly blessed.

Ronan was already sitting on the shore of Inishtrahull Island when Michael emerged from the ocean. He watched his boyfriend walk toward him and did his best to control his anxiety. Michael sat down and allowed his bare, wet shoulder to graze against Ronan's, but kept his eyes transfixed on the undulating ocean. He knew Ronan was going to tell him his final secret. He knew he would listen to every word that Ronan had to say, but he didn't think he could watch him as he spoke. He just didn't think he was that brave.

Ronan, however, knew better. He touched Michael's hand softly and turned him so they could face each other. He was so beautiful. Aflame with The Well's power, Michael radiated strength, both physical and emotional. Yes, Michael was nervous. He was unsure of what Ronan was going to tell him, unsure that he even wanted to hear it. But just by looking at him, his face stoic, his eyes compassionate, Ronan was confident that Michael would hear his words with both an open mind and heart and that he would ultimately accept his words with grace and thankfulness. Once he heard Ronan's story, he would understand why it was so important that it had to be shared.

"I need to tell you about Morgandy," Ronan said. "Morgandy van der Poole."

Michael had never heard of the name before and yet he knew it was the name of his enemy. The reaction was primal, instinctive. Somehow, he also knew that it was the name of Ronan's first soul mate.

"He was the eldest son of a major Atlantian family. He was preordained to become a Guardian of The Well," Ronan explained. "And I loved him."

As unhappy as Michael was to hear that last bit of information, that news didn't come as a shock either. Michael had known there was someone who had come before him and Nakano, someone who Ronan had been in love with. Giving that love a name didn't change the past. It did, however, make it more permanent and make it more difficult for Michael to ignore the fact that he wasn't Ronan's only love.

"I can't lie and tell you that I didn't think I would spend all eternity with Morgandy when we asked The Well to join our souls," Ronan admitted. "At the time it was what I wanted." His next words caught in his throat, and Ronan paused. It had been a long time since he had said Morgandy's name out loud. He thought it would be easy; he didn't think it would conjure such a wellspring of emotion and make him feel as unstable as a wave caught in the tide, but he was wrong. He looked away from Michael and watched the waves roll closer, then recede. Michael knew Ronan had no interest in watching the ocean's dance; he was pausing to find the strength to continue. Michael would wait as long as it took.

"Until I learned the truth," Ronan resumed, his voice stronger now. "Until I learned that Morgandy never loved me, he never wanted to be my soul mate. He merely wanted to betray our people and the sanctity of The Well."

Breathing deeply, Michael felt the sun and salt water in the air. It almost made him feel as good as it did to hear the honesty in Ronan's voice. Ronan meant it when he said he didn't want there to be any more secrets between them. He was keeping his promise not because he felt a need to confess, or because he was scared that Michael would one day stumble upon his secret, but because he loved and trusted Michael and wanted to share every detail of his life with him, the good and the bad. "It wasn't until after we pledged our souls that I discovered he was secretly working for David."

Michael had not expected that twist to Ronan's story, and the surprise revelation forced him to break his silence. "Morgandy was one of *Them?*"

"Physically he was still a water vampire," Ronan explained. "But spiritually he was part of David's race."

A gentle breeze blew past, cooling the fire that was beginning to consume them. Ronan accepted this intrusion as a reason to rest, calm his mind; Michael accepted it as a reminder that Ronan was his sole purpose now and that he needed to embrace every opportunity to let Ronan know that he would never leave his side. Michael held Ronan's hands tighter. He stared at his face until Ronan had no other choice but to return the gaze. When he did, Ronan saw nothing but love in his eyes.

"That must have really hurt," Michael said.

Nodding slightly, Ronan answered. "Yes, it did." Ronan caressed Michael's hands and noticed that they felt stronger than before. They were still incredibly smooth, but as if stone lived under the flesh. "He was my first love. He was handsome, charming, worldlier than I was."

Michael couldn't help but smile. "I know exactly how that feels."

Blushing, yet alarmed, Ronan hadn't realized those same words could have been used by Michael to describe Ronan in the early days of their relationship. He had to make him understand that beyond the superficial description, there was no comparison. "But Morgandy didn't love me like I love you," Ronan said, his voice so earnest it almost broke Michael's heart.

"I know," Michael said. "I didn't mean to suggest..."

He didn't want to keep talking, so Michael kissed Ronan, softly, but long enough to make Ronan understand he had not meant to compare him to Morgandy. Ronan was grateful, and one kiss turned into another and then several. It was splendid kissing Ronan on the beach, their bodies drenched in sunlight, but Michael wanted to know what had happened to Morgandy once his duplicity was revealed. Pulling away from Ronan, Michael asked, "So what happened once you found out his real agenda?"

"The Well intervened," Ronan replied. "It showed Morgandy and every other Atlantian just how powerful It is."

Michael tried to wait for Ronan to continue, but he couldn't; he was dying of curiosity. "So what exactly did The Well do?"

"The Well gave us back our souls, and our connection to each other was forever broken."

Although Ronan spoke the words simply, Michael knew the emotions that surrounded them had to be complex. He must have been heartbroken, Michael realized, devastated that someone he loved could turn against not only him, but his entire race. That's how Michael would feel if Ronan ever betrayed him. The thought filled Michael up with such despair and fear, he shook his head to unleash it from his mind.

Unfortunately, Michael knew there was more to the story. "So what happened to Morgandy?" he asked. "After, you know, The Well separated the two of you."

"I don't know," Ronan said, shrugging his shoulders, the anxiety finally released from his face. "He was cast out and banished from ever living among water vampires again. Truth is, I don't even know if he's still alive."

Contemplating it for a moment, Michael didn't think Morgandy's survival was possible. "How could a water vampire live without being connected to The Well?"

Ronan wanted to feel Michael's warm embrace, and so he turned him so his back leaned into his chest and wrapped his arms around him. "I don't think it's possible, love," Ronan said. "Along with human blood, it's the life force that keeps us alive."

Just when Michael was getting comfortable with the silence and the feeling of Ronan's heart beating into his own skin, Ronan resumed his story. "Right after that my mum wanted me and Ciaran to go to Archangel Academy together," he said. "She blamed herself because she was living in France near Saoirse's school and wasn't keeping her eye on me. Not that she could've seen anything coming. Everyone thought that my future was set."

His eyes closed, it looked as if Michael was sleeping in Ronan's arms, but he had heard every word. "Because Morgandy was supposed to be this Guardian and you were going to be like the Guardian's husband?"

He really finds humor in the most impossible situations, Ronan thought. "Something like that," he said, nuzzling his lips against Michael's warm neck.

Once again their kisses grew in number and passion, and soon Ronan was lying on top of Michael, their bodies moving as fluidly as the ocean. "I'm sorry Morgandy lied to you," Michael said. "But at the same time I have to give him a big fat thank you wherever he is."

Ronan understood. "Me too."

"Otherwise, I might not find myself in this position," Michael said, grinning widely. "Or this one." Unexpectedly, Michael rolled over so Ronan was now pinned against the sand and Michael was lying on top of him.

Looking up, Ronan squinted at the image of Michael's angelic face, his blond hair almost white as it disappeared into the sun's glow, the same distinct color as Morgandy's. No! Ronan was thankful that the glare of the sun obscured his shock from Michael's view. How could he think that Michael bore any resemblance to Morgandy? They didn't share any of the same qualities, not in mind, spirit, not even in body. Ronan shut his eyes tight, and when he opened them he saw that Michael looked the same as always. "Forever beautiful, forever mine."

Michael laid his body flat against Ronan, and they rose and fell in one breath. "Thank you," Michael whispered. "Thank you for telling me about your past and especially about Morgandy."

"You're welcome, love," Ronan replied. "And I probably don't have to say this, but you have nothing to fret about. I don't have any feelings for Morgandy."

Hmm. Michael needed to be sure Ronan was indeed telling the truth. "You may not love him, but don't you hate him now?"

Without hesitation, Ronan replied, "Not at all. All my feelings for him, good and bad, died a long time ago. That part of my life is over."

Michael accepted Ronan's kisses, but not his words. He knew Ronan believed what he said was the truth, that Morgandy was part of his past, part of every water vampire's past. But somehow he also knew that was wrong.

chapter 5

Michael hated to admit it, but his father had excellent taste in cars.

The Mercedes Benz SUV was sleek and formidable, like a metal and chrome chariot that had been drenched in crimson blood. The color choice was hardly subtle, but picked to arouse Michael's senses. Despite his resistance, it was working. Michael imagined that sitting in the driver's seat would be like being in the center of a bloodstained cloud. He pictured himself perched high above the ground, gripping the steering wheel and leaning his body into the contours of the black leather seat as he drove into Eden waving to his classmates and strangers. He imagined the look of shock that would appear on R.J.'s face if he ever pulled into the gas station driving this instead of his grandfather's beat-up Bronco. That would be priceless. Everyone who saw him would be jealous of his luxurious car. Everyone who saw him would know he was special.

But if someone did see him drive the car, if someone saw him just sitting in it, wouldn't they really be admiring his father? The first question anyone would ask would be "Where'd you get such an awesome car?" And Michael would be forced to reply, "It was a birthday gift from my dad."

As he stood in front of the Benz, his hands buried into the front pockets of his shorts so they wouldn't reach out and feel how insanely smooth and magical he knew the hood of the car had to feel, the rest of the imaginary conversation played out in Michael's head.

"Your father got you a Benz for your birthday?!" the stranger would say. "Dude, you must have the best dad in the world."

"Not really," Michael would tersely reply.

"Come off it," the stranger would press on. "Do you know how expensive that thing is?"

"He's just trying to buy my love."

"C'mon, cut the guy some slack."

"Should I also cut him some slack for brutally murdering my mother and making everyone think she committed suicide?"

Michael waited for the stranger's response, but none came. But really, what could anyone say after a comment like that even if the conversation was only being played out in his mind? *No! This had to stop!* Michael told himself. He didn't want to think constantly about what his father had done; he didn't want to be reminded constantly that his father had destroyed his family so callously, so definitively. Michael shook his head to force the negative images to leave. But as he pushed the unpleasant thoughts from his mind, another filled the space, one that was much more disturbing than all the others combined. Even if his father had done nothing to his mother, Grace would still have killed herself that night; her note was proof. So his father's actions, while vile and deplorable, had only accelerated his mother's death; they weren't the primary cause.

Stunned by this revelation, Michael's body froze as his mind reeled. How could he think such a thing? It was horrible, shameful, and yet, sadly, it was true. Is this how a vampire thinks? Logically, coldly, without allowing human emotion to corrupt the basis of understanding? Ronan wasn't like that. No, not at all. Well, that wasn't completely true, Michael realized. Ronan wasn't inhuman with him, but he did have another side. His views about some people and situations were much more analytical than Michael's were. Sure, he got hotheaded about certain things, like when he talked about the complex relationship between water vamps and David's race, but he could also approach a topic quite impersonally and remove all sentiment from the solution. Maybe it was just because Ronan was older, raised much differently than he was. Or maybe it was just because vampires were coldhearted as well as cold-blooded.

Were he and Ronan destined to become like Vaughan and David? Or would their connection to The Well ensure that their humanity would remain intact as long as they walked the earth disguised as humans? Michael was more confused than ever. *How in the world did I get from thinking about my car to thinking about my morality?*

All thoughts—simple and complex—were forgotten when Michael saw a patch of fog raise from the ground. Phaedra! She hadn't abandoned him. She knew he needed to be rescued, and she had returned. He watched the fog spin like a baby cyclone, and anticipation swelled in his heart. But just like in his dream, the fog turned out to be nothing unnatural. In this instance, merely the dusty remnants of someone who had raced toward him with incredible speed. Someone he had never expected to see.

Thanks a lot, Phaedra! Michael thought. *This has got to be some sort of cosmic joke.*

"I heard Fritz blethering on about your fancy new car, so I thought I'd check it out for myself."

Michael hadn't seen Nakano since the end of school. He didn't know if Nakano was spending the summer on campus, if he had moved in with Jean-Paul, or if he had returned home to be with his family, if he even had a family. Staring at the boy, Michael suddenly realized he didn't know very much about Nakano other than the basic facts: his motives were suspect, his hair was once again too long, and he hated Michael. The last item made it difficult for Michael to understand why Nakano was standing next to him. Not as difficult to understand, however, as why Michael didn't just leave. But why should he? After all, he was there first. Nope, he was staying put.

"Well, take a good look at it," Michael said. "If that's what you came to see."

Nakano stared straight ahead, his hands also tucked into the pockets of his shorts, which were jeans cut off just above the knee, and he lifted his chin to study the car. He looked like a surveyor inspecting a plot of land. "For once Fritz wasn't talking through the back of his neck," Nakano declared. "Freakin' awesome car you got there."

This made absolutely no sense. *Why was Nakano here? Why did he care about my car? And why am I talking to him?* "Thanks," Michael said in a voice halfway between surprised and sincere.

"My bum dad doesn't even send me a card on my birthday," Nakano admitted. "Not even sure he knows what day I was born."

So that was it! Nakano wasn't paying Michael a compliment; he was praising Vaughan. And why not? They were more like family than Michael and his father were. "First gift I got from him in seventeen years," Michael said.

"Kind of makes up for it if you ask me," Nakano replied.

Well, I didn't ask you! Michael thought. *I don't even know why you're here. We're not friends. It's not like I care what you have to say.* And yet Michael was listening to every word Nakano said. He hadn't asked him to leave, nor had he left Nakano alone to admire the car he so obviously coveted. For some reason despite all their previous differences—and those differences were huge—neither boy felt the urge to escape each other's presence. Maybe because they were tired of running in the opposite direction? Or maybe because they both knew that it was time to end their feud and accept the fact that they actually had more in common than they wanted to admit?

"So are you going to drive it?" Nakano asked. "Or just stare at it?"

"I haven't decided."

Nodding as if he understood Michael's dilemma, Nakano continued. "Cars aren't allowed on campus you know, against the so-called rules and all."

"Yeah, David informed me that I have to move it," Michael replied.

Finally, Kano turned to face Michael and spoke to him directly for the first time. "So what's the problem? You got your license, didn't you?" he asked, knowing full well the answer. "Not that you needed anything so . . . human."

Why couldn't anybody understand the importance of having a driver's license? "Ever since I was a little kid I always thought being able to drive would give me freedom."

"Blah, blah, blah, blah, blah." Nakano crossed his arms in front of his chest, one thin, sinewy arm on top of the other, and tilted his head back and forth when he spoke. He looked and sounded like a child in a schoolyard mocking his playmate.

As odd as he looked, this was the Nakano Michael had come to know. "So you just came here to make fun of me?"

Abruptly, Kano stopped moving his body and stared at Michael as intently as he had previously been inspecting the car. "Let it go, Howard," Kano said.

"Let *what* go?"

"Your license, this car, your relationship with your father even," Nakano explained. "None of that really means anything, does it? Not sure why you're making them out to be so bleedin' special."

It was weird enough to be standing next to Nakano having a semicivilized conversation, but it was completely insane to think that Nakano might have offered him a solution to his problem when no one else could. Nakano's comment offered him solace. "That actually makes sense."

"Of course it does," Kano replied, turning his attention back to the Benz. "You got your powers and your immortality and . . . Ronan. This car and everything it represents means nothing to you."

It was true, and suddenly Michael felt foolish for making the car seem much more important than it actually was.

"It can only have a hold over you if you let it," Kano added. "No matter how sweet the car looks, it's still just a car."

Michael turned to Nakano and said two words to him that he never, ever thought he'd say. "Thank you."

In response, Nakano shrugged his shoulders and mumbled, "Don't mention it." It was an attempt to be cavalier, to try to act and sound as if Michael's words, his appreciation, weren't welcomed.

Looking at the car, Michael could finally see it for what it was, an extraordinary piece of craftsmanship, but not the ticket to his freedom or public admiration. "I really mean it, Nakano, thanks a lot." Nakano stepped forward and pressed his face against the driver's side window. "If you really want to thank me," he said, his breath fogging up the window. "Why don't you take me for a ride?"

Michael felt his forehead crinkle; it was just about the weirdest proposition he had ever been offered. But Michael had learned to embrace the weird. "Okay."

Without a second thought, Michael took the keys out of his pocket and clicked the button that released the locks on the car doors. Nakano was already sitting in the passenger seat before Michael had a chance to open up the driver's side door. He turned the key in the ignition, and the Benz proved to be as beautiful inside as it was out; the car hardly made a sound when it started.

"Niiiiiiiiiiice," Nakano said approvingly.

"Guess that's what they mean when they say an engine purrs," Michael added. The hum was soft and smooth and not completely unlike the vibrations of The Well. Despite the odd choice of Nakano's being his very first passenger, Michael took the sound as an omen that he had made the right decision.

He drove to the parking lot slowly, not because he was scared or being careful, but because he wanted to savor the experience. It was the first time in his life that he was driving without an instructor. It was a milestone, and he wanted it to last as long as possible. When he saw Saoirse near the edge of campus, he also realized how much he really wanted to share it with everyone. Beeping, he waved his hand wildly out the window. "Saoirse!"

Startled, the girl turned her head, but instead of waving back or running toward the car to greet Michael, she ran in the other direction, into the woods. "What the hell?" Michael muttered. He beeped again, but she was already out of sight. "Why'd she do that?"

Holding his arm out the window to feel the soft breeze caress his hand, Nakano remarked, "Because girls are freakish."

Michael turned back to see who Saoirse had been talking to. He could have sworn he had seen her lips moving as if she had been talking to someone who must have been standing just behind the large oak tree, but no one was visible. "Did you see anybody with her?" Michael asked.

"Nope," Kano replied. "Just enjoying the ride."

And what a smooth ride it was. Only a short distance, but Michael could tell the Benz handled the road a lot better than Blakeley's old Honda. Proudly, Michael parked the car in an empty spot in the small parking lot behind the headmaster's office. He turned to thank Nakano again for giving him the push he needed and making him realize what a fool he was being. But Nakano was already gone. *Girls weren't the only ones who could be freakish,* Michael thought. It didn't matter. He didn't need Saoirse or Nakano to acknowledge him or go crazy over his car to make him feel like the luckiest kid in the world. There was only one person he needed to do that.

When he got to St. Sebastian's Ronan was there as he had suspected. However, he hadn't expected to see him sitting on the side of the pool, his feet dangling in the water; he had thought he would find him swimming. Ronan didn't need to practice to maintain his form, but he enjoyed spending as much time in the water as possible. "You keep practicing like that," Michael said, "and I'll have no problem beating you this year."

Smiling, Ronan reached out his hand, and Michael took it. He kicked off his flip-flops and sat next to him, submerging his feet in the cold water. "Ooh that feels nice," Michael remarked.

"Not as good as this," Ronan corrected. He pulled Michael closer and kissed him on the lips, only once, then rested his forehead onto his. Michael loved how Ronan's skin felt— strong and warmed by the sun that flooded the gym. Their noses pressed against each other, their breaths instantly adjusting to the other's rhythm.

"I made a decision," Michael whispered.

"What's that, love?"

"My father isn't going to stand in the way of my freedom and ruin my life," he said. "I drove my car."

"Good for you," Ronan replied, genuinely happy.

Michael broke their connection and sat back. "And you'll never guess who drove shotgun."

"Who?"

"Nakano."

"Seriously?!" Ronan shouted, genuinely surprised.

"Believe me, I'm more shocked than you are," Michael replied. "I'll tell you all about it later."

Smiling, Ronan said, "However it happened, I'm glad you finally got behind the wheel."

"Me too," Michael agreed. "But just because I did doesn't mean I forgive my dad. It just means that I like to drive, and of course I had to park my car properly before David had another hissy fit."

Ronan closed his eyes. "I'm glad you understand that the relationship between parents and their children can be complicated."

Ronan's tone had hardly changed, but Michael knew he was no longer talking exclusively about him and his father. "Um, you don't have another secret to tell me, do you?" Michael asked, only half-kidding. "Like maybe somebody else came before Morgandy?"

Opening his eyes, Ronan shook his head. "No, you know about everyone from my past now."

Well, if it wasn't Morgandy or another boyfriend, what could it be? "So then what's wrong?"

Smiling wistfully to cover up a sigh, Ronan covered Michael's hands with his own. "I still haven't heard from my mum."

"After all this time she still hasn't gotten in touch with you," Michael said. "Even, you know, just a telepathic 'Hey, how ya doin'.' "

Ronan kicked his feet in the water, his body as restless as

his spirit, and the pool was immediately filled with tiny waves. Up and down and up and down, the water kept rising and falling, slapping into the sides of the pool so hard that water sprayed over onto the gym floor even after his legs stopped moving. "I tried reaching out to her telepathically, I tried calling her cell phone, I even tried calling her private line that she instructed us to use only if it was a dire emergency and we didn't want to risk someone's tapping into our minds, and nothing, not one word from her!" Ronan blurted. "It's like she's deliberately blocking me out."

Angry and frustrated, Ronan let go of Michael's hands and leaned forward. His body hunched, tense, he stared into the pool, the surface once again calm, as if the water could unlock the mystery of his mother's silence. The water held no answers, but Michael did.

"Let's go."

Looking up, Ronan saw that Michael was standing next to him, towering above him, his hand outstretched. Still lost in his own emotions, Ronan was too confused to respond right away. "I said, let's go," Michael reiterated.

The firmness of Michael's voice propelled Ronan into action. He took his hand and stood up, half on his own and half relying on Michael's strength to hoist him upright. "Where are we going?" Ronan asked quietly.

"To get to the bottom of Edwige's vanishing act," Michael proclaimed. "Now that I've sort of made resolution with my father, it's time you did the same with yours." Michael smirked, "Well, with your mother, but you know what I mean."

Always the romantic, Ronan kissed a few knuckles on Michael's hand. "Yes, I do."

Resisting the urge to roll his eyes, Michael once again repeated himself. "Now come on, let's go visit your mother."

As Michael made a move toward the front entrance of the gym, Ronan lurched toward the back door. "Why are you going that way?" Ronan asked. "Someone might see us sprinting off campus."

Smugly, Michael smiled. "We're not going to use our water vampabilities to visit your mother's flat. I'm taking you for a drive."

"You can't drive to London," Ronan protested, his voice shrilly echoing in the gym. "You heard what David said."

Michael grabbed Ronan's hand firmly. "And don't you remember what I said? Rules were made to be broken."

Yes, they were, Ronan thought. *Weren't they living proof of that?* "Well, all right then," Ronan agreed. "Let's go to London."

Just as they were about to step outside, Michael turned to Ronan, his eyes wide with excitement. "And don't you love my new word? We've got water vampabilities!"

This time it was Ronan who had to stop himself from rolling his eyes. He couldn't, however, stop himself from teasing Michael. "You are off your dot," Ronan said, giving Michael a playful push. "Do you know that, Howard?"

Proudly, Michael responded, "Yes, Glynn-Rowley, I most certainly do."

Just before Michael started the engine he got nervous. What if David was lurking in The Forest? What if he was standing in his office, peeking through his blinds, watching them right now? Or what if one of his minions were spying on them? Anything was possible, Michael thought; any scenario could be real. And just like that Michael thought any alibi could be the truth.

He started the engine, and as the sound of the Benz's delightful purr filled his ears, Michael decided that if David approached them, he would simply say they were driving into Eden since it was Friday, which was technically considered part of the weekend. A bit of a stretch—well, an out-and-out lie—but Michael thought it would suffice as an explanation.

Turned out his preparation was unnecessary, and no one stopped them as they drove toward the front gate. But just as they were about to cross the metal entrance gate and exit the Archangel campus, they faced another obstacle. "Stop!" Ronan cried out.

As Michael slammed on the brakes, the boys lurched forward and then were flung back into their seats. "What the hell's wrong?!" Michael asked, not at all happy at the interruption.

"The electronic fence!" Ronan shouted back. "Just because it's summer doesn't mean it's been shut down."

Seriously? That's why you made me stop? "That can't hurt us," Michael said.

"No, not us, but the car might not survive the shock."

"Oh yeah," Michael said dejectedly. "I hadn't thought about that." Disappointed, Michael didn't want to give in, but it looked like he had no choice. "Guess we'll have to travel the old-fashioned way," Michael said. "On foot."

Just as he was about to put the car in reverse and return to the parking lot, Ronan ordered him to stop once again. "I have an idea." He jumped out of the car, shut the door, and ran to the metal gate. Silently, Ronan explained his idea to his boyfriend. *"I'll absorb the shock of the electronic current as you drive through the fence."*

Michael's face lit up. "That's brilliant!"

"I know," Ronan said, smiling. "You think up funny little phrases, and I think up smashingly brilliant ideas."

If Ronan had been sitting next to him, Michael would have kissed him. *"That's why we're the perfect team,"* Michael replied. *"Ready?"*

Standing to the side of the entrance gate, Ronan grabbed onto the metal pole. *"Go for it!"*

Michael took his foot off of the brake pedal and placed it on the gas, all the way down until the car zoomed under and past the front gate, untouched by the electronic current. He turned back and saw Ronan, equally unharmed, pumping his fist underneath the twisted metal lettering that spelled out Archangel Academy. They did it; they found a way around yet another hurdle. They were so excited they were acting as if they were going for a joyride instead of in search of a missing person.

Jumping into the front seat, Ronan was beaming. "Take me to London, James."

Michael kept his eyes looking forward as he drove onto the cobblestone road and away from school. "You do know that my name is Michael, right?"

Staring out the window as the countryside rolled alongside him, Ronan stifled a laugh. "Just drive."

Finding a parking spot in front of Edwige's flat proved to be as effortless as the long drive itself. It was partly due to Michael's enhanced reflexes and vision and partly due to his growing confidence, he mastered the British highway system and maneuvered the car through city traffic like an expert. If Ronan hadn't been so anxious he would have told Michael how impressed he was, but after the thrill of their getaway had passed all he could think about was what he was going to say to his mother, how he was going to tell her off for ignoring him all this time. He was going to give her an earful the second after she opened her door.

After the third knock it was apparent he wasn't going to get the chance. "She isn't home," Ronan observed.

Instinctively, Michael took hold of the doorknob and twisted. The door was open. "Are you sure of that, Ro?"

Anxiety, curiosity, fear, all wriggled around inside Ronan's head and in the pit of his stomach. If her door was open she had to be home and if she was home why didn't she answer him? Was she that determined to stay out of his life? Was she that angry with him for some unknown reason that she wouldn't even respond to his call? Or was it simply that she wasn't home?

They entered the living room, and it was like entering a morgue. The whole apartment in fact was still, quiet, and, after a quick look into every room, Edwige-free. "What the hell is going on?" Ronan asked, fear rising to the surface amongst all the emotions he was experiencing.

"I . . . I . . ." Michael stuttered, searching for the right thing to say. Then he realized nothing he said was going to sound right. "I don't know, Ro. It doesn't make any sense that she's ignoring you, it doesn't make any sense that her door's open, but she isn't here."

"It doesn't make any sense that her painting's gone."

Ronan's comment made Michael look up at the living room wall, and he noticed that it, like the apartment itself, was missing something. "You're right!" Michael exclaimed. "The painting's gone!"

The painting that depicted two men in the Atlantic Ocean, their bodies suspended side by side, their skin touching, forever connected, was indeed missing. It was one of Edwige's most prized possessions and one that she would never part with; it reminded her of Ronan and Michael, of her own heritage, of her species' future. "Do you think she was robbed?" Michael asked. "Somebody could probably get a lot of money for that thing."

It was a valid theory, but it was wrong. There hadn't been a robbery; no one had broken into the apartment to steal that one item. Edwige had taken it with her when she left. Ronan was sure of it. "She's gone."

Michael heard the certainty in Ronan's voice, but he didn't understand it. "What do you mean?"

"Look."

When Michael turned around he saw what Ronan was pointing at. The only thing on the surface of the wooden table that stood next to the window was dust. Gone was the mahogany box that housed Saxon's ashes and gone too—for the moment anyway—was any hope of finding Edwige. "Wherever she went she has no intention of returning," Ronan said. "That's why she took those two things with her."

Standing next to Ronan, Michael placed his hand in the small of his back so he would know that even though his mother had apparently left him, that she had apparently decided to take a leave of absence from his life, he wasn't going anywhere. Michael also hoped Ronan knew that he would remain by his side and scour the earth until they found her if that's what he wished to do.

"Nooooo!!!" Imogene screamed in the middle of her song as if another set of fangs had been plunged into her neck, as if once again the life was being torn from her spirit. "Leave me alone!!"

Climbing into the coffin, Brania took hold of Imogene and cradled her in her arms to try and comfort her, try to calm her down. "Imogene, what's wrong?" Brania cried.

Cold sweat poured down the sides of Imogene's face, plastering her jet-black bangs against her forehead. Her body convulsed, turning her skin an even paler shade of white. "It's Edwige," Imogene said, choking on the words. "She's here."

As she whipped her head around, Brania's fangs descended over her lips as quick as the flick of a switchblade. Her eyes darted wildly, left, right, left, but she didn't see anyone else with them in their cave. Since they were safe for the moment, her fangs retracted, and she turned back to her ward. "No, it's just the two of us."

Imogene's body shook more violently as if reacting to the lie. "She's right in front of me! Can't you see her!"

Brania held onto Imogene tighter. Whatever the girl was seeing, whatever the girl was going through, she prayed it would pass, because even with all her incredible strength she had no idea how to make it stop. All she could think to do was try and find a way to console her. "Please, Imogene, look at me, look at Mother and everything will be all right."

Imogene turned her head to face Brania and abruptly her body became motionless. Her expression did change, but not in the way Brania had hoped. Her fear turned to contempt, and words poured out of Imogene's mouth like daggers into Brania's heart. "You *should* suffer for what you did to me! You should burn in hell like the witch that you are!"

What? No, no! *Imogene would never speak to me like that,* Brania reasoned. *She trusts me, she loves me.* "Imogene, don't say that," Brania cried out desperately. "You can't mean it."

And Brania was right.

"You're getting everything you deserve, Edwige!" Imogene ranted. "And this is only the beginning of your suffering!"

She wasn't talking to Brania. Somehow, in some unexplainable way Imogene was communicating with Edwige. Watching her adopted daughter's face coil into a mask of pain, Brania couldn't help but feel relieved. Not only was she not the source of Imogene's anguish, but she had discovered that Imogene and Edwige were linked.

Even as she held Imogene and whispered in her ear that there was nothing to be afraid of, Brania began formulating a plan, a plan that would exploit this newfound connection and restore her birthright. She was overcome with a sensation of peace, because in no time at all she would be back where she truly believed she belonged, sitting on the right side of her father.

chapter 6

"Welcome back home."

Standing at the podium, David knew that every person in St. Sebastian's—student and teacher—was looking at him, listening to his voice, and he reveled in the attention. He only wished he could reveal his true self to them. How they would gasp when they saw his magnificent black wings and saw that he possessed powers beyond comprehension. But there would be time for that. Now, he had to welcome the students and faculty members back to Archangel Academy for yet another school year. This year, however, would be more special than ever.

"And welcome to our Tri-Centennial Celebration." David waited for the applause to subside before continuing. "This year we will commemorate three hundred years of academic excellence here at Double A." He paused again, knowing that the students would cheer at his use of the school's nickname. He personally disliked colloquialisms, but it made the students feel more comfortable in his presence, as if he were one of them. He laughed to himself and couldn't believe how incredibly easy it was to deceive people, even those who knew he was a vampire, with only a few choice words. What fools they all were.

When it was once again quiet, David explained that even though Archangel Cathedral and some of the main buildings were built in the fifteenth century, Double A had begun life as a monastery, a religious enclave where monks and those seeking sanctuary could worship without fear of persecution. Conveniently, David didn't mention that not every monk had spent his days praying to God, but rather to what he considered to be a superior deity. That wasn't a truth that needed to be disclosed just yet, but when the time was right, he would savor the opportunity to introduce them all to Zachariel's power. Until then he would stick to the more mundane facts. "It wasn't until three centuries later that the school itself was created," David said, his voice soft yet commanding. "But since that time Archangel Academy has been one of the most prestigious educational institutions in the world, a school that I consider myself lucky to have attended and a school that I am proud to call my home."

Ronan heard the cheering all around him, but he couldn't join in. Yes, he also loved Double A; yes, he also considered it home; but no, he couldn't uphold David's testimonial with applause. He knew David was lying and that to David the school was nothing more than a hideout. David didn't value education; he didn't care about the school's reputation or the students' prosperity. It was simply that Double A and the land that it was built upon, land that extended all the way into Eden, had been christened long ago as hallowed ground where his kind could walk in the sun as if they were worthy of its glory. Anger reddened Ronan's alabaster cheeks, because he knew David wasn't worthy of such a gift. The only light that should warm his skin should be created by the fires of hell.

"*So much for maintaining the peace, Ro,*" Michael commented silently, obviously tapping into Ronan's far-from-peaceful thoughts.

Caught, Ronan smiled and tilted his head. "*Guess I should practice what I preach.*"

"*Nah, it's more fun to throw your words right back at ya.*"

Ronan was delighted. Not only was Michael willing to hold a mirror up to him to expose his flaws, but he would tease him about them as well. "*That's my boy!*" Ronan said silently.

His laughter, however, was drowned out by David's booming voice. "And how do you honor three hundred years of being the best school in the world?" David asked rhetorically. "Prepare yourselves for a celebration that none of you will ever forget!"

The over-the-top pronouncement was met with a variety of responses. Michael and Ronan instantly felt uneasy, knowing that any festivity would most likely be camouflage to cover up another attempt by David to find The Well; Ciaran was hopeful that he would be able to uncover the true meaning of Atlantium before then so he and David could celebrate his breakthrough along with the school's anniversary; Fritz was scared that he would wind up attending his third school function in a row without a real girlfriend; and Nakano was surprised to find himself excited not only for the upcoming gala, but for the new school year.

On the other side of the bleachers, Saoirse sat next to a girl with flaming red hair and prayed the party would be a formal affair so she and her new best friend could go shopping for a special outfit. It was clear that everyone had a different priority. At the moment, David's was to steer the assembly away from talk of school festivities and to the introduction of the latest addition to Double A's staff.

"Now please help me welcome Dr. Oliver Sutton."

A slight shuffling noise followed David's statement, which turned out to be the sound of shoes scuffing against the lacquered wood of the gym floor. From the locker room emerged a small man who possessed none of David's majesty nor his predecessor's disheveled appearance. The man who would replace Lochlan MacCleery as the school's doctor was impeccably dressed, but the accent was on neatness and not style.

His dull gray suit fit his slight frame perfectly, but had been bought at a discount. His tie, the same color, but faded with age, held no pattern, and his black loafers were made of industrial strength plastic. His physical appearance was just as unfortunate. His eyes were small, set too close together, and the pupils and irises melded as one to create the same shade of black. The end of his nose hooked slightly and presided over thin lips set against a backdrop of ashen, pockmarked skin. Topping everything off was a scalp that was largely bald except for some wiry strands of black-gray hair combed over from left to right that didn't completely conceal a cluster of brown age spots on the crown of his head. If he hadn't been standing in front of the podium, he would have still commanded attention. But only for being unattractive. When he spoke, however, his voice did not arouse much interest.

"Hello," Oliver said.

Although amplified, he hardly made an impact. His sound wasn't enthralling like David's or as gruff as Lochlan's had been. It was nondescript.

"Thank you for letting me join your family," he continued meekly. It was an unnecessary statement since no one present—other than David presumably—had been asked to vote on or consider Oliver to fulfill the vacant position of school doctor. And when he took to the makeshift stage there had been no applause. Thanks did not have to be given. "It is a true honor to follow in Dr. MacCleery's footsteps as your new school physician."

Ronan wanted to stand up and shout that there was no way that he could replace Lochlan; there was no way that this meek imposter could be as courageous and honorable as MacCleery had turned out to be. For most of the time that they had known each other, Ronan and Lochlan hadn't trusted each other. They thought they were enemies; they had been wrong. The doctor had taken an oath to protect mankind from all kinds of evil, and even when he discovered that he was surrounded by some who didn't fit that description, who existed outside the boundaries of what would be considered human, he still fought to keep them all safe. He was murdered for his bravery. Staring at Dr. Sutton, Ronan knew intuitively that he was an unfit replacement.

"I will do my utmost to uphold good Dr. MacCleery's memory," Oliver droned. "And make him proud."

Positioned behind the newest staff member, Coach Blakeley sat amid the other school personnel. He, like Ronan, didn't approve of the new doctor. His relationship with Lochlan had been outwardly antagonistic, but he had admired him greatly. Leaning to the left he whispered into Sister Mary Elizabeth's ear, "I know it isn't very Christian of me, but I don't like the bloke." Although she remained silent, it was clear by her expression that she shared Blakeley's point of view. It was an endorsement that Professor Joubert, sitting on her opposite side, couldn't help but notice.

Bored, Michael felt his mind drift. Physically, he remained sitting in the bleachers; mentally he had journeyed somewhere far away, to a place where it was raining. One drop, two drops, three drops, four. One raindrop after another fell from the sky and plopped onto the ground, its sound echoing like a distant boom, loud, dissonant, but far enough away that it didn't present any immediate danger. Involuntarily, Michael turned his head and looked around as if he would be able to find the cause of the phantom sound in the gym. He did.

Dr. Sutton was still standing at the podium, but that was one of the only things that had remained the same. Every person in the gym besides Michael and Oliver was frozen, immobile, the victim of some time-stopping trick, and while Michael looked the same as he did moments before, Oliver had undergone a transformation, one that Michael was all too familiar with, but still found grotesque nonetheless.

It looked as if the doctor's body had shrunk and gotten thicker. His shoulders, no longer bony, curved forward, hunkered down by newly acquired muscle. His neck was like the trunk of a small tree, and the increased bulk threatened to pop open the top button of his shirt. The rest of his body strained at his suit's threadbare material, and Michael couldn't believe it wasn't ripping at the seams. Most horrific, however, was his skin.

Oliver's veins pulsated. They were filled with so much blood that they had grown almost an inch in height to create rippled lines all over his flesh. The excessive quantity of blood also discolored his skin, darkened it, so it looked like he was streaked in charcoal. As the fluid raced throughout his body, his veins trembled and spasmed, making it look as if leeches were crawling between flesh and bone. The man looked sinful.

As expected his eyes were now completely black, but his fangs were stained yellow and chipped. Michael assumed they were the jagged, tarnished remains of centuries of battle. A continuous stream of blood fell from one fang to the gym floor, creating the sound that had caught Michael's attention in the first place. The sound that he wished would stop reverberating in his ears. The sound that drew him into a private conversation with this vile creature.

"Michael." Oliver's voice was now unrecognizable, almost unidentifiable; it was like a gravelly hiss, like nothing Michael had ever heard before. "Isn't it time that you forgave your father?"

The words seeped into Michael's brain, contaminated his blood as quickly and stealthily as if Oliver's fangs had pierced his flesh. The seed was planted, a command was given, and Michael shook as the words pulsed through his body. He wanted the connection to end; he wanted whatever power this thing had over him to recede; he wanted to be free. And in an instant he was.

The applause was tepid and perfunctory, but at least it signaled the end of Dr. Sutton's turn as public speaker. Michael couldn't believe that the frail-looking doctor's true image was something so intimidating, so formidable. But Michael was just as formidable. He knew Sutton had tried to control his mind, brainwash him into making peace with his father. It wouldn't work. Whatever mind-bending powers Sutton had, they weren't going to force Michael to act against his will. Michael was so proud of himself he laughed out loud and he hoped the doctor understood he was laughing right at him.

"What's so funny?" Ronan asked.

"The new doc's a vamp," Michael told Ronan silently. *"Ugliest one yet! Looks more like a demon if you ask me."*

"Brilliant!" Ronan cried. *"I see somebody's trying for an A in vampire skills 101."*

Michael pressed his knee into the side of Ronan's thigh and replied, "I expect to collect my gold star later on tonight."

Before the flirting could escalate any further, Fritz and Ciaran surrounded Michael and Ronan on either side, and they descended the rest of the bleachers like a four-person barricade with Nakano taking up the rear. When they got to the bottom, Fritz pointed at something across the gym. "Check out the ginger bird."

Michael did a quick translation in his head of British to

American slang. Ginger equaled red and bird meant girl. He looked over and saw Saoirse approaching them, walking arm-in-arm with a very pretty, red-haired girl.

"That's Penry's twin sister Ruby," Ciaran announced, unable to take his eyes off of the girl.

The mere mention of Penry's name made them all become silent for a moment as they remembered their friend. He was dead barely a year. Sometimes it seemed like the tragedy had just happened; other times it was as if he had been gone for years. For Nakano, however, it was an event that replayed in his mind at least once a day.

Question after question invaded his mind. Why was Penry's sister here? Had she come for him? Did she know that he was responsible for her brother's death? *She has to know that I lost control!* Nakano wanted to scream, he wanted to tell Ruby that he was sorry. But what good would that do? It would be a waste of time. Just like it was a waste of time to feel anything for a lowly human, but he did. He knew his actions had been wrong; he knew he should ask for forgiveness, but ask whom? Who in the world would listen to him and who could ever make him feel like anything more than a murderer? *I'm a vampire!* Nakano reminded himself as he did every day. *I'm above humans! They mean nothing to me!*

Michael didn't hear Nakano's internal shouting, but he knew Ruby's presence and bringing up Penry's name would be upsetting to him. At least he hoped it would. When he turned around to see how Kano was taking the news he caught a glimpse of him running out the back door. *Good,* Michael thought. *At least he felt something.*

"Doesn't she go to some swanky boarding school in Switzerland?" Fritz asked, breaking the silence.

"She did, until the boating accident," Ciaran explained.

"What boating accident?" Michael asked.

As Ciaran relayed the details, he continued to stare directly at Ruby. "She was with her family on a small boat in the Atlantic Ocean. Weather turned out of nowhere, and they capsized," Ciaran explained.

"How do you know so much about her?" Fritz demanded.

"Maybe if you read the newspapers instead of comic books all the time, you'd be better informed," Ciaran shot back.

"Eh, newspapers are depressing," Fritz said.

"What happened to the rest of her family?" Michael asked.

"Nobody was hurt except for Ruby," Ciaran replied.

"That's strange," Ronan remarked.

"Hurt badly too," Ciaran explained. "She was actually in a coma for a while."

As the girls got closer, Ruby's resemblance to Penry became startling. Same hair color, same facial features. It was like looking at a softened, more petite version of Penry with longer hair. "Looks no worse for wear, if you ask me," Fritz said.

"Look closer," Ciaran instructed. "She woke up from her coma blind."

The three other boys looked at Ruby to see beyond her physical beauty and the similarities to Penry and realized Ciaran was right. As she walked, her gaze was unfocused; her eyes weren't distracted by the kids cutting in front of her or any other activity that was taking place throughout the gym. She kept her arm firmly entwined with Saoirse's, and it was clear that she was being guided across the floor. What wasn't clear was what she was doing here in the first place. "Why isn't she at some sort of school for the blind?" Michael asked. "Or at least back at her old school where she knows the layout better?"

They all agreed that either of those solutions would have been smarter choices than to come to a brand new school she had presumably only visited a few times before. Ciaran explained that her parents had wanted to send her to a top-notch school for the visually impaired, but Ruby had refused and insisted that she enroll in Penry's old school. "That's potty, don't you think?" Fritz asked. "She won't know her way around the place."

"True, but Saoirse told me she can be quite stubborn," Ciaran added.

Ronan peered into the girl and examined her with a vampire's eyes. He didn't uncover much of anything except that physically she was a carbon copy of his friend. Turning around to face Ciaran, who was standing behind him, he asked, "And just how does our sister know so much about her?"

Tapping Ronan on the shoulder, Saoirse declared, "Because your sister is Ruby's dorm mate." Ronan turned around and was so surprised to see that his sister and her friend had caught up with them so quickly that he was momentarily speechless. The others couldn't find their voices either, but for different reasons entirely. Saoirse didn't have that problem, and now that she had the group's full attention, she presented Ruby as if she were a prize that she had just won at a state fair. "Boys, may I introduce you to Miss Ruby Poltke."

Examining Penry's sister up close they saw that despite the physical similarities she shared with her late brother, she really wasn't his *identical* twin. While her hair was the same vibrant red, it was parted at the side and fell in thick waves just past her shoulders, the color almost matching that of her full, curvy lips. Her skin color was lighter than Penry's, like creamy milk, and her cheeks, prominent but softly rounded, were dotted with constellations of delicate freckles. While Penry looked younger than his age and fresh-faced, Ruby appeared older, and even without a stitch of makeup on, she had the glamorous look of an old-time movie star. But it was her eyes that commanded the boys' attention.

They were the color of a tranquil lake illuminated by the sun's rays, a collection of blues that shimmered and twinkled.

The loss of their function only made her eyes more alluring, more compelling, more difficult to resist. They drew the boys in, each one of them, and they found it impossible not to stare. Ruby's expression was mostly blank, but her lips were pressed together as if smiling, satisfied, as if she knew she was commanding their attention and, even though she couldn't see their admiration, she approved of it. She may have been Penry's sister, but she was definitely the more complex twin.

"Hello."

One word from Ruby triggered a cacophony of sound. Michael, Ronan, Ciaran, and Fritz all spoke at once. "Hi." "Pleased to meet you." "Welcome to Double A." "Blimey! Penry never said you were such a dish!" Luckily the last comment spoken by Fritz blended into the crowd's vocal onslaught so Ruby couldn't hear it properly. Her smile just grew even more satisfied at hearing the flurry of verbal activity her simple greeting provoked. As did Saoirse's. Proudly, the younger girl explained how she had become Ruby's first and, so far, only friend at Double A.

"Now that Phaedra left us like the wind, you know, so to speak," Saoirse explained, "Sister Mary put Ruby in with me."

Now everything made sense to Ronan. "So this is why we haven't seen that much of you," he said. "You've been getting Ruby acclimated to her new surroundings."

"That's my brother Ronan," Saoirse clarified. "You'll notice that his accent's a little less refined than mine."

"Shut up, Seersh!" Ronan exclaimed.

"As is his demeanor," his sister added.

When Ruby laughed her eyes seemed to sparkle even more. "Hello, Ronan," Ruby said. She thrust out her hand, and Ronan noticed that it wasn't the awkward movement of someone who couldn't see, but rather graceful, confident. "My brother told me that you're quite the swimmer," she continued. "And the best captain the team could hope for."

Ronan took Ruby's hand, and, while it was feminine and soft, her grip was strong. Clearly, this was a girl who was not going to let her unfortunate condition weaken her. "Thank you," Ronan replied, moved by her remark. "Penry was a right fine mate."

Eager to keep the introductions moving and maintain her role as impromptu hostess, Saoirse gently turned to the left to draw Ruby's attention away from one brother to the other. "And this is Ciaran," Saoirse announced. "My other brother."

"How do you do?" Ciaran asked, regretting the formality of his tone and his choice of words the second they were uttered.

"I told you he was a lot more like me," Saoirse commented, then pulled Ruby in closer as she whispered, "We're the sophisticated ones in the family."

When Ciaran took Ruby's hand in his all feelings of embarrassment evaporated. He didn't hear the good-natured laughter that filled the air around him; he only felt Ruby's gentle touch. It was exciting and familiar at the same time, and he was filled with an odd thought: he was glad that she was blind so she couldn't see how he stared into her eyes. He couldn't believe eyes that looked so beautiful, so perfect could be flawed. The scientist in him wanted to make them right; the teenager in him simply wanted to make her his. Unfortunately, he had competition.

"I'm Fritz. You sent me Penry's comic books last year."

Abruptly, Fritz took hold of Ruby's hand, but even though the force of the interruption made her body shift toward him, her gaze didn't move, she continued to stare in Ciaran's direction. Everyone, except Fritz, noticed that the connection wasn't severed. The only thing Fritz noticed was that Ruby's hand felt very much like Phaedra's, soft, inviting, and was a touch he wanted to get to know much better. "I've actually picked up where me and Penry left off and wrote a bunch of new comics," Fritz prattled. "I'd love to show them to you sometime so you can see how I turned Penry into Double P, this kind of superhero. I think you'd really like them."

"Fritz, if you haven't noticed, Ruby's blind," Saoirse corrected. "The girl can't see anything."

This time it was only Fritz who became speechless. Thinking quickly, Ciaran decided to use the rare pocket of silence to his advantage. "Just a figure of speech," he said. "The comics are quite fine actually. Penry would be proud."

"I'm sure he would be; he loved to make up stories," Ruby replied, smiling. "Perhaps you can read them to me."

"I'd fancy that!" Fritz shouted, reclaiming his power of speech and the romantic reins from Ciaran. "We can start with the zombie invasion, most popular issue yet."

"I'm sure that'll be the highlight of her day," Saoirse mocked. She glanced at Ciaran and saw that he was trying not to show his disappointment at being upstaged by Fritz's more aggressive behavior. She wished she could think of something to say that would give him the lead over Fritz, but all she could think of doing was to change the subject and make the final introduction. "And this is Michael," Saoirse declared. "He's Ronan's *homme de l'amour.*"

"Which is French for 'his boyfriend,' " Michael translated.

"Thanks a lot, Michael!" Saoirse chastised. "I was trying to be subtle."

Laughing, Michael joked, "You wouldn't know subtle if it whacked you across the side of your head!"

Hints of red colored Ruby's plump cheeks as she laughed heartily. She gripped Saoirse's arm tighter and pulled her close to her body. Michael wasn't sure if she was always so physical, so carefree with her movements, or if the loss of her sight made her react without the usual self-consciousness he found apparent in most girls he met. Whatever the reason, he sensed that she possessed the same joy and playfulness that he had come to admire in Penry. He thought it would be a lot of fun to become friends with this girl.

He was wrong.

The second their hands touched Michael went blind. However, instead of his eyes being covered with a veil of impenetrable blackness, all he could see was white. He held on to Ruby's hand tighter as he felt himself grow dizzy and his knees buckle. It was as if he was back in The Well when it was consumed with a bright white light, but it wasn't a comforting memory. Originally, he had thought the white light was a godsend, some sort of message of hope that The Well was trying to convey, until the light revealed itself to be a vastly different form of communication. It had been an unwelcome warning. It was The Well's way of advising Michael that he was changing, and if he wasn't careful, if he wasn't true to his real self, he could evolve into something deplorable and unwanted. Holding onto Ruby, seeing nothing but dense, thick white, he knew that he was being given another message; he just didn't know if it was good or bad.

"It's a pleasure to meet you, Michael," Ruby said quietly. "I've heard so much about you."

When Ruby spoke, Michael's sight returned. Gone was the absence of everything and filling the void was Ruby's face, her lips smiling slightly, her dead eyes seemingly alive. He was relieved that things were back to normal, but he wasn't naïve. He wasn't always happy to admit it, but he had learned that everything—every dream, every vision, every bizarre coincidence—happened for a reason. Ruby was connected to the same white light that had emanated from The Well; how and why he didn't know. But at least he was aware of the connection; that was a start. "Pleasure's all mine Ruby," Michael lied. "I think we're going to be great friends."

Even though Fritz knew that Michael's heart belonged to Ronan and he couldn't possibly be a rival for Ruby's romantic affection, he also knew that gay boys and straight girls could develop powerful friendships that were incredibly difficult to break. Might as well make a preemptive strike and declare his intention before anyone else had the chance. "I know a great way to show you around campus, Ruby. Let's go on a double date," Fritz suggested, though his tone sounded more like an order. "Me and you and Saoirse and her new boyfriend."

Three heads snapped in Saoirse's direction. Michael, Ciaran, and especially Ronan were surprised by this pronouncement, and their shock was so palpable even Ruby could sense it. "Lawks!" she cried. "Something tells me Saoirse's kept news of her new boyfriend under lock and key."

"That's because I don't have a new boyfriend!" Saoirse protested.

The three boys studied Saoirse's face for signs that she was lying, but unfortunately Saoirse had become such a good liar that they couldn't tell if her protestation was based on truth or a ploy to cover up a revelation she preferred remain undisclosed. Ronan hoped it was the former, because even though Saoirse was sixteen, he felt that she was too young to have a boyfriend. In contrast, Michael thought she was lying. It now made perfect sense to him that the reason she ran off into the woods when he saw her while he was driving was because he had caught her rendezvousing with her secret boyfriend. And all Ciaran could think about was the fact that his little sister might already be in a relationship and, thanks to Fritz's intrusion, it looked like he might never be.

"You do too have a boyfriend!" Fritz griped. "That blond bloke I saw you with."

Once again Saoirse's response was inscrutable. *"Him?"* she replied. "I was helping him with his French."

"Oh is that what they're calling it these days?" Fritz asked. He laughed so loudly at his own joke that he hardly realized he was the only one laughing.

"You have to watch out for that one, Ruby," Saoirse said confidentially. "Your brother wasn't the only one who liked to make up stories."

For a split second the smile left Ruby's face, and her expression hardened. "Don't worry," she responded, her voice deeper, her British accent thicker, less reserved. "I may be blind, but I'm far from dumb."

When Saoirse laughed everyone joined in except Michael. He knew her comment wasn't meant to be a joke. Like the white light, it was meant to be a warning. And how appropriate that one warning should follow another.

"I'm so glad you're all getting to know one another and reconnecting after the summer break, but if you dawdle any longer you'll be late for class," David announced. "And that's hardly the way to begin the new year."

"Right you are, Headmaster," Fritz replied, his voice dripping with respect in an attempt to impress Ruby and not the person he was addressing. When David smiled approvingly, Fritz decided it was a path worth continuing. "Headmaster, would it be all right if I walked Ruby to her class?"

David smirked. "Mr. Ulrich, you're proving to be a gentleman, if not a scholar."

"Thank you, sir." Fritz beamed, completely missing David's barb. "I'll take over from here, Seersh."

Saoirse tried to catch Ciaran's eyes to let him know that she was sorry; she had no choice but to hand Ruby over to the enemy. But Ciaran was staring off to the side, looking across the gym at nothing in particular, just anything other than watching Fritz take Ruby's slender arm and enfold it within his. He had witnessed defeat often enough; no need to watch it again.

Fritz led Ruby outside and on her way to her first class of the semester, an advanced elective in horticulture that Fritz had absolutely no interest in, but claimed to be fascinated by. Grabbing Ciaran's hand, Saoirse gave him a tug as if to yank him back to reality. His melancholy only lasted a moment after seeing his sister's smiling face. "C'mon, Ciar. Let's follow them and eavesdrop," she ordered. "Betcha five pounds

Fritz blabbers on about the Venus flytrap who devoured half the school in issue seven."

Ronan watched his siblings depart the gym and was happy that they had each other. It was important to have someone who always made you feel good even when you were unsure of yourself. It's what Michael did for him. Sometimes, however, it worked the other way around.

"She's dangerous," Michael said.

Crinkling his forehead, Ronan was surprised by Michael's comment and even more surprised by the serious look on his face. "She's just a kid," Ronan countered. "Saoirse's a handful, but she's harmless, you know that."

"I'm not talking about Saoirse," Michael replied. "I'm talking about Ruby."

"Ruby?" Ronan asked incredulously. "We were just introduced to a vampire doctor who looks more like a demon and you're worried about a blind girl?"

Michael looked at Ronan and was surprised that he didn't share his concern. "Trust me, Dr. Sutton we can handle," he said. "But that girl is dangerous."

Crossing his arms, Ronan tilted his head and examined Michael. He was completely befuddled by his behavior. "Why in the world would you think Penry's sister is dangerous?"

"Because she's not Penry's sister," Michael declared. "And whatever she is, she isn't human."

chapter 7

"What do you mean Ruby isn't human?!"

"How many times are you going to ask me that, Ro?"

"Well, you can't just drop a bomb like that and toddle off to class!"

"I was going to be late."

"Michael!!"

"I'm signing off, class's already started."

Michael closed part of his mind so Ronan could no longer communicate with him. He was surprised how easy it was to do, since only a few weeks ago he had still been struggling with telepathic conversation. It was almost as if when he stopped trying to make something work he was successful. He'd have to remember that when practicing the rest of his vampire skills—stop thinking about doing them and just let his new natural instincts take over. He wished he could adopt the same strategy with his classes. But as a student he had, for the most part, to respond like a human, which meant he had to read his assignments, take notes, study, and listen to lectures. Even when he knew they were wrong.

"The only true immortal creature is God," Professor Joubert proclaimed. "The rest of us have an end date."

Standing in front of the class, Joubert didn't have to make such outrageous proclamations to look impressive. He was so tall, almost 6'5", that the top of his head was only a few inches below the stone ceiling. The theology building was one of the oldest on campus, but also one of the smallest. Joubert looked like a giant, intimidating, powerful, but even still, he wasn't beyond reproach.

"According to the Bible, didn't Abraham live for like seven hundred years or something loco like that?"

Michael didn't see who asked the question, but he knew the voice belonged to Diego Fuente, the chubby Spanish kid, whose shirt was always wrinkled, who always sat in the back corner no matter what class he was in, and who always interrupted a lecture. The professors had learned to take his interruptions in stride, and Joubert was no different. "Seven hundred years or something *loco* like that is indeed long," Joubert responded, twirling a piece of chalk in between his long, slender fingers. "But I think Father Fazio would be disheartened to hear that you haven't grasped the concept that immortality transcends numerical calculation."

"What do you mean?" Diego replied, evidently unable to follow Joubert's reasoning. "Father Faz teaches math."

"He means because he's a priest, you dumb clot!" Nakano barked. He didn't mean to be so snarky, but when he saw Michael smile at his comment he was glad he hadn't censored himself.

When the classroom chuckling subsided, Joubert continued. "As most priests believe, whether they're teaching something non-secular or something as mundane as math, the only viable alternative we can hope for is resurrection."

Gazing at the thin, gold crucifix that hung on the wall in the front of class, Michael thought about everything he had learned at church in Weeping Water and how most everything he had learned was proven false when he came to Archangel Academy. The only thing he knew for certain was that no matter what any priest believed or preached, God didn't have a monopoly on immortality.

"What about vampires?!" Diego cried out, seemingly oblivious to Joubert's cutting remark.

Involuntarily, Michael locked eyes with Nakano and then whipped his head around to face the kid who had made this bold statement. Did Diego know that there were vampires sitting a few seats in front of him? Was Diego a vampire himself? No, that was impossible. Well, not impossible, but not probable. Wouldn't Michael know if Diego was a vampire? Wouldn't he get some indication that he wasn't mortal? Unable to divert his stare, Michael kept his gaze on the loudmouthed boy, desperately searching for a clue that would offer proof as to what kind of creature he was. Nothing. Maybe Michael's skills weren't as finely tuned as he had thought.

"Vampires," Joubert said as he began to walk around his desk, tapping his piece of chalk on the tabletop with each stride, "are products of fiction." Diego opened his mouth to ask another question, but Joubert ignored him and continued speaking. "And while they are beguiling literary inventions, they are limited."

"No, they're not!" This time it wasn't Diego who blurted out a bold statement; it was Michael. He knew that everyone in the class was looking at him, none more intently than Nakano, but he kept his focus on Joubert. He didn't want to play such a dangerous game, he didn't want to act recklessly, but his pride got the better of him and he had to stand up for his people and contradict such an ignorant comment. All that was left was to see how his professor would respond to his unexpected outburst.

"And why, Mr. Howard, would you make such a statement?" Joubert asked. "And, may I add, make it so passionately."

It had been quite a while since Michael had felt the prickly tingles of fear ride up and down his spine while sitting in a classroom. It was a common feeling no student was immune to, but he was no ordinary student. He felt his heart rate quicken and he tried to control it, slow it down, but the more he tried, the more the opposite occurred. He felt his heart beat even faster, and the chill on his spine spread out to envelope his whole body. *Stop thinking,* he commanded himself. *Just let instinct take over.*

When Michael finally spoke, his voice was steady, even if his body wasn't entirely calm. "Because immortality, which, you know, is the primary characteristic of vampires, doesn't have any limits."

"What about a vampire's inability to walk in the sun?" Joubert asked. "Or the necessity to drink human blood for sustenance? Aren't they testimony to a vampire's limitations?"

Only a certain inferior type of vampire, Michael wanted to reply. Wisely, he kept that thought to himself. He had already made one stupid comment; no need to compound it with another. He knew that he couldn't get into a discussion about the different varieties of vampire species, not in mixed company, not among people who would think he was insane or worse, among people who might be members of that certain inferior race themselves. Michael was no longer confident that he knew the truth about those around him. It was unsettling, but at least it reminded him that he had to be cautious.

"Well, I guess that's, you know, kind of true," Michael replied, trying to infuse a dose of humility into his tone.

When Joubert spoke his voice was free of humility; it was

the sound of a professor who once again was able to demonstrate to his students that he was smarter than they were. "So let us not forget that immortality is not a synonym for invulnerability and that vampires can die, just like a mere mortal," he claimed. "Which brings me back to my original statement, God is the only true immortal creature. And though it may be difficult for some of us to admit, none of us even comes close."

Once more Michael tried to decipher Joubert's expression, but failed. Was he mocking him? Was he speaking to him in some code? He was definitely looking in his direction, but so what? Naturally Joubert would direct his summation at the student who had contradicted him; there was nothing unusual about that. And yet Michael couldn't shake the feeling that his lecture wasn't random, but held a deeper meaning.

The confrontation over, Michael ran his fingers through his hair and stopped to massage his scalp. Much better. Exhaling deeply, he felt the sense of dread begin to dissolve. It was still present, but no longer as profound. Obviously, he was more flustered by Ronan's telling him about Morgandy as well as Ruby's arrival and apparent inhumanity than he had originally acknowledged. But he had to get control of his emotions. Just because Ruby was hiding a secret and no one knew what had happened to Morgandy didn't mean everything had to be a mystery. Then again maybe it did.

Following Professor Joubert's instruction to turn to page twenty-five of their textbook, the chapter that explored the idea of resurrection and its significance in the Bible, so that they could continue their discussion on immortality, Michael found the birthday card from his father. It was no longer ripped in two and Michael had no idea how it got in his book.

Curious, Michael looked at the cover again, a colorful fireworks display that spelled out the number 17. Inside, Vaughan had written "Happy Birthday, son! Ad infinitum! Love, Dad." The message no longer made Michael feel angry, but rather conflicted. He now thought the sentiment was lame, accurate, even sweet and all at the same time.

As Joubert rattled on about how resurrection was symbolic for a religious cleansing, a new beginning, a kind of a spiritual do-over, Michael wondered if finding his father's card right at this moment might also be symbolic. Maybe it was a sign that he should forgive him, forge a new beginning with the only relative he had who still wanted anything to do with him. But despite the signs, despite Dr. Sutton's earlier attempt to manipulate his emotions, despite Joubert's timely lecture, could he really forgive his father? Could he really forget what his father did and reestablish some sort of relationship with him? Before Michael could ponder that thought any further it appeared that another old relationship might be looking to reestablish itself as well.

Looking out the window, Michael saw that Jean-Paul looked the same as he always did. Tall and lanky, long, dark brown hair tucked behind his ears, eyes half-open, his lips slightly parted, the only physical difference was that his skin looked darker, as if he had gotten a tan over the summer. He was clad in his typical uniform: a tight-fitting white shirt, unbuttoned at the top, his skinny, black tie loose at his neck, and black jacket, pants, and shoes. Standing in the middle of the field outside St. Joseph's, holding his chauffeur's cap in front of him, he looked as if he was dozing off standing up.

What did I ever see in him? Michael asked himself.

There was no argument, Jean-Paul was extremely handsome, but not nearly as handsome as Ronan. Michael saw that clearly now, but there had been a time when it wasn't so obvious to him. There had been a time when Michael was hypnotized by Jean-Paul's good looks, overwhelmed by all the changes that had taken place so quickly in his life, and he barely escaped making a terrible mistake by betraying the love that he and Ronan shared. He was lucky; he had learned his lesson and was confident he would never make that mistake again. And anyway, Jean-Paul didn't look that hot. Not with blood dripping down the front of his shirt.

A stream of blood oozed down the left side of Jean-Paul's otherwise clean shirt, about the same width as his tie. He didn't move and looked unaffected by the disturbance, but the blood continued to flow from some unseen origin, growing slightly and beginning to cover more of the shirt's surface than before. The blood seemed to disappear at Jean-Paul's waist, but then one drop, two drops, three drops, four, fell onto the lush, green grass at his feet. As the blood drops splattered around his shoes and accumulated on the ground, their size grew, and Jean-Paul was standing in a puddle of his own rich, red blood.

Suddenly, Michael felt very hungry. The blood looked sweet and inviting and so incredibly necessary even though he didn't need to feed for several more weeks. He closed his eyes hoping the desire would pass. When he opened them, his craving was gone and so too was the source. Jean-Paul's shirt was as crisp and clean and bloodless as it always was.

Thank God, Michael thought. His hunger now completely subsided, Michael could once again think logically. Jean-Paul looked normal, not wounded, not near death, so maybe Michael's vision didn't mean anything. When he saw Nakano staring at him, Michael knew his expression meant that Kano was pissed off.

"It's not what you think," Michael said silently, hoping that he could reach Nakano nonverbally the same way he could reach Ronan. He couldn't. Nakano's expression changed, but only for the worse, and Michael thought Kano was going to transform right there and pounce on him for staring at his boyfriend. But he was wrong.

As he turned his gaze toward Jean-Paul, Nakano's face straddled the fine line between human and vampire. The whites of his eyes remained, but his irises practically emanated a black light. His teeth vibrated and fought the urge to allow his fangs to descend, while his fingers gripped his desk so tightly that the flesh on his hands turned into a swirl of red and white. Although Michael was impressed by Nakano's self-control, he wished he could think of something to say to let him know it wasn't necessary. He was forced to speak, however, but only in response to a question posed to him by Professor Joubert.

"Do you believe in resurrection, Mr. Howard?" his professor asked. "Or do you think it's merely biblical hyperbole?"

Michael didn't want to sound flippant, but he had to speak the truth. "Sir, I've come to believe that anything is possible." Stealing a quick glance outside, Michael saw that Jean-Paul was gone; the field was empty. Then out of the corner of his eye he saw through the small circular window on the classroom door that Jean-Paul had merely changed position. He was waiting in the hallway. "No matter how impossible it might sound."

A bit surprised by Michael's reply, Joubert smiled and slowly sat on the edge of his desk. "Spoken like a true student of the arcane."

Before Joubert could continue to admire Michael's tolerance for the unknown, the bell rang, and the students grabbed their books, scrambling as one determined crowd toward the door. "Read chapter three for tomorrow's class," Joubert shouted over the din of voices and activity. His words were barely out of his mouth and the room was suddenly empty except for Michael, Nakano, and an unlikely visitor.

" 'ello Michael," Jean-Paul said, his French accent still thick, his voice friendly.

"Hi," was all Michael could muster in response, since he knew Nakano's eyes were drilling daggers into his back.

"Eet eez good to see you again," Jean-Paul added.

"Um, yeah, good to see you too," Michael mumbled. "Bye." Without looking back, Michael left. He didn't want to know why Jean-Paul was lurking around their theology class, and he definitely didn't want to know if his vision was going to come true. It wasn't his problem; it was Nakano's.

"Are you going to say 'ello to me too?" Kano asked. "Or are you just going to ignore me?"

Jean-Paul leaned against the wall, his head scraping against the arch of the doorway, his hair falling into his eyes. "Kano you 'ave become so...teedious," Jean-Paul sighed. "Eet eez time for you to grow up."

Shocked, Nakano actually took a step back. Jean-Paul had become aloof lately, but not snippy. But maybe he was right? Maybe Nakano should just be happy to see him? It's not like he had run off after Michael, nor did Michael really look that happy to see him. No, it was obvious, Jean-Paul had come to see him because he missed him and he wanted to make up for lost time. Or not.

"I 'ave come 'ere to see your professor," Jean-Paul announced.

"Why in the world would a chauffeur need to see a theology professor?" Kano blurted.

Jean-Paul's beautiful lips curled into a sneer filled with loathing and contempt. "Because we 'ave a lot in common. We're both French," Jean-Paul retorted. "And we're both vampires."

What?! Professor Joubert—a vampire!? The revelation shouldn't have surprised Nakano, but it did. Turning to the man he had always known was old, but never imagined could be ancient, Nakano asked, "Is that true?"

A slight nod of his head confirmed it. "May God strike us dead if my fellow countryman is telling a lie," Joubert replied. After a moment of silence, he added, "Either Jean-Paul speaks the truth or once again God has proven his powers to be greatly exaggerated."

And now the theology professor was mocking the very religion he spent hours every day teaching. Nothing made sense any more. Nakano heard himself mumble some lame excuse that he had to leave or he'd be late for lunch, and thanks to his supernatural hearing he heard Jean-Paul laugh in response. "I forget 'ow childeesh children can act sometimes," he snickered.

Luckily, Nakano could get to The Forest on autopilot, so in a few seconds he was deep in the woods, away from Jean-Paul, away from his face, his smell, his stupid chauffeur outfit. All he wanted was to be with someone who didn't think he was a jerk, someone who wouldn't judge him for every stupid thing he'd ever done, someone he could trust. The only person who even remotely fit that description was Brania.

"We have a visitor," she announced before Nakano even entered the cave. "How lovely."

Ever since she had voluntarily sequestered herself in these primitive quarters, Brania's preternatural senses had become even more heightened and her typical suspicious nature sharpened. She was constantly on guard for intruders. Or guests.

"Welcome, Kano," she said, crossing to greet him properly. "And to what do we owe this pleasant surprise?"

Fighting the impulse to let his tears flow freely down his cheeks, Nakano replied hoarsely, "Just needed to see a friendly face I guess."

Brania was willing to accommodate. Imogene was not.

Sitting in her coffin, her back pressed into the corner of the casket so severely the wood cut into her flesh, Imogene saw two images simultaneously, one from the present, the other from the past. Nakano was standing there in front of her talking to Brania, but he was also crouched on all fours like a wild animal ripping Penry's throat apart with his fangs. Imogene didn't care which image was current and which was memory, they were both real to her. And after months of doing nothing but sitting and singing and obeying, she was beginning to feel strength and courage once again invade her body, and she was determined to use them.

"Noooo!!!!"

In mid-scream, Imogene sprang from her tomb like a coil that refused to remain pressed down any longer. She flew through the air with incredible speed and landed on top of Nakano before he even had a chance to defend himself. His back crashed into the hard earth with such force that his body buckled, head and legs flying upward. Imogene used the momentum to her advantage, clinging onto his shirt to pull him close to her face, then slamming him back down onto the ground.

Unable to hide her amusement, Brania chided her ward. "Imogene! Is that any way to greet our guest?"

Poised on top of Nakano, Imogene held tightly to his shirt and pressed her knees into the sides of his stomach. She turned to Brania, her face a mask of rage. "He killed my Penry!"

Brania wished she didn't understand the fury that was causing Imogene to act so violently; she wished she didn't comprehend the need for revenge that was turning her into something unrecognizable, but she understood all too clearly. She was no different than Imogene, except she had learned during all the centuries she had lived how to be patient. "Yes, he did," Brania said, her voice as calm as if she were telling Imogene a bedtime story. "But that was an unfortunate mistake."

Imogene, however, wasn't in the mood to be consoled. "It was no mistake!" she shrieked. She lifted Kano's body again and slammed him down once more, his head thumping into the ground. "He wanted to kill him, and he left me for dead!"

Underneath the girl, Nakano struggled to get free. *This was ridiculous,* he thought, *I'm a vampire and she's just human.* Well, she was human; now she was literally half dead, so Nakano didn't know the technical term for what she actually was. But she was a girl; he shouldn't be having so much trouble wrenching himself free. It was as if his hands were caught in steel traps and several tons of concrete were pressing down on his chest. He simply couldn't escape. The only chance he had was for Brania to intervene, and the only thing she was doing so far was talking; that wasn't enough. "Get her the hell off of me!" Nakano cried.

Uninspired by Kano's appeal, Brania stood motionless and watched him thrash about, wriggle his body as best he could, as Imogene held firm and hardly reacted to the movements underneath her. As disturbing as it was to see her daughter act so callously, so viciously, it was also amazing. Her actions were completely out of character. But then Brania felt the blood drain from her face as she realized she was wrong. Imogene was doing nothing out of the ordinary. She was merely acting like her old self.

As Nakano continued to fight for his freedom, Brania remembered how heroically Imogene had fought against her and Edwige, before Edwige ultimately won and infused the girl with her own hybrid vampire blood. She also remembered how Imogene had killed Jeremiah. She hadn't witnessed the assault, but she knew Jeremiah had possessed superhuman strength, so for Imogene to defeat him she couldn't have just been lucky. She was seeing a side of the girl she had thought was dead and buried, but in truth had only been asleep. She was watching the resurrection of her feisty spirit, and while it filled her with pride it also filled her with fear. Brania knew firsthand how dangerous an uncontrollable daughter could be.

"Enough, Imogene!" Brania cried. "You've proven your point."

The girl didn't budge. "Not until he's dead."

Cautiously, Brania took a step forward. She didn't think

Imogene would strike her, but she couldn't be sure. "Remember Nakano could've killed you too," she said quietly. "Isn't it better to be like this, the way you are now, than to be dead?"

The words had their desired effect, and Imogene loosened her grip on Nakano as she pondered Brania's interpretation of the facts. It was all the time Nakano needed to strike back. Finally able to get one hand free, he rallied his strength so he could punch Imogene in the jaw. But his swing hit nothing but air. Imogene was no longer on top of him.

"Imogene!" Brania cried out, having witnessed the girl disappear before her eyes.

Stunned, Nakano scrambled to his feet and looked all around the cave, waiting for the girl to strike back at any second. Left, right, behind, Imogene was nowhere. Just as they were about to run out of the cave, Brania saw a light flicker in the coffin, and then a shape began to materialize, a shape that turned into Imogene's body. Without saying another word, Imogene sat back down in the casket and leaned into the corner, bringing her knees close to her chest.

"What the hell just happened?" Nakano asked, his body still shaking.

Proud, yet truly frightened, Brania replied, "I think my daughter can turn herself invisible when she feels threatened."

Shaking his head, Kano started to pace the width of the cave, the words gurgling out of him like puss from a wound. "I came here from a run-in with Jean-Paul to seek refuge," he spat, "only to come face to face with some half dead, invisible, po-faced git!"

With one eye on Imogene, Brania sat down on a boulder that was lodged against one of the walls and smoothed out her black leather skirt. "Oh come on, Kano," she scolded. "She hardly looked glum. Vengeful yes, glum no."

Taking in the surroundings and this latest unexplainable event, Nakano was flabbergasted. "Seriously?! You like it here?"

Laughing at the boy's honesty, Brania replied, "For the time being this place suits me perfectly." Glancing over at the now-peaceful girl in the coffin, she added, "And Imogene is a lovely companion. We rely on each other implicitly."

Still unable to stand still, Nakano continued to pace, making sure to stay as far away from the open coffin as possible. "Bollocks! I don't believe a word you say!" he shouted. "I trust you less than I trust Jean-Paul!"

Not if I told you that Jean-Paul has been lying to you and he's really David's bastard son. Brania wanted to share that piece of information with Nakano, but thought it best to keep it secret for now until she could use it to her best advantage. She did, however, recognize an opportunity when she saw one and realized that Nakano's vulnerable state was ripe for exploitation. "Has Jean-Paul told you why he's so chummy with my father?" Brania asked.

At last Nakano heard something that made him stop moving. "No," he replied. "Tell me, what exactly is going on between them?"

Brania felt like a spider watching a curious little bug step onto her web. "I can't figure out what it is," she said, sounding helpless and unsure. "I thought you might know something since you're so close to Jean-Paul."

Exhausted, Nakano sat on the boulder next to Brania. "We're not that close anymore."

Feigning shock, Brania replied, "I don't believe that." She reached out and touched Kano's hand. It flinched slightly, unused to such tenderness. "I've seen the way he looks at you."

Nakano was drenched in a wave of hope, so he disregarded the rational part of his mind that questioned Brania's comment. He wanted to believe what Brania was saying, he wanted to believe that there was still a chance for him and Jean-Paul as a couple, so that's what he clung to. "Really?"

For just one second when Brania heard Nakano's voice crack did she contemplate telling him the truth. But then she remembered she needed to keep her heart out of her plans and only think with her mind. "Absolutely," she said. "There is no way that Jean-Paul can look at you and not see the wonderful man you're becoming."

Nakano could no longer look into her eyes, so he gazed down at the dirt at his feet and started counting the pebbles so he wouldn't cry. When he felt like he could speak again without blubbering, he did. "I'm trying."

Brania stared at the ground as well, hoping her movement would translate as contemplative and not mimicry. "You know, I've made a lot of mistakes myself, and I know I haven't always been the most trustworthy person, not to you, not to a lot of people actually," she said softly. "But I'm trying to change, too. I'm trying to become a better person just like you are."

This time when he felt Brania's fingers touch his chin, he didn't flinch, he allowed them to rest there and turn his face toward hers. She looked at him with such kindness, he wished he could bottle it and take it with him, so every night before he went to sleep he could open the bottle up and have kindness watch over him while he slept. "You really think I'm becoming a better person?"

"You're doing more than that," Brania corrected. "You're succeeding."

Brania grabbed Nakano's hands and made him stand up. "You're an adult now, and you can make your own decisions," she said. "You can trust whomever you want. I just hope that someday you come to trust me."

Deep within him, hope was churning into happiness, and impulsively he hugged Brania. Startled, she didn't hug back right away; her arms floundered for a few moments until her mind clicked in and advised her to return the gesture. She wrapped her arms around Nakano and was surprised to find that his warm, needy flesh felt good. But after he left, Brania wasn't sure if what had just transpired was indeed a good thing. Imogene knew it was not.

"He isn't an adult," she hissed.

Pulled from her musing, Brania crossed over to her ward and knelt beside the coffin. She placed her arms on the white satin edge and rested her chin on her clasped hands. She looked like a lazy schoolgirl kneeling in church and leaning on the back of a pew. "No, he isn't, darling," Brania agreed. "But he doesn't know that yet, because he's still a child like you."

Rising, Brania stood before Imogene and was happy that she had remained tranquil after her outburst. Brania would have to observe her more closely and try to find out what other powers she possessed, but right now she was hungry. "I need to feed," she announced. "But Mother will return shortly."

A few minutes after Brania left the cave, Imogene felt anger and resentment boil inside her. She looked at her skin expecting to see blisters, but it was as pale and smooth as always. Even still, she knew she was transforming into something different yet again. She didn't know what was happening to her, but she knew one thing for certain, that sooner rather than later, Brania was going to find out that the rules had changed.

The mere thought of Brania's name made the rage within her grow even stronger. Imogene knew that Brania didn't care that that thing had killed Penry. Brania didn't care about her; she just wanted to control her and do God knows what to her. The thought of it made Imogene feel threatened. She felt as if she were in danger and that even though she was alone she had to defend herself in any way possible. Rising, she felt her hand grip the side of the coffin without commanding it to do so and heard a deafening creak as the lid was ripped from its hinges. She felt her arm involuntarily swing to the side and heard the lid crash into the wall of the cave. She heard herself shriek, "I AM NOT A CHILD!!!"

And then she felt herself disappear.

chapter 8

"I am not a child!"

Despite Saoirse's protestation, her tone was indeed child-like. So was her stance for that matter. With one hand she held the door to her dorm room open, while her other hand was balled into a fist that dug into her hip. Her lips were pursed together and her head cocked to one side. Amused, Ciaran half-expected her to stomp her foot.

"I never said you were, Seersh," Ciaran clarified, walking past his sister and into her room.

Behind him he heard Saoirse sigh heavily and then the sound of the door closing. She might not be happy about it, but at least he was in. A quick look around the room, however, showed him that it might all be for naught. "She isn't here," Saoirse said.

Turning to face his sister, Ciaran tried to make his voice sound as innocent as possible. "Who?"

Now she did stomp her foot. "Don't give me that!" she yelled, waving a finger at the air in front of Ciaran's face. "You're not here to ask about Mum. You want to try and get a glimpse of the pretty little blind girl!"

"Don't call her that!" Ciaran demanded.

"Why not?" Saoirse asked, plopping onto her bed. She lay back, her blond hair spread out around her face, blending into the lemon-yellow bedspread. "She's pretty, she's little, and she's blind." Disregarding Ciaran's shocked expression, she expanded her reasoning. "She's also ginger-haired, but that would be one too many adjectives."

Suddenly Ciaran had a disturbing thought: Ruby could be in the bathroom right now and overhearing every word they were saying. He was sure that Ruby had gotten a taste of her impudent nature, but the girl hadn't been blind for very long, and blindness was not something that should be treated casually or in a way that could be interpreted as disrespectful. "It's rude," Ciaran whispered, his eyes bulging as he looked over at the closed bathroom door.

Rolling her own eyes as she rolled off the bed, Saoirse opened the door with a dramatic, sweeping flourish and announced grandly, "The ginger-haired princess ain't in the lavvy!"

Ciaran acknowledged the disappointment that filled his body, but since it was not an uncommon feeling, he didn't need to dwell on it for very long. Instead, he used his energy to channel the playfulness of his sister. "Well, she probably jumped from the tower to escape the evil, blond-haired witch." Saoirse's laughter was silenced only when the pillow Ciaran threw hit her squarely in the face.

When she picked up the pillow, Ciaran thought for sure that she would attack him with the goose-down weapon. Instead she tossed it on her bed and ran into her brother's arms to give him a quick hug that was filled with more awkwardness than spontaneity. "Sorry, Ciar," she said. Pulling away from her brother she crossed to the mirror on the other side of the room. When she saw her reflection she immediately started to tame a few strands of wayward hair. "Ruby isn't here. Fritz beat you to it and came by about ten minutes ago to walk her to the library."

"Oh that's great," Ciaran said, deflated. "I'm glad she has someone to show her around."

Saoirse knew he was lying, but she didn't want to discuss his latest romantic disappointment, so she kept her gaze focused on her unruly hair to avoid looking at her brother's sullen expression. Unfortunately, he was only going to make it harder for her to avoid eye contact. "What about you?"

"What do you mean?" she asked, reaching for her tortoise shell hairbrush.

"Anyone showing you around lately?" he asked. "You were M.I.A. most of the summer."

A few brushes and her hair was perfect. She dropped the brush back onto the vanity top and searched for another distraction. "No, you wanker, just doing girl stuff," Saoirse mumbled as she grabbed a barrette and began to clasp it in her hair. "And, you know, trying to keep up with all our beastly summer reading."

Ciaran couldn't argue with that. For whatever reason Double A felt it important that every student read five new books over summer vacation, but did not require them to spend any time doing lab work. It didn't make any sense to him. Though very little made sense to him lately, in or out of school.

"And I haven't heard from Mum either," she said. "So I hate to break it to you, but this was kind of a wasted visit."

She thought her words would act as a dismissal, but looking in the mirror she saw that they had the opposite effect.

Ciaran propped up the pillows and sat on her bed, his arms and ankles crossed. She was about to tell him quite sternly that she didn't want his shoes on her comforter, but she knew that he had seen her jumping on her bed—and his bed and Ronan and Michael's bed—countless times before with her shoes on, so it would be a request without merit. The only option she had was to continue the conversation. At least one part of it. "It isn't as strange as you're making it out to be."

"What isn't?" Ciaran asked.

"Mum's silence," Saoirse replied, sitting at the foot of the bed. She lifted up Ciaran's feet and placed them in her lap. She raised her one knee and then the other and watched his shoes rise and fall, thinking it was better to focus on them than look at Ciaran, so he wouldn't see that she was now lying. "It's quite normal when you think about it, and anyway isn't her silence gobs better than her stroppy attitude and nasty insults?" It was a smart plan, but even though Ciaran had not grown up with Saoirse, he was proving to be a very insightful and observant brother.

"You don't believe that," he said. "Your upper lip is twitching like it always does when you're nervous and lying."

Saoirse was too touched by Ciaran's comment to try and convince him he was wrong. Despite being caught, it was nice to have someone know you very well, not completely, but nearly. "Well, fine then," she said, squeezing the tip of one of his penny loafers so tightly that it made him wince.

The sound Ciaran made was a mixture of a cry and a laugh. "Ow!"

"It is flippin' strange," Saoirse said, releasing her hold on him, "but that's Mum. She's a strange bird."

Swinging his legs off Saoirse's knees, Ciaran bounced once and sat on the edge of her bed next to her. "Strange, yes, and if she was just being elusive toward us, I wouldn't think twice about it," Ciaran confessed, pressing his shoe into the floor as if that was going to soothe his toes. "But Ronan hasn't heard from her either, not in months."

The twitching stopped, but Saoirse's concern only grew. "Months?"

"Ever since your impromptu birthday party," Ciaran replied. "Regardless of how she can act sometimes, I'm worried about her."

And now Saoirse was worried too. She hadn't given her mother's absence much thought. While she boarded at Ecole des Roches, there had been long stretches of time when she hadn't seen her mother and only had the briefest of phone calls in between visits. Edwige wasn't a typical parent and could not be described as maternal, Saoirse knew that, but she also knew that her mother was always reachable. She always knew how to get in touch with her even if she never took the initiative. What was most disturbing was that she also knew that Edwige was never out of Ronan's life for very long. If that was now the case, if she had suddenly cut off communication with her eldest child without any explanation, then something was definitely wrong. Unfortunately, Saoirse didn't have the time to investigate it. "I guess we'll just have to wait until Mum decides it's time for her to make a return engagement," she said.

That's exactly what Ciaran had told Ronan initially, but after thinking about it for a while he had come to realize it was hardly the most effective course of action. If he had learned anything through his lab work, it was that you had to try and seek out a solution to a problem. If the first experiment failed, you started another and continued on until one succeeded. "So, we just do nothing?"

Saoirse didn't know what to do about her mother, but she did know how to handle Ciaran. The most effective course of action in dealing with her brother was to be direct. "For now, dear brother, the only thing I have to do is write a paper on some daft, recently discovered F. Scott Fitzgerald short story," she announced as she walked toward the front door. Opening it, she leaned against the frame, both hands holding the doorknob behind her back. "And since you are not the literary genius in the family, you can't help me."

"Sorry about that," Ciaran replied, slowly standing up.

Relieved that Ciaran had taken the bait, Saoirse relaxed a bit. "Dumbarse Yankee should've kept his bad work hidden better, so I could have a free afternoon."

Smiling at his sister, Ciaran wished that he possessed her ability to rebound so quickly, to allow bad news and worry to roll off his back as easily as a fallen leaf can be swept up by the wind. But he was more like a tree whose roots burrowed deep into the earth. "Please tell Ruby that, um . . ."

"That you stopped by to offer your services as Seeing Eye bloke," Saoirse said, finishing Ciaran's thought in her own inimitable style.

Blushing a little, Ciaran smiled. It was not at all what he was going to say, but his sister's less formal approach might actually work better. Just as Saoirse was about to shut the door behind him, Ciaran whipped around and held it open. "I almost forgot."

"What now?" Saoirse cried, unable to hide the exasperation in her voice.

"You need to come to the lab so I can run another test."

Thankfully Saoirse had years of training hiding her true emotions, so she was able to keep her expression blank and not offer her brother a clue that his suggestion was inappropriate in-the-hallway conversation. "I don't know, Ciar," she whispered. "I think I'm done with all that."

Ciaran pushed on the door a bit harder, but Saoirse held tight to the doorknob and pushed back. She even went so far as to raise her hand against the doorjamb so Ciaran would understand that she didn't want him to come back in her room so they could continue their conversation in private either. It worked; Ciaran got the signal, but he wasn't yet finished with the topic. "You have to," he persisted. "I found out some stuff about Michael, and I need to run another test to compare the two of you."

Knowing that Ciaran wouldn't leave until she agreed to once again be his guinea pig, Saoirse reluctantly conceded to his request. "Fine! Make an appointment with my girl, and she'll put you on my calendar," she joked. "Now go!"

Not taking the chance that Ciaran would ask another question or come up with another reason to prolong his visit, Saoirse slammed the door in his face. She held her breath and pressed her ear against the wood to make sure she heard him bound down the stairs. Only when she heard the outside front door shut did she turn around, just in time to see another boy come out of her closet. "I thought he'd never leave!"

"Sorry," she said, awkwardly shoving her hands into the side pockets of her school skirt. "I didn't want to be rude."

Maybe it was because of the easy way he leapt onto her bed and fell back against the pillows or maybe it was because he wasn't her brother, but Saoirse had no desire to tell him to get off. She didn't care if he had his shoes on; she didn't care if he rumpled up her bedspread. He looked good sitting there, like it was where he belonged.

"You didn't mind lying, though," he said. "You didn't tell him the real reason you haven't seen much of him lately."

Slowly, Saoirse walked over and sat on the foot of the bed. She was self-conscious that her skirt rode up a few inches above her knee, but she stopped herself from pulling it down. That was something a less confident girl would do, and she was determined to prove that she wasn't nervous. "I thought you wanted to keep things between us a secret," Saoirse replied, her finger tracing some imaginary pattern on the bed-spread. "Until we know for sure that this isn't just a passing fancy."

The boy smiled, and his hazel eyes gleamed, green and brown and even amber all sparkling together. He ran his fingers through his loose curls for no other reason than because it felt good and latched onto one exceptionally curly strand of hair, straightening it and then letting it go, letting it bounce back against his cheek. If his jaw hadn't been so square and his nose so thick and flat, he would have looked like a girl. When he spoke, however, there was no denying that he was all guy.

His voice was deep for a seventeen-year-old, a rich baritone, and Saoirse thought he could be an opera singer or someone who talks on the radio for a living, the sound was so beautiful. She loved to listen to him talk. Because English wasn't his first language, he would often put the accents on some words in the wrong places. So even on those occasions when he talked about himself for way too long, rambling on about his Scandinavian heritage or his opinions about world politics, she wouldn't listen to the words, but only to the sound. It was sometimes more interesting. "And until I'm more than just the new kid on the block."

"Which should be any day now, right?" Saoirse asked. Part of her enjoyed having a secret life, but the other part wanted to let the whole wide world know that she had a boyfriend.

"Well, I have some tryouts today," he said. "So if I make one of the teams, I guess it'll mean I'm part of the 'in' crowd."

Looking at his body, Saoirse had no doubt her boyfriend would make any team he tried out for and possibly give Ronan competition as unofficial top athlete on campus. He wasn't as muscular as Ronan was; he actually looked more like Michael, but way more defined. He had broad shoulders, a small waist, and long legs with lines and lines of fine blond hair all over his thighs and calves that Saoirse had found herself staring at all summer long. Shaking her head, she focused on the boy on her bed who was dressed in the Double A uniform and not the one in her mind who pranced about in a tank top and shorts. "Even if you don't make it, you'll still be part of the 'in' crowd," she said. "I'm sure of it."

Unexpectedly, he sat up and pushed Saoirse down on the bed. She was startled by the sudden movement, but when she saw his face smiling down at her, adorned with a crown of curls, looking like a cross between an angel and a scalawag, she knew he was only being playful. His question, however, was a bit more businesslike. "What kind of secret lab work are you doing with your brother?"

Blast you, Ciaran! I knew someone would hear us. "Ooh you make me sound like a spy," Saoirse teased. Her stomach flipped when she thought about the implications of her comment. If it were true, wouldn't that make her boyfriend her enemy?

"Seriously," he continued. "Sounded rather cryptic. What's up?"

Desperate to change the subject, Saoirse thought that if his smile could work wonders on her, hers might put a spell on him as well. "Why so many questions?" Saoirse asked, smiling as seductively as she knew how.

It didn't work. "Why aren't you answering me?" he retorted.

Boys! They really could be infuriating. Always wanting to have their way, always thinking their questions were super important, never considering for a second that they didn't have to know everything in the entire world. Infuriating, but really cute too. If only Saoirse's hands weren't being held down, she could just reach up and touch those curls, marvel at their softness. And then touch the little bit of stubble on his chin and marvel at its roughness. Infuriating, cute, *and* disorienting. If she was a spy she was the worst one in the history of spydom. Time to take back some control.

"Well, you know us spies, we don't like to be interrogated." And if her words didn't do the trick, her actions might. In one easy move, Saoirse flipped her boyfriend on his back, his curls spilling out onto the bed like little curlicues of sunshine. The sight made her heart skip a beat, even though she knew she had to keep her wits about her until all talk of lab work and experiments had passed. When she felt his chest and stomach move underneath her and heard his deep laugh, she knew she was safe.

"That's what I like about you," he said. "You're not like other girls; you're fearless."

Suddenly self-conscious about lying on top her boyfriend, she rolled off of him. She stared at the ceiling and wished there were a mirror up there so she could see how they looked lying side by side, their hair freely mingling together, his a few shades lighter than her own blond hair. It must be a beautiful sight. "I've learned this past year that there isn't anything in this world that I need to be scared of," Saoirse admitted.

"Except maybe a boyfriend."

Saoirse wasn't completely honest when she replied, "I'm not scared of you."

"Not yet," he said. Turning to face Saoirse, her boyfriend wrapped his arm around her waist and pulled her close to him. He closed his eyes and let instinct take over so his lips could find hers. Saoirse kept her eyes open, but only because she liked how weird his face looked so close up. His eyelashes were outrageously long, and the pores on his nose looked huge. The examination was brief because the kiss ended as quickly as it had begun. "Let's just keep us a secret for a little while longer," he said.

Nodding, Saoirse touched the side of his face and slid her fingers deep into the labyrinth of his curls. She pulled her hand away and was transfixed by how white some of the strands looked. "I've got a lot of secrets, Morgandy," she said. "Why not one more?"

chapter 9

So this was what it felt like to be blind.

Eyes closed, Fritz walked down the center aisle of the library in total darkness, his fingers scraping against the spines of one book after another. It wasn't so bad; in fact it was kind of interesting to feel the world instead of see it. Thick, thin, leathery, smooth, he had no idea what books he was touching, but he was amazed at how different they all felt. He had never noticed that before. Of course none of them felt as good as Ruby did.

Her arm was entwined with his, and although he could only feel a small patch of her skin, it was incredibly smooth. He figured she must use mounds of moisturizer to get it that soft. His skin, in contrast, was kind of rough in places.

He opened his right eye, just a crack, to take a peek at her. Amazing! She was one of those girls who looked just as good in profile as they did if you looked at them straight on. Fritz thought it had to do with her nose. Ruby's was perfect—not too big and, thankfully, not too small, not one of those little pug noses some girls had that Fritz hated, that made them look like they were always putting on airs, thinking they were too fancy for their own good. Her nose was even prettier than Phaedra's, and Phaedra had a really nice one. Ruby's best feature, however, were her eyes.

Peering at the girl through one half-closed eye, it was like he was spying on her through a keyhole. Fritz only saw a sliver, but it was enough. He could only see her left eye, but even from this angle it was sparkling blue, filled with light, and though it was useless it appeared to have focus. Unblinking, Ruby glided down the aisle like somebody who could see. She didn't stumble; she didn't trip; she didn't question her path. Fritz figured it had something to do with the expertise of her guide.

A smile formed on Ruby's lips, and she slowly turned to face him. Wow, he thought, she looked like she was really looking at him, like she could really see him. But if she could, then she could also see that his eyes weren't closed like he had said they were when they started to walk down the aisle. Maybe he was being paranoid, but Fritz got the strong sensation that Ruby knew he was lying.

He shut his eyes tight and was engulfed by darkness once again. He faced front, and his fingers now held onto the edge of the bookshelves for support as he walked, every once in a while getting whacked by the partitions that separated the various collections. Fritz was so discombobulated he couldn't even remember what book Ruby needed to find, let alone what section they were supposed to wind up in. Was it history? No, that wasn't it. Maybe classical mythology? He had no idea, so of course he started to panic and pick up speed. If you have no idea where you're going, might as well try to get there as fast as possible. Until you crash into something and get knocked to the ground.

"What the . . . !"

When Fritz opened his eyes he saw Ruby staring down at him and Ciaran lying in a similarly awkward position at his side. "Eaves! What the hell?!" Fritz cried out. "Why'd you knock me down?"

"I didn't knock you down," Ciaran shouted back. "You knocked into me."

"I didn't even see you!"

"That's 'cause you had your bloody eyes closed!"

"He was doing it for me."

Ruby's voice shut both boys up and reminded them that they weren't alone. Scrambling to stand, they both automatically started to brush their hair back into place and tuck their shirts in, even though the object of their admiration couldn't tell if they were unkempt or picture perfect.

"Hi, Ruby," Ciaran said, a bit out of breath.

"Hi, Ciaran," the girl replied, staring right in his direction. "Fancy meeting you here."

Not fancy at all, calculated actually. After his rather disappointing conversation with Saoirse, Ciaran had decided to take action and make a move before Fritz made too much headway in his pursuit of Ruby. Turned out to be a worthwhile risk. "I'm always here," Ciaran lied. "Working on a paper or something."

"Then maybe you can help me," Ruby said, reaching out to touch Ciaran's arm. "Would you happen to know where the science books are?"

Science! Fritz finally remembered where they were supposed to be heading.

"I need to do some research on a horticulture project, and Professor Chow told me the library actually had some books in Braille on the subject—not a complete section, but mixed in with the regular books about science," Ruby explained. "And it seems that Fritz has lost his way."

"I did not!" Fritz protested. "I know this library like I know the back of my bleedin' hand."

"So were you, uh, taking the scenic route?" Ciaran asked.

Fritz felt like pushing Ciaran against the bookshelf for making such a crack, but when he heard Ruby laugh he realized it *was* kind of funny, so he just joined in. "Guess the blind really shouldn't lead the blind."

Shocked, Ciaran couldn't believe how inappropriate Fritz could be, but surprisingly, Ruby laughed hardest of all at the joke. Both boys were impressed with how well she was transitioning; neither one thought they could be as resilient. But both thought they could be a better escort.

"Take my arm," Fritz and Ciaran said at the same time.

Proving to be as diplomatic as she was attractive, Ruby offered a compromise. "How about you each take one arm?"

Flanking the girl on either side, the boys guided her to the small section in the far end of the library that contained books on horticulture. Fritz had never been in this part of St. Joshua's before, but Ciaran knew it quite well; it was the only part of the library that housed any type of scientific reference book, the bulk of them being stored in the Einstein Wing. "I think this might be what you're looking for," Ciaran said, pulling out a very thick, oversized book that looked more like a giant photo album than a textbook.

"Blimey, that thing is huge!" Fritz remarked as Ciaran passed the book over to Ruby.

She ran her fingers over a series of raised bumps on the book's cover and said, "This *thing* is called *Horticulture: Principles and Practices*." She flashed a wide grin at Ciaran. "This is exactly what I need, Ciaran, thank you."

Smiling proudly, for Fritz's benefit of course and not Ruby's, he replied, "My pleasure."

Fritz made a face and mouthed the words "my pleasure" to mock his friend, which only made them both start to laugh. "What's so funny?" Ruby asked.

Not wanting to rat on his friend, Ciaran made a generalization that he hoped Ruby would understand. "It's just Fritz being Fritz."

"I can only imagine," Ruby replied, clutching her book close to her chest. "My brother told me all about how cheeky you can be."

Despite his reputation, Fritz tried to defend himself. "Penry called me cheeky?!"

For a moment Ruby seemed distracted. She was staring directly in between both boys, almost as if she was trying to look through the bookshelf to see what or who was on the other side. Neither boy noticed, however, as they were too busy staring at Ruby themselves. After a few seconds, Ruby refocused and tilted her head toward Fritz. "I know you've been on your best behavior, but I know all about your shady past," she said in a hushed whisper. "Remember, Penry and I were twins. If he didn't tell me something, I just had to read his mind."

If touché had a facial expression, it was being worn by Ciaran. Fritz, on the other hand, looked like he had just been force fed several jumbo pieces of humble pie. After a long pause, Ruby burst out laughing. She didn't need sight to know that her little hoax had had its desired effect. "Gotcha, Ulrich!"

Using Fritz's silence to his advantage, Ciaran led Ruby over to an empty table in a corner of the library. As he watched her deftly pull an assortment of objects out of her backpack, he realized this girl was quite self-sufficient and didn't need an ounce of anyone's pity. What she did command, however, was respect.

"What's that?" Ciaran asked as Ruby placed a small device that looked like an e-book with a detachable keyboard on the table.

"It's a blind student's best friend," she replied, attaching the keyboard to the tablet. "An electronic notebook. I can type in notes, and then it'll play them back to me with text-to-voice software."

"That's amazing!" Fritz exclaimed.

"It really is," Ruby agreed. "I don't think I could survive here without it." Once again she looked at the boys as if she could really see them. "Or without my new friends."

"Ruby!"

The girl had even more friends than she knew. Or could hear. Imogene was going to run out from behind the bookshelf, but she was so happy to see Penry's twin sister that she ran right through it. Another benefit of being invisible. "Ruby, it's me, Imogene!"

"What was that?" Fritz asked.

With one touch of a button Ciaran quashed Imogene's hopes that she could be heard, if not seen. "My watch alarm," Ciaran explained, pressing a tiny button on the side of his watch. "Sorry, Ruby, can't be late for swim tryouts."

"Do you, um, need someone to walk you back to your dorm later?" Fritz asked, hoping he didn't sound too obvious.

Smiling, Ruby replied, "Saoirse's picking me up, and we'll head to St. Joe's for dinner."

Without anything else to say and knowing that Blakeley would have their heads if they were late for tryouts for the new season's team, Ciaran and Fritz left Ruby with her book and newfangled device and rushed out of St. Joshua's. They had no idea that they weren't leaving her alone.

It was so good to see an old friend and be out of that gloomy, damp cave that Imogene didn't even care that she couldn't be seen or heard. She didn't understand why, since others could see her. The only explanation she could come up with was that Brania and Nakano had played major roles in the events that had led up to her death, so she somehow remained connected to them. Whatever the reason, it was obvious that she was changing yet again. And Imogene really didn't care; she just wanted to sit next to the girl she had once called her friend. However, it wasn't a simple task.

Imogene tried to pull out the chair next to Ruby, but once again her hand went right through the wood. It didn't matter, as long as she could be somewhere other than that cave. When Brania yelled at her just a few moments ago, Imogene didn't know where she'd wind up after she disappeared. She assumed she materialized here in the library because it was one of the places where she had always felt safe. Her head ached trying to make sense of it all, so she stopped. She wanted to enjoy every second of this respite for however long it lasted. Curious, she watched the blind girl's fingers dance over the raised bumps at an incredible speed and was overjoyed when she saw Ruby look up at her. Although Ruby couldn't see Imogene and Imogene couldn't make physical contact with Ruby, it was clear that they were each aware of the other's presence.

Imogene thought it was a good feeling, safe and familiar. Just as familiar as the scent of fresh roses that suddenly and inexplicably filled up the room.

chapter 10

The overpowering smell of chlorine filled up St. Sebastian's, which could only mean one thing: swim team tryouts were about to begin. Blakeley liked to add extra chemicals to the pool on the first day of tryouts to set the mood, let the kids know that even though they and the school were firmly planted on land, for a few hours at least, water reigned supreme. It was something Michael and Ronan already knew.

Breathing in deeply, Michael found the smell invigorating. Chlorine wasn't as intoxicating as salt water, but it was a close second. Ronan couldn't concentrate on anything other than Michael and how he looked in his swimsuit. "Crikey!" Ronan gasped. "I forgot how good you looked in your swimmers, love."

Smiling impishly, Michael didn't disagree. He had grown another inch over the summer and had worked hard to put on a few more pounds of muscle, so he knew he looked pretty good standing there in nothing but his Speedo. He had also noticed that a few dark-blond hairs had sprouted in the cleft of his chest and in a vertical line that started just below his belly button. Ronan had told him that even as a vampire his hair would continue to grow and his body would continue to show signs of improvement; he just didn't really know what to expect. Michael liked the changes. He knew they didn't make him human, but the connection to his old species was somehow reassuring. He felt even better now that Ronan had finally noticed them too. "You have to start paying closer attention," he joked.

Not to be outdone, Ronan made sure he had the last word. "I'll just have to remember to keep the lights on tonight."

Running out of the locker room, Ciaran joined them just in time to catch Ronan wink and Michael blush and figured he had stumbled headfirst into a private conversation. "Should I do a one-eighty and leave you two alone?" he asked warily.

"No!" Michael said, laughing and grabbing onto Ciaran's arm to ensure that he stayed put. "We could use a distraction."

Ciaran could handle that. After all, he was able to distract Ruby from focusing only on Fritz; surely he could entertain Michael and Ronan for a little bit. In fact, standing next to Michael he found it easy to relax and have some fun. Over the course of the last year he had learned that it was possible to celebrate the positive aspects of his life and not just dwell on the negative. It wasn't his natural tendency, but with practice it was getting easier. So was being silly for absolutely no reason.

Bowing regally, Ciaran said in a voice worthy of a character on one of those *Masterpiece Classic* miniseries, "Never let it be said that Ciaran Eaves did not comply."

"What news do you bring forth from the hinterland, brother?" Ronan asked, in an equally aristocratic voice.

"The *hinterland?*" Michael repeated.

Shrugging his shoulders, Ronan replied, "Leave me alone. I'm playing along!" Resuming his role, Ronan spread his legs farther apart and crossed his arms to face Ciaran. Despite being clad in nothing but a skimpy bathing suit, Ronan still managed to look like a king addressing one of his subjects. "Tell me the news, Lord Eaves, and pray, speak only words that will glorify your tongue."

Unable to hold his own tongue, Michael groaned, "Oh blimey!"

Ciaran slapped Michael on the shoulder, making it clear that he was enjoying the improvisation. Truth was he was simply enjoying the playful repartee with his brother. "On the breeze of the late summer wind comes news that one of our fallen soldiers will reenlist to fight for the sovereign once more."

This time Ronan couldn't hold his tongue, but it wasn't to mock his brother, it was to praise him. *"On the breeze of the late summer wind?!"* Ronan exclaimed. "That's brill! Have you been brushing up on your Austen lately? Sounds like something from *Pride and Prejudice.*"

"Actually I was imitating *Wuthering Heights,*" Ciaran explained, "which I just finished reading this morning."

Ronan's eyes bulged even wider. "Good for you, mate! 'Bout time you read something other than a textbook."

Clearing his throat, Michael interrupted. "Looks like the fallen soldier is entering the battlefield."

All three turned toward the locker room entrance and saw Blakeley marching into the gym, followed closely by Nakano, who was once again wearing the official swim team bathing suit—a navy blue Speedo with gold A's on both hips. Ronan was more impressed than ever with Ciaran. "Blimey! You weren't just being literary," he said. "You were being literary *and* dropping clues!"

Ronan might have been in high spirits, but Blakeley was even more pumped. Although Nakano remained at the far end of the pool, the coach took his one-man parade all the way around the pool, addressing the students without breaking a stride. "Mr. Kai here has come to his senses and decided to rejoin the team," he announced.

Every head in the room turned to look at Nakano to gauge his expression. Was this true? Was this some dumb joke? Was the volatile student going to freak out again, tell everyone to sod off, and run from the room? Just when the silence was becoming deafening, Blakeley spoke. "What do we think about that?"

No one except Michael noticed that Blakeley directed his comment toward him, as an obvious warning that he didn't want Michael to repeat his actions of last year, which had led to Nakano's abruptly quitting the team. *Don't worry, Coach,* Michael thought. *That won't happen again.* He didn't change his mind when he saw Nakano staring at him defiantly, almost willing him to say something nasty and pick a fight. Michael had no intention of doing that. He really wasn't sure why he was reconnecting with Nakano; he just felt it was the right thing to do. So right that Michael's applause led the group and soon the clapping turned into whoops and cheers. Those closest to Nakano were patting him on the shoulder and welcoming him back to where he was obviously missed.

Jostled by the crowd, Nakano turned and found himself staring at Michael, who was about to extend a hand to Kano as an olive branch of sorts. But before Michael could open his mouth to speak, Kano issued a promise. "Say one word, Howard, and I'll quit all over again."

Stunned, Michael telepathically confided in Ronan. *"I was just going to say that I was glad to see him back."*

Ronan just nodded and smiled at Nakano and then responded to his boyfriend. *"I think he already knows that."*

After making one complete lap around the circumference of the pool, Blakeley finally stopped. "Good!" he bellowed. "That's what I wanted to hear!"

In his hand he swung the metal chain with the whistle on it that he usually wore around his neck. *Swoosh, swoosh, swoosh,* it flipped in the air, swinging round and round as he surveyed the group. He eyed the students and knew that they were just that, kids, nothing more, but after the past year, after dealing with Dr. MacCleery's murder and the mysterious circumstances surrounding it, he didn't trust what he saw any longer.

He caught Ronan and Michael eyeing him, and for a second he lost his rhythm. The chain slipped and floundered in the air, the whistle bouncing off his knuckles and falling limp against the back of his hand. Blakeley knew that those two were at the center of all the chaos and disruption that had visited the school recently. He didn't know if they were the cause or if they would wind up being their salvation, but he did know that whatever had happened—and whatever would happen—they were and would be involved.

Look away, he told himself. *You're stronger than they are, whatever they are.* He whipped the whistle around in his hand with even more force. *Whatever they are?!* Where the hell did that come from? And what the hell was that supposed to mean? Blakeley had no idea what he was thinking; he had no idea where his mind was going. Damn, if everything was subject to question, then obviously, so too was his own sanity.

When he heard Alexei cough, he was pulled out of his thoughts and back to the present. He was a coach, not a philosopher, and he had a motley bunch of students to turn into ace swimmers. He might be going through his own private purgatory, but he also had a reputation to uphold. And he planned to do just that, as gruffly as possible. "Ya look like a bunch of pasty duffers, you do!" Looking into the group he looked for someone to pick on. "Especially you, Fuente!" he yelled. "Ya look like you spent the summer hiding under your bed."

Once again Diego displayed his ability to remain unflustered when berated by a teacher. "You know, it really is a fallacy that all Spaniards are dark skinned, sir," he replied. "Besides, my family's from the north."

Finally, things were getting back to normal. "I don't care where your bloody family's from! Ya look like a polar bear!"

The boys laughed so hard that Diego was unable to inform Blakeley that polar bears were expert swimmers and therefore he took his comment as a compliment. His thanks, however, would have to wait as Blakeley had more announcements to make.

"As you all know, we have a new school doctor," he said, his voice not as harsh as before, "who's got some new school rules."

Michael cringed at the mention of Dr. Sutton, but cringed even more when someone responded to Blakeley's comment by crying out from the crowd, "Coed swim team?!"

Smirking unprofessionally, Blakeley replied, "You yobs don't know what to do with girls on land. How the bloody hell do you think you'd know what to do with them in the pool!?"

"Some of us know," Michael whispered to Ronan. "We just don't care."

Smirking just as wickedly as Blakeley, Ronan responded by bumping his hip into Michael's butt.

"And one of those new rules is that the new doc is enforcing mandatory physicals for each student athlete," Blakeley continued. "I think it's a bloomin' foolish idea, but I'm just the daft gym teacher, not some medical expert."

Another cold tingle sprinkled down Michael's spine. *"Ronan, this means we'll be exposed!"*

Another smirk graced Ronan's face. *"And so will the good doctor."*

The cold tingle was replaced with the warm sensation of relief. *"Oh yeah ... I forgot about that."*

One thing Blakeley didn't forget was to save the best announcement for last. "Awright, shut it! I got one more thing, and it's the biggest of 'em all."

Like any good leader, Blakeley waited until the murmur in the crowd subsided, until he could feel the tension grow in the gym, until he had everyone's full attention before he spoke again. "This year the National Swim Team Competition is going to be held right here at Double A."

As he expected, that's all he had to say. Everyone knew what an honor it was to host the competition and that teams from schools all over the United Kingdom would come here for a weekend to vie for the title of the best in the country. There were prizes given for each discipline—backstroke, breaststroke, freestyle, relay—and to the best all-around athlete, and the most coveted Team of the Year award was given to the team that displayed the best athletic skills as well as superior sportsmanship.

The guys went wild, screaming, jumping up and down, pumping the air with their fists. Alexei got so excited he did a flip into the deep end of the pool. Equally carried away, but less agile, Diego tried to imitate Alexei's move, but only wound up performing an elite-level belly flop. Blakeley was so satisfied with the amount of excitement his announcement created that he didn't even scream when he was sprayed with a wave of water following Diego's plunge. He just made a mental note to bench Fuente so he wouldn't be able to participate in any of the races.

"The competition will take place during the Tri-Centennial Celebration," Blakeley shouted, unzipping and taking off his now-wet track jacket and tossing it to the floor. "And since we're hosting I expect us to win Team of the Year!"

An even louder roar engulfed the gym and even more guys jumped into the pool, splashing around, dunking each other, and shouting incoherently. It was no wonder that when Fritz ran in from the locker room he thought he was missing a fight.

Slapping Ciaran on the shoulder, he asked, "Who threw the first punch?"

Under the din of the crowd, Ciaran filled Fritz in on what was happening, then wanted to know why he was so late for practice. "We left the library at the same time," Ciaran said. "What happened to you?" It was the same thing Blakeley wanted to know.

"I was helping Ruby Poltke get to the library, Coach," Fritz announced proudly, completely unaware that Ciaran looked utterly confused by his statement.

"You too?" Blakeley replied. "Eaves already told me he was helping her, and he was able to make it to practice on time."

Fritz's bronze skin turned a shade closer to red. "Well, I rushed out to help Ruby so quickly after class, I forgot my swimsuit and had to run back to my dorm to get it," he confessed, his voice smaller than usual. It only took him a moment to return to his usual brassy self. "You didn't want me to show up here starkers, did you?"

The crowd was split. Half of the guys grimaced loudly at the prospect of seeing Fritz naked, while the other half let out a collective "awwww" to make fun of Fritz and his obvious crush on the girl. He laughed along with them, taking the ribbing in stride, what did he care? Despite Ciaran's showing up at the last minute and literally crashing into their private outing, he was the one who got to hold her arm and waltz her around school like she was his girlfriend, which he hoped very soon she would be. It didn't even matter to him that she was blind. He had thought it would at first, but when he was around her, she never acted like she had a disability. She was almost more self-assured than he was.

"Did you know that she reads Braille?" he informed the group.

"Yes!" Ciaran cried. "I was the one who found the book for God's sake!"

Alexei's voice broke right through the laughter. "Looks like Ruby had a two-for-one sale!"

Ignoring him, Fritz went on to extol Ruby's achievements. "She told me personally that she learned it in a bloody month! Do you know how hard that is to do?"

Although none of them had given it much thought before, they all imagined that it was a major accomplishment, learning a completely new language based on raised bumps on a piece of paper. However, none of them offered nearly the same level of excitement as they had when they heard about where the swim team competition would be held. Michael and Ronan were subdued because they knew Ruby possessed skills that were beyond human definition, so her mastery of Braille was not as impressive as Fritz thought. Ciaran refused to add to Fritz's elation by praising Ruby's triumph in front of an audience. He would tell her how impressed he was when he was alone with her, *if* he was ever alone with her. No, he corrected himself, no more negative thoughts. *When* he was alone with her.

"Hey, Nebraska! I think I'm going to get her to help me write an issue of my comic book in Braille too!" Fritz declared. "How brilliant will that be?"

Michael could tell by Ciaran's grim expression that he didn't think that was brilliant at all and, in fact, that the last thing Ciaran wanted to hear was that Fritz was anything more to Ruby than a tour guide. Dammit! Michael realized that both his friends had feelings for whoever this girl was who was claiming to be Penry's sister and that worried him greatly. There was nothing he could do except keep tabs on them all and see how the relationships developed before either of them got in over his head. At this point, however, Fritz was so enthused about the possibility of having a girlfriend and Ciaran was so disappointed at possibly losing out at the chance that nothing Michael said would resonate with them. All he could do was smile and tell Fritz that a Braille edition was inspired.

"And I know Penry would think it was a corking idea too!" Fritz added.

That name again! Every time Nakano heard someone mention Penry's name it was like a knife to his stomach. He didn't know why it unnerved him so much. Penry was human, nothing more. He was part of a species that was put here on earth as rations for vampires. That's it, end of story. Well, if that was true, why was he getting so upset about taking Penry's life? He fed on his blood; he didn't murder him. Wasn't there a huge difference between the two?

But one look at Michael and Nakano knew exactly why he was feeling guilty; he was lying to himself. He hadn't attacked Penry for his blood the night of the Archangel Festival; he had attacked him because he thought Penry was Michael. He thought that he was doing what David had wanted him to do—rid the world of water vamps one hybrid at a time. He didn't even look to make sure that it was Michael before he bit into Penry's neck; he just ravaged his flesh, confident that he was draining blood from the correct host. He had been wrong.

He knew he had crossed a line, but there was nothing he could do about it. More than that, he didn't know how much longer he could stand these feelings that he was having every time someone mentioned the dead kid's name. He couldn't take it anymore, and he wished that Fritz would stop blathering on about how proud Penry would be that he and Ruby were carrying on his bloody comic book. Blakeley saw to it that Kano got his wish.

"Ulrich!" Blakeley shouted. "Since you were the last to arrive, you'll be the first one to get a physical from Dr. Sutton."

Fritz was in such a good mood from spending time with Ruby, the news hardly fazed him. "Might as well start with the best physical specimen in the lot!" he shouted, giving his firm stomach a hard slap.

Watching him walk toward the locker room, Ciaran was plagued by an awful thought. For an instant he hoped Dr. Sutton would find some deadly virus running through Fritz's blood or discover that a major organ was about to fail, anything that would mean Fritz would be out of Ruby's life so Ciaran could finally make his entrance. Oh God! How could he think such a thing? Was any girl really worth spending even a moment wishing harm on a friend? Shocked that he could so easily consider such a notion, by how quickly his mind wandered into such evil territory, Ciaran said a quick prayer to try to counteract his thought. Sure, he wanted to get close to Ruby, but never at Fritz's expense. Hopefully it was just a momentary lapse and not an indication of his true nature.

Luckily, Blakeley wasn't concerned about anyone's psychological makeup at the moment; all he wanted to do was test their physical abilities. "Nakano, Alexei, Glynn-Rowley, and Eaves," he shouted. "Take your places for the first practice meet of the season!"

As the guys who were called broke free from the crowd to stand on top of the starting blocks, Michael leaned in and whispered in Ronan's ear, "Don't be too hard on them."

Responding in an even huskier whisper, Ronan let his lips brush softly against Michael's ear. "You know me, love. I only show off when it counts."

Michael was so distracted by Ronan's flirtatious comment

and by the feelings it aroused in the pit of his stomach that he didn't notice David enter the gym from the back entrance until he was standing at the opposite end of the pool. He looked so out of place, not only because he was formally dressed in his usual suit and tie, but because right behind him was a student that Michael had never seen before.

Based on his attire—he was wearing the official Double A swimsuit like every other kid in the gym—it was obvious that he wanted to try out for the team. Even though Michael didn't recognize the newcomer, it was obvious that he wasn't a stranger to everyone. Ronan, Ciaran, and Nakano looked like triplets; they were all wearing the same expression as they stared at the kid with the curly, blond hair: they looked as if they were staring at a corpse who had risen from the dead. It was only when David finally spoke that Michael understood why.

"I'd like to introduce Double A's latest student and the newest member of our swim team," David announced. "Meet the former national champion of Sweden, Morgandy van der Poole."

chapter 11

Ronan was lost in a memory. Sunlight poured down on the stranger like a sudden rainstorm. Ronan had to squint, and still he couldn't see him clearly. What he could see, however, made him feel different, better than he had ever felt before, like a man, an adult, even though he was hardly either. He knew the vision, as hazy as it was, would change his life forever.

The stranger was moving closer toward him, still a blur, still unidentifiable, still filling Ronan with excitement. The day, like so many others spent in the small village a few miles in from Inishtrahull Island, had been uneventful, so Ronan had figured it would pass without anything interesting or significant happening. When the stranger stood before him and the harsh sunlight was finally covered by a thick canopy of clouds, Ronan knew he had been wrong. It was like his mother always said, Ronan was special and greatness would come to him; he just had to be patient.

Sitting down on the ground next to him, the stranger asked, "What's your name?"

Dry mouthed, Ronan had to swallow hard in order to speak. "Ronan Glynn-Rowley."

The stranger smiled as if the name meant something to him, something good. "I'm Morgandy van der Poole."

Ronan didn't recognize the name, nor did he like it, too fancy, but the sound of Morgandy's deep voice intrigued him. Morgandy didn't possess the common accent, the Irish lilt he had been hearing since he was born. His voice was flatter, the words streaming out of his lips like a horizontal line and not rising up and down like sounds floating on top of a rough sea. His voice wasn't the only thing that was refreshing. The color of his hair was less blond than it was blinding sunshine, and the hair fell in a mass of curls across his forehead and past the nape of his neck, wild and reckless; it made Ronan dizzy. "I could use a pool on a day like today," Morgandy said. "Bloody sweltering."

Ronan felt a bead of sweat trickle down the side of his face, but before he could wipe it away, Morgandy touched him right below his earlobe with his finger and followed the perspiration's route along his jawbone, underneath his chin, down the center of his throat, and into the soft pit in the middle of his collarbone. Never had Ronan been touched like this before, so simply, so purposefully. It felt both wrong and right at the same time, and Ronan was disappointed when Morgandy stopped; he wanted his finger to travel to more parts of his body. "Would you like to swim inside of me?" Morgandy asked.

Apparently Morgandy's assertive approach wasn't confined to just his touch. "What?" Ronan said, trying not to sound as shocked as he was.

Turning away, Morgandy stared at some trees that swayed in an unexpected breeze. He stared so intently, it appeared as if the trees, bowing to the wind, held more interest to him than the handsome boy he was sitting next to. When he spoke, the intensity of his words proved otherwise. "Wouldn't it feel supreme to get lost forever in the waves of my emotions? Hold on to me for dear life because you're afraid I might make you drown?"

This was another first. No one had ever spoken to Ronan like this before, so simply, so poetically. Ronan had no idea what Morgandy was talking about, but he knew right then that he would risk drowning to find out, to get closer to this boy, hear more of his words, feel more of his touch. He was just about to say that yes, yes, yes, it would be perfection to swim inside his emotions when he heard a noise that ruined everything: he heard Morgandy's laugh.

The sound was so deep and hearty it didn't seem to belong to the boy; his delicate features should produce a more refined sound, not the noise Ronan was hearing. "I'm just fooling with you," Morgandy confessed, his hazel eyes blazing in the hot sun.

"I knew that," Ronan lied, abruptly looking away toward the trees that were now hanging lifeless in the stagnant air.

Morgandy leaned forward until his face was practically in front of Ronan's, until Ronan had no choice but to look at him once again. "You can't lie to me," Morgandy corrected. "You thought I was serious."

Ronan wasn't sure if it was the steely look behind Morgandy's smile or his own desire not to conceal his emotions that prompted him to tell the truth. "Yes, I did."

Satisfied, Morgandy sat back and pressed his palms into the dirt, extending his legs. He was wearing loose-fitting cargo shorts, and they rode up to the middle of his thigh. Ronan liked how Morgandy's blond hair looked almost white against his golden skin and how his muscles converged to create a curvy terrain that continued up and over his knee and down and under to his calves.

"You're beautiful." Ronan forgot all about Morgandy's body and concentrated on his words; it was the first time anyone had ever told him that. "Now I'm being serious," Morgandy added, just so there would be no confusion.

Speechless, Ronan didn't know how to respond. A few seconds ago he had been determined to speak honestly, and now he was about to change the rules to cover up the barrage of emotions and sensations that were being released inside of his brain and his body. Whoever this Morgandy was, he was whittling away at his confidence, altering the way he thought.

"You can tell me I'm beautiful too," Morgandy said. "I've heard it many times before."

The spell half-broken, Ronan wasn't sure if he should laugh or comply. Honesty was attractive; vanity less so.

"But never from someone who actually meant it," Morgandy added.

The sadness in Morgandy's voice touched Ronan deeply. In one sweeping rush, he understood everything he needed to know. He knew that Morgandy's bravado was a cover-up to mask his loneliness; he knew that Morgandy ached to have a companion, a boyfriend, a soul mate, just as much as Ronan did and that despite his obvious beauty an even more beautiful spirit existed underneath his flesh. "You *are* beautiful," Ronan replied.

Morgandy's eyes looked almost as sad as his voice sounded. "Thank you." But then the sadness evaporated like sweat that burrowed deep into skin. A trace of its residue lingered, but it was unseen, transformed, and even though Morgandy still looked like he might cry, it was in response to overwhelming joy, not sorrow.

Thrown by the unsettling encounter, Ronan needed confirmation. "Why are you looking at me like that?"

Sitting up, Morgandy shifted his legs so his bare knee

rested upon Ronan's. "Because I've finally come face to face with my destiny."

Ronan crumpled up the memory and buried it deep within his mind. He couldn't believe his eyes. It was Morgandy, looking exactly the same as he had the last time Ronan had seen him, right here in St. Sebastian's. He never thought he would see him again, even when he was telling Michael about their relationship, divulging the details of their past; he didn't think the mere mention of his name would conjure up his appearance. He saw that Ciaran and Nakano were both equally stunned, so he knew that it wasn't a hallucination. Somehow—and definitely for some specific reason—Morgandy had returned.

"Mr. van der Poole has transferred here from Sigtuna, one of the best schools in Stockholm, because his parents found an even finer academic institution," David announced.

Despite David's officious tone, Ronan knew he was lying; there was much more behind Morgandy's arrival. "Did you know about this?" Ronan whispered so both Nakano and Ciaran could hear him.

Slightly amused, Kano shook his head. "Not me."

A bit more concerned, Ciaran replied, "I didn't think he was still alive after what happened."

"Morgandy could not have joined us at a more propitious moment in Archangel Academy's history," David continued. "Just in time to help us celebrate our Tri-Centennial *and* help us win the National Swim Team Competition!"

Once again the mention of the upcoming contest caused mild pandemonium. The students cheered, applauded, Diego went so far as to rush up to a startled Morgandy and shake his hand furiously. He, like a few others in the gym, seemed thrilled to have Morgandy as a teammate, taking David's endorsement as gospel. Michael wasn't one of them. He was finding it hard to ignore the pangs of jealousy that were hacking into his brain. Sure Ronan had told him about Morgandy, but he hadn't told him everything. He left out the part about how incredibly handsome he was. And how he kind of resembled Michael. Or was that the other way around?

Standing at the edge of the pool, the sunlight from the windows fanning out behind him like a golden, windblown cape, Morgandy looked like he could be Michael's older brother. They shared many of the same physical traits, except that on Morgandy they were more pronounced, grown up, manlier. His hair was same color but curlier. His eyes had a green hue to them, but other colors as well, making them more complex. His red lips were just as full, but in a mouthwatering shade that looked exactly like blood diluted with water. And then there was his body.

Standing next to a fully dressed David, Morgandy looked practically naked even though he was wearing the same attire as every other guy in the gym. What was disconcerting was how poised he stood, almost defiant despite the fact that he knew he was being scrutinized by an unfamiliar pack. He definitely didn't lack any confidence, and as Michael inspected him a bit further it was easy to see why. Morgandy was an inch or two taller than he was, more muscular, hairier (although the hair running along his forearms, legs, and stomach was gossamer thin and translucent), and his bathing suit barely concealed the rest of him. Despite his recent minigrowth spurt, Michael felt ganglier and less attractive than ever. Ronan's expression didn't help matters.

No, his boyfriend wasn't looking at *his* ex-boyfriend with lust or desire, but he also wasn't looking at him with disgust. What was he thinking? It took Michael a few seconds to remember that he could simply ask him without anyone else hearing his question.

"What the hell is going on?"

Ronan didn't look in Michael's direction; his eyes were transfixed on the ghost from his past. *"I have no idea, love,"* Ronan replied. *"But stay alert because this cannot be good."*

And it was about to get worse.

"Swedish champion, eh?" Blakeley said, his tone dripping skepticism. "Why don't we put those credentials to the test?"

Prickled by the insinuation that he had exaggerated Morgandy's talent, but never one to cower from a challenge, David walked toward Blakeley. He made sure his heels hit the gym floor harder than usual so each step sounded more like the approach of an enemy. "What exactly do you have in mind, Coach Blakeley?" David asked, the vein in his neck pulsating slightly despite his overall look of calm.

Perhaps it was because Blakeley was in his comfort zone or perhaps it was because, after MacCleery's death, fear and panic were no longer a luxury or perhaps it was simply because he disliked the headmaster. Whatever the reason, he didn't back down even when he had to raise his head to look David in the eye. "Let's see how brilliant he is against our best man," he replied. "Two lap race, Morgandy versus Ronan."

A low roar emerged from the crowd, starting softly, but erupting quickly into whoops of encouragement and support. Blakeley wasn't the most intelligent teacher at Archangel Academy, but he had the most street smarts. He knew his audience and how to rouse them, and he knew how to provoke a man, especially one as cocky and pompous as David, in a way that could only end with his agreeing to his terms. "A head-to-head race?" David asked rhetorically. "Your best man against mine so to speak?"

Although David punctuated his query with a smile, his intentions were obvious. He was making it clear to Blakeley, if not to the students who were eagerly awaiting their coach's response, that he understood he was being challenged. It was not something that Blakeley could take back, and no matter how this little exercise ended, David would remember who had been the first to throw down the gauntlet. Blakeley didn't flinch. He knew what he had done, and even though he knew the rules were changing, there was no way he was going to back down. Not to David, not to anyone. "Absa-bloody-lootely," he said. "Sir."

If Michael hadn't known Morgandy's history, he might have felt sorry for him. He stood on one end of the pool alone, his hands clasped behind his back, his expression stoic, while on the other end, Ronan was practically lost within the ecstatic crowd that surrounded him. No one had anything against Morgandy personally, but no one questioned their allegiance. Every kid in the gym wanted their team captain to beat this newcomer. Even Nakano.

"This should be another easy win for Ronan," he said.

Michael didn't detect a trace of sarcasm in his voice, and yet he wasn't convinced Kano was speaking the truth. There was something in the way Morgandy moved, with equal parts grace and swagger, that made him think Ronan might finally lose a race. Michael, in fact, had almost beaten him a few times, proving that his boyfriend was a powerful swimmer, but not invincible. Plus, Morgandy had been a water vampire for just as long as Ronan, so didn't that mean he was just as powerful?

"Shake hands," Blakeley bellowed, interrupting Michael's train of thought.

Watching Ronan walk toward Morgandy, Michael could tell he was moving reluctantly. He didn't want to do this, he didn't want to confront his past in this way, and he definitely didn't want to shake Morgandy's hand. But he had no choice, and after a slight hesitation, Ronan felt the flesh he never thought he would feel again. And then he had another flash of memory.

"I'm special you know," Morgandy informed him. "I'm The Guardian of The Well."

Humbled, Ronan resisted the urge to kneel. He remembered his parents telling him stories about such children when he was very young, how special they were, how some were born into the position and how others were called to the honor. But Ronan had never met one. And now the boy who he had spent the last several months kissing, falling in love with, was telling him he was part of that elite group. Or maybe not. "Is this another one of your fool jokes, Morgandy?"

Smiling, Morgandy held Ronan's hands in his. Soft and smooth and hard and rough all at the same time. "No, this is the truth," Morgandy said, his eyes just as serious as when he had first told Ronan he loved him. "I'm the last of the original Atlantians here on earth, and my place as The Keeper of The Well has been foretold."

Ronan couldn't believe what he was hearing. He couldn't believe Morgandy had never told him this before. But then he realized Morgandy had probably wanted Ronan to fall in love with him without knowledge of his credentials. Not that it would have mattered; Ronan would have fallen in love with him even if he were the child of penniless peasants. "I can't believe I've been snogging with The Guardian of The Well this whole time," Ronan whispered.

Morgandy bent his head, and a few of his curls fell onto Ronan's forehead. "I was sworn to secrecy until I knew for certain that you would be my soul mate," he said. "And now you take your place alongside me. Together we will protect The Well and our people for all eternity."

Pride surged through Ronan's body. When he woke up this morning he didn't think anything could make him happier than the thought of combining his soul with Morgandy's and offering the new mixture to The Well. But now he was being told that he would be more than just another water vampire; he would be a protector, a guardian. It was almost too much to bear, and he had to hold onto Morgandy's hands with all his strength so he didn't faint.

"Hey, are you trying to break my hand?"

When Ronan's eyes focused he saw that he was standing in the present, and he was indeed squeezing Morgandy's hand with all his might. "Sorry," he mumbled awkwardly.

This was surreal. Ronan was trying to keep his expression blank, not indicate to Blakeley, David, or the rest of his teammates that he was not being introduced to Morgandy for the first time, that they shared a past, intimate, painful, and clearly one that wouldn't stay buried. He looked deep into Morgandy's eyes to see if he was having the same struggle, but didn't notice anything peculiar, which actually made sense. Morgandy had known he would be meeting Ronan today; he had had time to prepare, and he wasn't taken by surprise.

"Men," Blakeley said. "Take your marks."

Standing on top of the starting block, Ronan adjusted his goggles, and then his body instinctively took position. He bent forward, crouched his knees, stretched his arms behind him; he looked like he did at the start of every race. But this was no ordinary race. He glanced over at Michael, Ciaran, and Nakano, all huddled together in one group looking befuddled and tense, and he could tell that they knew it as well. The time for thinking, however, was over when he heard the splash and saw Morgandy descend under the water.

Diving in, Ronan had to play catch up and quickly. Already a body length behind Morgandy, Ronan felt the water pushing against him instead of how he typically felt, as if he was one with the current, the water almost separating in front of him to give him an uncluttered path. He could hear the shouting and rooting from above, but now it was a distraction. It didn't motivate him to swim even faster as it usually did; it reminded him that he was expected to beat the person swimming in the lane next to him, the person he had never thought he would see again, the person he had once loved.

He saw Morgandy a few strokes from the end of the pool and couldn't believe he was swimming so quickly, so easily, as if this was indeed nothing more than a race. How could that be possible? How could he be so focused with Ronan swimming right next to him? How could he already be flipping and pushing off the side of the pool to start the second lap?

As Morgandy swam in his direction in the other lane, their eyes locked. Ronan's body froze, and he felt suspended in space and time. He wasn't present; he was once again lost in the past.

"How could you do this to me?!" Ronan shrieked, clutching the edge of The Well for support. "How could you betray me like this?"

Rolling his eyes, Morgandy leaned against the side of the cave. The webbing in between his fingers still intact, he swirled a rock in his hand, making it spin in circles like a game of roulette. "Me, me, me, me, me," he said mockingly. "Don't you ever think of anyone other than yourself?"

Ronan felt his body buckle, and he fell to his knees, his webbed hand sliding down the cold, hard stone of The Well. This could not be happening. Their souls had been united right here in this very place, on this sacred ground, only a month ago, and already his dream had turned into a nightmare. This person he thought he would share eternity with had revealed himself to be a fraud, a charlatan whose sole purpose was to uncover the location of The Well and bring about the end of their race, the race that Morgandy had been born to protect.

"Morgandy, please, I don't understand," Ronan pleaded. "Why would you do such a thing?"

Tossing the rock aside, barely missing the belly of The

Well, Morgandy walked toward Ronan and squatted down next to him. He stared at him like a parent would look at an inconsolable child or a hunter at a defenseless animal, moments before slaughter. "Sweet, innocent Ronan," Morgandy said. "Don't you remember what I told you about destiny?"

And like an animal who was about to be killed, Ronan found courage he didn't know he had. Springing up, he grabbed Morgandy by the neck and ran until the stone wall prevented him from running any further. He pressed Morgandy's body into the wall so hard he heard the stones shift, and a light spray of rock dust fell all around them. "Yes!" Ronan cried. "I remember everything you told me about our destiny! You were born to protect The Well, and I was born to live by your side!"

Morgandy's limp body suddenly came to life. He thrust his arms upward and at the same time kicked his feet into Ronan's stomach, sending him hurtling across the harsh ground and into the wall on the other side of the cave. Winded, Ronan scrambled to his feet and turned just in time to see Morgandy standing in front of him. But it wasn't the Morgandy he remembered; this was something new and ugly.

His face twisted and transformed right in front of Ronan's eyes. His beautiful curls disappeared to reveal shorn locks that looked like a madman had pulled them out of his scalp. His eyes were black, surrounded by jaundiced irises. Only his teeth remained recognizable, pure white with two exquisitely chiseled fangs on either side of his mouth. The rest of his body looked deformed, burnt, and raw. Morgandy showed no signs of feeling any pain, but Ronan felt his heart break with pity and fear just looking at him. "Morgandy," Ronan said, his voice barely a whimper. "What's happened to you?"

His full lips now just a thin vertical, sliver of red, Morgandy smiled and opened his mouth to speak. Even before any words were uttered, a rancid smell rushed out to invade and claim the air, making Ronan wince. "That might have been your destiny, Ronan," the creature hissed. "But it wasn't mine."

Confused and frightened, Ronan watched this thing that Morgandy had turned into run out of the cave, leaving him alone, broken, and lost. Watching Morgandy swim past him, Ronan refused to let those feelings take control of him again.

Surging forward, he somersaulted and pushed off the side of the pool with every ounce of strength in his legs. It was enough to catapult him through the water so he was now a mere shoulder length behind Morgandy. Above him he could hear the crowd respond to the sudden shift in action, and using his preternatural hearing he could hear Michael cheering him on loudest of all. He also heard David mumbling something about an angel's wings, but he didn't have time to decipher the headmaster's cryptic meditation. It didn't matter; Michael could do it for him.

Keeping his eyes focused on the match in the pool and not on David who was now standing in between two of the starting blocks, Michael blocked out all other sound so he could listen to what the headmaster was saying. Michael was startled when he realized he was eavesdropping on a prayer.

"O Zachariel, lord and master," David said so softly it couldn't be heard by a human ear, "give this child an angel's wings so he can fly in the water like you can fly through the clouds."

Abruptly the prayer stopped, not because David was finished, but because he noticed Michael staring in his direction. Involuntarily, Michael had been drawn to the odd words and failed at trying to act in secret, but he didn't care. Let David know that he had been caught; let him know that he couldn't always dupe everyone; let him know that he couldn't always emerge the victor. And neither could Morgandy.

After slamming one hand down onto the edge of the pool first, Ronan pumped a fist into the air. A roar went up in the crowd, and one by one the kids jumped into the pool and surrounded their team captain, who proved once again that he was undefeatable.

Michael, Ciaran, and Nakano held back and watched Morgandy reach up to grab David's waiting hand. With one easy pull the boy was lifted out of the water and onto the gym floor. David threw a towel around Morgandy's shoulders and whispered something in his ear. "Did you catch that?" Ciaran asked.

"Well, I saw it, but I didn't hear anything," Michael replied. "What do you think that means?"

Both he and Ciaran looked at Nakano thinking that he must know what David's motives were since he was part of his race, but they were wrong. "Don't look at me," he growled. "I'm in the dark, just like the two of you."

A few weeks ago Michael wouldn't have believed Nakano; he would have assumed he was concealing information. But having witnessed firsthand the subtle changes in his character, Michael knew Nakano was telling the truth. Even though it meant that Morgandy's presence was that much more of a mystery, it made Michael feel better. At least he could start to trust Nakano again, as weird as that sounded to him. He just wished he knew what Morgandy was doing here and why David seemed to be so interested in his arrival. Once again Blakeley put an end to such speculation and brought everyone back to reality. Well, him and his whistle.

Before the shrill sound stopped blaring through the gym, Blakeley raised Ronan's arm in the universal sign of the victor. He didn't need to speak. He didn't need to announce that Ronan had won and therefore maintained Double A's bragging rights. The kids got it, and they responded loudly.

"I guess our illustrious coach doesn't realize that it's a moot point," Ciaran said to Michael. "Morgandy's a student now, not a member of the Swedish team, so even if he won, Double A wouldn't have lost."

Thankfully the crowd was still cheering, so Michael just had to shrug his shoulders and smile. He didn't need to offer his suspicions that having Morgandy as their newest student meant just the opposite: their school was in more trouble than ever, and it wasn't something that should be celebrated. Blakeley had other ideas.

Still holding Ronan's arm up in the air, he grabbed Morgandy with his free hand and raised his arm as well. "And welcome the newest member of the A team!"

This time Blakeley's announcement was met with silence. "C'mon, you dumb gits!" he shouted. "He may be new, but with van der Poole on the bloody team, we're sure to take top prize at Nationals!"

That got the crowd going once again. Michael clapped along with the others, but as if he was at some old man's golf outing. He felt as uncomfortable as he knew Ronan must, having to stand a few feet away from the person who had practically destroyed his life. Finally, Blakeley let go of both boys and announced that along with Ronan and Morgandy, he and Fritz would be on the A team. Michael felt a crest of heat pulse up his neck as he realized Nakano was now relegated to the B team. Much to Michael's surprise, Kano took the news that he would join the B ream of Ciaran, Alexei, and Ralphie Torino, the Italian kid who did the backstroke faster than anyone, in silence.

Nakano didn't speak, even in the locker room, even when everyone was talking about how great Nationals was going to be, even when he overheard some other kids expressing their shock that Fritz got put on the starting team over him. He only broke his silence once, when Ronan asked him why he thought Morgandy was acting as if he had never seen him before.

"Guess time does heal everything, mate," was all Nakano said.

One by one the kids left the locker room, patting Ronan

on the shoulder or giving him a high five. Michael didn't understand why Ronan was moving so slowly; he was usually the first one dressed and ready to leave. When he saw Ronan look over at Morgandy, who was slipping out the side door, he knew why.

"Follow me," Ronan said to Michael telepathically.

In the first shadows of dusk, they saw Morgandy sprint into The Forest, and, without speaking to each other, Michael and Ronan chased after him, careful not to step on a twig or make any noise to give themselves away. At some point, Michael reached forward as Ronan reached back and their hands met; they traveled as one until they came to a small clearing. Hovering over the ground for a few seconds they landed gently and silently on the grass, positioning themselves behind a cluster of oak trees to watch Morgandy feed on a man, who, by his dirty appearance and the state of his tattered clothing, appeared to be homeless.

Morgandy held the man tightly, his mouth fastened to his neck, until all color and expression left the man's face. The body dropped to the ground with a thud, and Morgandy leaned back on his haunches, twisting his neck from side to side so his head moved like that of a cobra. Then, slowly, his long, black tongue flicked the stray drops of blood off of his chin and lips until his face was clean.

Expecting Morgandy to rise and travel to The Well to complete his feeding, Ronan tapped Michael on the knee, and they stood up together. To their surprise Morgandy didn't move. They heard a rustling and saw some of the treetops flutter even though there was no wind, and finally Morgandy moved, but only to turn toward the trees and wait. When they saw David, wearing only his dress pants and carrying his shirt in his hand, emerge from the thicket on the other side of the clearing, they realized he had been expecting company. Taking cover once again, they also realized David and Morgandy were more than headmaster and student.

"Did you enjoy your meal?" David asked, his massive chest slowly rising up, then down.

"He was surprisingly tasty," Morgandy replied, "for a vagrant."

Laughing grotesquely, David ran his fingers through the thick mass of red hair on his chest and replied, "Every man does have a purpose."

Peeking around the side of the trees, Michael and Ronan saw David circle Morgandy and carelessly step onto the dead man's leg, the bone snapping in two underneath his weight. It was when he turned around, however, that they were really shocked. He had two deep gouges in his back, vertical in shape and on top of his shoulder blades. They weren't bloodied, but congealed, like scar tissue, and must have been old wounds, because the rest of him was unscathed. Plus, when he put his shirt on they saw that there were no rips or tears in the cloth. They didn't want to ponder the many reasons why David would be wandering through the woods without his shirt on, so luckily he interrupted their thoughts.

"This is just the beginning, my son," David said, placing his hands on Morgandy's shoulders. "So many more surprises await you."

Reading Ronan's mind, Michael got glimpses of information that helped him understand that Ronan was incredibly perplexed. Morgandy had been The Guardian of The Well, destined to protect it; now he was one of Them. It didn't make sense; more than that, it violated rules. Michael couldn't grasp everything at once and deliberately blocked out the images and thoughts that were invading his brain. Leave them for Ronan for now; he could ask questions later. The most important thing to do was to get out of here before they were seen. Or before Ronan accidentally exposed them.

So frazzled, Ronan forgot where he was and allowed his emotions to lead him. Impulsively, he stepped forward, not looking at the ground, and heard several branches crunch

under his feet. Yanking Ronan back, Michael pulled them behind the thickness of the trees just as David and Morgandy
looked up to find the source of the noise.

Ronan's heart beat loudly against Michael's chest, and
Michael could feel him shake in his arms. He wasn't going to
scold Ronan for acting foolishly. The events of the day and
the incredible stress had finally gotten to him. All he needed
to do was hold his boyfriend until the danger passed.

Several seconds later it did just that, and they heard David
and Morgandy retreat deeper into The Forest. For the time
being, thanks to Michael, they were safe.

chapter 12

After spending a few hours in his own bed Ronan finally felt safe. Unfortunately, he also felt restless. He couldn't concentrate on his reading. As far as he was concerned Edith Wharton had abandoned the English language and had written *The Age of Innocence* in Russian. He saw letters on the page, and he knew that they formed words, but his mind was so troubled, his body so worked up, that he couldn't comprehend one sentence of the novel. He had read the same paragraph over three times and still had no idea what she was trying to say. Maybe it was because his age of innocence had been over a long time ago, ever since Morgandy took it away.

Not eager to start philosophizing about his own complicated history, he slammed the book closed, startling Michael who was sitting at the desk typing up a Latin essay for Professor Volman.

Turning around, Michael thought Ronan looked like he

was just taking a break from reading. He was leaning his head against the cherry wood headboard; his arms were wrapped around the book that lay on his chest; his eyes were shut. But Michael knew better, he knew that Ronan was trying once again to get in touch with his mother.

It was all he had talked about when they first got home from The Forest. *I have to talk to my Mum. I have to let her know that Morgandy's back and he's one of Them. She'll know what to do.* That's all Ronan kept saying. Michael remained quiet and just nodded, knowing that Ronan was too anxious to listen to anything he had to say. It was interesting—more often than not Michael was the one who was revved up and unable to listen to reason or logic. Now the roles were reversed, and even though Ronan was lying quietly in their bed instead of pacing the floor of their dorm room, he was just as incapable of being calmed down. Michael had no other choice but to watch and make sure he was there for Ronan when he needed him.

Turning back to his laptop, Michael resumed typing his report on Latin etymology and didn't see Ronan frown and his body twitch. Try as he might, Ronan couldn't connect with Edwige. She wasn't responding to any of his telepathic messages. Now that so much time had passed since he had last heard from her, there could only be two reasons for her silence: either she was hurt and physically unable to reply or she was simply ignoring him. And Ronan knew it couldn't be the latter.

"Mum's done a lot of things," Ronan said. "But she's never deliberately ignored me."

Pia, matris quod filius, amour mater. His mind focused on Latin word origins, Michael didn't hear Ronan speak. So much for being there when his boyfriend needed him.

"Michael," Ronan said. "Don't you agree?"

He typed one last sentence at lightning speed, then turned away from his laptop and crawled onto the bed. "Sorry, what did you say?" Michael asked, placing his hand on the bed-spread just above Ronan's knee. He watched as the waves in the ring Ronan had given him moved up and down as he massaged the bone and skin through the thick material; it was as if they were from the sea and not bound in silver. Michael hoped his touch would release a little bit of Ronan's tension, but Ronan's expression didn't change.

"She must be hurt," Ronan said quietly, trying to keep his voice strong. "I can't think of any other reason why she would disregard me like this."

He didn't want to agree, but Michael had come to the same conclusion. "This might sound stupid, but do you think you can ask The Well to intervene?" Michael asked. "I mean it's connected to all water vampires, right? Wouldn't it be able to tell us where Edwige is?"

Despite his growing fear, Ronan smiled. It wasn't because Michael's suggestion was a brilliant solution; it was because of the use of one word—*us.* Ronan wasn't alone; he had Michael by his side, so no matter what had happened to Edwige, whether it was good or bad, he would be okay. "You're right about The Well's connection to our people, but I don't think it works like a GPS, love," Ronan said, placing his hand on top of Michael's. "I wish it did, though, because I don't have a good feeling about this."

Tossing Edith Wharton's tome to the side, Michael got under the covers with Ronan. They lay on their sides facing one another, enveloped in silence and shadow. Michael realized that for all Ronan's strength and muscles and preternatural abilities, his eyes still shined with the ideals of a little boy. The only real safety a child could know came from his parents. When that link was severed, it was like being plunged into an unquiet darkness, each step unknown, each step bringing with it uncertainty. Michael knew exactly what that felt like, and he wished he could spare Ronan the same fate.

Wrapping his leg around Ronan's, Michael held his hands, rubbing his thumb against Ronan's smooth skin. He knew a kiss wouldn't resolve anything, so instead he spoke. "I've been thinking about reaching out to my father," Michael whispered.

"Really?" Ronan said, unable to conceal his surprise. "What made you change your mind?"

"Edwige."

Ronan figured that all the talk about his mother's disappearance from his life had made Michael realize that even a parent who was wildly flawed was better than no parent at all. That was only part of it.

"If something *has* happened to Edwige, and that's a really big *if*," Michael started, "we know that David and his people are behind it." Ronan's body tensed up a bit, and he held onto Michael's hands harder. "My father's one of Them, so he's got to know what's going on, and if he doesn't know he can find out, especially if he sees how worried his son is."

Now that was a brilliant plan. And the perfect excuse for a kiss. "Thank you," Ronan said, his breath lingering hot on Michael's lips.

Their bodies moved closer together. One of Michael's hands disappeared inside the sleeve of Ronan's T-shirt and caressed his shoulder while Ronan's fingers stroked Michael's chin. "Honestly, I don't know if I can ever forgive him," Michael confessed. "But I don't know, I just thought that maybe I should make an attempt before it's too late."

"I'm really proud of you," Ronan said, his leg rubbing against Michael's softly. "It'll be bloody hard, no doubt, but even if he knows nothing about Edwige, I think it'll be worth it."

Running his hand up and down Ronan's arm, Michael could almost feel the blood race underneath Ronan's hard flesh. His boyfriend was trying desperately to remain calm, but he was so agitated, Michael half-expected him to scream out loud.

Not too far away in a secluded enclave, Imogene did just that.

"Nooooo!!!!"

This time Imogene's cry didn't fill Brania with interest, but with irritation. Yes, she understood that her ward's uncontrollable and highly vocal actions were the first steps in her plot for revenge against her father, but they were still annoying and disruptive. Children should obey and display good manners; they shouldn't rip lids off of coffins or scream bloody murder on a quiet evening. Staring at Imogene, Brania didn't feel an ounce of maternal affection.

Not when she saw her grip the sides of the casket as if she was holding on for dear life.

Not when she saw panic etch into her face.

Not when she heard her wail once again echo throughout the cave.

None of that affected Brania. None of that prompted her to walk toward Imogene and try to console her, not until she heard the girl speak.

"I know where Edwige is," Imogene declared.

Now that, Miss Imogene Minx, is a reason for me to move, Brania thought.

In less than a heartbeat, Brania was at Imogene's side, prying her fingers off of the edge of the cold, metal casket. She held the girl's icy hands in between hers and rubbed warmth into them. "Imogene, tell me where she is," Brania said, getting right to the point. "Tell Mother everything."

When Imogene shook her head in silent refusal, Brania involuntarily rubbed her hands harder, all the while keeping her face a mask of concern. "Please," she begged. "Let me help you."

Imogene's eyes darted around the cave frantically, looking

at everything, focusing on nothing. "I don't want anyone else to hear."

Afraid that if she kept rubbing Imogene's hands she would separate flesh from bone, Brania let go of the girl. She let her own hands drop inside the coffin and grazed her fingers across the white satin interior. The smooth, silky touch was calming, and after a few seconds Brania was able to speak in a more reassuring tone. "Darling, we're all alone," she said. "It's just you and me."

Imogene's eyes were still wide and untrusting. "You can't be sure of that," Imogene corrected, then added in a hushed whisper, "Not everyone can be seen."

The girl had a point. Brania had lived for centuries, and even she didn't know all of the supernatural species that roamed the earth. She also knew that like humans, God's other creatures could evolve and transform; Imogene had done that earlier by proving she could turn invisible, seemingly at will. Chances are she wasn't the only one who possessed that power. No, Imogene was right, and if Brania's plan were going to succeed, she would have to move forward with an overabundance of caution.

"Then let's play a game," Brania said cheerfully.

Despite her attempt to lighten the suffocating mood, Imogene's expression didn't soften. "I don't understand."

Climbing into the casket, Brania sat cross-legged facing Imogene. She looked as if she were setting herself up so they could play a game of patty-cake like two little girls in a field of snow. The game Brania wanted to play, however, was not nearly as innocent. "It'll be like our very own secret game. Won't that be fun?" she said. "All you have to do is whisper right into my ear and tell me where Edwige is."

Imogene leaned in close; she breathed in deeply and could smell the heat rising off of Brania's neck, sultry and familiar, but abruptly she sat back. "And you promise no one will ever know the truth?" Imogene asked desperately.

Brania couldn't promise that, and so she didn't. "I promise," she replied, "that I will never tell another person."

Finally satisfied, Imogene leaned in again and didn't stop moving until her lips brushed against Brania's anxious ear. Then she told her where Edwige was.

After she spoke, it was as if a great weight had been lifted from Imogene's shoulders. She felt relieved and, more than that, grateful that Brania was both her protector and confidant. She rewarded her in the best way she knew how, in song.

As Imogene's voice, mellifluous and strong, floated in the damp air, it surrounded Brania, but for the first time the sound couldn't penetrate her thoughts. She was still reeling from what Imogene had told her about Edwige's whereabouts. It was so obvious, but she would never have guessed it. Now that she knew the truth, all she could think about was that Imogene wasn't the only little minx around.

chapter 13

Michael felt like he was being followed. He didn't feel as if he was in danger, but he knew that despite the early morning hour he wasn't alone. The fall weather had already turned, and the dew on the grass was thick. It hadn't turned to ice, but it wasn't only moisture. It meant that when the grass was stepped on there was noise, even when it was stepped on by an immortal being.

Unafraid, Michael didn't turn around. He kept walking, walking, walking and didn't stop until he reached the imposing, wooden door that was the entrance to Archangel Cathedral and gave a nod to the carving of his namesake that majestically adorned the apex of the door. He looked up and marveled at how the faint sunlight was turned into a burst of fiery colors as it bounced off of the stained glass window. Standing there awash in the natural spotlight, Michael turned around out of curiosity and not concern and was surprised to find the grounds leading up to the cathedral were empty.

He was sure someone was behind him. Switching from human to vampire vision, Michael peered into the surrounding area, but still he could see nothing except for a few proactive squirrels gathering nuts in preparation for the upcoming winter. Maybe he was letting Ronan's anxiety rub off on him. When he entered the cathedral he realized he had been right all along.

How did she get here first? Michael asked himself.

Even though her back was to him, Michael knew it was Brania sitting in the last pew, and although two priests were lighting candles near the front altar, he also knew instinctively that she had been the one following him. How she got into the church before him, he couldn't say. Just another everyday mystery. Like the color of her hair.

Just outside the grasp of the light that poured into the church her deep auburn hair looked like blood mixed with dirt. It wasn't entirely unattractive, but definitely was not the vibrant shade it had been the first time he saw her in his father's hotel room. Perhaps he just remembered it looking more luxurious or perhaps Brania was starting to show her age. It was time for a closer look.

Sitting next to her he saw that not only was her hair darker, she was also showing signs of emotion. Her eyes were bloodshot, and if she hadn't just finished crying, she looked as if she would start at any moment. Brania didn't turn to face Michael. She didn't need to; she was well aware of his presence. However, neither of them was ready to speak, so they both breathed in deeply, their lungs filling up with the smell of incense that clung to the air just as Dr. MacCleery had once clung to the gold cross hanging above the tabernacle.

"My father murdered the doctor," Brania said, her harsh

words tarnishing the serenity of their holy surroundings. "Even if he wasn't the one whose hands got bloodied."

Was this remorse that Michael was witnessing? He couldn't be sure, so he took another deep breath to prevent himself from speaking and fought hard to latch on to his self-control. He had learned in one of his classes that silence is the best weapon to coerce your opponent into speech. It proved to be an accurate lesson.

"I don't know why he felt compelled to do something so bloody unnecessary, so . . . so vile," Brania said, ignoring the tears that now fell down her pure white cheeks. "But it was the first time I realized he had become something I could no longer love."

Michael knew exactly how she felt, and he could no longer remain silent. "Fathers do terrible things, really, really awful things," Michael said. "And they do them totally convinced they're justified."

Looking at Michael for the first time, she asked, "How can they justify murder?"

The irony of her statement wasn't lost on either of them. "Well," Brania said, shrugging her shoulders, "you know what I mean."

Michael did. MacCleery wasn't killed for food; he was killed for sport, as a warning. What Michael hadn't known until this very moment was that Brania didn't support her father's actions. He had assumed she had fallen in line behind him, in theory and in practice, and approved of the vicious murder. He never imagined that she not only disagreed with her father, but that she would admit her condemnation, especially to him. Maybe they had more in common than he thought.

"I can't believe I'm saying this," Michael started, "but he's still your father."

Her laughter startled the priests in the front of the church, their robes swaying as if caught by a breeze as they turned to inspect the intrusion. "I guess it's hard to let go of human optimism."

It was Michael's turn to shrug his shoulders. "And human truth," he replied. "I'm learning that just because you're a vampire doesn't mean you can live without your family."

Gazing up at the cross again, Brania almost glowed. If Michael hadn't known any better, he would have thought she was having some sort of holy revelation. The plaintive look on her face was really starting to freak him out, but of course it was so compelling he couldn't turn away. "What if you have no other choice?" she asked. Michael wasn't sure, however, if she was asking him or God. "What if you were forced to live out the rest of your life alone? Banished to an eternity of solitude and isolation?"

"Your father's banished you?"

Brania rubbed her palms on her skirt, introducing the scent of leather into the air. It mingled with the incense, and Michael felt himself get light-headed, though he wasn't sure if it was because of the smells or the revelation that David had turned his back on his only child.

"My father is more clever than that," Brania said. "He would never speak the words, but his actions don't carry with them any hint of doubt."

The thought came to Michael quickly, with such force that he almost forgot where he was; he was almost knocked unconscious. Despite how contentious his relationship was with his father, he still held onto the hope that the situation could be reversed, that it wasn't final, that things could go back to the way he had always dreamed they would be and he could have the father of his dreams. The reason his hope was possible was because his father had made it known that he wanted Michael in his life and that everything he did, all his actions, were based on his love for his son. Obviously, Brania didn't know that comfort. "I'm sorry to hear that," Michael replied.

Smiling, but unable to look Michael in the eye, Brania mumbled, "Thank you."

She leaned back in the pew and looked around the church. Michael imagined it had been quite some time since Brania had seen the inside of this or any cathedral, so he allowed her to spend some peaceful, undisturbed moments gazing at the elaborate stained glass windows, the lifelike sculptures of the various saints, the convergence of marble and wood in the dome that loomed over their heads. These were all images that brought Michael comfort, and he hoped they did the same for Brania, since she clearly couldn't find comfort anywhere else. She had a similar hope for him.

"I know you don't really like your father," she said. "But I think you know that down deep Vaughan is a good man." Before Michael could agree with or argue the point she continued. "He's imperfect, as most men are, but considering how evil he could be, I don't think he's all that bad."

Michael thought he knew what Brania was getting at, but he waited for her to clarify her point. "Before things become irreversible like they have for me," Brania added, "you may want to pay him a visit and see if you can...patch things up."

He listened to her words as if they were a prayer. "I told Ronan the other night that I was thinking of doing just that," Michael said, more convinced than ever that a reunion with his father was the right course of action. "I wasn't sure why I was doing it, I thought...Well, I had my reasons, but you're right, I should do it to get our relationship back on track."

"At the risk of sounding like a daft little girl instead of the all-powerful vampire I am," Brania said, her eyes finally smiling, "family is all we have."

Michael should have been confused, but he wasn't. Despite the threat of danger that came directly from Brania's people, Michael felt safer than ever before. He was on friendly terms with Nakano, he had just had an amazing conversation with Brania, and now he was going to make peace with his father. "You're absolutely right, Brania," Michael said. "Now if you'll excuse me, I have to go put those words into action."

Exercising her newfound caution, Brania waited quite a while after Michael left to laugh so he wouldn't hear her. But when she did she laughed so heartily and with such joyful abandon that the windowpanes shook and the priests crossed themselves thinking the ground was being assaulted by an earthquake. They had no idea they were merely witnessing a girl relishing the success of her plan. Michael didn't realize it, but he was going to do exactly what Brania wanted him to.

chapter 14

"Are you sure this is what you want to do, love?" Ronan silently asked.

Michael's knuckles were an inch away from banging on the door to his father's suite at the Eden Arms Hotel. He held them in midair and turned to face his boyfriend. *"I thought you were all for this?"*

"Well, yes, of course, I completely support you," Ronan replied. *"But..."*

"Why is there always a but?"

"Buuuut... I just want to make sure you're not doing this because I've been, you know, in a hump but because you really want to reconnect with your dad."

Shaking his head, Michael realized that as wonderful and sweet as boyfriends could be, they could also be exasperating. *"I'm sure,"* Michael said. *"And anyway it's not like I can back out now."*

Ronan grabbed Michael's fist and pulled it away from the door. *"Nobody knows we're here,"* he reminded Michael. *"We can be back at school in an instant and track Ciaran down to make him write that bio lab for me."*

"I didn't think vampires got cold feet?"

"I don't have cold feet!" Ronan protested.

"And you shouldn't. It's my wayward father we've come to surprise."

"Fine then," Ronan replied. *"I'll knock."*

"I don't need you to knock for me," Michael said. *"I'm perfectly capable of knocking on a door all by myself."*

Ignoring each other, Michael and Ronan both knocked on the door at the same time. When the door opened, they almost wished that they hadn't.

"Mum!" Ronan cried. "What the hell are you doing here?!"

Michael wasn't sure if he was more surprised to find Ronan's mother standing in the doorway to his father's apartment or to see that she was dressed in a plain black T-shirt and jeans. Every other time Michael had seen Edwige she was dressed impeccably; her clothes and accessories were all perfectly coordinated and perfectly expensive. Her hair, thanks to Marcel, was always expertly coiffed, whether it was blond or jet black as it was now. The color of her hair, however, was practically the only thing that was recognizable about her; she looked like a completely different person. And she sounded like one too.

"Please leave," she said. Her voice was hardly audible and caught at the back of her throat as if it didn't have the courage to create sound. Her eyes, usually clear and commanding, were glassy and lost. Michael was stunned by the transformation; it was that drastic. Ronan, however, had only noticed that he was finally looking at his mother once again.

"Why have you been ignoring me?" Ronan asked. "Haven't

you heard me? I've been trying to get in touch with you for months!"

Edwige tried to close the door, but Ronan's hand went up and stopped it from moving any farther. Michael thought she could have easily pushed back; he knew she was way more powerful than she looked, but she just stood there, eyes staring at the rug that surrounded her bare feet, her shoulders slightly hunched forward. She looked as fragile as she always did, but now she appeared weak, as if she could be broken. "Please, Ronan," she said, the words clearly an effort. "Leave and forget that you saw me here."

Anger was gradually replaced with worry, and Ronan's eyes and mind refocused. He was looking at his mother, but she was not the same. "Mum, what's wrong?"

Finally she looked up. The unexpected presence of her son and his companion was almost too much for Edwige to bear. She felt her body wobble, and she leaned against the door, not knowing where she found the strength not to fall into a heap on the floor. Placing her hand on her hip she tried to capture a pose from her past, but it only served to remind Ronan how small she had become since the last time he had seen her.

"Mum, please, what's going on?" Ronan pleaded. "You don't look right."

When Ronan reached forward to grab his mother's arm, Edwige lurched back and stumbled awkwardly until she grabbed the back of the couch. Ronan was about to run to his mother's aid, but Vaughan entered from the bedroom, and the realization hit him—his mother had left her children to live with one of Them. "What the bloody hell is going on here?!" Ronan screamed.

Vaughan ignored Ronan's question and the boy himself. "Would you mind closing the door, son?" he asked. "Don't want to give the neighbors a show."

Absentmindedly, Michael closed the door behind him. When he turned around he saw Edwige's prized painting hanging on the wall across from the sofa. Clearly she wasn't just visiting his father's apartment—she was planning on living here for a while. The realization was as shocking to Michael as it was to Ronan, but he remained silent, not knowing what to say. Ronan didn't have that problem.

"Answer me!"

As if pushed back by the force of her son's words, Edwige slumped onto the arm of the couch. She only moved, flinched was more like it, when Vaughan placed his hand on her shoulder. "Your mother made me a very happy man and moved in with me."

The clock on the wall ticked, the blinds tapped against the kitchen window courtesy of a restless breeze, but there was no other sound in the apartment. Until Ronan felt that if he didn't scream he would lose his mind.

"You've abandoned your children! You've ignored me for months! And all because you're living with this . . . thing!"

Vaughan took a step forward in an attempt to defend his significant other. Edwige, however, preferred not to be rescued. She held up her hand, which looked slight against Vaughan's chest, as a silent request that he allow her son to vent, say whatever he needed to say, no matter how ugly the words might sound. Reluctantly, Vaughan agreed. But it didn't mean that he would remain quiet. "You should watch how you talk to your mother," Vaughan reprimanded.

The only reason Ronan didn't lunge at Vaughan was because he felt Michael's hand on his arm. They hadn't come here to incite violence; they had come here searching for peace. Granted the rules had changed when Edwige opened the door, but still these were their parents, and wasn't it some consolation to have finally found Edwige? She wasn't dead; she wasn't lost forever; she wasn't taken from Ronan like Michael's mother was; she was still alive, and in time their relationship could be repaired. Michael knew that Ronan couldn't see that now; he was too consumed with shock and anger. The best thing Michael could do was get him to leave, get him far away from the mother he had been desperately searching for.

"I think we should go," Michael said softly.

"I wish you wouldn't," Vaughan replied. "It really makes me so . . . bloody happy to see you again."

Michael had no idea how he felt. There was a part of him that was indeed happy to see his father again, but finding out that he was living with Ronan's mother, that maybe he was in love with her, had turned things around, changed things so drastically. He was filled with so many feelings, he was almost numb. He nodded his head, heard himself mumble something, and felt his hand tug at Ronan's arm to get him to leave.

"Michael's right," Edwige said. "You should go."

It wasn't going to be that easy. "Not until you tell me why you've abandoned your children!" Ronan demanded. "This is not how we act! We're not like Them!"

Before Vaughan could move to defend his race, Edwige stood in between her lover and her son. In between the two robust figures, she looked like a porcelain doll that had been tossed aside and had lain dormant for years. "You're better off without me," she answered. "You don't need me anymore."

Michael shuddered at the sound of Edwige's voice. It was so fragile, so lost, it sounded just like his mother's when she would shut down. Michael looked at Edwige closer and saw that she had some of the same physical characteristics that Grace had when she was depressed and despondent. He also knew from experience how quickly depression could turn into rage. Ronan was about to get his first lesson.

"You mean you don't need us!" Ronan shouted back.

"No, I don't!" Edwige shouted, her voice finally reclaiming some of its old thunder. "I don't need to have my children scampering at my feet, begging for my attention, tugging me to look at them when I should be looking at myself!" Edwige paused to take a breath and watch the color drain from Ronan's face. "I have spent more than enough time being mother, father, protector, problem solver, nursemaid, fool! I am done with all that, do you hear me?! I want to live my life, not yours! And this is the life that I've chosen!"

Edwige shook violently, but no one could tell if it was because her tirade had weakened her or had reintroduced her to her celebrated strength. The rush of excitement distracted her long enough that she didn't notice Ronan move until he was across the room.

"How dare you bring this with you?!"

When Ronan turned around, they all saw that he was holding a simple, mahogany box. And they all knew that the box contained Saxon's ashes. "How could you disgrace his memory by bringing him here?" Ronan asked in a voice that once again reminded Michael of a little boy. "To the home of one of the people who murdered him?" His mouth opened once more to ask another question, but no words came out. He had to try a few more times to be able to speak again. When he did, he was through with questions; he had nothing more to ask. "I don't understand how you could do that."

It was good that Ronan didn't have any more questions, because Edwige clearly wasn't going to answer her son. She only wanted one thing from him, the box he was holding. "Give that to me."

Michael watched as Ronan's grip on the box softened. His whole body seemed to cave in, and it looked as if he finally realized that he was holding his father's remains in his hands, the father who had died a violent and ghastly death, and that he was standing in front of the mother who he had thought might have suffered the same fate. Michael thought these revelations would bring Ronan peace, some odd comfort, maybe not now, but in the near future. Not a chance.

"I said, give that box to me!" Edwige shouted, sounding exactly like the woman she used to be.

"I'll give you exactly what you deserve!" Ronan shrieked. "TRAITOR!!"

Ronan flicked open the latch on the box and held the lid as he hurled the contents at Edwige. His father's ashes remained brown and black as they flew through the air, changing color only when they touched Edwige's skin.

"Ahhhh!!!!"

As the ashes touched Edwige's body they turned bright red and became flames that penetrated her skin. Michael, Vaughan, and even Ronan watched in horror as Edwige screamed out in agony, her arms outstretched, her head tossed back, as the little pieces of fire pierced her flesh, ripped through her, turned chunks of her body into pockets of flame. She screamed even louder when she saw Saxon suspended in front of her.

It was anguish enough to be reliving the physical pain that her husband had suffered, but casting her eyes once again on his face, she was also forced to relive his emotional suffering. Consumed with the flames that had once destroyed Saxon, Edwige reached out to try and hold onto the image in front of her, but it was only an apparition. She could only see Saxon; she couldn't touch him. Even still, she could feel every raw emotion that had coursed through his body while his life was being brutally destroyed.

"Saxon!!" she cried. She felt the fear that he desperately tried to keep hidden, his anger at her betrayal, his disappointment when he discovered that she had violated their sacred covenant. She felt it all, and it was more excruciatingly painful than the red-hot flames that were passing through her. "PLEASE MAKE IT STOP!!" she cried out to no one and to everyone.

Vaughan ripped the tablecloth from the dining room table—the pewter candelabra that sat on top of it crashing to the floor with a thud—and wrapped it around Edwige's shoulders. It was as if he had doused her body with gasoline; the flames exploded with more fury than ever, and Ronan and Michael had to step back from the heat that was blazing off of Edwige's body. They were helpless to do anything except watch the fire engulf and consume her.

Unmoving, Edwige stood, staring into the eyes of her dead husband, movement, sound, salvation, all unattainable. She felt that the pain of both the past and the present were deserved, so she did nothing except look at her beloved Saxon until his image faded when the last piece of ash pierced her heart and fell onto the pile of cinders behind her. Only then were the flames extinguished; only then could Edwige finally feel what had been buried within Saxon's soul: his undying and unconditional love. This knowledge, this unexpected gift that Saxon had loved her despite their years of separation and her duplicitous actions, was almost as blinding as the pain she had just been forced to bear, but at least it gave her renewed strength. "Get out."

Her voice was quiet, but stern. Her body had returned to normal despite having been ravaged by the unnatural fire, and in fact the experience seemed to invigorate her. She no longer looked weak, vulnerable. She had her husband's spirit inside of her, and that was all the strength she needed. Ronan's strength, however, had been drained by witnessing the horror he had caused. It fled his body, and if it hadn't been for Michael pulling him from Vaughan's apartment, he would not have been able to leave.

When the boys were gone, Vaughan bent down to help Edwige return Saxon's scattered ashes, which were once again the colors of charcoaled flesh, to their resting place. It was not the wisest thing he had ever done.

"Do not touch my husband!" Edwige shrieked as she grabbed Vaughan's wrist. It felt like his hand was caught in a steel vise. Only when Edwige was certain Vaughan would comply with her order did she let go of him. He lingered in the room for a few moments, but then felt as if he was intruding on a very private moment and retreated to the safety of his bedroom.

Alone, Edwige finished the task of returning Saxon's ashes to the place they had called home for over a decade. She looked at a handful of ash and acknowledged that the pain had been worth it. She knew that underneath all the hatred, anger, and confusion, her husband still loved her as much as she loved him.

Ronan felt the same way. Sitting on his bed, Michael next to him, he knew that part of Michael was upset with him, no, stunned really, that he could act so violently toward his own mother. That he could watch her writhe in agony and not lift a finger to help her. But he also knew that Michael understood why he had been paralyzed. Not that long ago Michael had gone through the same thing—a combination of experiences that left him overcome with emotions, bombarded with conflicting feelings that he didn't know how to handle.

Seeing Morgandy had stirred up old feelings that he had kept hidden, feelings of rage that he had been duped by his first boyfriend, who for some unknown reason wanted to destroy his people. And now after searching for his mother, he discovered that he had been betrayed once again. She had abandoned him just like Morgandy had in order to live with one of Them. For whatever personal reason she had turned her back on her people, her children. He was heartbroken.

He had no idea what he would do if Michael weren't sitting next to him, if he didn't feel Michael's arms around him, his kisses on his forehead, reassuring him beyond question or doubt that not every person you loved would betray you. He held on to Michael's strong arms and felt his love and compassion surge into his flesh, touch his heart, and because of that he was able to hold onto Michael and cry in his arms, unashamed, knowing full well that he wouldn't let go.

Because Ronan knew that when his tears had run dry, Michael, unlike everyone else in his life, would still be by his side.

chapter 15

A New Day

Outside, the earth was awake.

The first week of November brought with it a quick drop in temperature and an eager snowfall that covered the grass with a light, powdery dust. A fine layering, nothing substantial, just enough to announce that winter was coming, just enough to make Michael and Ronan want to spend the day in bed. A sound slipped into their room along with the chill: *da-da-DAH-da, da-da-da.* The meadowlark's signature melody was as clear as the sky, and Michael was thrilled to hear his old friend. It had been quite some time since he paid a visit. Unfortunately, he was only visiting his dream.

"Looks like you've found a new home," the lark said.

"Yes," Michael replied. "My true home, the place where I was meant to be."

"I know, I've always known." The meadowlark's wings fluttered even though it didn't move. *Da-da-DAH-da, da-da-da*. Michael could listen to that tune all day. "And now you have to hold onto it, protect it, use your new power and strength to make sure nothing bad ever happens to it."

Michael wasn't sure that Double A needed his protection, but he nodded anyway. "I will."

"Good," the lark said, its yellow feathers brighter than Michael remembered. "Because he's going to need you."

He? What's he talking about? The school was always referred to as a "she." "Archangel Academy needs me?" Michael asked.

The lark turned its head so Michael could see its clear, round eyes. "I'm not talking about your school. I'm talking about Ronan."

Opening his eyes, Michael couldn't see the lark. The only one in the room with him was Ronan. For a few seconds he lay still, hoping he was wrong, hoping it wasn't a dream and he would be able to catch the meadowlark's sound, even if it spilled into the room, into the present, from his memory, but there was silence. The sound was gone; only Ronan remained. The person he slept with, the person he loved, the person he had to protect. When Michael saw the time on the alarm clock next to their bed, he realized Ronan was also the person he had to wake up.

"Ro," Michael said, nudging him more than slightly. "We overslept."

Ronan stirred, stretched, but kept his eyes shut and his hands tightly clutching the covers. "We have plenty of time."

Out of bed, Michael was already starting to dress. "Not if we want to be on time for first period."

Reluctantly, Ronan opened one eye and mumbled, "Really, we're that late?"

"When have you known me to get up early?" Michael

asked, flipping the covers to the side, revealing Ronan's near-naked body. "Now get dressed. You can't go to class in your underwear."

"Why not?" Ronan asked, stretching and yawning loudly. "I think I look bloody fantastic."

Knotting his tie, Michael tried not to smile. Ronan looked beyond fantastic. They both knew it, and they both knew that Michael would like nothing more than to spend the entire day staring at him. Well, maybe not the entire day; even that could get dull after a while. Michael was in love, he wasn't obsessed; he did have other things going on in his life. Like school which, sadly, started really early in the morning and required a more conservative attire. "And you look equally fantastic in your uniform," Michael said. "So get dressed."

Not just yet. Michael didn't see Ronan's arm reach out and grab him, but it must have, because the next thing he knew he was lying on the bed with Ronan on top of him. Clearly, his boyfriend still had some moves he hadn't yet seen. And some lines he hadn't yet heard.

"To look at a thing is quite different from seeing a thing," Ronan recited, his blue eyes clear and unblinking. "And one does not see anything until one sees its beauty."

Wrapping his fingers around Ronan's arm, Michael knew those words weren't original and that Ronan was quoting their favorite writer. It didn't lessen the sentiment; on the contrary, it strengthened it because it was their own private connection. "That's gotta be something Mr. Wilde wrote."

"From *An Ideal Husband*," Ronan confirmed. "But he could've been writing about you."

It was hard for Michael to respond while Ronan was kissing him, but he got a few words out. "Haven't read that far."

"That's okay," Ronan whispered as he kissed him deeply. "I know your boyfriend can be a distraction."

Despite how marvelous the bed and Ronan's body felt,

Michael couldn't afford to be late again and so he needed Ronan to be fully dressed. Commanding all his willpower, Michael pushed Ronan away from him. "Stop kissing me."

Miffed, Ronan stared down at Michael. "Why, love?" he asked. "Is my breath rank?"

Rolling out from underneath him, Michael laughed. "Well, a little, but, seriously, you have to get dressed! Joubert'll get all pissy if I'm late again, and you have to get all the way over to the lab," he said, crossing the room to grab their backpacks. "If we're both late, people are going to talk about us."

"They *already* talk about us," Ronan said, jumping into his trousers.

"Well, let's not give them more ammunition," Michael replied. "Now stop yakking and finish."

"I'm waiting for you," Ronan said.

Michael turned around, and of course Ronan was fully dressed, standing at the door with his coat on, acting as if Michael were the one who had delayed their departure. Tossing his backpack to Ronan, Michael walked past him and opened the door. "You think you're funny, don't you, Glynn-Rowley?"

"I know I'm funny, Howard," Ronan said, smiling as he closed the door behind him.

Michael was already starting to race across campus when Ronan heard him shout, "You're the only one!"

Jumping into his seat in theology, Michael could still hear Ronan's laughter, louder than the class bell. As much as he didn't want to, he had to turn off his connection with his boyfriend so he could concentrate on Joubert's lecture, no matter how boring it might be. He listened as his professor tried to excite his students by focusing on the Bible's more glamorous section, the Book of Revelations, but as an immortal Michael found the whole "end of days" apocalypse to be anticlimactic. As usual, things only got interesting after class.

"Looks like your boyfriend just can't stay away," Michael whispered.

Nakano turned around and saw Jean-Paul standing in the doorway, the rest of the class filing out past him. Shoving his books into his messenger bag, Nakano debated whether he should tell Michael the truth, that he hadn't seen much of Jean-Paul lately. Even though they had never officially broken up, calling him his boyfriend in their theology classroom would probably be considered a venial sin. In fact, he was certain Jean-Paul wasn't here to see him, but to have another confab with the vampire professor. Not so.

"Kano," Jean-Paul called out. "Do you have a moment for me?"

"A moment, an hour, a week, an eternity," Michael joked, throwing his pack over his shoulder. "Have fun, Nakano."

Walking past Jean-Paul, Michael was happy that his stomach didn't flip, his heart didn't skip a beat, and he found it very easy to speak to the man he had once found incredibly distracting. "Hi, Jean-Paul," he said. "Good to see you again."

Nakano was less sure of himself. Walking over to meet Jean-Paul at the doorway he felt like he was hobbling. He ran a hand through his hair and wished that he had let it continue to grow and not gotten another buzz cut. He threw his shoulders back as far as they could go, and he wished that he were just a few inches taller so he wouldn't look so short. Jean-Paul was so tall, so handsome, so confident, so at ease as he twirled his chauffeur's cap in his hand. Really, what could he ever want from Nakano? A date, a reconciliation, a kiss. How about an answer?

"Where eez Brania?" Jean-Paul asked, one outstretched finger still circling round and round, making his cap flip over and over in the air.

Startled, Nakano turned around and saw that Professor Joubert's hunched back was to them. He was ignoring them, not by choice, but because he was being questioned by

Diego. Nakano hadn't even noticed that the Fuente kid was still in the room; he thought he had left with the rest of the class. But at least his presence kept Joubert preoccupied so Kano could have a semi-private talk with Jean-Paul. But Jean-Paul didn't want to talk. He just wanted an answer to his question.

"Are you deaf?" he asked. "I said, where's Brania?"

This time Nakano was startled, because Jean-Paul's eyes turned as ugly as his tone. "I don't know."

"You're lying."

Glancing behind, he saw that Joubert was still talking to Diego. Joubert, looking tall despite being seated, held some papers, most likely Diego's answers to the essay questions on their latest test; the kid was always questioning why he had gotten a lower grade than he had expected. He was the type who went through life thinking that he should be rewarded just because he had tried. It didn't matter that he wasn't good enough, that he wasn't smart enough, that he wasn't hot enough to get the top prize. Nakano knew exactly how that felt. "So that's why you've come to see me?" he asked. "To find out where Brania is."

The cap suddenly stopped moving. Jean-Paul leaned over and smiled, and Nakano could see his teeth, so white and perfect; he could smell his breath, so thick and hot; he could hear his response, so blunt and hateful. "Pleeze, the only reason I'm 'ere eez because David asked me," Jean-Paul hissed. "And I weell ask you only one more time, where eez Brania?"

So there wasn't going to be another date, there would be no more kisses. The only reason Jean-Paul was standing in front of him was because he had been given orders. He might be an adult, he might be gorgeous, but he was nothing more than a lackey, a servant who did exactly as his master commanded. How unattractive was that? There was no way that Kano was going to go out with a guy who couldn't think for himself, who only did what he was told to do. No, this conversation was over.

"And I already told you, I don't know where Brania . . . eez," he replied.

Feeling smug, Nakano didn't care if he offended Jean-Paul. He didn't even care if Joubert and Diego heard every word he said. He had had enough of being treated poorly. Laughing out loud, he thought he might be having his own mini biblical revelation—if you want to be treated properly, you have to start treating yourself with respect. So not only was this conversation over, but so too was this relationship. "One more thing," Kano said, his voice no longer hushed. "Just so there's no confusion in that pretty, little pea-brain of yours, I'm dumping you."

Jean-Paul didn't protest or laugh, but he also didn't let Nakano leave. Extending his arm, he grabbed onto the doorjamb and denied Kano a dramatic exit. Leaning in a little bit further, his hair falling from behind his ears, looking greasy instead of smooth, Jean-Paul offered one last warning. "Be careful who you are loyal to or you might wind up like your leetle friend Penry."

Shocked, Nakano had had no idea that Jean-Paul knew about Penry. It wasn't something that they had talked about, and Jean-Paul hadn't been in town when the incident happened. Maybe it was something that vampires all over were talking about; maybe Nakano had become something of a legend, a rogue vampire who defied protocol and killed by his own rules. "Don't act surprised," Jean-Paul sneered. "David tells me everything. And . . . how do you say? *Oui,* vice versa."

Images of Jean-Paul and David ripped through Nakano's brain, both real and imagined. He didn't know what kind of relationship they had; he didn't know if they were friends or lovers; he didn't know anything anymore except that he had to get out of this room and the hell away from this guy. He didn't care how it looked to anyone else, he just grabbed Jean-Paul's arm and flung it violently to the side before running out of the classroom. Go tell that to David!

Catching Joubert's eyes, Jean-Paul shrugged his shoulders puckishly. He then tilted his head toward Diego, who was still rambling on about how he should receive at least partial credit for attempting to answer one of the essay questions, disregarding the fact that he had failed to explain in an insightful manner the symbolism of the color red in the Bible. "Mr. Fuente, I'll increase your grade by three points," Joubert rather wearily announced.

"Excellent! Thank you."

Taking Diego by the elbow, Joubert ushered him to the door, his huge frame dwarfing Diego. "Bear in mind, however, that your new grade doesn't reflect a reassessment of your intelligence on my part," he added. "But a nod to your perseverance."

Standing just outside the classroom, Diego had no idea his meeting with his teacher had ended. "Just one more thing. . . ." Those were the last words Diego uttered before Jean-Paul slammed the door in his face.

"Gwendal, how in ze world do you 'andle being surrounded by leetle children all day long?" Jean-Paul asked, his back leaning against the door. "I don't theenk anytheeng could be more annoying."

Ronan could argue with that statement. He had spent the last hour sitting next to Morgandy in chemistry feeling as if he was sitting next to a stranger instead of next to one of the most influential people in his life. The actions of the guy sitting next to him had shaped Ronan, turned him into the person he was today. He couldn't believe that Morgandy was able to keep up this pretense that they didn't share any history. It was absolutely maddening. Just like his questions.

"What's your name again?" Morgandy asked.

"Are you bloody kidding me?!"

Morgandy reeled back on his lab stool as far as he could without tumbling over. "Sorry, I'm the new kid, way too many names to remember," he replied. "You're Rowan, right?"

Ronan was holding the pencil so tightly in his hand it was about to break. "Wrong. I'm *Ronan*."

Slapping his hand down on the countertop, his curls bouncing a bit, Morgandy apologized yet again. "That's right, really sorry, truth is I'm no good with names." He turned his focus back to the microscope and took out the glass tray that was covered with a foul-looking brown and green substance. He held it gingerly so as not to spill the contents and placed it on the counter next to the others, which all held matter that looked equally gross. Turning back to his lab partner, he asked, "Do you have the next specimen . . . Ronan?"

Hearing Morgandy speak his name again made Ronan cringe. *How can he say my name as if it doesn't mean anything? How can he act as if he doesn't know who I am? How can I let him get away with this?* "Stop playing games, Morgandy."

Morgandy's brow furrowed. Confused, he shook his head and was finally able to respond, but his voice was way too casual for Ronan's liking. "Not playing games, just trying to finish up the assignment."

A clean snap and the pencil in Ronan's hand broke in two. "Stop acting as if you don't know who I am," he demanded, his voice quiet, but seething. "Like you don't remember me."

Morgandy's confusion didn't completely lift, but it was slowly being erased by irritation. "Look, I don't know what your problem is," Morgandy said. "But I don't remember you because we never met before."

"Seriously?!"

"Is there a problem over there?" Professor Chow asked from across the room.

Looking around, Ronan saw that his outburst had not only caught the attention of his teacher, but the rest of the class as well. "No, sir," he muttered. "Just really excited about this lab."

Despite the chuckles from a few of his classmates, most of the students shared Chow's look of disbelief. Ronan wasn't a very good actor and definitely not nearly as good as he believed Morgandy to be. "This is seriously how you're going to play this."

Morgandy looked around the room for support, for the right words to appease Ronan; he didn't find either. "I don't know what to tell you," he said finally. "You got me mixed up with some other guy."

"I think I'd remember the guy who shared my bed for almost a year," Ronan seethed.

So that was it! It was all a come-on. Morgandy had heard through the school grapevine that Ronan was gay, but he also thought he had a boyfriend, the blond kid from the swim team. Morgandy, like most all the students at Double A, didn't care about someone's sexual preference as long as they weren't pressured to do anything against their will. Like Ronan was obviously trying to do. "I think I need to call a time-out," Morgandy replied. "I don't care what you are or how you like to get off, but I don't swing that way."

Infuriated by Morgandy's blatant refusal to acknowledge their history, Ronan banged his fist on the counter and jumped off his chair, knocking it backward. "You bloody liar, you most certainly do swing that way!"

Now Ronan was acting violent, and Morgandy no longer thought his flirtations were harmless; he was afraid. "I'd like a new lab partner please!"

From across the room, Chow made his authoritative presence known. "Ronan! What's going on over there?!"

Fury prevented Ronan from speaking, so Morgandy explained the situation, censoring it for a public audience. "Mild disagreement over procedure, sir," he said. "But I think it's best if we switched partners."

Again, Chow didn't believe a word of it. Like most teachers, however, he had learned that it's often better not to pry and just to accept a student's version of the truth at face value and act accordingly. Just as he was shuffling around partners, pairing Alexei up with Morgandy, and a quiet kid from the Netherlands with Ronan, the bell rang. Chow was grateful; he knew the crisis wasn't solved, but at least it was postponed for another day.

Unlike Chow, Ronan didn't have an academic's patience. He wanted to corner Morgandy. He wanted to know once and for all why his one-time soul mate was acting like they had never shared a connection, like their past had never existed. But Morgandy had other plans and refused to comply. By the time Ronan got outside, Morgandy had already disappeared into The Forest, swallowed up by the trees and the dusk, which was darker than usual for this time of day.

The clouds above were sliding back and forth in the sky restlessly like they couldn't decide in which direction to travel. They were gray, outlined in black, ripe and ominous. Obviously, a storm was brewing. Let it storm, let it rain, let the whole sky fall down for all Ronan cared, all he wanted was a bloody answer. He was about to try and follow Morgandy's footprints in the bits of snow that were still on the ground, but out of the corner of his eye he found a better strategy.

"Nakano!"

Tired of running, Kano ignored his instinct and stayed put. He had no desire to talk to Ronan, but he also didn't want to dwell on Jean-Paul any longer. Isn't this what grown-ups did all the time? Choose the lesser of two evils? When Ronan caught up with him he recognized his expression—super strong, almost silent, totally taking himself too seriously. Nakano thought he had the perfect antidote. "What can I do you for on this beautiful day, chum?" he asked in a tone that was wedged perfectly between sarcasm and a friendly teasing.

It was like throwing a feather at a brick. Ronan's expression didn't change. "Do you know why Morgandy's acting like he doesn't remember me?"

Nakano tried again. "No, and honestly, mate, it's a little long for a song title."

Springing forward, Ronan made Nakano retreat further back into The Forest. Nakano wasn't scared; he just didn't feel like getting trampled. "I'm not bloody fooling around!" Ronan cried. "Ever since he got here it's like I'm a stranger to him."

An ex-boyfriend acting indifferent, yeah, Nakano had no idea what that was like. "Maybe you weren't worth remembering," he quipped. "I've blocked out most of the time that we spent together."

This time when Ronan lunged forward he wrapped his hands around Nakano's throat and lifted him two feet off the ground. He kept moving until Kano's back was rammed into the side of a tree. "I'm trying very hard to control my temper," Ronan growled.

Lodging several fingers in between Ronan's hands and his throat, Kano was able to breathe. "You could've fooled me," he gasped, his legs swinging freely in the air.

Coming to his senses Ronan realized what he was doing, taking out his frustration on someone who might not be entirely innocent, but who definitely didn't deserve to be on the receiving end of his wrath. He let go, and after a split second Nakano fell to the ground easily, as if he had jumped off a curb. Even still Ronan didn't give him a moment to catch his breath before grilling him further. "What do you know about it?"

Wow, two ex-boyfriends in one day demanding answers from Nakano. He had never been so popular. "Why are you asking me? I hardly remember the guy."

Exhibiting self-control, Ronan didn't grab Nakano. Instead he gripped a low-hanging branch and bent it until it almost broke in two. "Because I know he's working with David!" he explained. "Which means he's also working with you."

The day was turning out to be one surprise after another. Nakano had had no idea that Morgandy was now one of Them, yet another secret David was keeping from his tribe, just like his real relationship with Jean-Paul. Whatever was going on with Ronan's ex was none of his business, and that's how Nakano wanted to keep it. "Then I suggest you ask David, because I don't bloody well care about Morgandy," Nakano advised. "And we all know that David controls everything."

Watching Kano disappear into The Forest, Ronan felt oddly relieved. It wasn't the response he had been looking for, but at least it was honest.

It was much more than what his sister was dealing with.

"What are you doing here?" Saoirse asked.

"Is that any way to greet your boyfriend?"

Morgandy didn't wait for a reply; he just walked into her room, hesitating only slightly when he saw Ruby sitting at her desk, her fingers gliding over an open book. "Don't mind me," she said. "I'm just reading about the medicinal properties of Northern European flora."

"It's Braille," Saoirse explained in response to Morgandy's quizzical look.

"Of course," he said. "Sorry to just barge in." Turning his back to Ruby, he took Saoirse in his arms. "But I just had to see you."

A jumble of emotions fluttered in Saoirse's stomach. She was delighted to see Morgandy, surprised that he had showed up unannounced, and slightly embarrassed that he was kissing her in front of Ruby. "What was that for?" she asked, pulling away from Morgandy's kiss.

"Just a reminder that not everything is weird and complicated," he said.

Pulling back even farther, Saoirse replied, "Well, I guess it's nice to know that I'm not weird or complicated."

"You're anything but," Morgandy confirmed, holding her closer to him.

Saoirse, however, wasn't in the mood to kiss or hug, not because Ruby was in the room, but because she was tired of being the phantom girlfriend. "No, I'm just anonymous," she said, plopping on her bed.

Glancing over at Ruby, who was still in the same position she had been in since he showed up, Morgandy sat next to Saoirse and spoke in a quieter voice. "Can we talk about this some other time?"

She really didn't have to answer the question as her body language did it for her. She folded her arms and shook her head, but not one to be subtle she followed up with a verbal explanation. "No. I'm bored with this whole secret relationship thing," she admitted. "I want to go public, you know, give the fans what they've been asking for, and I know the perfect venue for the reveal, at the Archangel Festival."

"There isn't going to be one this year," Morgandy said, relieved, but knowing full well that he hadn't dodged the bullet entirely.

"What do you mean there's not going to be a festival?!" Saoirse exclaimed. "I got a swanky new dress and everything!"

Morgandy tried to grab Saoirse's hand, but she slapped his hand away. "Sorry, but David cancelled it, said it would take away from the Tri-Centennial Celebration."

Saoirse was so incensed by the stupid decree she didn't notice that Morgandy had called David by his first name instead of Headmaster or that Ruby's fingers had stopped moving. The girl turned her head slightly, suddenly more interested in her friend's conversation than her book. "Well, that's just bloody idiotic!" Saoirse cried.

Watching his girlfriend pace the room, Morgandy couldn't help but smile; she really was a spitfire. "Might be, but it's going to be announced by the end of the week," he said. "I, um, heard it from some of the guys."

Pouting, Saoirse plopped on the bed. "Isn't there any way we can make him change his mind?"

Brushing her hair away from her face, Morgandy was struck once again by Saoirse's beauty. He had nothing against being gay; he just had no idea why a guy wouldn't want to kiss something as delicate as a girl's lips, and so he did. "Sorry, Seersh," he said quietly. "But from what I've heard, whatever David wants, David gets."

And by the way that Ruby was leering at Morgandy and the very peculiar way that she was reacting to David's name, it appeared that she understood that as well.

chapter 16

Michael was definitely more handsome than an angel. Yes, even an archangel. At least that's what Ronan thought when he took a good look at the carving of the saint etched onto the mirror frame that hung in the anteroom to David's office. Sure the depiction of Michael the archangel was heroic looking, complete with strong features, billowing hair, and a muscular body, but it lacked something. Ronan almost laughed out loud when he realized that it lacked imperfection; the archangel was flawless. It was hilarious because he always said his boyfriend was perfect. Staring at the dark brown oak tribute to the iconic figure, Ronan realized his Michael was better than perfect—because he was real.

"And because he's yours."

Ronan didn't know who spoke the words, but when he glanced at the sculpture he saw the archangel looking up at him from the bottom of the frame, still looking perfect and heroic, but now he was smiling. Luckily, he was so transfixed by the saint's changed expression that he didn't see Zachariel, in the right hand corner of the frame, staring at him, his face a portrait of evil, his eyes so cold and hateful they could have frozen the sun that framed his head. It was identical to the way Vaughan looked when he entered the anteroom from David's office.

"Ronan."

"Fancy meeting you again, Mr. Howard," Ronan replied, his voice as icy as the chill that clutched Vaughan's chest. "And so soon."

Before Vaughan could answer or exit, David opened his door, holding a small, black leather box wrapped with a single red ribbon. Unlike Vaughan, when David saw Ronan his smile didn't fade; it actually widened. "My, my, my, the prodigal son returns."

Unable to conceal his disgust, Ronan retorted, "Thankfully I was never your son in any sense of the word."

If possible, David's smile grew even wider. "Perhaps if your lovely mother would have surrendered to her true feelings and married me," David said, "you would have benefited from my fatherly tutelage."

At that very moment Ronan was unable to decide which man he loathed more: the man Edwige had once lived with or the one she was living with now. Looking from one vile vampire to the other, he was about to consider it a draw until David finished his sentence. "Since poor, dear Saxon was taken from you so unexpectedly when you were such a young lad." That comment clinched it. No one could be more heinous than David.

"Regardless of when my father was taken from me," Ronan said, his voice practically a growl, "no one, not even you, could ever be the man that he was."

David chuckled heartily as if he were once again at a lady's tea party in Victorian England. Ronan, like the women who had once attended those gatherings, amused him. But while this brief interlude was enjoyable, it wasn't the reason he had left his office. "Vaughan, my good fellow," David said, "you ran off before I had a chance to give you a token of my appreciation."

As he took the leather box from David awkwardly, it was clear that Vaughan was not expecting a gift. "Oh, why, thank you," he stuttered. "You're . . . you're too kind."

Like a benevolent benefactor, David shook his head, unwilling to accept Vaughan's praise. "No thanks are necessary," he replied. "The permanent contact lens implants you have supplied us with have been a great success. Think of this as a symbol of my gratitude."

All three of them understood the significance of the gift. David never rewarded his subjects for their efforts; he expected all those beneath him to toil unceremoniously until he was satisfied with their actions. For him to bestow a gift, no matter how small, on one of his underlings meant that he or she had achieved something that even David was unable to. Ronan quickly surmised that Vaughan's factory and these implants made it possible for non-water vamps to walk in the sun on Archangel Academy grounds without having to take any precautions to protect their eyes. Vaughan offered David's people something David could not; he offered them independence.

Watching Vaughan bask in David's unprecedented warmth, Ronan wondered how quickly the temperature in the room would drop if he mentioned the name of Vaughan's live-in houseguest. Not only would David be furious that Vaughan was fraternizing with the enemy, but his enormous ego would be wounded to know that Vaughan had captured the woman he was unable to. Sensing that Ronan was contemplating revealing the secret of his living conditions, Vaughan decided it was time to make a quick exit. "I am humbled, David."

It was now Vaughan's turn to act as if he had been spirited back to a bygone era. Holding the box in one hand, he extended the other to his side and slowly bowed. He kept his eyes firmly fixed on the floor for a few seconds to allow David the thrill of witnessing, without question, his subservience. As Vaughan expected, the gesture delighted David, his chest puffing up like a peacock, but it was a flamboyant move that harbored an ulterior motive. Rising halfway, Vaughan nodded at David one final time and then grandly turned so he could face Ronan. Without stopping as he left the room, he whispered, "Tell Michael I hope he's well."

Consumed with pride that one of his flock had displayed to a member of the lower species how to behave properly in the presence of their ruler, David didn't hear Vaughan's comment. He merely gloated and invited Ronan into his office. Ignoring the feeling that he was walking into a trap, Ronan entered and quickly scoured the room with three of his five senses. A few seconds later he was calmer, as he didn't see, hear, or smell anything that aroused his suspicion. He was confident when David closed the door behind him that they were the only creatures, human or otherwise, in his office. After David spoke his confidence was replaced by confusion. "I'm disappointed in you, Ronan."

Ronan assumed he had disappointed David in many ways over the years, but couldn't figure out which specific disappointment he was referring to at the moment. "And why is that?"

Gazing out the window, David saw there was a small tear in the green velvet drapes. He would have to get that imperfection fixed, but there were so many other things to do, so many more important things that needed to be accomplished before mending window treatments. If he folded the material slightly perhaps no one would notice the flaw. "Oliver tells me that you and Michael missed your appointments for your school physicals," he replied as he readjusted the position of the drapes. "You know they are mandatory for all students regardless of their unique physical composition."

That's what he was talking about? Ronan would hardly call that a disappointment, more like a diversion, a tactic so David could have control of the conversation. Fine, let him think he's in control. "We didn't think there was any point," Ronan replied, "since we all know what the final result would be."

Satisfied that the drapery's flaw was sufficiently hidden, David turned around, his smile courteous, condescending. "Yes, Ronan, we all know what the examination would have uncovered," he said. "But Oliver was so looking forward to studying the two of you . . . What were the words that he used? Ah yes, up close and personal."

Ronan was sure that David's smile had turned into a leer, and he was disgusted at the thought of Michael and himself being examined by the wizened, lecherous doctor. He chewed on his lip for a second to prevent himself from saying exactly what was on his mind: that the foul doctor was never going to get his hands on him or Michael unless it was in a fight to the death. Instead he replied, injecting his words with as little sarcasm as possible, "Tell Sutton we didn't mean to spoil his fun."

"He'll be happy to hear that," David said. "And you'll be happy to know that Oliver submitted your results to Coach Blakeley and told him that you and Michael passed your physicals with flying colors."

Not wishing for the meeting to be filled any longer with unnecessary chatter, Ronan decided it was time to get to the reason he had come to enemy territory in the first place. "Why doesn't Morgandy remember me?" he asked.

One of the things David hated most was being blindsided. Another was ignoring his gut instinct. David knew Ronan hadn't dropped by for a friendly visit; he knew the boy had come armed with a purpose, but he had let himself get distracted by unimportant issues. Now he was paying for his stupidity, for his weakness; he was standing in front of this inferior creature and being forced to hide a look of shock, a look of surprise. *Enough of this acting like a child. Remember who you are,* David chastised himself. *Headmaster, leader, Zachariel's chosen!* When David spoke he allowed all the hatred he was feeling for himself to seep into his speech. "Because of that repulsive Well of yours."

Yes, that felt better. Turning his back to Ronan, David lifted the top off of a sterling silver decanter that had a neck as long and slender as a swan's and filled up a matching goblet with blood. He didn't see Ronan's reaction, but he didn't need to; he knew such a blasphemous proclamation would elicit a powerful response. When he turned around he saw that he was right. Ronan's entire body was fighting the urge to defend the holy icon. David knew his silence would only infuriate Ronan even more, so instead of speaking, he drank.

Ronan felt his fangs tingle as he watched David's throat rise and fall. God, he's such a pig, Ronan thought, drinking blood like it was brandy and not the precious liquid it was. These people really are disgusting! "The Well has nothing to do with this."

David ran his index finger along the inside of the goblet, and when he lifted it up it was covered in blood. Just as David was about to stick his finger in his mouth, lick it clean of every crimson drop, Ronan lurched forward and grabbed his wrist, sending the metal goblet crashing to the floor. It bounced several times before careening into the leg of a chair where it stopped. And then there was no sound in the room as they both called upon willpower to adjust their next moves. Ronan commanded his fangs to stay hidden, and David, feeling the tingle in his back, begged his wings not to unfurl. This was a time for confrontation, not showmanship. It was also a time for a reminder.

With a flick of his massive wrist, David threw Ronan's hand flying into the air, the momentum causing him to lose his balance and teeter backward. It was not that David didn't like to be touched; he just preferred to make the first move. "Touch me again, Ronan, and I will forget that you are not used to playing the role of the scorned lover," David seethed. "Morgandy doesn't remember you, because when he chose to join the ranks of the more powerful, your vindictive Well wiped his memory clean."

Could it be that simple? Ronan had never heard of that happening before, but it made sense. If Morgandy wanted to be one of Them, The Well wasn't going to allow him to cross over knowing all its secrets or maintaining all the benefits bestowed upon their race. If this was true, he was beginning to learn that The Well was more powerful than he had ever imagined.

"So not only did you abandon him, Ronan, but your Well erased all his memories. Swimming like a pack of oversized fish, waking up each morning wrapped in your glorious arms, all those memories were taken from him and he was cast out," David continued. "Why, he was discarded as callously as if he were a crippled newborn."

"I didn't abandon him!" Ronan cried. "He betrayed me!"

Once again David turned his back on Ronan, not to pour himself another drink, but to resume his place behind his desk. Like the insipid ladies of the long-ago tea parties, this young man was starting to bore him, and he wanted their conversation to end. "That is your interpretation, not that it makes a difference," David said. "Morgandy van der Poole is born anew, unto a far superior race." Dipping his quill pen into an inkwell, David shifted his attention to the small pile of papers on his desk. "And even though you've lost him forever, dear boy, never fear, he may become part of your family after all."

"What the hell are you talking about?"

David loved when he piqued an adversary's curiosity with a simple turn of phrase. He relished the look of confusion on Ronan's face for several moments before speaking. "Your former paramour has been searching for his freedom," he announced. "And I believe he may have finally found it."

"I have to be free, Michael," Saoirse declared. "That's what my name means, you know, it's Irish for freedom."

Slinking deeper into the brown velvet couch in the front room of St. Joshua's, Michael sighed. "And in English does it mean stupid?"

"I am not stupid!" Shocked, Saoirse threw her notebook at Michael. He deflected it expertly with the tip of his finger, sending it flying a few feet up in the air, and waited until it started to descend before reaching out his hand to grab it before it fell to the floor. They might not be in the library proper, but there was still no need to cause a ruckus.

"Then why are you keeping secrets from your brother?" Michael asked. "Haven't you learned that around here that's really not the smartest thing to do?"

"This is different," she said, jumping up from her chair and jumping onto the couch next to Michael. "This doesn't have anything to do with the V word."

Michael tried to stop himself from laughing, but couldn't. "The V word?"

Failing to find the humor in her euphemism, Saoirse replied, "Would you prefer I use the proper word? Because I can, you know. It rolls off my tongue right easy."

"Oh shut up!" Michael said, playfully hitting Saoirse in the arm with an embroidered pillow. "Look, I get why you don't want to tell Ronan that you have a boyfriend, he'll get all big brotherly and stuff, but you can't keep it a secret forever. You have to tell him some time."

"Well, I was planning on making the big reveal the night of the Archangel Festival," Saoirse said as she braided a few strands of her hair. "But David the arsemaster canceled it."

This was news to Michael, news that was really disappointing. "No Festival! Why not?"

"Because it'll outshine his daft Tri-Centennial shindig," she replied, releasing the three strands of hair and watching them spin.

Now it was Michael's turn to pout. Wrapping his arms around the pillow, he held it close to his chest. "But that's kind of our anniversary, me and Ronan."

"Anniversary?" Saoirse asked. "Of what?"

Thinking back to the first night he and Ronan spent together, Michael was reminded yet again that there were certain memories that should absolutely remain private and secret. "Um, well, never mind."

Proving that she could read minds even if she didn't possess the power of telepathy, Saoirse grabbed the pillow and whacked Michael in the head with it. "That is downright goppin'!" she exclaimed, her face scrunching up as if she had just smelled something foul. "You calendar that?"

Wrestling the pillow from Saoirse before they got thrown out of the library, Michael tossed it onto the wing chair. "Officially changing the subject now," he declared. "Have you seen Diego? We're partners on a history project in Willows's class, and we have to do some research."

Saoirse halfheartedly looked around the room and shook her head. "No Fuente presenté," she joked.

With or without his study partner, Michael had to enter the bowels of the library and start doing some actual schoolwork; the time for chatting with his favorite blonde was over. Well, almost. "I've got a great idea!" he announced. "Let's go on a double date. Me and Ronan and you and the mystery boyfriend."

Before she responded, Michael knew she loved the idea.

Her clutching his hands and jumping up and down kind of gave it away. "I love it!" she squealed. "We'll go into Eden and hang out somewhere and be all adult-like. It'll be cracking!"

She was a handful, but she really was a lot of fun. Hopefully, her boyfriend was worthy. "And don't worry, I'm sure Ronan is going to get along with this guy," Michael said. "Whoever he is."

Flopping onto the couch like it was her bed, Saoirse laughed. "You know me, I never worry."

Which is exactly why Michael was worried. Just as he was about to leave in search of a book on the Franco-Prussian War, Michael suddenly remembered something else that caused him concern. "Where's Ruby?" he asked. "Aren't you supposed to be with her during your free period?"

"Not since the creation of the Ulrich Doctrine," Saoirse announced.

"What?"

Braiding her hair again, Saoirse translated. "The charter that Fritz drew up christening himself Ruby's bloomin' twenty-four-hour-a-day chaperone," she said. "He's gone a bit potty over that one, I must say."

Luckily Saoirse was more interested in her hair, so she didn't see Michael's alarmed expression. Well, there wasn't anything that he could say or do that would convince Fritz to ease up on his courtship of Penry's sister; Fritz was determined to make her his girlfriend. Walking into the library, Michael consoled himself with the fact that just because Ruby wasn't human, didn't necessarily mean that she wasn't also harmless.

As hopeful as that thought was, it was wrong.

Looking at the girl from behind, Brania thought she was looking at herself. Same wavy hair, same auburn color, same curves. When the girl entered a clearing in The Forest and wasn't shrouded in tree shadow, Brania realized there were some differences. This girl's hair was much redder, much more like the color of Brania's hair when she was a young girl, and her shape, while womanly, wasn't nearly as voluptuous as hers. Still, from her current point of view the girl was attractive and would probably make a delicious meal.

Hunger pains ripped through Brania's body, determined to make her act. Usually she had control over her cravings, but now it took every ounce of restraint not to act like a cheetah and pounce on the unsuspecting girl, gently brush aside her red hair, and pierce her neck with her fangs. Take her blood, take her body, take her life. Before she realized it, Brania was right behind the girl, her fangs longing for release, her own body desperate for blood. So desperate that if Ruby hadn't turned around at that exact moment Brania would have devoured every drop of her blood in one inhuman swallow.

"Hello, Brania."

Clutching her own throat in surprise, Brania stepped back. It wasn't the resemblance that alarmed her—besides the color of her hair and the shape of her body the similarities ended—it was the fact that Brania didn't know what kind of creature she was; all she knew was that she wasn't human. Other than that, she hadn't a clue. Her eyes were completely white; not a pigment of color invaded either socket. Her skin was beyond translucent, and when she reached out her hand, Brania saw that it was covered in a shimmery substance. Her entire body was outlined in a white glow, making her look ethereal. The fact that this being knew her name made Brania think she was probably sinister as well.

"How do you know me?" she demanded.

Ruby smiled, her red lips parting slightly to show teeth that didn't contain fangs, but were whiter than any Brania had ever seen before. "I've known you your whole life," she replied, even though her lips didn't move. "It's so nice to finally meet David's daughter."

So that was it, she knew David. If that were true, she had to be sinister, no doubt about it. "How do you know my father?" Brania asked, her voice losing all of its calm. "Answer me!"

This time Ruby laughed, but her body didn't move, and if her eyes laughed along with her voice Brania couldn't tell; they were still pure white, the color of total absence. "I've known your father for a very, very, very long time," Ruby said. "And now I'd like to get to know you."

When Ruby touched Brania's hand, she felt the world around her disappear. Gone was The Forest, gone was this strange girl who claimed to know her father, gone was everything except a white canvas. For a few seconds she felt like she was floating within a cloud, protected, hidden, comforted, and then she hit the ground. Immediately, she tried to get up, but her body refused. She felt that her own flesh was rebelling against her, but she quickly understood that it was merely being controlled by someone else.

Looking down at Brania, Ruby was disappointed. She had thought that Brania would resemble David a bit more. Ah well, the girl wasn't as young as she looked; age did change the body somewhat, even when that body belonged to a vampire. She did wish Brania's hair were less auburn and more of a true red, more like the coloring of her hair. And David's.

She began to walk in a circle, and Brania noticed that when she moved a white light appeared behind her like a laser beam. What power that beam possessed or signified, Brania had no idea. She just knew it wasn't normal. When Ruby had traveled once around Brania's body, she stopped and stepped back so the light could connect and create one complete circle in the air. She raised her arm and, as if it were connected, Brania's body also began to rise, not stopping until it was level with the circle of light.

Unable to move even her eyelids, Brania was consumed with fear. She was one of the most powerful creatures who walked the earth and here she was immobilized by some girl without eyes, incapable of doing anything except staring up into the bit of sky that was still visible and not blocked out by the trees. Whatever this thing was, she was stronger than Brania, much stronger, so along with her fear, Brania also offered her respect.

There was a sudden noise from within the wood, just a rabbit scurrying away, uninterested in the spectacle, but enough to distract Ruby. When she turned, the spell was lost. The light disappeared, and Brania fell to the ground, her body hitting the dirt hard, her mind losing consciousness. The sounds of The Forest grew louder as Ruby watched Brania's motionless body, the wind, the chirping, the rustling, just the sounds of nature, sounds that would continue no matter what Ruby chose to do. But looking down at Brania, she remembered what David had always taught her: timing is everything, nothing can be rushed, and if something is important it's worth waiting for.

Yes, David was right. It would be better if she introduced herself to Brania another day. Satisfied that it was the right decision, Ruby walked further into the depths of The Forest, leaving Brania alone so she could sleep in peace. As she walked, her right hand swirled to create a circle in the air, a faint white light emanating from her fingertips. At the same time a circle was formed around Brania's body, a circle that was made up of the most beautiful white roses.

chapter 17

At first, Michael thought his eyes were playing tricks on him. He wanted so badly for it to be true that he thought he was hallucinating. But when he saw the funnel of gray fog slice through the clear, dark sky only to stop and hover in front of him near the edge of The Forest, he knew it was real. Phaedra had returned.

"Hi, Michael."

Thrilled to see his friend again, Michael was speechless. He threw his arms around Phaedra and hugged her, immediately noticing how warm and soft she felt. She was definitely more efemera than human. It didn't matter; it still felt wonderful to feel her, see her once again since he had thought she was out of his life, all their lives, forever. But here she was standing before him dressed in the familiar St. Anne's uniform, her hair still a mass of unruly curls, her eyes still gray-blue and peaceful. Even though her reappearance brought

Michael joy, he knew she hadn't returned simply to pay him a friendly visit. Her homecoming must have been prompted by a far more important purpose. "I've come to warn you about something," she said.

"Before you tell me why you're really here, can't we just hang out for a while?" he asked. "Can't we take a walk so I can fill you in on what's been happening since you left?"

A breeze blew past them disrupting her curls even further, and she tucked the wayward strands of hair behind her ear. It was a simple gesture, but it filled them both with sadness because it reminded them of the teenager she used to be and how she would never be that young girl again despite her convincing appearance. She was an ancient spirit with a message, a message that Michael had to hear even if he thought it was old news. "Ruby isn't what she seems," Phaedra said.

Nodding his head, Michael agreed. "I know. She isn't human."

"That's only part of it."

Intrigued, Michael sat down on a boulder, the same color as the fog Phaedra so effortlessly transformed into. "What do you mean?"

Phaedra hesitated only slightly before she sat down next to Michael. She was reluctant to get comfortable because she knew she couldn't stay long. She shouldn't even be here now; she should be at the Holding Place awaiting instructions, finding out who she had to protect next. Another breeze enveloped her, bringing with it an annoying voice that whispered in her ear, reminding her that no one could be more interesting than Michael and no surroundings could be more welcoming than Double A. That's because Fritz wasn't a student at any other school.

"Phaedra, what do you mean?" Michael repeated.

Focusing on the boy sitting next to her and not the one occupying her mind, Phaedra replied, "Because of what Ruby sets into motion, you're going to be challenged like never before."

Intrigue had graduated into full-fledged concern, and Michael was starting to realize the gravity of the situation. "What is she going to do?"

A few yards away, a twig snapped. It was a random noise, probably just an animal in search of a warm place to sleep, but it reminded Phaedra that she was breaking rules, defying the universe's orders. If she wanted to stay here on earth any longer, she had to take precautions. "I think we should take that walk," she said, abruptly getting up and walking into The Forest.

Michael was quick to follow and even quicker to understand her motives. "You don't want anyone to see you."

"I *can't* have anyone see me," she corrected. "I'm not supposed to be here."

"Then why did you come?" he asked. "You must know that I figured out Ruby wasn't human the first time I saw her."

Leading Michael away from a well-worn path and into an area more densely populated with trees and bushes, Phaedra finally stopped when she was satisfied she would be camouflaged from prying eyes. "To remind you that you can only trust yourself and Ronan and to remember the things that he's told you."

Michael wished she didn't look so serious; he wished she would smile again. But obviously this wasn't going to be a happy, hugs and kisses type of reunion. He thought back to the many things that Ronan had told him and instantly knew what Phaedra was referring to. "You're talking about my dream."

"Yes," she confirmed. "If there ever comes a time when you have to make an impossible choice, listen to your heart and you'll find the answer."

His heart understood the command; it had ever since he first heard Ronan speak the words in his vision. His brain was having a bit more difficulty comprehending the message. "Of course I'll protect Ronan, you know that," he replied, twirling his ring around his finger with his thumb. "But he's so much stronger than I am, I can't imagine he'll ever need my protection."

Finally, there was her smile. Unfortunately, it was borderline condescending. "Michael, you really have to let go of this idea that immortals are invulnerable," she said. "It's sort of like being human. Humans have free will, but that doesn't mean they're not going to sin."

Michael turned the comparison around in his head. "So just because you're immortal doesn't mean you can't die?"

"Exactly," she replied. Phaedra didn't want to frighten Michael, but she had to make him understand. "And despite that knowledge you must choose to do what your heart and your destiny command."

A cold chill clung to the early evening air, but Michael didn't feel it. His body erupted in an explosion of heat, heat that housed fear and panic. Phaedra was telling him something he didn't want to comprehend; she was telling him that Ronan could die. It was an unimaginable thought. Ronan was a vampire; he was amazingly powerful; he couldn't die. And yet those weren't the reasons Michael wanted him to remain impervious to mortality. It was because without Ronan by his side, Michael didn't know if life would be worth living. She was also suggesting something incomprehensible, that Michael must stand by and allow it to unfold. He knew he could never let that happen. "Phaedra," Michael began, surprised to hear himself speak when it was so difficult to breathe, "if you know something, if you know that something is going to happen to Ronan, you have to tell me."

Looking down at her pleated skirt, she pulled on the material and stretched it out a bit. How she loved wearing this uniform, how easy it was to slip back into it. "Even if I knew exactly what was going to happen, I couldn't tell you," she replied. "I'm only here because you're my friend and because Ruby cannot be trusted."

Michael rubbed his sweaty palms on his thighs and tried to shift his mind from worrying about Ronan to figuring out the truth about Ruby. "You have to give me a few more clues about her," Michael pleaded. "I don't think she's a vampire, she hasn't shown any signs of being an efemera, but she is immortal, right?"

In many ways The Forest resembled the Holding Place, not at all in appearance, but in feeling. Both places held secrets, both places offered refuge from the real world, but both places were only meant to be resided in temporarily. "I have to go," Phaedra announced, standing in preparation to transform back to her natural state.

"No, please, you just got here!" Michael cried, grabbing her arm, saddened that it felt as light as air. "And you haven't told me anything that I didn't already know. Ronan may someday need my protection, and Ruby's immortal."

"Just remember that immortal creatures aren't bound by morality," Phaedra replied. "They can have their own agendas and may be here on earth for their own reasons."

Suddenly it made sense to Michael. His friend's return had nothing to do with otherworldly warnings or supernatural pronouncements; it had everything to do with good, old-fashioned human emotion. "You're jealous of Ruby."

Phaedra was so stunned by Michael's allegation that her body fluttered. Part of it turned to mist, while the other part clung to its more solid shape. "That is so not true."

Gleeful, Michael wanted to jump up and down, but curtailed his excitement by shoving his hands into his pants pockets and forcing his body to remain still. "You sound more like Fritz's ex than you do some ancient paranormal creature."

Just as she knew everything there was to know about Michael, he knew all about her. Phaedra couldn't lie to him, and what made her different than most efemeras was that she didn't want to. She considered him her friend. "I miss Fritz," she confessed. "Actually I miss what we could have shared. We never really got to any of the good stuff."

Now this was the type of conversation Michael wanted to have. "Then stay! Pick up where you left off!" Michael shouted. "Guaranteed this thing Fritz has for Ruby is totally a rebound because he's never gotten over you."

Another breeze, another wave of sweet emotion. It was all beginning to be too much to bear. As much as Phaedra loved this place, as much as she missed being a part of Michael's life, seeing Fritz every day, living as a teenage girl, that chapter of her existence was over. "I do miss Double A more than I thought possible," she said.

"Then that settles it!" Michael declared. "We'll make up some excuse that your parents were sick and you had to leave school. . . ."

A few more words tumbled out of Michael's mouth before he realized Phaedra was holding up her hand in front of his face as if to block the sound. She couldn't hear about the possibility of returning to the life she had almost chosen because it was the life that she had given up. She had made her choice, and she had to stick to it. As much as she looked the part, she wasn't a teenager who could flit from one decision to the next just because she had changed her mind; where she came from things didn't work that way. "I'm sorry, Michael," Phaedra said, her words as faint as her appearance, "I gave up my chance to ever be human, and I can't stay here as what I really am."

Before Michael could protest or debate the reasons why her decision was dumb and foolish and just had to be discounted, he saw her body disappear before his eyes. Her uniform, her curls, her sweet face, gone and replaced with a soft mist of smoke that undulated, rippled in midair until it turned into a column of gray fog. As the fog rose to travel to heights Michael could never imagine visiting he heard Phaedra's voice for one last time. "Remember what I said. Do not trust Ruby; she isn't what she seems."

In spite of the seriousness of Phaedra's tone and the urgency of her message, Michael couldn't resist one final comeback. "Yeah right, like anyone in this place is what they seem!"

An odd smell washed over him, and Michael thought Phaedra was answering him with some weird, cosmic joke. But then he remembered that the girl really wasn't one to play tricks. No, this smell was earthbound, and it was foul and repugnant. Not interested in trying to solve another puzzle, Michael walked in the opposite direction of the unpleasant odor, leaving the task of uncovering its origin for someone else.

Nakano winced as he inhaled something equally repulsive. Compelled to move toward the smell, he stopped in his tracks when he saw the source, his mind bombarded by a flood of questions. Why won't those bloody white roses just die? What the hell are they doing in The Forest and not clinging to the walls of St. Joshua's where they belong? And why is Brania sleeping on the dirt surrounded by a circle of those ugly things?

Kneeling down next to her, Nakano's knee squashed one of the roses, burying it into the earth, its delicate, stark-white petals ripped from its stem. He didn't even have to speak Brania's name and she woke up. Like a wild animal disturbed from a deep slumber, Brania clawed at the dirt, her arms and legs acting without thought, only purpose, to retreat and put space between herself and this intruder. When her eyes focused she realized her intruder was unexpected, but harmless. "Nakano, what are you doing here?"

"Crikey, Brania, I could ask you the same question," he

replied. "Did I, um, interrupt some dodgy fertility ceremony or something?"

Ignoring Kano, Brania scoured the land and her memory for some clue as to what she was doing in The Forest or why she had been sleeping inside a circle of white roses. She knew they held some unknown significance and they had not been placed there arbitrarily. Whoever did this to her did so for a reason.

The last thing she remembered was walking in the woods, hungry, in search of a meal, the silhouette of a girl in the distance. Brania closed her eyes and tried to envision what had happened next, but her mind was empty; all she saw was black. When she opened her eyes, she was stung by how white the roses were, almost blinding, not natural, which meant whatever had happened to her, whatever had taken place here was not going to be remembered simply by willing her mind to concentrate. Best to use the situation, as bewildering as it might be, to her advantage. "Thank you, Kano," Brania said, trying to sound like a confused victim. "I don't know what happened, but it looks like you came to my rescue."

Nakano was also thankful, thankful that the darkness hid his face from Brania so she didn't see him blush. "It was . . . nothing," he stammered. "But sure . . . You're welcome."

Walking toward him, making sure not to step on any of the roses, Brania grabbed Nakano's hand. "I owe you my life," she stated. "We both know The Forest is not always a safe place."

An image of Penry's lifeless body jammed itself into Nakano's mind, and he shook involuntarily. *Stop thinking about the past, need to deal with the present.* "Your father is looking for you," Nakano said.

Amazing, Brania thought. No matter how Brania tried to manipulate Nakano, he never noticed. "Thank you again," she replied. "How did you come about this information?"

"Jean-Paul asked me where you were, I guess because he knows that we're friends," Nakano explained.

Thankful that the darkness concealed the true nature behind her smile, Brania replied, "Indeed we are."

The color of his cheeks grew a deeper shade of red, but it wouldn't have mattered if they had been standing in the light of day. Brania wouldn't make fun of him; she was his friend. "He said David wants to see you," Kano continued. "He didn't say why, but you should be careful, because, well, you know David better than anyone."

That was true. Brania knew her father better than anyone. So she knew he had deliberately sent Jean-Paul as a messenger, knowing that Nakano wouldn't be able to resist the urge to run right to her. She also knew that he expected her to remain stubborn and stay in hiding, making him feel as if he had the upper hand. It was time to prove her father wrong. "Thank you for everything, Kano, but you should go home now," Brania said. "I need to teach my father a lesson."

A few minutes later when Brania stumbled upon the three men huddled over the massive buck, she thought it was the perfect illustration of why you should never turn your back on your enemy. David, Jean-Paul, and Joubert were all crouched on the ground, their fangs buried deep within the animal's flesh, each filling their bodies with as much animal blood as possible, unaware that they were being watched. "Looks like a feast fit for a king's fools," Brania declared.

Only David didn't jump at the interruption. He continued to drink the buck's tasty fluid until his hunger was quenched. He then took out a monogrammed handkerchief, the color of merlot, from the breast pocket of his jacket and wiped his mouth clean before turning around to acknowledge his daughter's presence. "Jean-Paul, you didn't tell me that Brania would be joining us."

Brania loved watching her brother fidget. Using her enhanced vision she could actually see the confusion spread over his face as he pondered how to handle his dilemma. Hmm, she thought she would save his pretty, little French head from having to make a choice. "Jean-Paul had no idea I would be crashing your party," she said. "He failed at the task you gave him."

Sitting on top of the now-dead buck, David crossed his legs at the ankles as if he were sitting on an antique settee. "Really?" he replied. "I told him that I wished to talk to you and here we are, talking."

Not moving from her vantage point of a small hill a few feet above the men, Brania cocked her head to the side. "Spin it any way you like, Father. Your son isn't the reason I'm here; Nakano is," she corrected. "He's the one you should thank."

David did his best to conceal his surprise, but Brania could tell by the way Jean-Paul flinched when she mentioned Nakano's name that David had had no idea his beloved son had hired a third party to do his bidding. Teaching was turning out to be kind of fun. Until David decided to alter the lesson plan. "I forgive you for killing Margaret," he announced. "I understand why you felt Nurse Radcliff needed to be terminated, and I have chosen to show you mercy. So you see, there's no need for you to remain in hiding from me any longer."

She felt her feet dig into the earth to stop her legs from shaking. She wasn't exactly sure why, since she felt no remorse for causing the nurse's death, but perhaps it was because she suddenly realized that if it came down to a physical confrontation, it would be three against one. Interesting, she realized, no matter how much you know there's always room for more knowledge. "I never felt I had to hide from you," Brania said. "You are after all my father. It's just that for the time being I prefer to be alone."

When David rose, the buck shifted slightly, and some excess blood slid down the animal's tongue and trickled out of its open mouth. Brania felt such derision for this group of men that she half-expected them to scamper on all fours and fight each other to see who could lick up the last remaining drop. But no one moved, not until David motioned that they should join him. "And so we shall concede to your wishes," he stated. "You may retreat to your solitary confinement, but I have one request."

Her feet dug farther into earth. "And what is that?"

"That you be at my side during the upcoming Tri-Centennial Celebration," David replied. "It is more than a matter of protocol. It is an auspicious occasion, and I would like to be surrounded by my children. Please don't disappoint me." David didn't wait for Brania to reply. He simply retreated into the woods, followed by Jean-Paul and Joubert.

Damn him! Brania hated allowing him to have the last word, but he didn't stick around long enough for her to say anything. And, now that she was alone with nothing in sight but the rotting corpse of a once magnificent animal, she had plenty to say. Her father should come back now, and she would show him how easily she could disappoint him. But she wasn't going to be given the opportunity to form any sort of rebuttal; she had other matters to attend to. Like finding out why Imogene was screaming so loudly she was threatening to disturb all of England.

Racing into the cave, Brania thought she understood the reason for Imogene's shrieks—Nakano was pacing in one corner of their hideout. "Don't look at me!" he cried. "Crazy ghost girl was screaming her bloody head off when I got here."

Not only was Imogene screaming, she was clawing at the sides of the lidless coffin as if she was unable to sit up, as if some weight were keeping her body flat against the bottom of the casket. The girl was going through yet another transformation, and Brania had a good idea who was responsible. However, she wanted to keep that person's identity a secret. "Kano, go home!" she ordered.

Flustered, Nakano didn't understand why he was being yelled at. "But I didn't do anything!"

Drawing upon every maternal instinct she had acquired while Imogene had been in her care, Brania spoke quietly but firmly to Nakano. "I understand that, but the truth is your being here upsets Imogene so I need you to leave, just so I can calm her down," Brania rationalized. "Could you please do that for me?"

Reluctantly, Kano agreed. "Yeah, sure."

He was hardly out of the cave before Brania jumped into the coffin and grabbed Imogene by the shoulders to try and force her out of her trance. "Imogene! What's happening? Tell me!"

Arms flailing, Imogene was clutching at the air, Brania's face, anything that would pull her out of whatever scene she was witnessing. "Dro . . . drow . . ." she gasped.

She was drowning. Brania's instincts were correct. Imogene was still linked to Edwige, and now Edwige was swimming deeper into the ocean on her way to The Well. "Look at me, Imogene," Brania ordered. "You're safe, you're with Mother." Either Imogene didn't hear what Brania was saying or she didn't believe her. Her arms kept moving as if she was treading water, trying to reach a surface that didn't exist. "Imogene, I need you to focus," Brania compelled. "Use Edwige's eyes and find The Well."

Suddenly her body stopped shaking, her arms fell to her sides, and her breathing returned to normal. "I see it," Imogene announced.

Brania stared at her in amazement, knowing that Imogene was gazing upon the elusive Well, the life force of all water vamps, the treasure that her father wanted to find and destroy. Holding Imogene close to her, wiping the sweat from her brow, Brania beamed. She wasn't sure if she was prouder of Imogene for her unprecedented connection to Edwige or of herself for the skillful way her own mind worked. It wasn't every day that she outdid herself, conceiving another plan that would teach her father that he had underestimated her. Soon he would discover that Brania was more powerful, cunning, and vengeful than he could ever hope to be.

chapter 18

Brania didn't expect to find anyone else in the cave when she returned from her feeding, which is why she was surprised to find that Imogene had company. She was even more surprised when she recognized the girl who was sitting with Imogene in her coffin. She only saw the girl from behind, but her hair was just as red and wavy as the last time she had seen it.

"You're the girl from The Forest!" Brania exclaimed.

"Brania, please, my guest's name is Ruby," Imogene corrected.

Turning to face Brania, her eyes no longer completely white, but now their normal blue, Ruby smiled. "Hello, Brania."

Recoiling just a bit at the sight of the girl, a torrent of memory assaulted Brania, and in an instant she remembered everything that this Ruby person had done to her. She didn't know why, she didn't know how, but she knew two things: She was connected to this girl, and this stranger was dangerous. "What are you doing here?"

Ignoring her question, Ruby instead extended her hand to Brania and asked, "Would you mind helping me out?"

Warily, Brania walked toward the casket and tried to hold onto the anger she was feeling and not give in to the fear that lay just underneath it. Fear was useless; it was for mortals, not for someone like her. Unfortunately, fear clung to her like a shy child clings to its mother. It simply would not let go. "Imogene," Brania said. "She's your guest, would you please help her out of your coffin?"

Thrilled to have a task, Imogene jumped at the opportunity. "Ruby, give me your hand," Imogene instructed. How wonderful it was to be able to feel someone else's hand. Imogene assumed that the reason she could touch Ruby and Ruby could hear her was because they were in the cave. This "straddling life and death" thing sure had its own rules. But as long as Imogene could touch someone other than Brania, she didn't care. She was so energized that by the time she and Ruby were both standing on the cave's floor, Imogene had informed Brania that Ruby had recently enrolled at St. Anne's school, she was blind, and she was Penry's twin sister. Finally, it made sense to Brania. "So that's why you've come here," Brania said, feeling the fear unwrap its needy little fingers from her body. "To avenge the death of your brother."

"Brania!" Imogene exclaimed. "That is no way to speak to my new friend!"

When Imogene saw Brania's head whip in her direction, her face filled with scorn and contempt, it reminded her of the way Brania had looked when she attacked her in her dorm room. Before Brania took her first step toward her, Imogene disappeared. "Imogene!" Brania howled. "I do not have time for these games!"

The game didn't last very long, because Imogene didn't

want to stray too far from Ruby. It was nice to look into the girl's eyes that were the same color as Penry's, so after a few seconds she materialized in her coffin. "Now stay there and do not move!" Brania ordered. Turning around to face Ruby, she spun so hard that her heel dug into the rock floor, a tiny cloud of dust floating around her shoe. "And you!" she barked. "Why have you come to me? I had nothing to do with your brother's death."

As if she could see exactly where the boulder was, Ruby walked toward it and sat down. She looked at Brania, and her bemused expression never changed; all that changed were her eyes. Gone were the blue irises, back were sockets of white.

"Answer me, Ruby!" Brania screamed.

"My name isn't Ruby, and I have no connection to this Penry," the girl replied. "However, I have returned because of my brother."

Clutching her knees closer to her chest, Imogene didn't believe a word the girl was saying. She looked just like Penry; she had to be his sister. "You're lying! You are Ruby!"

If Ruby heard Imogene's protest, she didn't give any indication. She stared directly at Brania. "Behind the picture across from the desk in your father's office you will find a book hidden in the wall," she said. "Give it to David and tell him that I would like him to read me a story."

Brania realized this girl had no connection to the dead kid whatsoever. Whoever she was, whatever she was, she was only using Ruby's body as a host, a conduit so she could walk the earth. And make contact with Brania's father. "Who shall I tell him is making this request?" Brania asked.

Just before she left the cave, Ruby answered. "Tell him that Rhoswen has come home."

Wasting no time Brania raced out of the cave and to David's office. She didn't see a trace of Ruby or Rhoswen or whatever her name was, not that she expected to. She also didn't care that she was leaving Imogene alone. Brania knew she shouldn't abandon her so abruptly since she was vital to the success of her overall plan, but she would make it up to her. Right now she had work to do.

Slipping inside the anteroom, Brania's shadow comingled with the black and gray projections created by the trees outside to form a surreal landscape in the mirror. Roused from their sleep, the archangels were curious to find an intruder in their midst, Zachariel most of all, but even he was ultimately helpless to stop Brania from entering David's office. By the way she moved, without hesitation and with purpose, it was clear that nothing could stand in her way.

Brania removed the painting and saw that its placement was more than ornamental; it concealed a small safe. With a thief's dexterity, she turned the knob and using her preternatural hearing listened for the telltale clicks. The first number was eleven, then twenty-five and sixty-four. *Such arrogance,* Brania thought. Of course David would use his birthday as the safe's combination. Although most people would not deduce that sixty-four referred to 1564, the year of his birth.

Peering into the safe, Brania saw several letters and a stack of faded parchment wrapped in strips of worn leather and marked with David's stamp, one unfurled wing made of red wax. Pushing them to the side she saw sepia-toned photographs, money of every conceivable international currency dating back to the sixteenth century, and finally, tucked behind an ornate silver and gold mask adorned with black ostrich feathers—an odd keepsake indeed—was a book. Even if Brania had seen it in an overstuffed library she would have known it was the book Ruby, well, Rhoswen, had instructed her to find. On the faded cover was a raised marble inlay, a remarkably detailed depiction of a white rose.

"Zachariel told me I had a visitor, but I had no idea it would be you," David said. As if of its own accord the door closed behind him as David took one step, two steps, three steps closer to his daughter, his expression slowly shifting from amused to incensed. "Or that I would find you rummaging through my personal effects." The only reason he stopped moving was because Brania held up the book in front of her, the marble rose a stronger deterrent than a sharp-edged wooden stake.

"What are you doing with that?" David asked, his voice a low, gruff whisper.

If it hadn't been for the flames from the fireplace that had ignited the moment David walked into the room, the silence would have been overwhelming. "I think the more appropriate question, Father, is who is Rhoswen?"

The name struck David like lightning, unexpected, quick, violent. He had known this day would come, he had sensed it for months now, but he had never entertained the thought that it truly would arrive. The day when he would have to acknowledge his past and remember the pain, the agonizing decision he had once made that brought him to his present state of glory. No! Not everything had to be revealed. Brania might be his daughter, she may be inquisitive and insightful, but she was still a woman and therefore insignificant. No, he only had to tell her enough of the story to keep her satisfied. "Rhoswen is my sister."

"What?!" Brania cried. "How come I've never heard of her?"

Give her another morsel, another benign piece of information. "She died when you were an infant," David replied as he sat in the mahogany armchair near the window, to the casual eye appearing calm and aloof. "It was heartbreaking and, like so many things that break the heart, her demise went unmentioned. Until now."

Brania stared at her father, certain that he was telling her the truth, but also certain that there was much more to the story. "How did she die?"

Crossing his legs, David traced the seam of his trousers with his finger to keep the rest of his hand from shaking. "She was murdered."

"Murdered!"

David was surprised to find that his hand lay still on his knee. Perhaps the memory no longer had power over him; perhaps enough time had passed; perhaps his mind had finally convinced his soul that he was innocent. "It was a barbaric time," he said. "Murder was a common, albeit, unfortunate occurrence. And in Rhoswen's case, random."

So her aunt, her father's sister, was a murder victim whose spirit just happened to be taking up residence in the body of the twin sister of a murdered student. Logically, Brania knew that was a strong enough link to connect the two, but emotionally she knew otherwise. "What's the significance of this book?"

Blinking his eyes to forbid the tears to appear, David knew that if he looked away from the marble rose Brania would correctly presume that it was more than decorative. It was a symbol, a symbol of his past, a past he wanted to stay dead and buried. But a past that clearly had a mind of its own. "The book belonged to my sister," he said. "The name Rhoswen means the white rose."

All the pieces finally fell into place. Brania understood why she had awakened inside a circle of white roses. There was a reason why Rhoswen's eyes looked like two round, white canvases. Her mind racing almost out of control she realized the scope of Rhoswen's influence was immense. The flowers that grew outside of St. Joshua's, that had grown there for centuries, were not an anomaly; they were not formed by nature but were the product of this supernatural spirit, who had endowed them with incredible, life-altering powers. Brania didn't know why, but she knew David held the key to unlocking all of Rhoswen's secrets. She had never been more grateful that she had her own secret with which she could barter.

"Rhoswen said that she's returned and she would like you to read this book to her."

When Brania placed the book in David's hands, it was as if she had branded him with a white-hot poker. He felt as if his flesh, his heart, even the remaining pieces of his soul were singed, and it took all his formidable strength not to let the book drop to the floor. "You've spoken to my sister?" David asked, sounding younger than Brania had ever heard him sound before.

"More than that," she gloated. "I've seen her."

A rumble began in David's stomach, so loud, so forceful, he thought for sure the sound would make his body shake uncontrollably, that Brania would think he was in the throes of an epileptic seizure. His vision started to blur, his head grew dizzy, and he had no choice but to close his eyes or else risk falling off the chair. *Use these frailties,* David commanded himself, *turn them into strengths.* Opening his eyes, he imagined he was looking at a world of wonder and possibility instead of the dubious face of his daughter. "This is a sign, Brania, a sign!" he gasped. "My family is coming together just in time for Archangel's Tri-Centennial Celebration!"

Never in all her years had she witnessed her father look so emotional, sound so affected by circumstances that he did not create. It was unsettling, and even though a part of her wished her father possessed such sentimentality, she knew the man's psychological makeup too well. This was all an act. An act that, for the time being, Brania felt she should play along with. "It will be a wonderful reunion," she said. Softly she touched his hand and immediately thought the gesture might be too much, but then figured if her father could play the scene to the hilt, why couldn't she?

"I have another surprise for you," Brania added. "I know how we can find The Well."

This time David did almost drop the book he was holding, but before it fell from his lap he grabbed it, his fingers gripping it so tightly they threatened to tear it in two. "How? Tell me!"

Oh what a beautiful sight to watch her father beg, to see him squirm like an anxious child. "All you need to know, Father," Brania replied, "is that your ex-lover, Edwige, plays an important role in my plan."

"Edwige!" Ignoring her father, Brania turned to leave, the clicking of her heels echoing through the room. Silence returned only when she reached the door. "When I speak with Rhoswen again, I'll tell her that you're waiting for her."

David didn't know how much time had passed after Brania left until the strength returned to his legs, but once it did, he rose, shakily, unsteady, and without direction. Brania, Edwige, Rhoswen! He was in a daze, his mind lost in the past, his body wandering in the present. What brought the two together was the sound of Zachariel's voice. "Control the women in your life or they shall destroy you!"

The harsh, resolute voice was all David needed to hear to propel him into action, allow him to take command of his body once again. The fury traveled like a missile from his toes to his brain, and the book was suddenly hurtling, hurtling, hurtling into the fireplace. Upon impact, the flames erupted like a raging inferno. It crackled like laughter heard within the bowels of an insane asylum; it changed color from orange to yellow to red; it shifted shape from fire to a woman's face.

Amid the bonfire emerged a specter, the true face of David's sister Rhoswen appearing the same way she looked the night she had died. "I've come home, Dahey," the face advised, calling David by his Christian name.

He was repulsed by the sight and sound of the past, but

unable to look away. David's skin was almost as white as the apparition. "NO!" he shrieked. "This can't be. You're dead!"

The phantom was now a full-bodied image. Rhoswen stepped out of the flames, her body, her hair, her long gown, all white, as she floated toward her brother. "So are you," she said, smiling impishly, "and that hasn't stopped you from roaming the planet for centuries."

Cowering, David clutched at his desk, holding up one hand in front of his face in a futile attempt to shield his eyes from the vision. "What do you want from me?!"

Rhoswen began to retreat back into the flames, her voice growing fainter the closer she got to the fire. "I'll let the girl, Ruby, explain," she said. "She's proven to be an amazing creature and has served me well." Even after Rhoswen disappeared into the flames, every trace of white consumed by red, she was still able to issue one final warning. "Do not underestimate her like you've underestimated me."

Now that his sister was no longer present, no longer posed a threat, David found his courage. "I killed you once!" he cried. "I'll kill you again."

As if in response to his tirade, the flames extinguished, and the room was plunged into almost total darkness, the only light from the full moon outside. It was enough, however, for David to see Rhoswen's book, unburnt and intact, fly out from the fireplace and land at his feet. The marble rose still white and immaculate and staring up at him like an accusation that simply wouldn't die.

chapter 19

"I cannot believe my little sister has a boyfriend."

"And I cannot believe you're finding that so hard to believe."

"But she's only sixteen!"

"And you had already found and lost your soul mate by that age!" Michael shouted, immediately realizing his words if not his tone were rather harsh. "Sorry, Ro, but it had to be said."

"You're right, love, it did," Ronan said, grabbing Michael's hand. He then gave it a squeeze, playful, but a tad harder than necessary. "But promise me one thing?"

"Sure," Michael replied, trying not to wince under the pressure. "What is it?"

"For the rest of the night, do not say anything that'll remind me of Morgandy," Ronan said. "It's going to be difficult enough as it is to have fun. No need to make things worse."

They continued to hold hands as they walked past The Apple Tree, remembering the first time they did so in public. They hadn't thought about it that first time. They hadn't been trying to be brave or make some sort of political statement; it had been natural. Their hands had found each other as they walked side by side just as their souls had found each other, even though they lived on opposite sides of the world.

Tiny clumps of snow were now piled onto the bronzed branches and leaves, making the sculpture look as if it were halfway between life and death, just like the boys who passed underneath its shade. Michael took it as a sign that they belonged there and that it was a perfect night for a double date. When he turned the corner, he changed his mind.

Stopping abruptly they allowed a stray black cat uninterrupted passage from the empty street into a narrow slither of darkness between two stone-faced buildings. Michael couldn't see the cat's face trapped within the black abyss, but he heard its hiss and realized it could be a warning that they should turn around and go home. Ronan took it as confirmation that the nagging ache he had felt in the pit of his stomach during the drive into town had nothing to do with his being an overprotective brother uneager to see his little sister as someone's girlfriend and everything to do with his gut feeling that the night was not going to end well. "So don't mention Morgandy," Ronan said. "And in exchange I'll make you a promise."

"What's that?" Michael asked cautiously as the unseen cat hissed once again.

Smiling, Ronan put his arm around Michael's shoulder and whispered into his ear. "If tonight goes as I think it will, I promise I won't say I told you so."

Eden was rather desolate for a Saturday night. And the town looked even bleaker since it was decorated for the holiday season. Almost every window twinkled with colored lights. Santas, snowmen, and Christmas trees had taken up residence in front of stores and on street corners. But Michael and Ronan were the only spectators, the only witnesses to the elaborate display. Despite the store owners' efforts, early December had failed to attract many tourists. Or people had just stayed away because they knew it wasn't going to be a night for celebration.

But then Michael looked across the street and saw that a huge, green wreath hung over the Eden Café sign. What could possibly go wrong when everything looked so festive? Glancing down the alleyway that served as a shortcut from the opposite direction to the café's entrance, he found out that decorations were no match for destiny.

"Morgandy?!" Ronan bellowed.

Down at the other end of the alleyway Ronan saw Saoirse walking toward them holding Morgandy's hand, her smile wilting when she heard the anger in her brother's voice. It disappeared completely when she saw Ronan and Michael sprint from one end of the alley to the other and stop mere inches in front of them. She expected her brother to be rude, boorish, unhappy to acknowledge that his sister was growing up. She didn't expect this. She knew that look; she had seen it only a few times before, but it still alarmed her. The way Ronan was looking at Morgandy, Saoirse knew he was resisting the urge to transform into his true image and rip a gaping hole in her boyfriend's neck with his fangs.

"Is this some kind of bloody joke?!" Ronan barked.

Shock finally segued to embarrassment. "Ronan!" Saoirse seethed. "This is my boyfriend."

"This is insane!" Ronan roared.

The force of Ronan's rage scared Michael, and he realized that if he didn't intervene there would be bloodshed. But what could he possibly say to placate Ronan? What words could possibly diffuse the situation, make it less offensive and, yes, less insane than it truly was? Morgandy was Saoirse's secret boyfriend? Just what kind of a sick game was this guy playing? Unable to find an appropriate word to utter, Michael simply placed a hand on Ronan's arm and was grateful that Ronan didn't flick it away. It was a good sign; it meant that Ronan hadn't given in to his primal instinct, he was in control of his emotions, his anger, and was willing to listen to reason. If any reason could be found. Finally, Michael found his voice. "Saoirse," he said calmly. "Don't you know who this is?"

Slowly she turned to face Morgandy. She searched his hazel eyes and loose blond curls. He looked so innocent, just a boy on the brink of manhood, but was it all a mask? Could he be harboring secrets that lay just behind that smooth skin and those soft lips that felt so incredibly good when they were pressed against her own? If she were a normal teenager, she wouldn't question Morgandy's intent; she would know that her brother was just overreacting. But she wasn't normal, and she knew better. What did Ronan and Michael know about Morgandy that she didn't? Suddenly Morgandy's silence was overwhelming, and his hand felt very heavy in hers. The connection felt wrong, and she wished that she were back in her room hanging out with Ruby, acting like the stupid little girl that she was beginning to think she was. "He's my boyfriend," she replied weakly.

"He was my soul mate!" Ronan cried.

"What?!" Saoirse heard her brother's words, but they didn't make sense. There was absolutely no way her boyfriend had once been Ronan's. That was so ... so ... It was so beyond comprehension that Saoirse didn't even have a word for it. It was so wrong that it had to be right. She had known all along that Ronan was never going to approve of her boyfriend. She had known he was going to convince her that she was too young to be committed to one person or that because of her unique heritage she should stay away from guys she met at school and only date guys that Ronan handpicked for her, who received her arrogant brother's water vamp stamp of approval. She had absolutely no idea he would go to such extreme lengths to try and break up her relationship. "That's flippin' ridiculous, Ro."

"It's the truth," he replied.

The simplicity of his words and the seriousness of his voice gave Saoirse pause. She didn't want to believe his accusation, but what was the alternative? That Ronan was staring at her—his face a disturbing blend of compassion and fear— and lying. He would never do that, would he? It took someone who loved her brother just as much as she did to make her understand, as painful as it was, that Ronan was telling the truth.

"You know you can trust Ronan, Saoirse," Michael said. "He would never lie to you."

Michael was right, that made sense. Holding Morgandy's hand didn't. She let go of it like she had just been zapped with an electric current, without thought, the will to survive taking over. Looking at Morgandy's angelic face, she couldn't believe he was the demon from her brother's past. "He's the one you and Mum never wanted to talk about?" she gasped.

"Yes," Ronan replied.

"He's the one you were living with while I was trapped in France and being ignored?"

"Yes."

Saoirse's body started to shake. Her voice grew from a breath to a roar. "He's the one who was so cruel, your race could never even speak his name?!"

"Yes!"

Michael wished he could reach out and hug the girl. She looked so confused, so young, and he knew exactly what she was going through. Not long ago he had felt the same way. The circumstances were different, but the emotions, conflicting, shattering, devastating, were the same. But Saoirse wasn't

Michael; she really was Edwige's daughter, and although she looked frail and destructible, she wasn't. Even now, gripped by emotional turmoil, she didn't want consolation; she wanted answers.

"Morgandy!" Saoirse's voice was part-shout, part-plea. "How could you do this to me?"

Finally, he spoke, his cavalier attitude belying the gravity of the situation. "Seersh, ya got it all wrong."

"Don't call me Seersh!" she screamed, her body jerking forward viciously. "Just answer my question! How could you deceive me like this?!" she cried, taking another lumbering step toward Morgandy, the intensity of her movement making him back away involuntarily. "How could you do it knowing bloody well that Ronan is my brother?!"

The sun had already set, and they were far from the brightly lit street, so the only light came from an uncovered work lamp that hung above a loading dock at the end of the taller brick building across from the café. Half of the alley was illuminated, the other half was dark, a slant of black that started from the work lamp and ended squarely at Morgandy's right foot, his body literally cut in half. His face and the right side of his torso were softened by lamplight; the rest of his body was drenched in darkness. "I figured out that he was your brother," Morgandy said. "Glynn-Rowley isn't the most common last name."

Saoirse wasn't the only one shocked by this revelation. "And you didn't think that was something you should mention to her?" Michael asked.

Morgandy looked at Michael with pity, his eyes condescending, like an arrogant teacher who knew the truth lay well beyond his student's grasp. "Ronan and I had a little . . . oh I guess you could call it a misunderstanding."

"Bugger that!" Ronan shouted. "There was no misunderstanding! We share a past!"

This time Michael didn't try to calm Ronan, not because he didn't think it was necessary, but because he couldn't. He was just as angry as Ronan was. Morgandy had betrayed Ronan. He had returned and betrayed Saoirse. And now that he was caught, he was taunting them, making a mockery of their outrage. How much of a freaking jerk could he be?

"You came on to me, and I rebuffed you," Morgandy said dismissively.

Luckily, Ronan didn't have to explain what had happened. Saoirse knew Morgandy was lying. She slapped him hard in the shoulder, making him scuttle back awkwardly into complete shadow. "Oh right, you just forgot that you and my brother offered your souls to The Well!"

"What the hell are you talking about?!" Morgandy replied, his face hardly visible, so it seemed like a voice had materialized from the ether. "I don't know about any well!"

"I don't believe you!" Saoirse shouted back.

"It's the truth."

Now Ronan was defending Morgandy? What the hell *was* going on? Saoirse was more confused than ever. Her eyes darted from Ronan to Michael, and she could tell from Michael's expression that he wasn't surprised by Ronan's outburst, so she figured her brother must be telling the truth once again. She took a step closer to Ronan and waved her finger in his face with such force that if it had been a knife she would have split the air into shreds. "You have one bloody minute to explain in simple bloody detail what the bloody hell is going on here!!"

Michael could sense that Ronan was about to reach out to his sister, put his arms on her shoulder, but Michael had an even stronger sense that Saoirse didn't want to be touched. He applied more pressure to Ronan's arm and thankfully he got the hint. Keeping his distance, Ronan laid it out as plainly as he could. "When Morgandy betrayed me and our entire race, The Well forbade us to speak of him again, which is why you never knew his name. The Well also wiped his memory clean, which is why he has no idea we were ever soul mates." Ronan paused, not only to give Saoirse time to digest the information, but to give himself time to breathe more evenly. "At some point David must have found him, I don't know when exactly, could have been before we were ever joined together or after he was banished, I don't know, but it doesn't really matter. All that matters now is that he's chosen to become one of Them."

Everything she had shared with Morgandy was a lie. Not one kiss, not one secret conversation had meant anything. Not one daydream that she had had of their future was ever going to come true. All because Morgandy was a sham, a creep, and worst of all, a fool. "I can almost get over the fact that you forgot you were gay and that you now think you're straight, but you gave up being a water vamp to be like those other... *things?*" Saoirse was so repulsed she could hardly look at Morgandy. "Just how bleedin' stupid are you?"

As he stepped back into the light, Morgandy's face was a scowl and had lost some of its innocent beauty. When he spoke his voice wasn't innocent or beautiful; it contained too much knowledge, it sounded too deep. "You have no idea how incredibly powerful David and his people are."

Saoirse's laughter made Morgandy's scowl harden. "Who do you think you're talking to?" she asked. "I know everything there is to know about Them." Her laughter grew louder, so uncontrollable it interfered with her speech. "I know... that outside this school and this quaint little town... those oh-so-powerful vampires have to scurry around like cockroaches afraid of the sun!"

When Morgandy spoke his tone had softened, but his face harbored the same harsh look. "No, Saoirse," he said. "Let me show you Their true nature."

Now when Saoirse felt Morgandy's hand on her arm she felt like she was being contaminated; it repulsed her. "Don't touch me!" But for all of her bravado, for all of her strength, she was still a teenage girl who had just witnessed her first love be exposed for the liar he was. "I'm gutted, Morgandy! Do you get that?" she cried, tears finally spilling from her eyes. "Bloody gutted, and it's all your fault!" And when Saoirse hit Morgandy again, this time with a fist to his chest, he hit back, slapping her hard across the face. His action was more than shocking. It proved Saoirse right—he was bleedin' stupid.

Acting as one, Michael and Ronan leapt forward, each grabbing an arm, and propelled Morgandy backward, ramming his back into the brick wall of the building across from the café. When Morgandy's face transformed into its vampire countenance, his eyes became so black, so filled with hate, that they actually created light within the dense shadow. "So is this how you girls play?" he hissed, his thin, coarse tongue slapping against a fang. "Two against one."

Michael and Ronan looked at each other, not surprised to see that their faces had undergone a change as well, and they smiled. They turned to face Morgandy so he could see the full beauty of their fangs, and in unison they responded, "Yes."

Without giving their opponent a chance to reply, they slammed his back into the brick wall again, this time harder, making some of the bricks wobble and shake. They continued the motion over and over, disregarding Morgandy's demands that they let go of him, hardly feeling his legs kick into their flesh or the bricks bounce off their bodies after they were wrenched from the wall. In sync, Michael and Ronan stopped at the same time, long enough to give Morgandy a false sense of hope, to think that their tirade had ended. When they saw that Morgandy's eyes were once again filled with the determination to fight back, and weren't just glazed over and in pain, they sent him flying in the air behind them. They didn't have to turn around to see the result of their actions. When they heard the crunch of metal they knew they had been successful—Morgandy's body had crashed into the metal bars that covered a boarded-up window.

Michael and Ronan smiled at each other. They were so far removed from their human form that they weren't bothered by complex emotions. They didn't feel guilty for hurting another creature. They didn't feel anything except delight that they were making Morgandy pay for his duplicity and for striking Saoirse. They never even heard the girl shout for them to stop.

Turning around just as Morgandy was rising to his feet, Michael leapt forward and grabbed his ankle. He swung him around, and Morgandy had to bend forward and hold on to the back of his knee so his head didn't slam into the wall on the first rotation. The second time around, Morgandy had acclimated to the motion, so when he flew past Ronan he reached out his hands to grab him, his fangs chomping at the air in hopes of piercing Ronan's flesh. The third time Michael whipped him around, Saoirse's command was finally heard.

"Enough!"

Obeying, Michael let go of Morgandy's ankle, and he was propelled halfway down the alleyway until gravity was victorious and he landed facedown on the ground. The powerful momentum made Morgandy's body spin wildly on the cobblestone until he smashed into the wall, bouncing against it like a wayward Frisbee, stopping only when movement was no longer an option.

Their desire for revenge, not entirely satiated, but for the moment abated, Michael and Ronan felt their bodies change. When they saw Morgandy stand up and stumble forward, they were looking at him with human eyes, their minds, however, still free from guilt. They had defended Saoirse from an enemy and would do so again. In fact, when Morgandy stood in front of Saoirse they were hoping for another opportunity.

Still off balance, Morgandy held out his hands slightly to steady himself. "I'm sorry," he said. "I shouldn't have done that." He shook his head as if to will his features to resume their human appearance, but it was as if his true self was too proud, too determined to remain in control, and he didn't change. The beautiful face Saoirse loved to stare at was nowhere to be found. "I never meant to hurt you," he said, his voice a rough whisper.

She wasn't frightened by his ugliness, by the deep black sockets that had replaced his eyes, by the thin, parched lips, or the scaly, scarred flesh. Looking at Morgandy now simply made her incredibly sad. "Guess I'll just have to take your word on that."

Stepping away from Morgandy, away from the darkness, and toward her brother and Michael, she seriously wished for the first time in her life that she were a vampire. Not so she could destroy the boy she used to call her boyfriend, but so she could use her power to get away from him as quickly as possible. "I want someone to take me home."

Feeling not at all triumphant, but pleased that Saoirse recognized that any kind of relationship with Morgandy was impossible, Ronan put his arm around his sister and led her away from the guy who had broken both their hearts. Her brother's strength felt wonderful. It was comforting, loving, and exactly what she needed. With Ronan by her side, it made turning her back on Morgandy easier than she would have imagined.

And more painful than Morgandy could ever have dreamed.

A guttural cry sprang from Morgandy's throat before his feet even left the ground. "Nooo!!!!" he howled. But before Morgandy reached his targets, Michael was already tackling him in midair and wrestling him to the ground. He allowed the protective instinct to be in full control. It was as if Michael was outside of his body watching it act. He saw himself crouched over Morgandy, pinning him down. He

saw his webbed hand cover most all of Morgandy's grotesque face and push down hard so the ground underneath
his skull started to crack. He saw a thread of saliva that ran
from his top set of teeth to the bottom vibrate as he spoke.
"Touch either one of them again, and I will kill you." It was
only when he saw that Morgandy believed he was speaking
the truth and not merely issuing an idle threat that Michael
saw his body release its hold on Morgandy and rise. When he
joined the others Ronan didn't have to say a word; Michael
saw the pride and even a little bit of awe flowing from
Ronan's eyes. "Go ahead and say it," Michael allowed, his
features back to the way they were when Ronan first laid
eyes on him.

Ronan smiled and whispered, "That I told you so?"

"Yup."

"No, love," he said. Ronan held Saoirse even closer to him
and kissed Michael softly on the lips. "It's just time for us to
go."

Looking around, Michael saw Morgandy was upright.
Even though he was stealing glances at them, his head was
down and his shoulders hunched. He was one filthy animal
that was retreating from a fight, not looking for another. Still
Michael needed to stay behind. "I'll catch up with you," he
said. "You two could use some brother-sister time anyway."

Unsure, Ronan looked down the alley and saw that Morgandy was gone. He didn't completely understand Michael's
motives, but he knew he'd be okay on his own. "Don't be
long, love. We have to feed."

"I have to speak with Edwige."

As much as Vaughan liked seeing his son, he had a large
ego, so his first impulse was to tell Michael that he should
come back when he had to speak to him as well. Before he
could respond, Edwige interrupted. "I'd like to talk to you as
well."

Outnumbered, Vaughan moved to the side and let his son enter his apartment, closing the door behind him. When it was obvious that no one was going to speak until he left the room he made an exit. "If anyone needs me," Vaughan said unnecessarily, "I'll be in the bedroom."

The first thing Michael noticed when his father left the room was how much better Edwige looked. He imagined it was because her secret was out, because she was no longer in hiding, no longer had to worry about her children finding out about her new alternative lifestyle. Her hair was still jet black, but it wasn't shaggy like the last time he had seen her; it looked like it had been recently cut and styled. And her makeup was the way Michael remembered, not applied with a heavy hand, but dramatic, and her outfit was worthy of a clotheshorse's wardrobe.

She wore a pair of emerald silk pajamas that were like something Michael had seen an actress who played the rich hostess of a house party in an old movie wear. The top resembled a man's buttoned-down shirt, except that the sleeves grew in width from the elbow to the cuff and flowed with the movement of her arm. In contrast, the pants were more form-fitting and cropped at the ankle. Ironically, she had finished off her pajama ensemble with a pair of gold, bejeweled sandals with a heel that Michael thought had to be at least three inches high, maybe four. Guess when you're a short woman you have to create an illusion of height. Sitting next to Edwige, Michael got the sense that that was the only illusion.

"The power of a makeover is remarkable, isn't it?" Edwige commented.

"Well, you do look like your old self," Michael happily agreed. "We were worried there for a while."

"I never meant to frighten any of you," she said, her voice compassionate but strong. "What's the human phrase? I had hit rock bottom."

"Headfirst, I'd say," Michael replied.

Laughing at Michael's honesty, Edwige felt comfortable enough to explain her actions more fully. "I had come to loathe myself and my life, Michael. It was a new and . . . all-consuming feeling," she confessed. "I felt as if I needed to be punished, and so I cast your father in the role of my jailer."

"Did my father keep you here by force?" Michael asked.

"No," Edwige replied firmly. "I possess that other very human characteristic of free will."

Surprisingly, Michael was relieved to know that Edwige's seclusion was self-induced and not a result of Vaughan's machinations. Maybe Brania had been right: His father really wasn't that bad after all. Reading his expression, Edwige concurred. "Vaughan is far from perfect," she said, "but when given the opportunity, he proves himself to be a very good man."

"I'm glad to hear that," Michael replied. "And I'm glad to see that you really look happy to be here."

Edwige didn't hesitate in her response. "I am." She also didn't hesitate to get to the real reason for Michael's visit, now that the air had been cleared.

"You're here to speak to me about Ronan, aren't you?" Edwige asked, knowing full well the answer.

"How did you know that?"

Relaxing into the couch, Edwige smiled. "Despite my re-connection with your father, the strongest connection that we share is our love for Ronan."

Michael surprised himself by blushing. When was the truth going to stop making him act like a little boy? Ah well, maybe that was the secret to love; it kept everyone eternally youthful.

"So tell me," Edwige said. "What could my son possibly have done that would bring you here to the so-called lion's den?"

Taking a deep breath, Michael wasn't really sure how to begin. When he found the words, he realized he needed to whisper so his father didn't overhear. "It's really about Ronan and Saoirse," Michael started, his words causing Edwige to sit upright. "Morgandy's back."

As Michael explained the situation and what had just transpired a few blocks away, the color drained from Edwige's face. Her green blouse began to work against her complexion, creating a dull pallor in her cheeks. When Michael stopped talking, Edwige had one simple request. "Keep him away from my children."

"I plan to," Michael replied. "But I'm not sure if I can do it alone. Morgandy has David on his side. I may need some help."

Edwige understood the question; she hoped Michael would understand the response. "For right now my children are better off without me."

"That isn't true! They need you, Ciaran needs you, and so do I," Michael implored. "We all wish you could just see that so you wouldn't feel so alone."

"But she isn't alone," Vaughan corrected. Silently he had entered the living room, curious as to what his son and his . . . well, whatever label he bestowed upon Edwige—girlfriend, lover, eternal life partner—were talking about or simply because he got bored sitting by himself. When he placed his hand on Edwige's shoulder, she didn't flinch at his touch, but she didn't melt into him, either, the way Michael and Ronan did. She simply remained sitting in the exact same position as if Vaughan wasn't touching her, as if he was somewhere far, far away. "She has me," Vaughan said.

In spite of Edwige's protestations to the contrary, this was a very odd relationship. Even if Michael could have stayed all night to talk through the pros and cons with them, he knew he still wouldn't understand it. He had other things to do anyway.

"I should get going," he announced, getting up, but not moving toward the door.

"I hope you'll come again, son," Vaughan said, not making a move either. "You know the door is always open for you." His next remark proved that, if he wasn't entirely fatherly, at least he was honest. "And perhaps next time you'll want to spend some time chatting with your old man."

It was time for Michael to be just as straightforward. "When I feel like chatting, Dad, you'll be the first to know."

Before Michael could exit on his own, Edwige spoke. "Let me walk you to the door." She grabbed Michael gently by the elbow, fully aware that Vaughan was scrutinizing her actions. At the door she positioned herself so Vaughan could only see her from the back, and when she spoke, she barely made a sound. "You did the right thing telling me about Morgandy. Thank you."

He didn't know if he moved first or if it was Edwige, but suddenly they were hugging. And he was speaking just as softly in her ear, his eyes deliberately avoiding his father's gaze. "We're going to feed."

Edwige knew she was being offered an invitation, but it, unfortunately, was one that she couldn't accept. "And may it be glorious."

Sitting on the shore of Inishtrahull Island, his arms wrapped around Ronan's still wet body, Michael realized Edwige was wrong—their feeding had been more than glorious; it had been the most passionate yet. He supposed it was simply that after the evening they had had, they needed to reclaim their love for each other, acknowledge it, explore it, taste it more deeply than ever before. Smiling before he spoke, Michael was happy this relationship thing was starting to feel completely natural. Things that might have been difficult to express a few months ago were getting easier to share. "I stopped by my father's apartment to speak with your mother," Michael confessed. "I thought she should know about Morgandy."

Not a flicker of disapproval appeared on Ronan's face, only delight. "Crikey, Michael, you really are trying to be the ideal husband, aren't you?"

Holding Ronan closer, inhaling deeply the heat and the ocean that clung to Ronan's body, Michael wasn't sure what he meant. "You have to stop speaking in that literary code of yours, Ro."

Turning to face Michael, Ronan explained himself. "Your relationship with your dad is still pretty baltic, and yet you went there because of me. Thank you."

Now that was about as direct as Michael could hope for. "You're welcome."

Michael wasn't the only one who was hopeful. Far off in the distance, Edwige was watching her son and his boyfriend and cried, quietly but joyfully, as she watched the easy way they held each other. She prayed that their love would last for eternity and that they would never experience the kind of pain she had endured when Saxon was taken from her. She didn't want any of her children to know such inconsolable grief. But she also knew that if it was meant to be, there was absolutely nothing she would be able to do to prevent it.

chapter 20

A new year, a new term, same old practice.

The minute school resumed after the holiday break, Blakeley started drilling the swim team like they were preparing for the Olympics. Swim Team Nationals was a prestigious event, but no matter many how many races Double A students won, no one was going to end up on a box of Wheaties or with a million-dollar endorsement deal. Bragging rights and a keen looking trophy were about all they could hope for, yet Blakeley refused to ease up. Standing on the side of the pool, Ciaran was catching his breath in between heats talking to Ronan who was putting on a pretty good show of looking equally exhausted.

His chest heaving, Ciaran wiped his forehead, not knowing how much of it was water and how much was sweat. "I still can't believe Mum didn't want to spend the holidays with you."

Ronan was bent over, his hands pressed into his knees, watching the water drip off his nose onto the gym floor. "It's her life, mate," he replied. "If she'd rather spend Christmas and ring in the New Year with Michael's father instead of her own children, well, that's her own bloody problem."

Ciaran knew Ronan's offhanded comment was only an attempt to hide his true feelings. No matter what he said, his brother was upset and hurt by their mother's actions. Ciaran, however, was used to being ignored by Edwige and had developed a much thicker skin as well as a self-serving philosophy. "I've resigned myself to the fact that for all intents and purposes I'm an orphan," he said, fully expecting the look of sorrow that spread across Ronan's face. "And don't make that face. You know I'm right."

Ronan held Ciaran's gaze for as long as he could, then shifted to watch a patch of water develop into a puddle on the gym floor. "Well, just 'cause I'm immortal doesn't mean I don't still need my mum," Ronan said quietly. Instantly he realized he didn't sound as flip as he had wanted. It wasn't that he was ashamed to speak so truthfully to his brother; he just didn't feel like having a heart-to-heart in the middle of St. Sebastian's, so before Ciaran could respond, Ronan made sure he got in the next word. "And if you repeat that to anyone, I'll deny it 'til my dying day," he quipped. "Which you know won't be coming round anytime soon."

Yes, Ciaran knew all too well that most of his relatives would outlive him by centuries at the very least. Unless, of course, something about his DNA changed, which he knew was a distinct possibility. Not one that he spent much time dwelling on, but one that offered him solace when he woke up in the middle of the night wondering what his future was going to be like. But at the moment, he didn't want to think about the future. Pressing a towel into his face, Ciaran stifled a sudden laugh when he remembered the recent past. "The only nice thing to come out of Mum's absence was that we all got to spend the holidays together," Ciaran remarked.

"A jolly good time was had by all," Ronan said, smiling and nodding his head in agreement. "I think the best part was seeing you razz up your guts after drinking too much whiskey."

Just the thought of it made Ciaran's head spin all over again. "Don't remind me!" he pleaded. He buried his face in the towel, which was not the wisest thing to do since the towel reeked of bleach and the smell, added to the memory of throwing up, made him cough fiercely. "Damn that Fritz for introducing me to the stuff."

Bending over again, but this time because he was laughing so hard, Ronan said, "I don't think you're supposed to wolf down three helpings of bangers and mash *before* drinking the whole bottle."

Ciaran snapped the towel at Ronan playfully. "I didn't drink the *whole* bottle."

"Well, no, not at once!"

"Aw stuff it," Ciaran said, now laughing just as hard as Ronan.

They could have spent the remainder of the practice session laughing over the dumb things they had done over their break—Ronan singing every single Christmas carol too loudly and disastrously off-key; Michael screwing up his mother's recipe for plum pudding so badly that even the deer in The Forest refused to eat it; or Saoirse, who proved she wasn't completely over Morgandy by making a snowman, putting a curly blond wig on its head, and then decimating her creation with a shovel until it was nothing but a small mound of snow and curls—but then they'd have to deal with Blakeley's wrath, since he didn't consider lollygagging a laughing matter. Like Michael and Fritz, who were sitting in the bleachers taking an unofficial break, were about to.

"You ladies want to have tea or do you want to win Nationals?" Blakeley bellowed.

Just as Fritz opened his mouth to speak, Michael kicked him hard in the shin. "Ow!" Fritz cried, clutching his leg.

Extending his own leg, Michael replied, "Just stretching out a cramp, sir."

Blakeley eyed them suspiciously. He knew they were lying, but they were also two of his best swimmers, so he was willing to cut them some slack the first day back. But just some. "Ya got five minutes," he shouted. "And I don't care if you're cramping so bad you need Dr. Sutton to make a house call. I want you both back in the water."

Still rubbing his leg where Michael had kicked him, Fritz exclaimed, "What'd you do that for?"

"A preventive strike," Michael said. "I know you were about to say that you could go for a spot of Earl Grey."

"Umbrage, Nebraska! I take umbrage!" Fritz protested, acting as if he was highly insulted before breaking out into a huge grin. "I was actually going to ask for a spot of orange pekoe," he clarified. "My grandmum makes it for me with the best homemade scones and clotted cream."

Michael just knew the basics about Fritz's family background, so he wasn't sure if Fritz was joking. "And would that be your grandmum on your German side or your Ethiopian side?"

"Grandmum Zara from Ethiopia," Fritz replied, as if it were the most normal response in the world. Noticing Michael's perplexed expression, Fritz filled in the blanks of his family tree. "She came to England when she was seven and worked as sort of an indentured servant in the house of some duke, at least I think it was a duke." Fritz thought for a moment, but it didn't help; he still couldn't remember. "Well, the bloody chap had some kind of a title, and she went on to become his head chef," Fritz explained. "She wrote a cookbook, and on the day it was published, the duke, or whatever he was, hung himself in the kitchen from one of those hooks they use to hold really big pots, because he had lost his fortune in a poker game."

"That's horrible!"

"For the duke, maybe, not his finest moment, for sure," Fritz granted. "But the timing helped turn Grandmum's book into a bestseller, and she made a couple million pounds."

No reason to be surprised. Of course a character like Fritz would have an ancestor who was just as colorful and entertaining as he was; that was expected. Michael had never expected Fritz to be insightful as well. "So fess up. What's going on with you and Morgandy?"

Startled, Michael wasn't sure how to answer the question. Ever since finding out that Morgandy was both Saoirse's and Ronan's ex-boyfriend and what his true identity was, they had all agreed to keep the complicated matter confidential. Clearly, Fritz had picked up on some of the tension. "Nothing's up between us. I don't even know the guy that well," Michael replied, unconvincingly trying to sound nonchalant.

"Nebraska, you lie!" Fritz accused. "Just like you lied when you told me my idea to give Double P super stretchy arms and legs was brill."

Thankful to be given a topic that would steer them away from Fritz's original question, Michael stomped his foot in a perfect imitation of Saoirse when she didn't get her way. "I did not lie," Michael protested. "I still say rubberized limbs are great powers that any superhero would kill to have." Turns out the idea was also perfect fodder for almost every Double A student seeking revenge on Fritz, the consummate prankster, and wanting to make *him* the butt of a prank for once.

"Tell that to my mum!" Fritz yelled. "I had to listen to her effing and blinding at me for almost a month when she saw all the rubbers everybody sent me."

Recalling the fiasco and the crazy amount of condoms the kids had stuffed in Fritz's schoolbag and flung through his bedroom window, all of which were found by Fritz's mother when she picked him up before the holiday break, Michael laughed harder than ever, stopping only when Fritz reminded him how they had stumbled onto the subject in the first place. "Don't think I forgot," he said smugly. "What's your beef with Morgandy? Did you guys tell him to sod off 'cause he was seeing Saoirse on the sly?"

Suddenly, laughing was the furthest thing from Michael's mind. He had to think. If Fritz knew about Morgandy's involvement with Saoirse, what else did he know about the guy? Unable to focus, Michael glanced across the gym and saw Morgandy chatting with Alexei and wished he could use his enhanced hearing to listen to what they were saying to each other instead of continuing his conversation with Fritz. But he didn't want to give his friend any more reason to be suspicious. "Where'd you hear that?"

"My girl, Ruby, told me," Fritz replied, deliberately putting extra emphasis on Ruby's name.

"Your girl?"

"That's right," Fritz declared. "You're not the only one with a love life, Nebraska."

As much as Michael was happy that Fritz was experiencing what it felt like to be romantically involved with someone, he couldn't give the relationship his blessing; he knew too much, about Ruby and about the other girl in Fritz's life. "That's great," Michael said, hoping he sounded more enthusiastic than he felt. "I just wish, you know, that things could've worked out between you and Phaedra."

Surprisingly, Fritz didn't make a joke or come back with a quick retort. He simply responded to Michael's observation honestly. "So do I, mate, but what's the bloody phrase? Just not meant to be."

Staring at Morgandy and then at Ronan, Michael was

thrilled that in their case that cliché had been accurate. If not, well, Michael didn't want to think about that.

"Maybe he'll just up and drop out too."

"Who?" Michael asked, not sure who Fritz was talking about.

"Morgandy," Fritz clarified, his voice a conspiratorial whisper. "The Swede Saoirse was sweet on."

Something else that Michael felt wasn't meant to be. David had brought Morgandy here for a reason. There was no way he was going to send him on his way or ship him off to another school because things hadn't worked out between him and Saoirse. No, as much as Michael would like it, as relieved as he would be, Morgandy definitely was staying put. Fritz wasn't as confident, and he really had good reason. "Give him some time, and he'll up and leave like all the rest," Fritz said. "Phaedra, Imogene, Hawksbry, Doc MacCleery. Even Diego—no one's seen the bloke since before that daft holiday of yours."

"Christmas isn't exclusively American."

"No, the other one," Fritz replied. "Where you hoodwinked the Indians and stole their land."

"Thanksgiving?"

"That's the one," Fritz said. "Don't know why you're all so bloomin' proud of yourselves over that coup. You stole their land you know."

"Oh, and the Brits never stole land that wasn't theirs?"

Smiling and leaning back into the bleachers, Fritz responded, "We did it for Her Majesty. You did it for corn on the cob."

"You're a lunatic, Fritz!"

Tilting his head in acknowledgment of Michael's praise, Fritz switched topics yet again. "Perhaps I am," he said. "But if I were in charge of this school, no one would ever go missing."

If only Fritz or anyone could ever have that power.

"Really?" Michael asked. "And how would you prevent that?"

"I'd inject every one of us with a GPS device, so when somebody goes missing, the headmaster'll be able to track 'em down." Fritz slapped Michael so hard on the back he actually felt the sting for a few seconds. "What a corking issue that would make!" Fritz exclaimed. "Double A turns out to be built on a bloody wormhole and more people start vanishing from the school than in a missing person's unit."

Little did both Michael and Fritz know that not all missing persons remained missing.

When Blakeley's whistle blew, Nakano jumped. When Blakeley announced that he wanted the A Team of Ronan, Michael, Morgandy, and Fritz to practice the four-man relay, he sat back down. When Blakeley stood with his back to the windows that opened out to The Forest and Imogene materialized behind him, Nakano ran out the side door.

Lucky for them Blakeley was fixated on watching the technique of his starting team and Kano could run faster than most people could blink, so he wasn't seen by anyone leaving the gym. He was, however, seen by someone entering The Forest.

"Get away from me, you murderer!" Imogene cried.

"Are you completely off your trolley?!" Nakano shouted back.

Imogene was furious that Nakano was ruining her excursion. When Brania had raised her hand to slap her, Imogene took the opportunity to fade out of that claustrophobic cave and fade into one of the places that had brought her so much joy when she was alive: St. Sebastian's.

"Nobody can see me unless I'm in that bloody cave!" she yelled. "And if somebody does . . . well, I'll just tell them I've decided to come back to school."

The verdict was in, and the jury had found Imogene to be

insane. Crouching behind some wild brush so he wouldn't be seen, Nakano tried to empathize with her plight and calmly talk sense into the girl, but failed miserably. "You're a walking corpse! A bloody ghost girl!" he shouted. "If you *can* be seen, you can't just tell people you got bored and decided to come back to school!"

"And you can't tell me what to do!"

The second Nakano ran forward, he knew what was going to happen, but he had no choice. Imogene wasn't listening to him, and it was clear that she wasn't going to take cover, move out of the line of vision of everyone in St. Sebastian's on her own. If she hung around in front of the windows much longer, there was a chance that someone would see her, and there was no way she was going to explain her whereabouts the past year or why she had chosen to return without winding up in a loony bin somewhere. Or worse, exposing the countless secrets she knew. No, Nakano had one choice: to grab her and drag her back to the cave. Unfortunately, when he ran toward Imogene, she had a foolproof defense. She disappeared.

Despite her unique talent, Imogene was predictable, and it didn't take a genius to figure out that she would return to the cave. She could only disappear when she felt frightened, she could wander around a bit on her own, but inevitably she would have to return home, to the cave. When Nakano burst into the hidden enclave, Imogene sounded anything but peaceful.

Standing in the center of her coffin, Imogene screamed, "When are we going to explore the world like you promised?!"

He almost didn't see Brania because she was sitting in the far corner on the floor, her legs crossed in a meditative position. Her weary expression made Nakano think she wished she possessed Imogene's migratory skills so she could evaporate and reappear anywhere else but here. "We *are* going to travel, Imogene," Brania said, her voice brimming with exasperation. "But not until our work is done."

"I don't have any work to do!" Imogene shouted as she began to pace the length of the casket, back and forth, back and forth, stomp, stomp, stomp. "All I do is sing! Well, I'm tired of singing, and I'm tired of listening to you!"

"Looks like shacking up in a cave ain't all it's cracked up to be," Kano joked. He was sitting on one of the largest boulders in the room, leaning forward, his chin resting in his palms as if he were watching the final scene in a riveting play. "How will it all end? Will the ghost girl disappear for parts unknown or will vampire lady be able to restore peace to her rocky kingdom?"

Nakano was so amused with himself he didn't even care that Brania looked like she wanted to tear his throat apart with her bare fangs. "Rocky! Get it?" he asked.

Ignoring Nakano, Brania walked toward the coffin, smiling compassionately. When she spoke Nakano realized she had decided to play the role of doting mother. "You don't have to listen to me, Imogene," Brania said softly. "But I wish you would."

Instead of being soothed by Brania's placation, the girl was incensed, stopping in mid-pace to whirl around and hurl an ultimatum at her keeper. "I will if you stop seeing that red-haired girl. She was my friend first!"

Brania gripped the side of the casket and felt the metal rim cut into her flesh. How dare someone as lowly as Imogene give her an order? Imogene was her subject, not the other way around. This was what happened when you showed someone tenderness, sympathy, and love. They turned on you and used your feelings to their advantage. If that's the game Imogene wanted to play, then she should be prepared to lose, because no one was a better manipulator than Brania. "Imogene, darling, there's no reason for you to be jealous of Ruby," Brania said. "You're my firstborn, my dearest, and that will never, ever change."

One layer of armor fell from Imogene's slender frame, and the girl's features softened, her entire body relaxed. "You promise you're telling me the truth?"

Climbing inside the coffin so she could hold Imogene close to her heart, Brania replied, "Of course it's the truth. A mother would never lie to her child."

Nakano only clapped his hands twice in applause before Brania's stare made him stop. She needed Imogene to be obedient in order for her plan to find the location of The Well to succeed, so she had to assuage her ruffled feathers. Nakano, while useful, wasn't vital, so she could pluck out his feathers one vindictive yank at a time. "Why don't you keep your hair short Nakano?" Brania suggested. "You really don't have the bone structure to wear it long."

Bitch! Why do I fall for it every time? Why do I always think that she's my friend and that I can trust her and then have to listen to her make a nasty comment? Wasn't I the one who found that idiot near the gym? Wasn't I the one who tried to get Imogene off of public display? When is somebody going to thank me instead of giving me grief all the time?! Thought after thought, rant after rant, bounced around Nakano's head. David, Jean-Paul, Brania, Imogene, he was done with all of them. They could burn in hell for all he cared!

The enthralling smell of blood and rotting flesh distracted him for a second, intoxicated him, and set him running off in the opposite direction, away from Double A and further into the dense, rarely traveled portion of The Forest. The smell was making him hungry, so why not feed early. Who needs to wait until sundown? He could make his own rules and explore new territory at the same time. Take that, Imogene!

The delicious scent was getting more pungent with each step he took. He breathed in deeper, deeper, deeper as he ran until the bouquet of decay mixed with blood consumed his lungs. He had no idea what he was going to find to be the source of the aroma; he didn't even waste the energy to speculate, because whatever it was, it was making him weak. So weak that when he reached Diego's corpse, he fell to his knees.

Half of his classmate's face was gone, eaten, devoured by the hordes of hungry animals that populated this area of The Forest, revealing bits of skull and mutilated muscle that were now a playground for maggots. The other half was eerily undamaged as if left there as a reminder of what the boy had once looked like. Nakano had never noticed that Diego had a birthmark below his right eye that looked very much like a six-pointed star. The rest of his body was twisted into odd, inhuman positions, and Nakano didn't know if that was the result of the initial struggle that killed him or from being out here exposed to the elements and vulnerable to predators. Diego had last been seen in November, so he had been lying here for at least three months. Nakano hoped that he had spent most all of that time dead.

Instinctively, Kano looked at Diego's neck for signs that he had been the victim of a vampire killing, but the portion of his neck that hadn't been eaten away was unbruised. He thought there might be the possibility that Diego had been killed by less supernatural means until he saw his fingers.

What remained of his left arm was outstretched, and the two fingers that were still attached to his badly decomposed hand were lying in a pool of blood surrounded by dirt and snow. Leaning forward on his hands and knees, Nakano saw that within the concoction of natural elements was a word— *the*—that he imagined Diego had written as a message while he lay dying. But *the* what? What in the world could it mean? If he was going to try and communicate from beyond the grave, why would he choose such a common word? Why not write something specific, something that had meaning? Nakano gasped out loud when the inspiration came to him. If the word didn't hold any meaning, perhaps the blood that wrote the word did.

Lowering his body so his face was inches from Diego's blood-encrypted message, Nakano opened his mouth and traced the letters with his long, slender tongue. By the time his tongue rounded the curve in the letter *e*, Nakano realized his inspiration had real consequence. He was no longer living in the present, but was hurtled back in time and was witnessing Diego's death.

It was as if he were within Diego's body, traveling as a passenger, as the boy ran wildly into the thick brush, tripping over unearthed rocks and running into low-hanging branches, his breath coming in quick, fearful gasps. When Diego turned around to look behind him, face whatever was running after him, hunting him down, Nakano understood what word Diego had been trying to convey. His message wasn't complete; he died before he finished it. He didn't want to use his blood to trace the word *the*. He was trying to spell out *theology*.

As if looking out from behind Diego's panicked eyes, Nakano saw Professor Joubert and Jean-Paul racing after him, their faces transformed, fangs displayed, and gaining speed with every step. They had no intention of letting their prey get away. But why were they chasing after him in the first place? What could Diego have possibly done to provoke such an attack?

When Diego's body tumbled, Nakano felt as if his own bones hit the earth. He wasn't certain if he was in the past or the present until he felt a hand turn him over violently and he was staring up at Jean-Paul's face. "That weel teach you not to spy on your professors."

"I . . . I wa-wasn't sp-spying," Diego stuttered, fear making him incapable of speaking clearly. "I . . . I . . . j-just wa-wanted to sp-speak t-t-to Professor Jou-Jou-Joubert."

Jean-Paul pressed his knees harder into Diego's shoulders, and Nakano felt the pain. "Then thees eez your lucky day," Jean-Paul declared. "Because Professor Jou-Jou-Joubert eez right 'ere."

Nakano had to look hard to connect the face he was staring at with the face that he saw every day in Theology class. Very little was the same. But when he looked into the professor's eyes, even though they were glassy and tinged with a yellow hue, they were filled with pity. Whatever he was about to do, he was going to do it reluctantly. "Diego, you shouldn't have followed me," he said. "You shouldn't have come upon us when we were feeding."

The vision started to blur when the tears escaped from Diego's eyes. "P-p-please, sir," was all Diego could say until he could catch his breath. And then he begged. "Please don't hurt me."

There was silence, not a sound was heard. It was as if the entire world were waiting to hear how Professor Joubert would respond. Even Nakano, who knew the outcome, knew how the scene inevitably played out, held his breath hoping that the past could be rewritten. It couldn't. "I'm sorry, Diego," Joubert replied, his voice filled with as much kindness as possible. "I can't let you live after what you've seen."

"You c-c-an make me l-l-like you," Diego said.

In spite of what he knew, Nakano was filled with a ray of hope and even pride. Fuente wasn't as dumb as he had always thought. Pinned to the ground, looking up into the face of a vampire, an extraordinary creature he had probably never imagined truly existed, Diego had the quick sense to bargain for his life. Joubert looked impressed as well and, yes, thankful that his student had given him an option to avoid outright murder. But Jean-Paul thought differently.

"Gwendal," Jean-Paul said, pushing the professor aside. "Look at heem. We do not need a fat, ugly peeg to join our ranks."

It was at that moment that Diego knew his life was over. Nakano's body twisted as Diego tried to free himself from underneath the weight of the two men. He tried to form words, attempt another tactic, but each time he seemed to give up before he began. After a few seconds, Diego had given up all hope. His body stopped moving, and something died within Nakano's heart. He couldn't believe how palpable the fear was that was consuming Diego, and he couldn't believe how evil the hatred was that flowed through Jean-Paul's veins.

"Let's use theese fat peeg for dessert," Jean-Paul said, his voice erupting into a cruel laugh, which only ended when he buried his fangs into Diego's neck and took every drop of blood his body could digest.

Somehow Diego clung onto life as he watched the two men walk away, Jean-Paul strutting off as if he had just bedded another conquest, Joubert's tall frame hunched over, moving like a man who had given in to a vice he so desperately tried to resist. Nakano wanted the vision to stop; he had seen enough. But Diego was still alive, still trying to communicate with whoever would find his body. Nakano thought he felt his own tears race down his cheeks when he realized Diego was acting the same way he always did in class, refusing to give up. Which is exactly what the boy had done until all life drifted from him.

Diego's soul floated up and through Nakano's body. It was like feeling goodness, but not being able to hold onto it. Nakano knew that sensation, and the vision would haunt him forever. Not only had he witnessed a senseless murder, not only had he seen how evil the man he had once loved could actually be, but he finally understood what he had done to Penry. And he knew because of that one horrific, misguided act, he would never be worthy of forgiveness.

chapter 21

Saoirse was bored. Ever since she had broken up with Morgandy her life just wasn't as interesting. There were no more secret dates, no more rendezvous in the middle of the day, no more chances to test herself, to find out just how far she was willing to let herself go when the two of them were alone in her dorm room. All of that was gone; all of that was ruined because Morgandy wasn't just a secret boyfriend, he was also a lying boyfriend. On top of all that he had also been her brother's boyfriend. Like Saoirse said, it was "goppin' disgusting."

It didn't matter that Morgandy couldn't remember anything about Ronan, that he didn't have a trace of memory of the time they had spent together as a couple, as soul mates. He was still a liar. Morgandy might not remember the facts about that time of his life, all the little details and events that made up his daily existence, but there was no way that Saoirse was going to believe that he could forget his feelings, the ones that told him he was gay or that he was duplicitous enough to betray someone he professed to love. That's who Morgandy was, and that's why Saoirse couldn't forgive him no matter how desperately she wanted to.

Before his memories were taken from him and scattered to points that were just out of his grasp, Morgandy had made choices. Some were natural, like choosing to honor his true self and spend the rest of his life with Ronan, another guy. Others were unnatural, like choosing to betray Ronan's love and destroy The Well and the entire race of water vampires along with it. Why'd he have to be such a jerk?! Sure it would have been weird to continue to date him knowing that he had previously romanced her brother, but Saoirse was willing to accept the fact that Morgandy had fallen in love with her despite her gender. But how to get past his quest for, what was the technical word? Oh yeah, *genocide.*

When she had first learned of his outrageous plot, of course, she flipped out. Her brother, her mother, so many of the people she had known as a little girl were water vampires. She wasn't one hundred percent sure, no one really was, but if The Well were ever destroyed, the chances were pretty darn good that they would be destroyed too. And destroyed as in killed, gone forever. The surprising thing, though, was how personally she was affected. She had been surrounded by water vampires her entire life, but never considered herself part of their race. Until now.

Sitting in St. Albert's lab, she had a wicked revelation: maybe she was just like Morgandy. Not that she craved super mass destruction, but maybe facts didn't matter; only intangibles were important. Maybe the truth about her unlikely entry into this world, about why she was physically one of a kind, would never be uncovered by gathering scientific data or conducting experiments just like she may never know why Morgandy was this wannabe mass murderer. All she really needed to know about herself was that despite being human, she was an honorary member of an inhuman race. Made sense to her.

"Ciaran," Saoirse said, taking a sip of her hot chocolate. "Don't hit me with a test tube, but I think I'm done with all this experimentation stuff."

Looking into his microscope at a swirling mass of red and yellow gunk that seemed to pulsate and change shape every few seconds, Ciaran wasn't surprised by Saoirse's comment. He knew she was growing impatient. She was just like David, just like most everyone else. No one shared Ciaran's love for research; they were only interested in results. What they didn't understand was that results took time, perseverance, and sometimes, in some cases, results never came. Research sometimes produced even more questions that needed to be examined further. In some instances, however, all that hard work and patience paid off. "Well, if that's what you really want."

Now just hold on for a second! Something about the way Ciaran sounded, something about his too-casual tone didn't sound right. Could he have found something out? Something important? "Well, it's not what I really want," she protested. "But you know this whole affair, well non-affair with Morgandy, has kind of got me permanently narked, and I am a girl, if you haven't noticed, and I want to have some fun."

The red and yellow gunk shifted in shape again, becoming a slender oval. "Don't know what you expected from a guy whose nickname is Morgue."

"I didn't expect him to be one of Them," Saoirse replied, flicking some whipped cream at Ciaran that fell short of hitting its target and fell to the floor. "And I didn't expect you to *not* be able to find out why I'm a human born to two vampires. Honestly, I thought you would've come up with something by now." She waited for Ciaran to look at her, but evidently his specimen was more interesting than his sister. "I mean I really do want to know why I'm this misfit, so if you found something in your tests, tell me."

Scribbling in his notebook, Ciaran didn't even look up when he spoke. His voice the same flat monotone as before, he said, "You're special."

"Zzzzz, yesterday's news," Saoirse said, licking a chunk of whipped cream off of her finger that she had scooped out from the top of her drink. "But blimey, maybe I'm just supposed to be this mystery that, you know, can't be figured out."

Almost under his breath, Ciaran muttered, "Well, I have figured *something* out."

Saoirse almost snorted whipped cream through her nose. "You did?!" she exclaimed. "When were you going to tell me, ya dumbarse?"

Now that he had his sister's full attention and interest, Ciaran finally raised his head from his work and faced Saoirse. "I wanted to make sure I completely understood my findings before I said anything."

"I don't care if you don't completely understand it!" Saoirse shouted. "Tell me what you found!"

Ignoring her outburst, Ciaran continued speaking as if he were a lecturer who had unexpectedly found himself with a captive audience. "Before making any sort of announcement, a good scientist always repeats his experiments several times to make sure he comes up with the same result," he replied. "The most disappointing thing in the world is to find out that you have a false positive."

"No, Ciar, the most disappointing thing in the world is to find out your boyfriend is an amnesiac who shagged your brother," she declared. "Now tell me what you know or I swear to God I'll start breaking things!"

If Ciaran hadn't believed his sister would follow through on her threat, he would've laughed. Instead he disclosed his scientific findings. "I've isolated an unknown gene that I found in your blood."

"Unknown?"

"Yes, unknown."

Saoirse took another sip of hot chocolate. She wasn't thirsty; she was merely trying to collect her thoughts, take a moment to see if this news was as incredible as she thought it might be. "So what you're saying is that it's something that can't be found in any of those really big books you read all the time?"

"Correctomundo!" Ciaran loved when his work sparked curiosity in someone else, when his findings piqued another person's interest and for a moment they shared a common bond. It was nice not to be alone in his own fascination even if that other person was only fascinated by her own celebrity.

"So that means I'm the only person in the world to have this unknown gene?" Saoirse reasoned. The way she posed the question it was clear that any response other than "yes" would greatly disappoint her. Unfortunately, Ciaran had to do just that.

"No."

Outraged, Saoirse felt as if Ciaran had slapped her in the face just as Morgandy had. Why was nothing turning out the way she wanted it to? Boys totally sucked. All they did was play games. "What do you mean 'no'?!"

"The gene is unknown to the scientific world," Ciaran explained. "But you're not the only person who has it."

"Which doesn't make any sense!" Saoirse cried, slamming her mug onto the countertop.

So much for trying to create an air of intrigue. If Saoirse just wanted the bottom line, well, then that's what Ciaran would give her. "I found the same gene in Michael's blood."

Disregarding the complex ramifications of this discovery or the physiological randomness that she and Michael could both possess the same scientific anomaly, all Saoirse could think about was how cool it was that she and Michael were somehow linked. She really liked her brother's boyfriend and was thrilled that they had grown close this past year and that Michael had become more like her sibling than just her friend. How wild that they might be even closer than anyone had ever imagined! Maybe science wasn't all boring, complicated experiments after all. "So tell me more about this unknown gene."

It worked. Ciaran had hoped Saoirse's interest would skyrocket when he mentioned Michael's name. He had done what every smart scientist did who wanted to create excitement about his discovery; he had made his findings personal. He hoped to make them irresistible as well. "It's water-based, so I call it Atlantium."

"Oooh Atlantium," she cooed. "That's brill!"

Now that it was clear that Saoirse was as excited as he was, Ciaran didn't have to hide his true emotions. "It gets even more brilliant." He pulled out a small metal box from the cabinet drawer and placed it on the countertop. Unlocking it, Ciaran turned it around so Saoirse could see what was inside. "These are all the samples of your blood that I've taken."

Resting on her elbows, Saoirse peered into the box as if she were fawning over a particularly fine piece of jewelry. "And all of that contains the mysterious Atlantium?"

"No."

"What do you mean no?" she snapped. "Ciaran, you're really starting to tick me off! You just said . . ."

"I said that I found the gene in a sample," Ciaran interrupted. "I didn't say that I found it in every sample."

Saoirse scrutinized her brother to see if he was testing her.

She would never become a scientist, but even she knew his statement sounded wrong. "Doesn't that like defy the laws of nature?"

"Completely," Ciaran said, a bit surprised that Saoirse had gotten it so quickly. "It makes absolutely no sense at all. It goes against the human physical composition," he said, unable to control his enthusiasm. "Every sample of a person's blood should be the same; it should all carry the same DNA and genetic breakdown." He pushed the box closer to Saoirse and waved his hand over it like he was conducting a magic act. "Yours doesn't."

Ciaran might be smiling, but how could this possibly be good news? Yes, Saoirse had always known she was different, a freak, but all the people around her—the vampires, water vamps, efemeras—they were all a little freaky too, so what did it matter? In the grand scheme of things she was a lot more normal than they were, and she had always found comfort in knowing that she was human. Now her brother had uncovered confirmation, proof, that she might not be that human after all. She wasn't just an honorary member of an inhuman race; she might very well be their missing link. "So what does all this mean?" she asked, not certain she wanted to know the answer.

Ciaran hated being vague, but he had no other choice. "I don't know yet."

"You have to know!" Saoirse screamed, slamming her mug onto the table once more. "You're a lab rat. This is what you do!"

Quickly, Ciaran closed the metal box and returned it to its storage, worried that it would be doused in Saoirse's drink if she got any more excited. "What do you think I've *been* doing?! Running tests, retesting, comparing your blood to that of other species."

"And what did you find?!"

"There's no evidence of Atlantium in my blood or even in Ronan's, but I found traces of it in all of the samples of Michael's blood that I've been able to examine. Every one of them is the same."

"Unlike mine," Saoirse said.

"Yes, unlike yours," Ciaran confirmed. "But don't you see how bloody amazing that is?!"

He just didn't get it. "No, Ciar, I don't," Saoirse replied. "And amazing is not exactly the word I'd use to describe what's going on inside of me."

She just didn't get it. "Saoirse, it's like your blood, your physiological makeup, is constantly changing!" Ciaran beamed. "Almost like it's vibrating on a level no other human being has ever reached, vibrating like I've heard Ronan say The Well vibrates. So I don't care what you think, but that's bloody amazing!"

If Saoirse had wanted to be special, if she had wanted to be some sort of abnormal legend, she would have been happy to hear what Ciaran was telling her; she would have embraced it. She would revel in the fact that she was like Phaedra and her mother and all the others and wear her badge of inhumanity with pride. But it wasn't what she wanted. Ever since she had come to St. Anne's and especially since she had started dating Morgandy, all she wanted to be was normal. She wanted to be average. She wanted to go to school without worrying that people were staring at her or wondering if they could turn her into their kind of vampire or use her as a living specimen to uncover the unknown. Unfortunately, she also knew from experience that you could not escape who you are or what you were supposed to be.

"I don't understand it in its entirety, but I believe Atlantium is what connects you and Michael to The Well," Ciaran said, his voice positively reverential. "And somehow this gene is what links The Well to the human world."

" 'Scuse me, Science Boy, but that's fanciful talk, don't ya think?" Saoirse quipped.

"When you're presented with facts that make no logical sense," Ciaran replied, "the next logical step is to think illogically."

Gulping down the rest of her hot chocolate, Saoirse hoped the warmth would make her feel better, like she had no troubles. Concentrate on the sweet mixture of cream and cocoa and let it trick her into thinking they were just chatting about the nonsensical stuff siblings are supposed to talk about and not genetic anomalies and interspecies correlations. It actually worked, until Ciaran completed his thought. "I think you and Michael are somehow destined to play important roles in the world of all water vamps," Ciaran said, "as well as in the future of The Well itself."

Saoirse stared at Ciaran for quite some time, and she only replied when it was clear that he was serious. "You have got to be kidding me, boyo."

Ciaran couldn't help but laugh at his sister's reaction. "I know it sounds daft," he admitted. "But I'm convinced the only way to decipher why you are what you are is to think beyond science."

Giving her hair a good, arrogant flip, Saoirse replied, "And belly flop smack dab into the middle of science fiction."

It was time for Ciaran to play the game by his sister's rules, time to act bored and disinterested instead of charged up like he really was. Bit by bit he started to put away his paraphernalia, and never once did he look Saoirse in the eye. "Be cheeky and call it what you want, science fiction, fantasy, whatever," Ciaran said. "All I know is your body negates scientific fact in a way I've never seen before, and it's my expert opinion—and we all know I'm an expert in these things— that the answer lies outside of the box so to speak." He knew by Saoirse's silence that he was starting to make sense to her, so he wrapped up his summation as succinctly and, hopefully, as enticingly, as possible. "And right inside that little round Well of theirs."

After a few moments of silent deliberation, Saoirse figured she had come this far, why not take it a few steps further, even if she suspected her brother was leading her by the hand directly into Barmyland. "Fine, but no more needles."

Ciaran resisted the urge to hug Saoirse and swing her around the room and fought hard to maintain his blasé composure. "I'll only need to draw one more sample of blood."

"One more and that's it! I feel like I'm cutting myself all over again and not getting any of the attention!" Saoirse screamed, rubbing her hand over her forearm as if she was soothing a sudden pain.

"Since there's no way we can get to The Well, the next test will be conducted at the pool at St. Sebastian's," Ciaran explained. "It's a long shot, but I want to test your blood to see how it reacts after your body's been in a pool of water."

Could this get any worse?! "Blimey, Ciar! The chlorine'll turn my hair green!" Saoirse shouted.

Laughing at his sister's priorities, Ciaran remembered that she might be a rare, uncommon individual, but she was still a teenage girl. And he wasn't against using that fact in his favor. "Morgandy is still on the swim team, remember?"

El Disgusto, Morgandy van der Liar, on the swim team? Who cared? Saoirse did. Despite everything she felt about her ex, whenever she had a daydream, she just couldn't help herself and cast him in the leading role. It might be nice to accidentally bump into him at the pool and see him in his skimpy bathing suit, his curls plastered wet against his forehead. She wouldn't talk to him, of course, never, not again. Why give him a chance to spew more lies? But it would be nice to look at him. And if she were standing there in her own revealing bikini, like maybe the blue-and-white-striped one that she totally rocked, she could show him what he was missing. No matter what kind of results the test produced, Saoirse thought it was what business people called a win-win situation. "Never let it be said that Saoirse Glynn-Rowley stood in the way of scientific progress."

Taking that as a yes, Ciaran finally let his true emotions break through his deadpan veneer. "You won't regret this, Seersh!" Hugging Saoirse tightly and swinging her in circle after circle after circle, he couldn't believe that he was one step closer to finding out the truth about his sister. He was even closer to finding out the truth about himself.

Once Saoirse agreed to the next phase of the experimentation, Ciaran felt the strong desire, a compulsion really, to inform David that his plan was moving forward. It made no sense. He knew David was manipulating him, he knew that David wanted to use the information from his research to destroy instead of enhance, and yet all Ciaran wanted to do was make sure the headmaster knew that he had put his trust in the right person and that Ciaran could deliver as promised. The more Ciaran tried to fight against going to see David, the quicker he ran.

Taking a shortcut from St. Albert's, Ciaran came around the back of David's office. There was only a light dusting of snow on the ground, so while his footprints were recorded, they made no sound. Just as he was about to turn the corner and move along the front of the building, where he'd be in plain sight of anyone entering or exiting the Archangel Academy gate, Ciaran noticed something strange partially buried in the snow.

He bent down and saw a black feather, jutting out from a mound of white powder. Not that strange, but for some reason he was drawn to inspect it further. Picking it up he expected it to be an inch or two in length, probably a loose feather from a crow's wing. He never expected it to be several feet in length and almost a foot wide. The thing was huge and had definitely not fallen from a crow.

Tracing his fingers along one side of the feather, Ciaran couldn't believe how soft it was to the touch. It couldn't possibly be real; it had to be fake, part of a costume, part of somebody's get up for the Tri-Centennial Celebration. That's what he thought until he saw the dried droplets of blood clinging to the edges near the end of the feather, the part that had once nestled against skin. Whatever creature this feather had once belonged to had been in a fight.

Ciaran look around to see if the bird was nearby, but he couldn't see anything on the ground except snow. He was about to start digging to see if the animal or its nest had been covered by the snowfall, but his curiosity was interrupted by voices. Looking up he realized he was crouched just below a window, and the voices were coming from David's office. He was still curious, but no longer about the bird and its lost feather.

"Why didn't you tell me that Ronan was my ... my ..." Morgandy stuttered, his voice travelling in an angry staccato rhythm just over Ciaran's head.

"I believe the word you're choking on is *boyfriend*," David replied.

Was that David? His voice was off. Maybe it was because Ciaran wasn't looking him in the eyes, he wasn't in his magnetic presence, so he could hear the sound for what it truly was. It wasn't that different; it was still deep, commanding, imperious, but underneath all that was something Ciaran had never noticed before: anxiety. David didn't sound like he was upset with Morgandy. It was more like he was gravely concerned about something else. Ciaran knew that he would only be able to determine what it truly meant if he continued to listen.

"And I didn't tell you because it wasn't necessary for you to know," David replied. There it was again. His voice was a little strained, the cadence of his speech a little quicker than normal. The headmaster might be addressing Morgandy, but there was someone else on his mind.

"Not necessary?!" Morgandy cried. "This is my life you're talking about! I have every right to know, and it wasn't your decision to make!"

Whoa! Morgandy must be certifiable. Nobody talked to David like that, not without serious repercussions. It took a few seconds, but it came. Ciaran heard the sound before he saw the silver decanter crash through the window, and he had just enough time to raise his arms to shield his face and eyes before the shards of glass started to shower down upon him.

While flying through the air, the decanter twirled on its side, and just as it began its descent the top detached from the long, swan-like neck and flew in the opposite direction, landing near the entrance to The Forest. The decanter itself continued to twist in the air, its contents spilling out from its spout like a lasso of blood. Crimson drops decorated the side of the building, the snow, even Ciaran's body until the decanter finally landed on an embankment, blood pouring from its mouth, turning the snow pink, and burrowing into the hungry earth.

Then there was silence, no sound, no voices, nothing. Ciaran stood still so he wouldn't make a noise, wouldn't step on a piece of glass from the shattered window. He saw that his jacket and hands were speckled with blood, but even in his frozen position he was able to see that he hadn't been cut. That was a relief. Then again maybe not. With two vampires a few feet away, he wasn't exactly comforted to know that he was stained with blood. Ciaran's discomfort only grew when David spoke again and he noticed that the timbre of his voice was even more unrecognizable. What the hell was wrong with the headmaster?

"Your past was destroyed by the cruel hands of time," David growled. "And time is an evil mistress! She lurks, she waits, but she never disappears! Never! She always comes back, and she always comes back wanting revenge!"

Time is an evil mistress out for revenge? David must be reading one of Ronan's potboilers.

"What the hell are you talking about?" Morgandy asked, rather impudently. "Time had nothing to do with my losing my memory. It was taken from me by that Well."

Another eerie silence passed, and Ciaran imagined that David was either searching for the right word or something else to fling out the window. "Yes, yes, of course, I know that The Well has been cruel to you," David rambled.

"And so have you."

Oh okay. Now Ciaran understood. Morgandy was a vampire with a death wish. Why else would he keep attacking David if he didn't want him to strike back? How stupid could he be? Didn't he know how powerful David was, how incredibly strong, unpredictable, and evil? If all that was true—and Ciaran knew that it was—then wasn't he even stupider than Morgandy? The urge to flee, to run back to the safety of St. Albert's, was overwhelming, but no, he must have come here for a reason. *That's right, Ciaran, treat this like a routine experiment, wait it out, wait for the result, and maybe you'll finally be able to comprehend what is happening.*

"How dare you speak to me in that tone!" David bellowed.

"Then don't talk to me like I'm a fool! Like I'm some *human!!*" Morgandy spat back, his voice even deeper and more repugnant than David's. "You told me when you found me wandering through the back alleys of London, filthy, alone, feasting on sewer rats to stay alive that you were my salvation!"

"I am your salvation," David whispered, his voice hoarse, strained like it was about to snap.

"Then start acting like it!" Morgandy howled. "Stop forcing me to take on these stupid roles.... Saoirse's boyfriend, where did that get me? Nothing but a waste of time."

"Do not question me!"

Ciaran seriously thought he was going to have a heart attack. Or a stroke. Or be killed. David was breathing so heavily that when Ciaran looked up he was certain that he would find David gazing down at him from the window, but no one was there. Even still Ciaran could hear David panting, struggling to control his breathing. Was this the real David? A frightened man instead of a frightening ruler?

"I'm not an idiot, David! I know that you didn't stumble upon me in London accidentally," Morgandy stated. "I know that somehow we were partners before that damned Well wiped my memory clean. Why don't you just admit it?!"

This time when Ciaran heard the crash he knew nothing was going to fly out the window because he felt the side of the building shake. Whatever David had hurled against the wall, it hit low to the floor, and the vibration sent Ciaran heaving forward, his hands slamming into the ground, a jagged piece of glass piercing the fleshy part of his left hand between his forefinger and his thumb. "Ahhh!" Ciaran cried. The only thing that saved him from being heard was that David cried even louder.

"YES!!! We were working together!" David admitted, his voice positively tremulous. "You were destined to be The Guardian of The Well, but you were also destined to be its destroyer."

"So you used me," Morgandy replied, his tone more a statement than a question.

"I guided you *after* you came to me!" David corrected. "*After* you begged me for my help! We are kindred spirits, you and I, of the same mind, and so few . . . SO FEW understand our desire, our destiny!"

"Then let's destroy it once and for all!" Morgandy shouted.

"It will be destroyed!" David declared. "Together our ranks will find The Well, obliterate it, and celebrate the end of all water vampires!"

Ciaran couldn't stop shaking. None of this was new, not really, so then why was he acting as if he was learning it for the first time? Sure, hearing Morgandy possessed with vengeance was startling, but Ciaran had known what David's intentions were all along, and until now he had been willing to help him with his plan. Mouth agape, he fell back against the cold stone wall. *What in God's name am I doing?*

Then it hit him. He was finally, *finally,* breaking free from David's hold over him. Hearing David speak, hearing only his words and his rage, but not being in his hypnotic trance, made Ciaran hear for the first time how barbaric and irreversible his message was. Horrified and ashamed, Ciaran clutched his head with his hands. He was no better than David; he was just as sick and cruel. How could he ever have considered working with David? How could he ever have agreed to hand over his research, his results, to a man who wanted to murder his family?

Yet for the longest time he had thought about nothing else. But how? One, two, three slaps to his forehead, the blood from his cut staining his skin. How could he have let it come this far? Some part of him had to have known what kind of monster David was. Did he simply ignore the truth because he wanted to be accepted, because he wanted approval? How pathetic could he be?! Well, no more! That was it. The pathetic, lonely boy who could be mesmerized by a madman, Svengalied by some psychopath who stroked his ego, was officially dead. He was absolutely going to continue on with his research, because that's what Science Boys did, but there was no way in hell that this Science Boy was going to give any information to David. Not even if David threatened to kill him or worse, turn him into one of Them.

David could take his body, do whatever his sick, twisted, blood-guzzling mind wanted to do with it, but there was absolutely no way that he was going to get his dirty, unholy hands on Ciaran's soul.

chapter 22

Standing at the foot of their bed, Ruby didn't think a more beautiful couple could possibly exist. It had nothing to do with their physical appearance, though Michael and Ronan were both quite handsome. Ruby saw beyond their exteriors. She didn't possess sight, but she could see into their hearts, and even deeper, into their souls. She could see their souls despite the fact that they were no longer housed within their bodies, but had been offered to The Well and currently existed within its cold, shiny waters. Ruby was able to see their souls, intertwined as one, because she wasn't really Ruby; she was being possessed by a spirit. It was just one of the things she thought it was time that Michael and Ronan should know about.

"My spirit name is Rhoswen," she said.

Asleep, Michael and Ronan each saw Ruby in their dreams. When she spoke to them, her lips didn't move. When she opened her eyes, they both saw they were completely white. When she took them each by the hand, they accepted her touch and felt themselves being pulled out of their beds. Standing on Inishtrahull Island, the boys knew they were staring at Ruby's body, but whoever had led them here was definitely not Penry's sister.

"I have been watching the two of you and so many others from afar," Rhoswen explained. "The time had come for me to join you, and to do that I had to borrow Ruby's body."

Even though this Rhoswen spirit used the word *borrow,* they knew she hadn't asked Ruby's permission before taking over her body and forcing Ruby into a state that resembled being in a walking coma. Surprisingly, that wasn't the most important piece of information the boys wanted their guide to divulge.

"Who are you?" Michael asked, his lips as still as Rhoswen's.

"And what do you want?" Ronan added as silently as the others.

Rhoswen smiled, delighted by the questions, heartened by the fact that these two acted as one. She brought their hands up to her cheeks so she could feel the cool flesh against her skin for a moment and then set them free so they could fall. "I am a friend," she answered. "And I have come, in part, to remind you of your destiny."

The boys looked at each other. Their expressions were mirror images of doubt and skepticism, and Michael spoke for them both. "What about the *other* part?"

Just as Rhoswen reeled her head back and roared with laughter, a huge wave crashed noisily onto the shore, and neither boy thought it was a coincidence. They also knew instinctively that they weren't going to have their questions answered to their satisfaction. Ruby or Rhoswen, or whoever they were looking at, was in control of this dream.

"The other part of my journey is none of your concern,"

she replied, her voice friendly, but final. "All that you need to know, all that is important to you, will be told."

The boys watched Ruby's hair and nightgown blow softly in the early dawn breeze, and this time they didn't need to look at one another to know they shared the same look of impatience. Rhoswen saw it too, and she responded to it. "Now."

She clutched their hands and once again they travelled. This time their distance was short, but their destination symbolic. Hovering over the ocean, The Well somewhere underneath their bare feet hidden by the miles of water below them, Rhoswen held onto Michael and Ronan, and together, hand in hand in hand, they floated effortlessly as small waves crested and rippled just inches from their toes. Despite Rhoswen's benevolent smile and the bucolic setting, Michael had an uneasy feeling; the last time one of his dreams took place in the ocean it had ended in horror and left him unsettled for days. Sensing his apprehension, Rhoswen understood it was time to honor her promise.

"The prophecy of The First and The Other is your destiny," she announced.

This was not the first time Ronan had heard this theory. Edwige had told him the very same thing when she became aware that he had fallen in love with Michael, an outsider, but hearing it from Rhoswen and not his mother made it sound like possibility and not interference.

"The legend of The First and The Other describes the origin of my people," Ronan said. "Are you saying that Michael and I are destined to be part of that legend?"

"You're already a part of it," Rhoswen confirmed. "You were from the day you were both born."

Ronan reached out to grab Michael's hand; he just had to touch him, and the three of them formed a circle above the ocean. "I knew from the first night I saw you, love, that it was fate."

Odd, even though they weren't alone, even though he was holding Rhoswen's hand and she looked just like Ruby, Michael wasn't embarrassed by Ronan's sweet confession, perhaps because it was the truth.

"It isn't a coincidence that you are both from places of water," Rhoswen continued. "Ronan from Inishtrahull Island and Michael from Weeping Water."

Then again, maybe it was all a lie. Michael was glad he didn't have to speak the words; he barely had the strength to think them. "But I wasn't born in Weeping Water. I was born in London."

The human circle didn't come unbroken, but it definitely lost some of its tension. Michael and Ronan felt as if a spiteful wave had just slammed into them and they were struggling to maintain their balance. Rhoswen merely smiled. "But where were you conceived, Michael?"

What? His conception was not something Michael had ever thought about. Besides the fact that he knew it wasn't immaculate, he really didn't want to know anything else about it. "Um, where I come from, Miss Rhoswen," Michael stammered, "that's what we call a really personal question."

Another hearty laugh, another watery explosion. The wave rose, and Michael and Ronan felt its power shudder through them and crash onto the ocean's surface, yet they remained dry. And Rhoswen remained amused. "Didn't your mother travel to the other shore that touches this same water when she was a young woman? And wasn't it there that she met your father?"

Ronan was staring at Michael who was staring at Rhoswen, but he could still see his eyes grow wide and his jaw drop. "Oh . . . my . . . God! My mother came to Atlantic City to be in the Miss America pageant when she was a few years older than I am right now!" Michael exclaimed silently. "You're saying she was pregnant with me before she got married?"

A nod of Rhoswen's head explained everything. "You

were both conceived on shores of the ocean where The Well resides," she explained. "Created out of love, christened by the same sea, bestowed with the same destiny."

Amazing and yet so simple. And very reassuring. At least now Michael had proof that his parents had truly loved each other, for a brief time anyway. Their love might have died when Grace found out that Vaughan planned to become a vampire and wanted his firstborn to follow in his eternal footsteps, but for a while they had been happy, and when he was conceived his mother must have known happiness in his father's arms. He was grateful for that knowledge even if it made his head throb.

Slowly the three of them began to move, their bodies floating in a circle as one united group, swirling like the water within the body of The Well. The more Rhoswen spoke, the faster they spun. "Ronan, The First, and Michael, The Other, you were destined to be together," she said, her silent voice sounding like an ancient chant. "You are meant to be where you are, you are meant to lead your people to a victorious future, and never doubt your connection or fear that your strength won't be enough to survive."

They were spinning so fast now Michael and Ronan could no longer see Rhoswen; she was a blur, red hair, white nightgown mixed in with the blue sky behind her, smeared colors trapped in a never ending circle. Michael lost hold of Ronan's hand just as Rhoswen's grip grew stronger, and when she spoke for one final time Michael knew he alone could hear her. "And no matter what happens to Ronan you must never be afraid."

Back in the stillness of their bed, Michael and Ronan woke up at the same time facing each other, their hands clasped together. Unlike other mornings their first connection wasn't a kiss, but a memory.

"Rhoswen?" they said jointly.

Quickly nodding their heads, they realized they had just

shared the same dream, just been spirited away by the same supernatural guide and given insight into their future. But could the information that had been bestowed upon them be trusted? "I don't want to put a damper on our dream," Michael said, "but Phaedra kind of insinuated that Ruby couldn't be trusted."

Rolling onto his back, Ronan stared at the ceiling for a few seconds contemplating Michael's comment. As much as he hated to admit it, his boyfriend's visions were usually accurate, no matter how much of a downer the takeaway message might be. But if you think about something hard enough, you can usually find a loophole. "But Ruby isn't really Ruby. She's Rhoswen," Ronan reasoned.

Michael scrunched up his face. "I'm sure Phaedra just used her earthly name because she didn't want to confuse me by calling her Rhoswen, you know, her spirit name, which until now I had never heard of."

Smiling, Ronan pressed his forehead into Michael's and gave him a belated good-morning kiss. "I have no idea who this Rhoswen is, but I have a feeling she was telling us the truth," Ronan whispered in between fits of laughter that brought their bodies even closer together, "which is why I'm so happy you weren't conceived in the middle of some desert."

"Speaking of conception," Michael said, "I betcha thought I forgot again." It could have been a result of their dream-journey, but Ronan had no idea what Michael was talking about until he exclaimed, "Happy birthday!"

Glancing at the calendar, Ronan saw that it was indeed March 15. What do you know? It was his birthday. "I told you, love, birthdays aren't a really big deal," he said.

"Maybe so, but I wanted this one to be special," Michael replied. "You know, to make up for last year."

Before Ronan could remind Michael that he wasn't holding a grudge because Michael forgot his previous birthday,

Michael jumped off the bed and pulled out presents from underneath it. "Open this one first," he said, giving Ronan the larger of the two boxes, the one wrapped in a brown paper bag and twine. "I was going for retro chic," Michael explained. "But it just turned out looking cheap."

Ronan had to agree. "Guess it won't matter if I tear the paper to shreds then," he said, doing just that. But once he saw what the wrapping was concealing, it didn't matter how terrible the wrapping was. "Blimey, Michael! I love it!"

And Michael had known he would. It was the complete Oscar Wilde collection, each book bound in black leather and sporting the title of the work in silver lettering on the spine. Making it look even more impressive was the fact that the entire collection was housed in a sterling silver sleeve that made it display-worthy. Jumping off their bed, Ronan shifted some books on his shelf and placed the gift above his desk. "It's perfect! I can't wait to reread every one of them," he said, bounding back to the bed to give Michael a thank you kiss. But Michael wasn't done bearing gifts.

"Not yet," Michael replied, handing Ronan a much smaller box that was unwrapped but topped with a little red bow. "There's a part two."

Beaming, Ronan began to rethink his long-held belief. Birthdays might lack significance to vampires, but maybe they shouldn't be a human-specific holiday. After opening his second present, however, Ronan thought that maybe humans were the only ones who could understand them. "I don't get it," he said. "This is the ring I gave you for your birthday."

"Nope, it's a replica," Michael explained, waving his left hand in Ronan's face and showing that he was still wearing his ring on his index finger. "I had one made for you."

"Two perfect gifts in a row!" Ronan grinned. "It's beautiful and thoughtful just like you." This time Michael didn't interrupt Ronan when he leaned in to kiss him. Ever the romantic, Ronan asked, "Would you put it on my finger?"

Blushing a little, Michael reached for Ronan's left hand, but Ronan extended his right. "No need for us to be matching ring buddies," Ronan said with a smile. So much for being Mr. Romance! Slipping the ring onto Ronan's finger—on his right hand—neither boy was surprised to find that it was the perfect fit, just like their relationship.

And what a perfect start to the day. The only thing that nagged at Michael was Rhoswen's departing words, her final warning. He didn't want to dwell on it; he only wanted to celebrate Ronan's birthday. But why not combine the two? Yes! The only way to find out the truth about Rhoswen was to find out more about Ruby. What better way to do it than in the guise of a birthday celebration!

"I know how to get to celebrate your birthday *and* get to the bottom of this whole Ruby / Rhoswen situation!" Michael shouted.

"Sounds exciting, love," Ronan said. "What's the plan?"

"We're going on another double date!"

chapter 23

Two days later and Ronan was still pouting.

"But I haven't stopped having nightmares from the last double date, love," he whined, sitting in the bleachers. "Can't we do something safer? How 'bout an intervention?"

"No can do," Michael whispered, patting Ronan's knee. "It's all set. Tonight, you, me, Fritz, and Ruby are going to the movies."

It hadn't even begun and the date already had disaster written all over it. "The movies?"

Michael craned his neck and used his vampire sight to see through the crowd of students in St. Sebastian's to find the other couple who was going to join them later on for a night of post-birthday fun, laughter, and of course, secret scrutiny of the spirit-possessed. No luck; he couldn't find Fritz and Ruby, but he saw Ciaran and Saoirse climbing up the bleachers and waved to them.

"Don't worry, Ro, we're not going to see some mindless action movie; I wouldn't make you sit through that," Michael said. "I think it's a romantic comedy. Or a horror film, I can't remember, but Ruby likes both so we're good."

Good? There was nothing good about what Michael was saying, nor did it make any sense. "Ruby is blind, Michael. How can she possibly like the movies?"

For such a smart vampire, Ronan sometimes didn't understand the ways of the world. "She fills in the pictures with her mind," Michael said as if he were drawing the most obvious of conclusions.

Moving over to make room for Ciaran and Saoirse, Ronan muttered under his breath, "Whatever the bloody hell she is, she's one strange bird that one."

Thanks to his mumbling, Ciaran didn't catch Ronan's comment, but since he looked exactly like the brooding, sulking teenager he had been before he met Michael, Ciaran knew he was interrupting some sort of disagreement between the two boys. "Lover's quarrel?" Ciaran asked.

"Nah," Michael replied. "Just me being the party planner and Ronan being the party pooper."

"Still?!" Saoirse cried. "Time comes when we all have to grow up and out of our childish roles, Roney." As if to illustrate her point, she smoothed out her hair and refastened a chic-looking black-and-topaz-colored Bakelite barrette that she had lifted from one of Edwige's jewelry boxes when she first came to town. "Look at me," she said, tossing back her hair. "Annoying little sister has grown into a sophisticated young lady."

Okay, let's see just how sophisticated. "The party planner arranged for us to go on another double date," Ronan conveyed.

"Blimey, Michael, are you barking mad?!" Saoirse asked, her shriek showing not an ounce of sophistication. "Seriously, are you a glutton for punishment?"

"Oh come on!" he protested. "What are the odds of this double date also ending up in disaster and having equally tragic consequences?"

"Um, I'd say the odds are slanted in the favor of tragedy," Ciaran deadpanned.

"Thank you, brother," Ronan said.

Shrugging his shoulders, Ciaran brushed off the praise. "Just speaking the truth."

Now it was Michael's turn to pout. Turning away from the group, he faced forward and crossed his arms. "Believe what you want to believe, but this date is going to be brill."

Saoirse slapped Michael in the shoulder. "Have you forgotten where you go to school? This isn't The Academy For The Sunny and Preternaturally Happy! It's Double A, Michael. If something bad or unexpected can happen, it probably will."

As much as he wanted to defend his plans for the evening, Michael had to admit that Saoirse had a point. Double A was a hotbed for unfortunate phenomena. Unfortunately, there was no way to cancel, especially when Fritz announced the plans were securely set in motion.

"I bought our tickets online, gents. Consider it a birthday treat," Fritz said proudly as he entered their row on the bleachers. Ruby was right behind him holding onto his hand, though it didn't look like she needed any help maneuvering her way through the crowd. "And you can buy the popcorn and soda for everybody."

Smirking, Saoirse whispered to Michael, "Your double date might be tragic, but since you boys don't eat, at least it'll be cheap."

As Ruby got closer Michael and Ronan couldn't help but forget about their disagreement regarding the evening's festivities and come together in like-minded focus. Working as one, their minds and eyes zeroed in on Ruby and tried to see beneath her pale skin and red hair, go beyond the distracting physical characteristics and the body that was merely playing host to an intruder, and try to delve into the girl's spirit, her soul, to connect with Rhoswen.

"Do you think Rhoswen is controlling her even now?" Michael asked Ronan telepathically. *"Or is she kind of asleep?"*

Ronan felt positively human. He couldn't pick up on any unnatural presence around Ruby. Either this Rhoswen was like Michael suggested and was asleep, or she was so powerful she could camouflage herself in plain sight. Funny, Ronan had always thought being a vampire meant he was the most powerful creature on earth; it was a humbling lesson to learn that he shared the planet with many other species that were even more powerful than he was. *"I don't know,"* Ronan answered honestly. *"But if Ruby is still blind and isn't acting as if she has no idea how she got here, then Rhoswen must still be in charge."*

Okay, Michael had to take it back. Maybe Ronan did understand the bizarre ways of the world after all. *"That actually makes sense."*

What made sense to Ciaran was that this was his chance to try and get closer to Ruby. Thinking quickly and acting even faster, he gave his sister's foot a kick and darted his eyes to the row behind them. Ever savvy, Saoirse got up and sat behind Michael, acting as if she was just giving Fritz and his girlfriend more room to spread out. What she was really doing was helping Ciaran secure a seat next to the girl he was pining over.

As Saoirse vacated her seat, Ruby leaned over and grabbed Ciaran's hand. "Did you cut yourself?" she asked.

For a moment, Ciaran was confused. How could she know? Then he realized she must have felt the Band-Aid in between his thumb and forefinger. "Oh that," he replied. "Just a cut, no big deal."

"I'm glad to hear that," Ruby said, smiling shyly at Ciaran.

Fritz didn't witness their connection, but Ronan did. Unfortunately, he didn't know if Ruby was smiling on her own or if she was just following some otherworldly order. Just when he didn't think it could get any more confusing, he noticed Nakano standing on the gym floor looking straight up at the group, but acting as if he couldn't decide which way to move. Glancing over to his left, Ronan saw the reason for his dilemma.

A few sections over, Morgandy was sitting in the crowd next to Brania, who Ronan figured must have finally decided to make a public appearance after lying low for months, and Alexei. When Alexei smiled arrogantly, revealing a pair of brand new fangs, Ronan was crestfallen. They had defiled another innocent student and added yet another body to their ranks. Turning back to Nakano, Ronan felt even worse, because it was clear Kano didn't know whose ranks he wanted to join.

Nakano knew that he would suffer repercussions, but he didn't care, he wanted to sit by Ronan, Michael, and the others. It wasn't like he was choosing sides, forfeiting his membership or something. It was just that Michael and Fritz and even Ronan's kid sister were a lot more enjoyable to spend time with than Morgue and the Mistress of the Cave. He needed a break, and he was going to take it, whatever the consequences. "This seat taken?" he asked.

Saoirse turned her hand over, palm side up, and waved it across the empty space on the bench as if presenting it to Nakano. "All yours, Nakanosan."

It felt good to laugh, and so he did. It was a nice distraction because the only other alternative was to look to the left and watch Brania, Morgandy, and the rest of their cronies glowering in his direction. And so what if they were? Who cared what they thought? Nakano didn't even turn his head when most of the kids in the gym started to cheer, signaling their headmaster's entrance. Whatever David was going to say was going to be boring; he just knew it. The only thing Kano cared about was that he was among friends.

David wished he felt the same way. As the headmaster took to the podium to address his students and faculty, he felt the entire universe working against him as the gym was plunged into darkness. Not just shadow like the other times when he had spoken in front of an assembly, but as if a switch had been turned off and it was suddenly nighttime at nine in the morning. Hidden in the blackness, David clutched the edge of the dais, and he felt the blood from the previous night's feeding drain from his face. Why was he suddenly weak? Why didn't Zachariel have his back? *This shouldn't be happening!* David heard the voice in his head whisper frantically. *Doesn't the world know who I am? The sun should be bursting upon my entrance, embracing me, not shrinking from view. This treason needs to end now!*

And it did. Ultimately, the interruption didn't last long. It hardly caused a commotion among those gathered, but it was enough to rattle David even further than he already was. He hated disturbance; it signified a lack of control. Ever since Rhoswen had returned, somehow returned from wherever the hell she had been all these centuries, he had felt his control slipping away. It was time to reclaim it.

"And then there was light," David said, as sunlight once again filled the gym. "I guess that makes me your headmaster and Mother Nature all wrapped up in one."

There was a large burst of laughter, with most of the faculty members standing behind David joining in appropriately. However, there were a few mutineers, including Coach Blakeley and Sister Mary Elizabeth, who even before David spoke noticed that his appearance lacked its typical perfection. His suit was slightly wrinkled, and his complexion was spotty. Sister Mary thought he might be coming down with the flu; Blakeley figured the pompous oaf was finally feeling the stress of his position.

In the bleachers, Brania and her troupe led the applause celebrating their leader's quick wit, but there were many who declined to join in the ovation. Ciaran refused to make eye contact with David and kept his eyes squarely on Ruby's hands, admiring her precise manicure, how the red paint was almost identical to the color of her hair. Fritz didn't even notice Ciaran's wandering eye, since he was too busy using the time to jot down notes for another issue of *Tales of the Double A*, this one having something to do with a sea creature who crashes the upcoming swim competition, but who in the end is defeated because even though he's super powerful, he's allergic to chlorine. Score one for humanity! In fact, score two, because despite Nakano's genetic connection to the speaker, he had no interest in listening to anything David had to say, and he and Saoirse were engaged in a cutthroat game of tic-tac-toe.

The only ones who looked at all interested were Michael and Ronan, but they weren't drawn to watch David. Instead they were transfixed on Ruby, even more than before. Ever since David had walked into St. Sebastian's, Ruby had followed him with her blind eyes as if she could see him enter from the locker room and take his place behind the podium. They would have simply thought she was being hypnotized by his magnetism like so many others had been, if it hadn't been for the slight sneer that gripped her face and the way she was breathing through her nose. She looked positively disgusted, and it only made Michael and Ronan certain that they were in the company of Rhoswen and that poor Ruby was nowhere to be found.

"In a few short weeks the Tri-Centennial Celebration will be upon us," David shouted, his voice a bit stronger but not nearly as powerful as usual. "We must be ready to show the world we are invincible!"

Stifling a laugh Blakeley turned his head slightly and whispered to Dr. Sutton who was standing behind him, "Bloke's gettin' a little full of himself." The coach kept his eyes on David, so he didn't see the doctor's angry expression or his fangs peek out slightly and press into his thin, chapped lips. "Takin' it right over the top he is," he added.

How Dr. Sutton wanted to teach the mortal a lesson, just like he wanted to teach most everyone in the room a lesson that they were all inferior, pointless. They might be God's creations, but they had been created before God realized his mistake and built a mightier race, a race that he wanted to see rule the earth. Full of himself? Of course David Zachary was full of himself, but only because he had every reason to be.

David wished he could remember all those reasons as he spoke. He knew his voice was booming throughout the gym. He could tell that many of the faces that stared at him were mesmerized. But there were too many that were drifting from him, gazing out the window, looking in another direction and not at him, not at his extraordinary face. He had to try harder, make them see that in a few short weeks the world was about to change.

"Don't worry, Father," he heard Brania silently call out to him. *"I will lead you to The Well. I can show you the way."*

"Yes! Show me the way!"

It was only after the words were out of his mouth that David realized he had spoken them out loud and not silently to his daughter. Finally, every face in the gym was looking at him, but for the wrong reason. They weren't staring at him like disciples eager to drown in his every word, hungry to devour whatever morsels of wisdom he chose to toss at their feeble minds. No, they were ogling him like he was a sideshow act, an abnormality, something that would entertain, something that was ludicrous.

A tiny bead of sweat trickled from his brow and traveled down the side of his face, turning inward when it met the edge of his beard, slipping toward the crook of his mouth. His sweat tasted salty, and it was innately repulsive because it reminded him of the ocean, home of those damned water vamps. That's all that was needed to turn things around. Despite the foul taste that clung to the inside of his mouth, David smiled, broadly, knowingly. He was about to show them all that he was still their ruler, he was still in control, regardless of his momentary stumble.

"In honor of Double A's three hundredth anniversary," David bellowed, "I challenge each and every one of you to show me the way to victory!"

It was done. He had corralled his hatred to overcome humiliation; he had survived a foe that was more vicious than any he had ever done battle with: his own fear. The battle, however, was only just beginning. As the students began the trek back to their classrooms, one face stood out among the crowd, one face that David knew could not be trusted.

"Headmaster Zachary, I'd like to show you something."

Flanked by Fritz and Sister Mary Elizabeth, Ruby stared straight ahead, her gaze meeting David's chest. If she had had sight she would have noticed that it was rising and falling in an increased rhythm; it was definitely something that Sister Mary noticed, but Fritz was too busy seeing who was watching him stand next to his girlfriend in front of the headmaster to notice anything important. "Of course, Miss . . ." David began, uncharacteristically forgetting a student's name.

"Poltke," Ruby offered. "Penry's sister."

"Yes, yes, of course." David was flustered. He knew the girl was a liar, but there wasn't anything he could do about it, not surrounded by all these people, not now. All he could do was search the gym for Brania, Morgandy, Dr. Sutton, a familiar face that could provide support. In the meantime while he waited he could busy himself by wiping away the additional beads of sweat that were starting to race down his face and make his temples glisten.

"Are you feeling all right, Headmaster?"

Damned inquisitive nun! In the instant that she spoke, David could not honestly say why he had let her live for so long. Religious zealot, fool! He wished he could pluck out her eyeballs with his fingernails instead of having to answer her condescending question, but he had to exhibit self-control, show them all how important it was to maintain composure and decorum. "I feel wonderful, thank you," he replied. "It is a bit unusually stuffy in here, however." Turning away from the old woman, David looked down at the girl. "What is it that you wanted to show me?"

Staring blankly ahead, Ruby bent down and placed her tote bag on the floor. She then pulled out a T-shirt and held it up by the shoulders. "I thought all the students could wear these for the Tri-Centennial Celebration," she said. When there was no response, she thought she was holding the T-shirt the wrong way; she thought the drawing that Fritz had helped her with was facing backward.

It wasn't. David just couldn't believe what he was seeing. Ruby was holding up a red T-shirt with the number three hundred written on it in white lettering, clearly in recognition of Double A's anniversary, except that the zeros in the number were white roses. "Fritz," she asked. "Am I holding it the right way?"

"Looks smashing, Rube," he said proudly. "I think the headmaster is just gobsmacked. Ain't that right, sir?"

They were staring at him, even the blind one, waiting for him to respond, waiting for him to give his consent, his approval, that their foul creation could be used as some sort of a school logo. And why not? What reason could he give to thwart their effort? Think, David, think! But David couldn't think. All he could see were the white roses, a symbol of every misdeed, every wrongdoing he had ever committed.

"Headmaster, what do you think?" Ruby asked. "I talked to Mrs. Lorenzo, and she said the art department's ready to silkscreen one for every student. She's just waiting for your official authorization."

David tried to convince himself that the image was merely a stupid drawing that didn't mean anything, but he knew that it meant everything. "Then Mrs. Lorenzo shall have it," he finally said.

Before Ruby and Fritz could thank David any further, Dr. Sutton, sensing his leader's discomfort, swooped in and made up some story about an administrative emergency that needed David's immediate attention. Brania waited until Sister Mary left the couple before approaching Fritz and Ruby. Just like her father, she was thrown by the girl's artistic efforts. Proving to be more resilient, Brania found her voice much quicker than David had. "White roses," Brania remarked. "How incredibly . . . clever."

"Thank you, Brania," Ruby replied. "I can't think of any image that is more iconic to Double A."

"How interesting that you would know that," Brania said, searching Ruby's eyes for a flicker of life. "Even though you've never even seen them before." Ruby's expression didn't change, but Fritz thought the air between the two girls was a wee bit thick. But Brania was kind of balmy and got along with very few people, so the tension was really nothing out of the ordinary. She just had to speak again for Fritz to recognize Brania was being her normal, prickly self. "It's almost as if someone's doing your seeing for you."

So that's what she was getting it. "That would be me," Fritz said. "Also known as the boyfriend."

Wasn't that perfectly conventional. Brania wondered if Fritz knew the truth about his girlfriend, but from what she knew of the boy, she knew he would never win a blue ribbon for being astute. No, he had no idea what he was dating. "I'm glad to see that Ruby's in such good hands," Brania said. The truth, however, was that Ruby was much more interesting when she was alone. "Don't forget to save me a T-shirt," she added as she walked back into the crowd, shaking her head. She would have to remember to add another item to the growing list of things that bored her: mismatched lovebirds.

Mismatched friends, on the other hand, could be quite amusing.

"I'm free after school if you want a rematch," Saoirse offered. "I know I probably bruised your ego winning all those games."

How this one was related to Ronan and Ciaran, Nakano had no idea. She actually had a sense of humor. "Don't get too comfortable wearing the tic-tac-toe tiara," Kano replied. "That was only the warm up."

How this one could be one of Them, Saoirse had no idea. He actually was fun to be around. "Bring it on, Kanosan! I'll even give you a handicap. You can start with an extra 'o'."

"I don't need charity," Kano said. "But if you fancy being a loser, I accept."

"Perfect! The tic-tac-toe tournament will resume in St. Martha's at three o'clock today," Saoirse announced. "Oh bollocks! Don't you have swim team practice for the big meet?"

Biting his tongue, Nakano made a decision to go against his nature and be upfront, tell the truth. "I think I'm bagging the swim team."

"Won't that be a little redundant?" Saoirse asked, as gently as she could. "You already quit once before."

Nakano felt weird, not because Saoirse had added an even deeper level of honesty to their conversation, but because he didn't feel the urge to run from her or to lash out. He really just wanted to talk. "Ever since I got bumped to the B team, Blakeley hardly knows I'm alive," he explained. "The swim team used to be fun and always a challenge to try and be as good as Ronan."

"And now?"

"It's turned into a couple hours waiting around for my turn to swim a lap or two," Kano admitted, surprised that it was so easy to be honest. "I guess part of it's not being on the A team, but the main thing is that I just want to have some fun again. And swim team isn't doing it."

Boy, did Saoirse know how that felt. Well, not the stuff about the swim team, but the wanting to have some fun. As they were about to leave St. Sebastian's, Saoirse saw two of her St. Anne's classmates, and she actually saw a lightbulb appear in a cute little thought bubble in front of her very eyes. It was a stroke of inspiration, and she couldn't wait to share it with her new friend. "You want to have some fun, Kanosan?" she asked rhetorically. "Then follow me."

Ronan was convinced he was not going to have fun, but he still followed Michael into the movie theatre. He really didn't have any other choice; Fritz and Ruby were waiting for them, and Fritz especially was looking forward to his large popcorn and soda. Ronan knew that if he snuck out the side entrance he would never hear the end of it from Fritz. Sometimes you just had to suck it up and like Saoirse said, grow up.

"Thanks, Ro," Fritz said, grabbing the tray from him. "Did you make sure they sprinkled it with three layers of butter and didn't just smother it on top?"

"Yes, Fritz."

"Did you watch them do it? Because they don't like special orders," Fritz revealed. "They're not the bloomin' Burger King."

"Yes, Fritz, I supervised."

"And did you make sure they only used a half a cup of ice in the sodas?"

"I measured it myself," Ronan replied tersely.

"No need to get snarky, mate," Fritz scoffed, though he softened his attitude when he saw Ruby was laughing at their exchange. "It's a dodgy practice, Rube, a trick they like to play on their customers."

"And what trick would that be, Fritz," she asked, sounding remarkably as if she actually wanted to know the answer.

"You see, what they do is they fill the cup to the rim with ice—sometimes the cubes stick out like a tiny replica of the bloody Arctic Circle—just so they can shortchange you on the soda," he explained. "Well, if I'm paying for a full cup of soda, I want a full cup of soda!"

"Well, you didn't bloody pay for it, Fritz," Ronan corrected, "so be happy with your Arctic Circle!"

"Boys, boys, you're both pretty," Michael joked. He held onto Ronan's arm tightly, not because he was afraid he was going to punch Fritz, but because he was afraid he was going to try and leave. "But Ruby and I are prettier, so we demand you stifle it."

Smiling at Michael, Ruby agreed. "Which translates to 'shut up, mates' because the previews are starting."

At that very second the lights in the theatre dimmed, and the first preview was projected onto the screen. "How did you know they were going to start?" Michael asked.

Leaning her head closer to Michael, Ruby whispered, "You know us blind girls; we have a sixth sense for these things."

Michael had no idea if the preview was for a foreign language art house movie or an animated cartoon. He was too shocked by Ruby's comment. *"Did you hear her, Ronan?!"* Michael asked. *"She just admitted she's got a sixth sense!"*

"Easy love, it's a figure of speech," Ronan replied. *"Now if she said she had six toes on one foot, that I would find interesting."*

Luckily the darkness of the theatre concealed Michael's smile, so he could continue to act as if he was annoyed with

Ronan. *"I've said it before, Glynn-Rowley, you've got no sense of humor."*

Ronan's hand found Michael's and their matching rings clinked in the darkness as he replied, *"Which is why I have you."*

Fritz had given himself a goal: He was going to kiss Ruby by the time the previews ended. But the third one had started, and he still had not made a move. Maybe this double date thing wasn't a good idea after all; there was so much added pressure. If he made a fool out of himself when he was alone with Ruby, she wasn't going to tell anyone, but if he did something stupid in front of Michael and Ronan, they might tell everyone. Then again, Ronan really didn't gossip and Michael was his friend, but Michael could slip when he was talking to Saoirse, and she had the biggest mouth of anyone he had ever met. Oh God, why was he thinking about Michael and Ronan and Saoirse when he was sitting in a darkened movie theatre holding hands with his girlfriend? Just stop thinking and kiss her.

"That was nice, Fritz," Ruby whispered, the taste of butter still on her lips.

"Yeah, it was," he replied, his voice a bit gruff.

"I wouldn't mind if you did it again."

Sassy! Fritz Ulrich had found himself a sassy girlfriend, and he couldn't have been happier. The feeling, however, wasn't universal.

In the middle of their second kiss, there was a huge explosion of sound, and for a second Fritz thought he was hearing the buzzing in his head, some sort of residual effect of a really hot kiss. But it was quickly evident that the sound was real. Someone had pulled the fire alarm because the theatre was filling up with smoke.

Curl after curl of gray, smoky fog filled the theatre, rolling in from somewhere within the bones of the building. It entered the theatre defiantly, determined, as if it were on a mission, the smoke rolling, rolling, rolling, devouring everything in its path, and soon it was impossible to see the movie screen. Gray tendrils split apart from the huge cloud of smoke that hung in the air in the front of the theatre and began to slip in and out of the seats, wrap themselves around the legs of the moviegoers who were desperately trying to get out of the theatre, and swirl around their faces, making them cough and their eyes burn.

Piercing through the frightened screams of the patrons, a voice boomed from a loudspeaker and instructed everyone to follow the ushers and quickly, but calmly, evacuate the premises. "Don't let go of my hand, Ruby," Fritz ordered, bravely keeping his fear to himself.

"I won't." And true to her word she didn't, not even when she turned around to face Michael, not even when her eyes turned into two orbs of solid white, and not even when she hissed through lips that never parted, "This is all because of your friend."

Stunned, but not really surprised, Michael watched Fritz lead Ruby out the side exit, his arm around the girl's slender shoulders, protecting her from the swarm of people bumping into them. For a second Michael breathed in deeply and listened intently. He neither smelled nor heard the crackle of fire, and he knew there was nothing natural about this interruption. Still, he instinctively reached back to grab Ronan's hand and make sure he was right behind him. He wasn't, but another familiar face was.

"Phaedra! I knew it was you!" Michael yelped. "And by the way, Ruby knows it's you too. So would you mind explaining what's going on here?"

To the untrained eye, Phaedra looked like just another patron whose night at the movies had been ruined, but Michael could tell that she was different. He could see the blue veins underneath her skin, and her hair, still curly and slightly disheveled, seemed to be floating around her face like the wisps of fog that it truly was. It was a depressing sight because Michael realized she was, without a doubt and without reversing the trend, more efemera than human.

"I'm sorry, but I had to do something," Phaedra said, her voice floating in the air like a wayward piece of cloud.

"This is all you could come up with?" Michael asked, slightly dumbfounded. "You know shouting fire in a crowded movie theatre is illegal, not to mention highly dangerous."

"Ruby is dangerous," Phaedra countered.

Michael wanted to touch Phaedra's hand, but he knew it would only make him feel sadder; he knew it would be like trying to hold onto air. "We know that. Why do you think we're here?" he said. "We're actually doing some spiritual reconnaissance work."

If the situation hadn't been so grave, Phaedra would've laughed, but her time was limited. "You have to be careful around her," she implored. "And you need to keep her away from Fritz."

He should've known. Once a teenage girl, always a teenage girl. "Okay, I get it. Is this how efemeras act when they're jealous?" Michael asked. "They turn a movie theatre into their own little playroom?"

"This isn't a game, Michael!" Even though Phaedra had tried to shout, her voice was hardly more than a sliver of sound. She was using all the strength she had just to appear in human form; she didn't have any strength left over to shout. "Listen to me, this is important," she said. "Wherever Ruby goes death will follow."

Talk about an exit line. Before Michael could question Phaedra further, get her to elaborate, find out if she was exaggerating or downright lying in an attempt to scare him so he'd do something that would break up Fritz and Ruby, he saw her fade away. There was so much commotion and so much smoke all around him that no one saw her evaporate.

It was almost as if he had experienced a hallucination, until Ronan confirmed that he wasn't crazy.

"You saw her too?"

"Yes," Ronan confirmed. "I held back because I figured she'd talk more openly to you if you were alone. Did she say anything important?"

Michael quickly relayed Phaedra's brief message. "I don't know, Ro," Michael said, suddenly confused. "I can't be sure if she's telling the truth or if she's just royally pissed off that Fritz's got a new girlfriend."

"Well, the only thing we do know, love," Ronan said as he threw his arm around Michael as they started to walk out of the theatre, "is that your double dates really do suck."

The drive back to school was mainly silent. Ronan wasn't known to be a jabberjaw, Fritz wasn't happy that movie night had been cut short, and Michael wasn't sure who was in his back seat—Ruby or Rhoswen—so he hesitated to start a conversation. There was some small talk, but it was forced, so Michael let out a sigh of relief when he parked his Benz in the lot near David's office and turned off the ignition. The night was finally over. In Michael's mind, it hadn't been a complete catastrophe. He had gained another piece of information about Ruby, albeit from a completely biased source, but still, it was something new and that's why he had arranged the evening in the first place.

Fritz's motives for their night in Eden had been much more basic: He had just wanted to snuggle next to Ruby during the movie. Since that hadn't worked out he'd have to settle for holding her hand as he walked her back to her dorm room. After they had exchanged their good-nights and Michael and Ronan walked in the other direction toward St. Florian's, Fritz thought he'd take the long way home to get as much one-on-one alone time with Ruby as possible. She had other plans.

When they reached the clearing behind David's office, Ruby stopped to face Fritz, and the boy almost fainted. Her irises were gone; only the whites remained. Even though her body wasn't shaking, he thought that maybe Ruby was having a stroke or something. Nothing was going to happen to her; it was Fritz who was being put under a spell.

"Leave Ruby alone and go home," Rhoswen ordered. "When you wake up tomorrow you'll remember none of this. You'll believe you walked Ruby safely to her door."

It was as if a see-through door had slammed shut in front of Fritz's eyes, like he was locked within an invisible cell; he could see the world around him, he just couldn't interact with it. He had no control over his body; he had relinquished it, unaware, to an unseen power. Without saying another word, Fritz started walking into The Forest; from behind no one would have known that he was being manipulated like an untethered marionette. And no one could imagine why his girlfriend would want to visit the headmaster at such a late hour.

As she walked past the mirror in David's greenroom, Rhoswen smiled at Michael, the archangel, who had always been her favorite. She looked up at the carving and took in his heroic face, his powerful body, Satan cowering under the weight of his boot, and she was overjoyed. Good always did triumph over evil. Sometimes it took centuries to win a battle, but what did several hundred years mean when the end result was victory?

Glancing at the other archangels that graced the mirror's frame, the feeling of joy grew. There was so much evil in the world that sometimes it was easy to forget that there was also good. That was because the evildoers penetrated every aspect of society, earthly and otherwise. She knew that Zachariel's eyes had turned bright red and were glowing in her direction, but she didn't feel the need to acknowledge his presence. He was one of those charlatans who had posed as virtuous, who had infiltrated a corps of peace-loving guardians, but was nothing more than a lowly, despicable creature and undeserving of her attention. She would never understand why her brother was so fascinated with him.

Silently, she entered David's office and spied him sitting next to the fireplace, its flames suddenly igniting, crackling enthusiastically upon seeing her again. David didn't look up. He didn't share in the flames' applause. He couldn't; he didn't know she was there, and so he continued to drink blood from a brandy snifter and remained deep in thought. Until his thoughts were interrupted.

"Hello, brother."

The snifter slipped through David's shaking fingers and crashed onto the floor. Pieces of glass flew in every direction, but the blood defied nature and didn't splatter. Like a crimson snake it slithered on the floor, curving slightly to the left, then the right, but maintaining its path, building speed as it traveled toward its goal, not stopping until it reached Rhoswen. When the tip of the blood trail was a few inches from her feet, it veered to the right and continued until it connected on the other side. Looking at the circle of blood that surrounded her, Rhoswen smiled. When she looked at her brother, her smile disappeared.

"It looks like the circle of blood that enveloped me the night I died," she said. "Do you remember placing me in its center, Dahey?"

The sound of his Christian name made David wince. He remained seated, his face flushed. The only visible movement on his entire body came from a muscle in his right cheek that twitched every few seconds. Of course he remembered the night Rhoswen had died. No matter how hard he tried to forget, it was a memory that would never leave him.

"Do you remember telling me to sit quietly in the circle

and to wait for Zachariel?" she asked, her voice becoming more agitated, less calm. "I was so young, so trusting. I had no idea that I was waiting for my brother to murder me."

Finally David was able to command another part of his body to move, and he slammed his fist into the arm of the chair. "It wasn't murder; it was a sacrifice!"

A slow smile formed on Rhoswen's lips. "Which is merely murder that comes with a reward."

Finally, David found the strength to stand. The ascent took longer than he had anticipated, and when he stood upright he felt his legs might collapse underneath him; they were amazingly weak, and so he didn't stray far from his chair. "What are you doing here?!" he asked, his voice unable to hide its desperation. "Why have you returned?!"

"Three hundred years is an awfully long time to be away from home, don't you think?"

When David saw Rhoswen's spirit step out of Ruby's body and walk toward him, he was grateful he hadn't ventured away from his chair. His legs gave out from under him, and he fell back down. His hands clutched the arms of the chair as he saw his sister for the first time in three hundred years. She looked as innocent and beautiful as she did in the dreams that had never ceased to haunt him.

With Ruby's body frozen behind her, Rhoswen kept walking toward David, and with each step she took she moved further away from apparition and closer to resembling the woman she used to be. Her long, straight black hair was parted in the middle and flowed down her back, stopping only when it reached her waist. On top of her head she wore a crown of white roses, robust, grand flowers that were in full bloom, each petal soft and the color of unblemished snow. It was the same color as her skin.

As she moved the gown she wore rippled at her feet as if she were walking on wind. The floor-length dress was made of two different kinds of material, one underneath the other.

On top the cloth was chiffon in a green color that resembled a flower's stem; under that was white silk that fell closer to her small frame. Around her waist she wore a belt made out of more white roses, but these were miniature, delicate, each petal bending inward toward the center, not yet ready to open up and greet the world. She resembled a living, breathing garden.

David gasped at the sight, at the visual manifestation of his memory, as he realized she was wearing the same dress she had worn the night she died, the night he sacrificed her soul to Zachariel in exchange for his own immortality. It was his own mad desire for supremacy over God, his own amazement that in Zachariel's promises he had found the key that could unlock his fantastic vision that led him to commit an unspeakable act, the murder of his own flesh and blood. But what choice did he have? It had had to be done if he wanted his bloodless flesh to live on forever. Zachariel had proclaimed that the only way for Brother Dahey to be transformed from monk into vampire was for Rhoswen's life to be sacrificed in a circle of his own blood. He wished it had been a harder decision to make.

Rhoswen was moving closer toward David, and the night she had died was replaying in his mind more vividly than ever before. He remembered thinking about how she looked that night, pure, youthful, unsuspecting. He remembered thinking how for the first time in his life he was thankful she was blind so she wouldn't question why he was cutting the vein in his arm and filling the silver goblet with his own blood. With her heightened sense of hearing she heard the blood pour from the goblet onto the floor of the building that was now St. Joshua's Library, and she had asked what he was doing. Instinctively he had lied. He had told her he was preparing a game that he wanted to play with her, and as always Rhoswen believed what her brother told her. She had never had any reason to doubt him before; she never thought she had any reason to that night. Only when she felt the knife plunge into her body, when she felt the ridged blade sever the flesh between her shoulders, when the world all around her went white did she think that she had misjudged her brother. But then it was too late. She was dead before her body hit the floor, directly in the center of the circle of her brother's blood.

"Get away from me!" David screamed. "Don't come any closer!"

David rose from the chair too quickly, and he felt light-headed. He stumbled and had to hold on to the fireplace mantel for support. *This is insane! I am more powerful than she is!* David shouted to himself. That might have been true, but Rhoswen had a distinct advantage over David: She wasn't crippled by her own guilt.

"Are you feeling remorse, brother?" Rhoswen asked. "Are you feeling guilty for killing me like a coward, stabbing me in the back in exchange for becoming a creature of the night?"

Racing toward the door, David didn't care how cowardly he appeared. He wanted to leave the room; he needed to escape, breathe fresh, uncontaminated air, but Rhoswen was not going to allow her reunion to be cut short. Just as David reached Ruby's motionless body, the door slammed shut. The last things he saw before the door closed were Zachariel's red, flaming eyes staring at him, filled with utter disappointment. When he turned around he saw Rhoswen holding the book with the marble rose on it, her blind eyes looking at him the same way they used to when she was alive, filled with hope.

It was too much to bear. Over the centuries David had pushed the memory of his sister from his mind, altered the way his brain remembered things to convince himself that he was an only child and had become a vampire without sacrificing the life of the only person he had ever loved. With Rhoswen standing before him he could no longer hide from the truth. "What do you want from me?" David begged, his voice breaking like a scared child's.

The only sound in the room was the crackling fire. It filled up the space while Rhoswen decided how she wanted to answer her brother's question. Did she want revenge or did she want comfort? It was such a difficult decision to make.

"For now, Dahey," she said, holding out the book to him, "I want you to read to me like you used to."

Vision after vision bombarded David's mind, all of them the same, all of him sitting in a chair, reading to Rhoswen. In every memory her head gently rested on his knee, her blind eyes staring into nothingness as her mind conjured up images of the stories David told her. Looking at Rhoswen now as she sat on the floor next to his chair and held her favorite book in her hands made David feel both ashamed and exhilarated. It was both his greatest fear and his greatest wish come true.

"Read to me like you did in the place that you now call St. Joshua's," Rhoswen said. "Where I let the white roses bloom in honor and remembrance of my name."

David took the book from her, and his hands were remarkably steady; it was a positive omen. Rhoswen's return did not have to mean misfortune; it could mean a chance to reconnect with his long lost sibling. Yes! Maybe all he needed to do was read her one story and she would leave and they would both have closure, both be able to move on. Maybe he would then be able to look at the white roses that grew outside of St. Joshua's and not be haunted by Rhoswen's memory. Maybe he could see them as a happy reminder of the blind girl whose only happiness in life had been hearing her brother read stories to her.

"Once upon a time there lived a beautiful princess," David said, his voice tentative as he read the opening line of Rhoswen's favorite story. He felt her head lying on his knee, and he could sense her delight at being in his presence once again after so many years. Three centuries later and she was still a child, still his sister, still his Rhoswen. He was so moved that the words of the next sentence caught in his throat, and he had to swallow hard in order to speak. And he was so lost in the wonder of the present and the familiarity of the past that he didn't notice Michael and Ronan looking into his office from the open window.

He didn't see their stunned expressions. He didn't know that they had overheard him and Rhoswen speak and had uncovered his greatest secret: that David was far from all-powerful, far from indestructible; he was vulnerable and weak. As Michael and Ronan held on to each other, unable to tear themselves away from the unbelievable sight, they both knew that at some point very soon they were going to use the information they had learned about David to their advantage.

Looks like Phaedra and Rhoswen were both right, Michael realized. The next time David and his army attacked them, death would surely follow. And now that Michael knew David was a fraud, there was absolutely no reason for him to be afraid.

chapter 24

Outside, the earth was alive. Anticipation hung in the air, as vibrant and as lush as the landscape.

The end of May was always a lively time at Double A. The end of the school year meant that the students were frantically studying for final exams and preparing for their summer vacations. The end of spring always meant that the campus grounds were in full bloom and brimming with a jumble of colors and smells. But this year the school was crackling with more excitement than ever before. The euphoria of hosting the National Swim Team Competition, the unofficial start of the Tri-Centennial Celebration, was about to be realized; the day had finally arrived. For some it had arrived earlier than expected.

"When I signed up for this experiment, I didn't think we'd have to be here at the crack of bloody dawn," Saoirse said, finishing off her protest with a yawn.

"Blame Blakeley," Ciaran replied, checking his bag for the third time to make sure that he had brought an extra syringe and backup test tubes. "Yesterday he called for an early morning warm-up session before the first race starts this afternoon."

"Why'd we have to wait until today, anyway?" Saoirse asked.

"I thought it would be symbolic," Ciaran replied.

"Now you want to be symbolic *and* scientific?" Saoirse questioned as she tossed her towel next to her backpack and shivered. Despite the early morning sun that was pouring into St. Sebastian's, the room was still chilly, and her bikini didn't offer much warmth. "I should be under my covers, Ciaran."

"You should be under the water," he corrected. "Now get in before the rest of the team starts to show up."

Standing on the top rung of the ladder attached to the side of the pool, Saoirse paused, her left foot dangling in the air an inch above the water. "Hold on, boyo! Wasn't that one of your selling points?" she asked. "So maybe a certain ex-boyfriend might see me in my cracking outfit?"

Oh yeah, right. Remembering that he had mentioned her participation might result in Morgandy's getting a glimpse of Saoirse like he'd never seen before, Ciaran backpedaled. "Um, yeah, but later, you know? When we're finished."

"Was Albert Einstein a liar too?" Saoirse asked, descending into the pool.

Ciaran had no idea. The only thing he knew for certain was that he was running out of time if he wanted to keep using the gym as his own private annex lab. "Take a few breaths, then a really deep one, and go under," Ciaran said, holding a stopwatch. "Stay down for as long as you can."

One breath, two breaths, three breaths, wait. "Is there any reason why we couldn't have done this in my bathtub?" Saoirse asked. "The water would've been a lot warmer."

Looking as if someone had presented him with an explanation as to how and precisely when the universe had been created, Ciaran replied meekly, "Oh I hadn't even thought of that."

Just before she took one last gulp of air and disappeared underwater, Saoirse snipped, "Guess you and Mr. Einstein have nothing in common after all."

Alone, Ciaran watched the long hand on the stopwatch click, click, click as it traveled from one number to the next. One minute. One minute, ten seconds. Eleven, twelve, and then they were no longer alone.

The noise spilled out into the gym from the locker room before the three boys did. "You wanted to be one of Them all along!" Ronan shouted. "Well, you got your bloody wish!"

"I didn't want to be cast out and left for dead!" Morgandy spat back.

Regardless of what he told Saoirse, Ciaran hadn't wanted to be interrupted. No one was going to believe he and his sister had just wanted to go for a swim before the competition started. He would've looked for a place to hide, but it was a foolish idea. The gym was one huge, open space and plus, Saoirse was in the pool. He couldn't just hide and leave her to fend for herself when she came up for air. No, he'd have to stay put and hope that the intruders were too wrapped up in their own drama to question their presence. So far it was working. Even Michael, who didn't seem to be engaged in the argument, hadn't noticed him yet.

When Ronan turned to face his nemesis, Ciaran could see that his brother was prepared for a fight. The muscles in his back were flexed, his hands were fists, his thick legs like tree stumps anchored into the floor. Morgandy, on the other hand, was like a hungry mosquito, flitting about, bobbing, flailing. "I was right to try and destroy The Well!" he cried, his deep voice so frenzied it seemed to make the gym shake. "I'm living proof of how vindictive and evil it can be."

"No, Morgandy," Ronan said, his voice so quiet it seemed to quell the shaking. "You're living proof that some people are simply born evil."

Ronan's words, his insight, penetrated into the very depths of Morgandy's mind and soul. Could that be his secret? Could that be what The Well had tried to erase? The fact that Morgandy had not been trying to uphold some personal belief or defend some popular ideology when he wanted to obliterate The Well, that he hadn't been swayed by David to abandon his birthright to be its guardian, but that he was merely succumbing to his true nature? He had never thought of himself that way, but could his be the face of pure evil?

Glancing at his reflection as it rippled on the surface of the pool water he didn't shield his eyes. He didn't shrink from the horror of seeing his soul exposed in all its tainted, sullied glory or beg Ronan to help him find the path back to goodness, because he realized in one liberating moment that goodness was not the place from which he had come. There was no reason to scurry back there, remorseful, repentant, to seek shelter and salvation; his destination was in the opposite direction. He laughed, the sound rough and coarse like jagged rocks chaffing against one another. As his body convulsed joyously, his curls bounced slightly, and when he placed his hands on his hips to steady himself, he wasn't surprised to feel that his flesh was hot, warmed not just by his latest victim's blood, but by the recognition of exactly who he was. He couldn't wait to share the revelation. "Oh my God," Morgandy whispered. "I never imagined that."

Ronan hadn't been expecting such a humble response, but he'd take it. Maybe he had reached Morgandy? Maybe he had finally gotten him to understand that The Well had given him the greatest gift of all by separating him from his memories, from his past, from his innate malevolence so he could start his life over? Or maybe Ronan just misinterpreted the

reply? "Thank you, Ronan," Morgandy hissed, "for reminding me of who I really am."

Distracted by his own hope that Morgandy might welcome the opportunity to change, he hesitated when he saw
him leap forward, arms reaching, fangs bared. Luckily, Michael had dispensed with hope where Morgandy was concerned. He had never expected him to express gratitude and
had known he would exercise his free will to retaliate against
Ronan's words with violence. Springing into action, Michael
tackled Morgandy in mid-flight, and together they twisted
horizontally and rested on the air for a few seconds before
plunging into the pool.

Underneath the water, they fought not as boys but as the
supernatural creatures they were. Michael whipped his webbed
hand in front of him and a second later Morgandy's head
snapped to the left. Morgandy kicked his leg up and after a
slight delay Michael somersaulted backward. When he regained his balance, Michael flipped his webbed feet once,
twice, and latched onto Morgandy yet again, this time holding him by the throat and ramming his back into the bottom
of the pool. Staring at them while wedged into a corner of the
pool, Saoirse screamed for them to stop. Her voice, however,
was silenced by the water and the commotion. She may not
have been heard, but she was definitely seen.

When Morgandy broke free and swam toward her, his face
cruelly distorted and tinged with a greenish-blue color thanks
to the chlorine, she screamed with even more force and never
noticed that her lungs were completely filled up with water. It
hadn't registered, but like the other beings in the pool, she
was having no trouble breathing underwater.

Michael had no idea what Saoirse was doing in the pool,
but he would have to figure that out later. Right now he had
to protect her, because from the ominous look on Morgandy's face it was obvious that she was about to become his
next victim.

Wildly, Morgandy leapt forward through the water, hands outstretched, eager to claim his prize. As he propelled closer to Saoirse, she screamed louder and pressed harder into the side of the pool. Morgandy's fingers grazed Saoirse's neck as Michael wrapped a webbed hand around Morgandy's ankle. At the same instant the water around them started to bubble. When Michael hurled Morgandy into the far end of the pool, it started to churn. And when Morgandy was flung by the current back into Michael's chest, they began to spin around, caught in the center of a mini-whirlpool. It felt wrong—a whirlpool in the middle of a pool—but it also felt safe. At least for Michael.

After a few rotations, Michael noticed that Morgandy was no longer struggling; he was unconscious. Michael remembered the last time he had had a pool fight, with Nakano, it was an altercation that didn't end well for either of them. Holding Morgandy's lifeless and now human-looking body as the water spun around them, Michael knew he had made his point; he had proved to his enemy that he and Ronan were a team. Strike one, prepare to contend with the other. As if the water was having the same thought, it abruptly stopped moving, and Michael knew it was time to bring this battle to an end. But he brought it to an end too hastily.

When Blakeley saw Michael's face he was so terrified the scream clung to the insides of his throat, refusing to be heard. Worried about Morgandy's condition, Michael had broken through the surface of the water without transforming back. His fangs were exposed, his face elongated, his eyes narrow slits, and the hands that placed Morgandy on the gym floor were webbed just like his feet.

"Transform!"

Ronan didn't have to say another word, in silence or out loud; Michael understood. He also understood that no matter how quickly he converted his appearance, the harm was done; his true self had been seen by a human. Well, there was nothing he could do about that now; he would have to deal with that later. Right now, Morgandy was lying on the ground not breathing.

Thankfully, none of the other kids had arrived yet for their pre-competition workout. The only other person in the gym was David, Blakeley's guest, specially invited to see how unbeatable his team was. The headmaster wasn't someone Michael enjoyed seeing unexpectedly, but at least he knew how to handle such a unique situation.

Racing over to Morgandy, David knelt beside him, placed his hands just below his ribcage, and pressed down and up several times. Michael wasn't sure if traditional resuscitation techniques could revive a vampire, but what did he know? He didn't think he had hurt Morgandy that badly, either. Their fight in the alleyway had been much more intense, and Morgandy had walked away from that scuffle more humiliated than bruised. What the headmaster was doing to reawaken Morgandy seemed like a waste of time. Until Michael realized it was all a cover-up for his next tactic.

Tilting Morgandy's head back to create an arch in his neck, David pinched the boy's nose and lowered himself until their mouths almost touched. Then, unseen by everyone except Michael, David allowed his own face to transform and his own hideous countenance to slither out of hiding. Michael winced, but didn't look away until he saw the headmaster's blood slowly slide down his cracked tongue and spill into Morgandy's open mouth. Disgusting! It was like a vampire blood transfusion.

One drop, two drops, three drops, four, until the blood flow increased and the fluid began to race down David's tongue and fill up Morgandy's mouth. Finished, David pursed his parched lips together, cutting off the blood supply, and shut Morgandy's mouth to allow the blood to funnel down his throat and traverse throughout his body, reinvigorate it. The tactic worked, and color returned to Morgandy's face. His chest started to rise and fall, and when his eyes opened they were clear and alert. "What happened?"

Helping Morgandy stand, David answered, "Minor accident, nothing more." David turned to face Blakeley, making sure that his appearance wouldn't put the coach into a further state of shock. "I'm taking him to the infirmary so Dr. Sutton can fully evaluate his condition." Blakeley could merely nod in response. Turning to face Michael, all David could do was control his rage. Walking with his arm around a still-weak Morgandy, David grinned salaciously and whispered to Michael, "Clean up your mess or I'll have to bring your beloved coach over to our side."

Not knowing how to diffuse the situation, Ronan and Ciaran individually decided to remain calm and allow Michael to act first. They would let him speak and then follow his lead. They didn't get a chance. Michael took one step toward Blakeley, and the coach found his voice. "Stay away from me!" he screamed. "I don't know what you are, but you ain't bloody right!"

"What are you talking about, Coach?" Ronan said, his face forming an odd-looking smile. "Michael and Morgandy just had a row, that's all."

Sticking up his hands as if to push back the air, push back what he couldn't comprehend, Blakeley's voice quickly rose to a panic. "They might've had a row, but that . . . *thing* that I saw come out of the pool, that wasn't Michael!"

"Of course it was Michael," Ciaran added. "You know, I think the stress of the whole swim competition thing has gotten to you."

"That must be it. You're seeing things that aren't there," Ronan joined in. "Stress is one powerful demon."

"Yes! That's what he is! Some kind of demon!" Blakeley cried.

"Coach, I'm sorry if I scared you," Michael said, trying to

remember what innocence sounded like. "But look at me, I'm no demon."

He was right; he didn't look like a demon or the devil; he just looked like a kid. But Blakeley knew what he had seen come out of that pool, at least he thought he did. Ignoring reason, ignoring his own sanity, Blakeley began to ramble, and for the first time the events that had taken place at the school over the past year started to make sense. "That's it! It's all because of you! Ever since you showed up things have been crazy around here!" Blakeley shouted, his finger jabbing the air viciously. "Ever since you came to Double A people have started to go missing or die. First Penry, then his girl-friend, Alistair, Lochlan, his nurse, that Amir kid, the girl with the really frizzy hair, and now Diego!" Panting, Blakeley stopped, almost too scared to finish. "Tell me, Michael, where the bloody hell is Diego?!"

Such a long list. Could Michael really be responsible? No. No, it was just coincidence, it had nothing to do with him. It just couldn't. "I have no idea, Coach," Michael answered softly.

Blakeley couldn't take it anymore. He couldn't explain it, he was in no way capable of rationalizing it, but he couldn't stay in the same room as Michael. If he stayed in the gym for another second he thought he was going to faint. "Oh really?" Blakeley said, running out of the gym. "We'll see about that!"

When Ciaran ran to the other side of the pool, they all thought he was chasing after Blakeley until he bent down and grabbed the pink towel adorned with a huge letter S. "Saoirse!" Quickly glancing at the stopwatch, Ciaran saw that Saoirse had been underwater for over five minutes. Way too long. Tossing the timer aside, he dove into the pool fully dressed. Underwater his eyes, wide and fearful, darted all over. Left, right, nothing, just water. Saoirse was nowhere to be found. Breaking the surface, he looked around the gym, but still not a trace of her. How had she left without being seen? Confused, Ciaran placed his hands flat on the edge of the pool and started to hoist himself up, but quickly got some help with his exit.

Ronan clutched the wet collar of Ciaran's shirt, and the way his eyes were flaring, Ciaran realized blue was the new color of anger. "What was Saoirse doing in the pool?" Ronan demanded.

Unable to come up with a lie quickly enough, Ciaran told a version of the truth. "We were testing her breathing," he said quietly so no one else could hear him. "You know how interested she is in her origin. I figured she's got to be connected to Atlantis somehow, so I thought I'd see how long she could stay underwater."

"And how long were you going to wait to share your results with David?" Ronan demanded.

"I . . . I wasn't," Ciaran stammered. "I wouldn't do that."

"Don't lie to me, Ciaran!" Ronan shouted. "I saw David come out of your lab. I know you're still working with him!"

"Was! I'm done with all that!" Ciaran cried. "I swear it!"

There was something in the tone of Ciaran's voice that Ronan had never heard before when they discussed David: fear.

"Well, it's about bloody time," Ronan said. He wasn't happy to hear that his brother was afraid, but Ronan was thrilled to hear that Ciaran had come to his senses. He wanted to ask Ciaran what had happened that made him finally accept the fact that David was no good, but at the moment he had to deal with his other sibling. "So where the hell is Saoirse?" Ronan asked.

"She must've made a run for it when things got wonky," Ciaran replied.

"I don't think *wonky* is the best way to describe the situation," Michael said, joining them. "More like fiasco, shambles. How about catastrophe?"

Rubbing Michael's shoulder, Ronan tried his best to cheer

his boyfriend up. "Don't fret, love, it's not like Blakeley saw you feeding," Ronan said. "He saw a glimpse of your true self, that's all."

That's all! "Isn't that enough?!"

Twisting his shirttail to drain some water from it, Ciaran agreed. "Ro's right. He can't prove anything. You just have to be more careful from here on out."

Although surprised by the positive spin they were putting on the disaster, Michael was grateful he had their support. Or did he?

"Um, Ronan," Michael started. "Any reason you left me on my own to do battle with the Morgue?"

"The Well told me not to interfere," he replied.

"So let me get this straight, brother," Ciaran started. "Your Well is now speaking to you?"

Ronan shrugged his shoulders and looked unintentionally impish. "It's not like He rings me daily," he replied. "But, yeah, I've heard from Him." Was that accurate? "Or Her, or is it It?" For all the times Ronan had pledged his love, support, and devotion to The Well, he really didn't know what pronoun to use to describe it. "Whatever it is, it told me to stay put."

"That's why there was a whirlpool!" Michael announced.

"A whirlpool?" the brothers replied in unison.

"Yeah, just like the one that sucked up Amir last year," Michael explained.

Ronan had never been prouder to be a water vamp. "That's why The Well told me not to get involved," he said. "Everything was under control, thanks to Him."

"Or Her, or It," Michael added.

"Whatever," they said, laughing as one.

Ciaran, however, failed to see the humor. Not because he wasn't a water vamp, but because he was a scientist. A scientist whose experiment had just exceeded his wildest expectations. "Boys, I hate to strip the gilding from your lilies," he interjected. "But this isn't about either of you. It's about Saoirse."

After a moment of silence, Ronan was the first to follow Ciaran's train of thought. "Blimey! You think the whirlpool meant that The Well was somehow protecting Saoirse?"

"Yes!" Ciaran cried.

"That would be borderline amazing," Michael shared. "Without, you know, the borderline part."

"Let me guess, Michael. Just before the whirlpool started, Morgandy was about to attack Saoirse," Ciaran hypothesized correctly. "Is that right?"

"Exactly!" Michael confirmed.

"I was right all along!" Ciaran shouted. "Saoirse *is* connected to The Well, but the relationship is even stronger than I ever imagined!"

"What do you mean?" Ronan asked.

"Saoirse didn't sneak out of here without anyone seeing her," Ciaran explained. "She was taken to a safe place. And there's no safer place than that Well of yours."

As Michael and Ronan ran out of the gym on their way to Inishtrahull Island to visit a particular spot buried deep within the Atlantic Ocean, Saoirse was sitting with her back against the cold, stone wall of The Well. Arms wrapped around her knees, Saoirse sighed, half-scared, half-bored, and wondered how in the world she had ever gotten there. And, more important, if she was ever going to be able to get back home.

chapter 25

In three different locations, three different revelations were beginning to unfold.

"What are you two doing here?" Saoirse asked.

"We should really be asking you that question," Ronan replied. And then, suddenly, he felt incredibly awkward.

Because they weren't visiting The Well after a feeding he and Michael remained clothed, wearing their Double A track pants over their swim team Speedos, all now soaking wet. They looked like they had gotten pushed into a pool and had only had enough time to rip their shirts off, a look that Ronan, especially, found to be a bit too casual in the presence of The Well. But it was more than that. Whenever they had made the journey to this sacred place it had been ceremonial and just the two of them; they never ventured here merely to visit, nor did they ever have company. Seeing Saoirse sitting on the ground and leaning against the base of The Well like she was resting against a tree trunk in The Forest in between classes was just a little too weird. "How did this happen?" he asked, his voice a hushed whisper.

Reaching overhead, Saoirse gripped the top of The Well and stood up. "You're asking me?" she snapped. "Aren't you the authority on all things water vampire-esque?"

Michael couldn't help but smile. Even here, standing in the shadow of The Well, the God-like entity that was worshipped by an entire race, Saoirse wasn't intimidated, not the least bit awestruck. Standing in her bikini, she rubbed her hands together to wipe away the sea grime and noticed some pieces of dirt still clinging to her skin. She dragged the palm of her right hand down the edge of The Well's rim and upon inspection wasn't completely satisfied with the result. "Guess the maid forgot to come in this week," she mumbled to herself.

This time Michael did laugh. Ronan, however, grew even more tense. Watching his sister act so informally in a place that commanded reverence and respect made Ronan uncomfortable. He knew The Well was protecting Saoirse, he knew that the two were indeed connected in some strange way, but he also knew The Well demanded obedience and decorum and could dispense punishment with the same ease as it bestowed mercy. Then again, maybe Ronan didn't know The Well at all.

He looked around the cave and saw that the rocks near the ceiling were shimmering with a golden light; he had never noticed that before. The ceiling itself was sprinkled with a silvery dust that sparkled and twinkled, making the entire cave glow. Ronan didn't know if he had never taken in these details before or if The Well was somehow changing the physical shape of its home, redecorating to welcome its latest guest. Was Saoirse really that special? When he heard the water within The Well ripple, sounding as if someone was plucking the strings of a harp, he was convinced The Well was laughing at him. *Now doesn't that just take the biscuit,* Ronan thought. *The Well's just like Michael. It finds humor in everything.*

Folding his arms across his bare chest, Ronan smirked. "My guess is that when The Well sensed you were in danger of being attacked by Morgandy, the pool turned into a portal and whisked you to safety," he explained. "Bringing you right here to home base."

If that were true, then they weren't kidding. This Well really did have super duper magical powers. Mimicking her brother's stance, Saoirse folded her arms. "Plausible, rabbit, very plausible, given, you know, the implausibility of our circumstances," she agreed. "Even though Michael was doing a jolly good job of rescuing me without any outside help." Saoirse felt the warmth of her flesh seep into her arms and was overcome with shyness, suddenly all too aware that she had never completely gotten over her crush on Michael and that her bathing suit was quite revealing. That was the last time she would ever be manipulated into trying to impress a boy. "This is all Ciaran's fault, you know?" she declared. "Him and his bleedin' experiments."

Glancing sideways at Michael, Ronan had to give their brother his due. "C'mon, Seersh," he said. "You have to admit, this one turned out to be pretty successful."

"We're like miles and miles below water, right?" she asked.

Marveling at the truth of the situation, Ronan finally unleashed his enthusiasm and grabbed his sister by her shoulders. Decorum be damned! "We're in uncharted territory, Saoirse!" he exclaimed. "Besides that, do you realize that you are the only non-water vampire to ever . . . ever! . . . cast your eyes on all of this?"

Unable to move her body, Saoirse twisted her head as much as she could, but all she could see was rock and stone. "You realize it's just a cave, right?"

Laughing hysterically, Ronan let Saoirse go, but held onto

his excitement. Needing some sort of physical contact he hugged Michael tightly, twirling him around a few times as Saoirse watched with a stunned expression. "She thinks this is just a cave!"

Equally bemused, Michael was laughing just as hard as Ronan. However, he also understood Saoirse's indifference. Even though the bulk of her family was comprised of water vamps, she was an outsider, excluded from this miraculous part of their lives. "It might look like just a cave, but it's sacred ground," Michael said, his voice more gentle than preaching. "I don't really know how it works or all of its mysteries, but trust me, Saoirse, your being here is nothing short of a miracle."

Saoirse did trust Michael, and she got what he was saying. She understood that she was standing amid majesty, touching blessed dirt. She just didn't feel anything. This place meant nothing to her. And for one of the first times in her life she understood that she should keep those feelings to herself. Ronan and Michael didn't want to hear that she would rather be back in St. Sebastian's or in her dorm hanging out with Ruby, so she self-edited and joined in with the merriment. "Well then, three cheers for Ciaran!"

"Professor Chow would probably give him full marks and an engraved plaque," Michael declared. "Heck he'd probably petition to have the Einstein Wing be renamed The Ciaran Eaves Research Laboratory For Things That Defy Explanation!"

"Brilliant idea!" Ronan beamed. "I second it!"

Rubbing the back of Michael's neck, Ronan held out his hand to Saoirse. Unsure of what her brother was staging, she held his hand and could feel the blood pumping through his veins. "This is an unprecedented event in our history," Ronan announced. "And I'm so bloody happy that I got to witness it." He squeezed her hand tightly. "Thank you, Saoirse."

"I should be thanking you guys," she stated. "This is all

really beautiful in its own way and peaceful and everything, but I thought I was going to be stuck here forever, so, um, thanks for showing up."

Michael grabbed Saoirse's free hand so the three of them were joined as one. "Why don't we go home and share the good news with the man of the hour?" he suggested. "Ciaran's gotta be dying to know what's going on."

"Good!" Saoirse declared. "Because I've got a pep rally to get to, and if we don't leave right now I'm going to be late."

Once again the water rippled, more intensely this time, and the cave was filled with a harp's flourish that indeed sounded like laughter. Clearly, The Well was amused by Saoirse's priorities. "Then let's go," Ronan said. The words were barely out of his mouth and he realized they might have a very serious problem. "Saoirse, I don't know exactly how you got here, but are you going to be able to hold your breath until we reach the water's surface?" he asked.

Saoirse didn't know *exactly* how she had gotten here either, but thinking back to how easily she had breathed underwater in the pool, she wasn't worried. "No need to fret, Roney," she assured. "Me and The Well here have got it all under control."

Standing in Sister Mary Elizabeth's office, Blakeley couldn't control his emotions. He was nervous, scared, and more than a little embarrassed. The first two feelings he was familiar with; the third, not so much. It wasn't because his trophy-filled office looked like it was a narcissist's retreat compared to the austerity of the nun's quarters. It was simply that it had been years since he had sought religious guidance. He didn't know how to begin.

Sitting behind her desk, Sister Mary recognized when someone was floundering. She placed her pencil next to her notepad and smiled. "Why don't you take a seat and tell me what brings you here?"

Blakeley could hardly stop pacing the small confines of the office; there was no way he was going to be able to remain seated. No, gotta keep moving, stay alert. Just because he was in a nun's office didn't mean he was safe; he knew better. "I'd rather stand, thank you."

"Whatever makes you most comfortable," she said. Knowing the coach the way she did, she knew that he was a no-nonsense man, so she adopted the same approach. She replaced her smile with a more serious look and asked, "So tell me, Peter, what's on your mind?"

How appropriate that a Christian woman would remind him that he had a Christian name. He hadn't been called Peter in years. To everyone—co-workers, students, their parents—he was just Blakeley or Coach. The sound of his own name made him feel like a child again. Had he really strayed that far from who he was? Had he really grown up to disregard everything that he had learned? Did it take something so . . . unnatural, so evil to remind him that he had once believed in things that required faith? He had no clue if this woman, this frail woman whose only weapon against the unknown was devotion, could help him regain his footing, help him rebuild his courage, but he had to try.

"Confession being good for the soul and all that tommy-rot?" he asked, his voice sarcastic to hide the flurry of emotions growing in his heart.

Clasping her hands, Sister Mary replied, "Just the simplest way to begin a conversation."

Blakeley found Sister Mary's straightforward attitude reassuring, if not entirely calming. Gripping the back of the only other chair in the room, he looked into the sister's unblinking eyes and found the strength to articulate the fear that threatened to consume him. "It's Michael Howard, Sister, he's not right," he blurted out. "He's trouble."

"Did you come to that conclusion on your own?" she

asked. "Or did you pray to God for guidance and understanding?"

"I don't know how to pray."

Sister Mary laughed more heartily than she or Blakeley expected. The sound was high-pitched and seemed to be released from not just her throat, but her whole body. "If you know how to talk," she said, "you know how to pray."

"This isn't funny, Sister!" Blakeley yelled, unable to control his anger. "I'm scared! And I think you know me well enough to know that that's not something I admit to very often."

"There's nothing wrong with being fearful, Peter," Sister Mary replied. Every trace of laughter was gone from her voice and had been replaced with a tone that was solemn and learned. "It's how we act when we're afraid that's key."

"Don't give me that! You've noticed it too. I've watched you!" Blakeley shouted, his forehead glazed with sweat. "You know there's something wrong with this Howard kid, and yet you're not afraid of him. Why?!"

Sister Mary wished she could hold Blakeley's hand and tell him he had nothing to be concerned about, that his fears were unfounded, but that wasn't the truth. Something bad was happening at Double A, and she was fully aware that Michael was at the center of it, but there wasn't a single part of her mind or soul that believed he was the cause; she believed he would be the salvation. Unfortunately, there was no way she was going to convince Blakeley of her beliefs. As with all faith-related teachings, he would have to come to his own conclusion in his own time.

"I know how I feel about Michael," she said. "What you need to do is search within yourself to find out how you truly feel about him."

Frustrated, Blakeley pressed harder on the back of the chair and pushed it down into the floor, the sound of wood scraping against wood interrupting the conversation. "So you got no answers for me then?" Blakeley challenged.

"I'm a nun, not an oracle," Sister Mary replied. She was hopeful that her laughter and slight irreverence would have more impact on her caller than a pious decree. "And I think you're a big enough boy to figure out the answers all on your own."

Brania wasn't sure what specific questions she should ask, but she knew if anyone could give her answers about her father's past it was his sister. That's why when Rhoswen showed up at the cave without warning or an invitation, announcing that it was time they went on a tour of the past, Brania was riddled with curiosity, even though she knew instinctively that it would alter the way she felt about her father forever.

Stepping out of Ruby's body, Rhoswen ignored Imogene's shriek and walked toward Brania, her green and white dress flowing around her, making it look like she was floating over the stones. The scent of the white roses that hung around her waist and graced her head drowned out the musty odor that occupied the cave. Her one outstretched arm, her one beckoning hand, was like an offering of unparalleled insight and knowledge, and Brania ached to grab onto it. But could she? Should she?

"I don't want to go with you," Brania said, inexplicably nervous about journeying into the unknown. It was an absurd feeling, but she sensed that wherever Rhoswen wanted to take her, whatever events she wanted her to see, would be horrifying. But how could anything be more horrifying than what she already knew about her father? He had made her do heinous things as a child. He had ripped purity from her heart and allowed the black blemishes of sin to settle into her soul, all because he was a coward, because he wanted to reap the benefits of someone else's wicked actions. Someone who he was supposed to love and protect and cherish. No, it was time to stop acting like the child she had never been and learn the truth. All she had to do was take hold of Rhoswen's hand. If it was so simple, why was she hesitating?

"Do you want to control your own immortality?" Rhoswen asked.

Brania's reply was immediate. "Yes."

"Do you want to break free from the harness your father has shackled you with?"

Again, Brania's answer came without thought. "Yes."

"Do you want to understand that the man who prevents you from fulfilling your potential is not worthy of your fear?"

Brania hesitated. Did she really want such knowledge? Did she really want to sever the ties that bound her to the man whom she loved and despised in equal amounts? She heard Imogene whimper, unnerved at watching Ruby's body remain frozen at one end of the cave and Rhoswen's ghost-like presence take up the other, and Brania found her answer. As much as she loved her ward, she never wanted to be that fragile, that despondent. If she didn't take this step, chances were that's what she would become. If she didn't take hold of Rhoswen's hand, she might never have another opportunity to escape that fate.

The moment flesh touched spirit, Brania and Rhoswen disappeared as easily as Imogene was able to when she was frightened. Hurtling into black space, Brania was blinded for a moment. Then she saw the world race by her like wisps of multicolored light. Nothing was clear; nothing was recognizable; she couldn't make out any landmarks, until she landed.

St. Joshua's looked the same, only the surroundings were different. There were very few buildings nearby, and the foliage was overflowing, wild, nothing like the meticulously manicured lawn today. Brania didn't know what time period she was in until she looked through the library window and saw her father as a teenager reading to a girl who was the carbon copy of the billowing spirit that stood next to her. The girl sitting on the ground next to her father was listening intently, devouring every word he spoke, all the while caressing a bouquet of white roses, stroking each petal and occasionally brushing a flower across her lips or her useless eyes.

"Your father would read to me every day," Rhoswen explained. "And with each new book he'd bring me a fistful of white roses."

The image was startling. David looked so gentle. Could this be the same man she knew? "He loves you very much," Brania observed.

"He did." Rhoswen clutched Brania's hand, her spirit-grip firm and secure, and they disappeared again only to reemerge standing outside the same building, only this time it looked different, slightly more modern. Brania realized they had traveled a few years into the future from the previous scene.

As the action unfolded before her eyes, Brania realized that this was the man she knew, this was the man she loved and hated and wanted to destroy. This was the man capable of performing acts of cruelty on those he claimed to love. Brania felt her heart pound within her chest as she watched Rhoswen sit staring into her own private darkness, smiling, unsuspecting, while a few feet away David cut himself and created a circle of his own blood. She felt her stomach churn as she heard him whisper in Rhoswen's ear that they were going to play a game. And she screamed out loud when David stabbed his sister in the back while she smiled.

The first thought that came to her mind when she stopped screaming was that her father didn't even have the courage to look Rhoswen in the face when he murdered her. The next was: Why did he do something so vile in the first place?

Reading her mind, Rhoswen explained. "Your father sacrificed me to Zachariel so he could become a vampire. As part of his reward, Zachariel made it so his race could walk in the sunlight on this hallowed ground." The blind girl smiled. "Ironically, only their eyes needed protection from sunshine."

Finally, Brania understood what was so special about this land; it was drenched in her family's blood. "He's destroyed everyone who's ever loved him."

Finally, Rhoswen knew her murder would be avenged. "Because he loves himself and his power just a little bit more."

She scooped up a handful of dirt and blood from the ground where her dead body lay and molded it into a ball. She threw it up in the air, and when it landed in Brania's waiting hands the ball of dirt had transformed into a gorgeous white rose in full bloom. "This flower will bring you more luck than any of my flowers have over the centuries," she advised. "Choose how you use it wisely."

By the time they returned to the cave and Rhoswen had once again assumed Ruby's body, Brania already knew what she must do. After Rhoswen left, she helped Imogene out of her coffin and sat the girl down next to her on the large boulder in the middle of the cave.

"I have good news," she said, though her expression was far more sinister than joyful. "It's time for us to get to work so we can reclaim our freedom."

chapter 26

Girls suck! Totally, completely, and without a bloody doubt.

Nakano looked from face to face to face, from the Italian girl to the Swede to the pretty Hindu girl with the pierced nose, and he couldn't believe he was standing in the boys' locker room surrounded by nothing but girls who wouldn't shut up. On and on and on they chattered about the stupidest things in the world; one dumb sentence after another tumbled out of their painted mouths. Nakano thought if he had to listen to one more word about clothes or makeup or the best feminine products his head would explode. The only girl he had any interest in talking to had double crossed him, the same girl who had gotten him in this mess in the first place, and the same girl who was running into the locker room from the back entrance.

"Saoirse!" Nakano yelled. "It's about time!"

"Sorry," she said, buttoning up her skirt. "I was, um, a little detained."

"Crikey! I thought you were going to stand me up."

"Kanosan! How could you think I would do that?" she yelled back. "I'm the one who set this whole thing up."

"Well, you're cutting it a little close, aren't you?" he said. "We go on in less than a bloody minute."

"I had stuff to do with my brother and Michael," she replied, fusing a lie with the truth. "But I'm here now and I'm ready to go. Isn't it exciting?!"

"No, it isn't!" Nakano's complexion turned even paler than normal. "I'm terrified."

And he had reason to be. Never before had Nakano been in a situation like this, not as a human or as a vampire, and he had been in some peculiar and unusual situations as both. This one, however, was odder than them all.

Huddled in the locker room, he wondered if he was about to make the stupidest mistake of his life. If he did he would have no one else to blame except himself. Well, and Saoirse too, because it was her idea and she was the one who had talked him into doing it, but at some point he could have said no. It was just that he didn't want to. He was having fun, and that's all he really wanted, to balance out all the stress he'd been under lately with some good times. Running his hand nervously through the bristly top of his crew cut, he had the feeling that those good times were all about to come to an end.

"Ladies! And Mr. Kai, here we go!" the Italian girl chirped excitedly. "Kano, you stay in the middle of the group like we decided, since you're our secret weapon."

The girl was Talisa Rondo, captain of the cheerleading squad, and she was leading Nakano out onto the St. Sebastian gym floor for his debut as the first and thus far only male cheerleader in all of Double A's history. Instead, he felt like he was being led to an execution.

David's voice boomed throughout the gym and spilled into the locker room. "Honored guests, distinguished rivals, I welcome all of you to the National Swim Team Competition and Archangel Academy's Tri-Centennial Celebration." He paused as the crowd roared, and the sound made Nakano sick. They were a rowdy group, filled with students and faculty members from schools all across Western Europe who had come here to win some swimming races, and as a side treat they were going to get to ridicule the lone boy who was cheering with all the girls. They would join in with Fritz and Ronan and all his other so-called friends at Double A to morph into one loud, angry, mocking voice that Nakano would hear in his dreams for the rest of eternity. This was so not worth it. "I can't do this."

Saoirse whipped around so fast that her ponytail whacked Nakano in the face. "Vamp up, Kanosan," she whispered. "We've been practicing and working our arses off for this moment for weeks."

Wiping away some cold sweat that was bubbling on his forehead, Kano nodded. "I know, and it's been great, Seersh, I've had a really great time with you and the squad, but I can't do this."

"Why? Because everybody's going to find out you're gay?" she asked, fists on hips. "We interrupt this pep rally for a school news bulletin, everybody already knows!"

"Yes, okay!" he admitted. "I'm proud of who I am, but why do I have to advertise it to the entire school? To every bloody school in Western Europe?"

Saoirse had no idea what it was like to be gay, but she did know what it was like to be embarrassed because of who you were, so she understood what Nakano was going through. She also knew that after the shock of seeing Nakano standing in a field of pom-pom girls wore off, the crowd was going to flip out watching Kano do all his acrobatic vampire tricks. She had to find the right words to convince him that if he chickened out now he would never forgive himself. Subtlety had never worked for her before, so why start now.

"If you wimp out now and watch this pep rally from the bleachers instead of showing this school and this whole crowd how brill your moves are, you will regret it for the rest of your life," she spat. "And when you're 192 and I'm dead, I'll come back as a ghost and make you remember that you gave up a chance to be a superstar cheerleader just 'cause you were scared." She took a breath to let her words seep into Nakano's brain and his heart, but saw no change; it looked like she hadn't made an impact. One last try. "Do not deprive these people of seeing the Kano triple twist backflip," she whispered reverentially. "It will make them believe in the impossible." What a terrific closing argument! Saoirse seriously thought she might try for a career as a lawyer, she could be very persuasive when she wanted to.

And successful. Nakano couldn't resist, partly because Saoirse's words and enthusiasm swayed him, but partly because he really did want to show off. Why not use his powers for good? Entertain the troops, make them see just how incredibly talented and superior he really was without plunging his fangs into any reluctant necks. It could be a nice change of pace. "Let's do this!"

Some girls marched, some pranced, others just walked out onto the gym floor, but all of them worked together to shield Nakano from the audience in the bleachers until Talisa gave the command and the squad parted to reveal who they were hiding in the middle of their huddle. That's when the crowd gasped. Collectively and loudly. And that's when Nakano's conviction waned. Saoirse's pep talk was forgotten, and all he wanted to do was flee, run into The Forest and never come back again. He peered into the crowd and saw his friends staring at him with their jaws open, incredulous looks etched into their faces. He didn't have to read their minds; he just had to use his vampire hearing to listen to what they were saying to one another.

"This is why Kano quit the swim team a second time?" Michael asked Ronan rhetorically. "To be a cheerleader?"

Shaking his head Ronan replied, "Funny, I never thought of him as the cheery type."

"Nakano's a cheerleader now," Fritz whispered to Ruby, who was just as surprised.

"I thought it was an all-girl squad," she remarked.

"Technically, it still kind of is," Ciaran quipped.

Oh really, Eaves, Nakano thought. *Tell me what girl can do this?*

On the first beat of the music Nakano took all the nervousness and anxiety and fear that he had been feeling and put it into motion, three continuous backflips to be exact. While the girls on the squad cheered, shook their pom-poms, and did cartwheels and some other basic gymnastic moves all around him, Nakano began a routine that would immediately attain legendary status at Double A. He flipped, he flew, he twisted, spiraled, and contorted in the air and at some point, possibly after his double flip over a small pyramid of cheerleaders, the audience forgot all about how weird it was to see a guy cheering with a bunch of girls, and they started cheering for him. Saoirse was beaming as Kano threw her up into the air so she could do a Russian split and land in his waiting arms.

"Told ya so," she said, a bit out of breath. Not waiting for a reply, she jumped out of his arms to join the rest of the squad and give Nakano ample room to finish the routine. The crowd was now screaming so loudly the music couldn't even be heard. No matter. Kano didn't need music, just the satisfaction that thanks to some encouragement from a friend he hadn't run.

Standing between Talisa and Saoirse, Nakano didn't have

to use any preternatural skill to know what the crowd thought of him. They were standing, stomping their feet, chanting his name. When Saoirse gave him a hug, he was so happy he couldn't speak. And when Fritz and the others ran toward him and bombarded him with accolades and praise, he just smiled and felt his cheeks grow warm.

"Blimey, mate!" Fritz exclaimed, his hands gesticulating wildly, even the one that was holding onto Ruby. "Where'd you learn to do all that stuff?"

When you're a vampire it sort of comes naturally. "Practice," Nakano replied.

"You were amazing!" Michael cried. "I can't believe you kept it a secret."

"I can't believe I had the guts to do it."

"Are you bonkers?" Ronan shouted. "You're Olympic caliber with moves like that."

"Thanks, guys," Kano said sheepishly, not at all used to such attention. "But you should all thank Saoirse. She's the one who convinced me to join the squad."

"Of course she did," Ronan said. "Always full of surprises."

Before they could all agree, Coach Blakeley announced that the first swimming race was about to begin and that all the teams needed to gather around the pool. As the group split up, Ciaran pulled Saoirse aside with Michael and Ronan close behind. When he spoke he made sure no one else could hear them. "So I heard someone had a right fine adventure this morning," Ciaran said, his eyes shimmering with excitement.

Fussing with her pom-poms, Saoirse confirmed the rumor. "I know, I know, first non-water vamp to see The Well," she replied.

"Which is bloody amazing!" Ciaran exclaimed.

"You're not missing that much, though," she said. "It's a bit on the cold side."

Ignoring his sister, Ciaran rambled on, his excitement

building. "No! You can breathe underwater, and The Well is protecting you even though you're human!" He turned to Ronan and Michael, who were still impressed by the morning's events. "Sis, I don't know what you are, but clearly The Well thinks you're bloody special!"

Now that she had actually seen The Well, seen with her own eyes what her family and their race prattled on about and praised, she wasn't sure she shared their opinion. If she was so special and if she had this unique connection to this thing, this mysterious and all-powerful entity, why wasn't she more excited? Why didn't she think her life had just gotten a huge upgrade and she was standing on the corner of Amazing Avenue and Smashingly Brilliant Street? Maybe because she had had more fun being tossed in the air by Nakano in front of a crowd of applauding spectators. She wasn't sure. Thankfully, boring self-examination could be postponed, because just then Blakeley's voice boomed over the loudspeaker. "Let the games begin!"

Sitting in the bleachers David tried to push all worry from his mind and concentrate on the mundane competition that was playing out in front of him. It was sheer willpower that prevented him from ripping those damned T-shirts that Ruby had designed from the backs of the students. Wherever he looked he was assaulted by a red T-shirt with the number three and two white roses that spelled out three hundred. It was like Rhoswen was all around him, suffocating him. He had to ignore them, act as if they weren't there, or else he'd lose his mind. He looked forward to watch the participants, marvel at their lithe, sculpted bodies, their muscular frames clad in tiny bathing suits in so many different colors, each representing a different school. He had no interest in them sexually, that was perverse, but they were a distraction, and he did appreciate and admire the discipline required to attain such physical beauty and supremacy. Nothing simple was ever achieved easily; he knew that better than most everyone. Except perhaps Brania.

"The competition is off to a rousing start," she silently declared.

Looking straight ahead, David didn't turn to the right where Brania was sitting next to him. He focused on Morgandy, in the middle lane of the pool, a few strokes ahead of his nearest competitor. *"Because I saw to it that it was planned meticulously."*

What a perfect segue, Father. Thank you. *"I have a plan,"* Brania said. She was also staring at Morgandy as he prepared to flip and swim the last lap of the race. She, however, had no interest in the match. She was merely acting like her father, aloof and indifferent, when just the opposite was true. *"Edwige is planning to feed tomorrow,"* she informed him. *"With my help you can follow her to The Well and do with it whatever your heart desires."*

David could no longer resist. He turned to face his daughter and was incensed to see that she still kept her eyes on the race.

"And just how will you be able to follow Edwige to The Well?" David asked.

"I have a secret weapon," Brania replied.

David knew better than to ask what Brania's secret weapon was. His only chance of finding out was to let his daughter think she had the upper hand.

"Excellent," David replied tersely. *"Then the time has come for you to be appropriately rewarded."*

"I was hoping you'd say that," Brania replied, finally deigning to look at her father. *"I'd like my reward beforehand, and since I know you're such a busy man, I've taken the liberty of picking out the perfect gift."*

David hated giving in to anyone, especially a woman, but

he had no choice. Brania, for the moment was in control. *"What would you like in return?"* David asked. *"Say the word, and your wish will be granted."*

"I think it's time that you made another sacrifice," Brania replied.

The word made David shudder. They both knew its significance. Somehow David understood that his daughter knew that he had sacrificed the life of his sister to ensure the fulfillment of his own desires. And Brania knew that David wouldn't want his secret to be learned by the masses. Even vampires have an ethical code, and the brutal murder of one's blind sister sort of crossed that line. Brania thought it was the perfect time to cross another.

"I want to be an only child again," she said, clutching the white rose that she had tucked inside her skirt pocket. *"I'd like you to kill Jean-Paul."*

"What!?" David cried.

The race culminated in a Double A victory so David's outburst went unnoticed by those around him. His shock, however, delighted his daughter.

"Please, Father," she said. *"Remember to use your inside voice."*

Brania's words kept repeating in his mind over and over again, like a record player whose needle had gotten caught in a groove. *Kill Jean-Paul. Kill Jean-Paul. Kill Jean-Paul. How could she be so cruel to expect me to kill my own son?* The answer came to him so quickly and with such brutal honesty that David had to grip his knees to stop his hands from shaking. *Because you taught her well.*

Indeed he had. Just like he had sacrificed his sister for the good of his people, he now had to sacrifice his son. The end—destruction of The Well, end of water vamps—would surely justify the means. There was only one problem: David couldn't trust his daughter.

"How do I know you'll keep your end of the bargain?"
David asked her.

"You don't," she replied. Hardly the answer he was looking for. *"You'll just have to take my word for it."*

Damn her! There wasn't any other way! This Imogene girl was linked to Edwige; she was the only one who could lead them to The Well, and she was under Brania's control. There was a very good chance Brania would double cross him, but it was a chance that he had to take. Unfortunately, if he thought about it much longer, the chance would slip by. *"Remember, Edwige feeds tomorrow, so there's no time to lollygag,"* Brania had reminded him. *"I'll call for you at daybreak and expect to see Jean-Paul's burnt ashes."*

This was treason! Blackmail! So many years David had ignored his son, preferring to dote on his daughter instead, and now that he had reconnected with Jean-Paul he was going to have to sever their ties. How could he possibly kill him? The mere thought of it was unfathomable. No, there was no way he could do that. He could, however, order his execution. Yes, that he could do. That he could do very easily. But first he would have to find an assassin.

After the first set of races was completed there was a break in the competition, and the crowd began milling about the gym. David found the person he was looking for standing alone near the windows.

"Nakano," David said. "I have an important assignment for you."

And just like that Nakano's perfect day came to an end.

chapter 27

Nakano knew something was wrong, David was being way too friendly.

During their entire walk over from St. Sebastian's to his office, David had talked nonstop, complimenting Nakano on his acrobatic exhibition, admiring how clever he had been to illustrate his incredible skills in public without calling attention to his preternatural abilities, even congratulating him on making the difficult decision to quit the swim team so he could showcase his talents appropriately. "A wise man knows when he is beaten," David had said. "But it is the courageous man who shakes off defeat to rise to victory."

No matter what David said, no matter how impressed or interested he might seem in Nakano's recent achievement, there was no way that he had brought him here to philosophize about his cheerleading debut. This meeting was definitely about something else. But David was taking his sweet time revealing just what that was.

"This was given to me by a geisha I once knew," David announced, admiring the ornate box that lived on the mantel of the fireplace. "She painted it herself." He turned it around in his hand, gazing, searching at each side of the small, rectangular object that was decorated with a different scene—a cluster of butterflies, a waterfall, a bevy of cherry blossoms, a stony brook—all snippets of natural beauty, all delicately hand painted. "Each one of these panels reminds me of her," he continued. "She too was an exquisite creature." Lifting the lid, which was topped with a vibrant blue and black Wanderer butterfly, its wings opened, but frozen in flight, David took a deep breath. "And loyal."

And just how is a stupid box loyal? Nakano thought.

David didn't hear Kano's question—he was peering underneath the lid, but he answered it anyway. "She filled this container with her blood as an offering," David said.

Well, yes, that could be considered an act of loyalty. Or stupidity, depending upon how you looked at it.

"I can still remember how she tasted. I can still smell her scent," he recalled. "As fragrant and alive as a Japanese garden."

Returning the piece to its rightful place, David motioned for Nakano to sit in front of the fireplace in one of the two side chairs that were made of distressed brown leather. The fabric was creased and the color faded due to age and frequent use, and as Kano sat he was struck by how the texture reminded him of David's face. The headmaster's typically smooth, age-defying complexion looked tired, strained as if tension and stress were lying just on the other side of his flesh. Maybe that's why he wanted to speak with him, to get something off his chest, ask him to share his burden? Or maybe he just wanted to tell him stories about a former concubine, thinking Nakano would get all nostalgic and want to hear more anecdotes about his home country's past.

The leather moaned slightly when David gripped the back of the chair opposite Nakano. David looked like he was going to make the same sound. "I hope you will prove yourself to be equally as loyal."

"Haven't I already proven my allegiance to you and our race?" Nakano sniped. "There's no reason for my loyalty to be questioned."

The time had come, however, for it to be tested.

Finally David relaxed a bit, as if a burden had been lifted, slightly, from his shoulders, and he smiled. "Good," he said. "Because I want you to kill Jean-Paul Germaine."

Something must be wrong with his hearing. There was no way Nakano had heard David correctly. "I'm sorry," Kano said. "You want me to do *what*?"

Despite the ache that was growing all throughout David's body, he made sure his smile didn't fade, in fact he willed it to grow even wider. "I believe you heard me the first time," he said. "It was, if I may point out, a very concise and uncomplicated request."

Uncomplicated?! This had to be some colossal joke. "Why would you want me to kill Jean-Paul?" Nakano cried in disbelief. "I thought the two of you were really close."

David's will collapsed, and his smile faded. "Are you questioning me?"

The words tumbled out of Kano's mouth before he realized how foolish they were. "Yes, as a matter of fact I am."

The movement was so reactive, so quick, Nakano didn't even know he was being pinned against the wall until he tried to touch the floor with his feet. It took him another second to realize that it was extremely difficult to breathe, which only made sense since David was holding him by the throat and squeezing so hard that his knuckles resembled chunks of ivory.

"I am your master!" David seethed, his foul breath sting-ing Nakano's eyes, his spit sprinkling onto Nakano's lips. "How dare you question me!"

Whenever Kano had been manhandled before, and the times had been many, he had always reacted in the same way, he would fight back, defend himself whether he was infuri-ated or frightened. This was different. He felt one of David's hands around his throat, the other pressing down hard onto his forehead. He saw David's vile, deformed face, and yet he felt nothing; he was numb. "I'm sorry," he said, the words sounding as if they were spoken by a very intelligent robot.

"Jean-Paul's death is necessary for our people to reach a higher purpose," David hissed. But the next words almost made him choke. "He needs to be killed!"

Images of Jean-Paul's beautiful face bombarded Nakano's brain. Bathed in moonlight, sheathed in passionate sweat, drenched in blood. No, not that, anything but that. Too many feelings were swarming inside Kano's mind; he loved Jean-Paul, he hated him, he was angry that their relationship was over, he was disappointed in his actions. He couldn't think straight, so he decided not to think at all.

"And I want you to do it," David instructed. "Bring his ashes to me by daybreak."

The ticking of the grandfather clock filled the room as David waited for a response that wasn't coming soon enough for his liking. "DO YOU UNDERSTAND ME?!" David was so furious, so disgusted with Nakano, with Brania, with him-self, that his cry resembled a madman's. His fangs were scraping against Nakano's skin, and all he wanted to do was tear the boy's flesh to shreds and savor every tender mouthful to satiate the pain that was enveloping him. But he couldn't, he couldn't destroy his servant. He needed Nakano to do his bidding.

And so Nakano agreed. "I understand."

Dropping to the floor with a thud, Nakano stayed in a

clump for almost a minute before finding the strength to get up. When he stood, he saw David was standing by the window, his eyes closed, sunlight pouring over him, calling attention to the lines and crevices that were now undeniable parts of his face. The headmaster suddenly looked old.

Nakano remained staring at his leader, and he was torn between the desire to embrace him or to push him through the window, hoping the glass would slice his face, further destroying the robust beauty he had once possessed. But he couldn't move to fulfill either thought. He was too confused, too blindsided. It was as if he were suspended in time and space and didn't know where to go, even though he had very specific orders to carry out. The grandfather clock ticked louder, each tick, tick, tick, more insistent than the last. Nakano wished he could turn back the hands of time to just an hour ago when people were applauding him, thanking him for doing something they had never even dreamed of doing. He almost laughed out loud. Now he was going to do something he had never dreamed of doing: kill his ex-boyfriend. It was absurd, it made no sense to him whatsoever, yet it was David's wish, and Nakano knew it was useless to try and defy his leader's mandate even though he might be showing signs of weakness. He might actually have an Achilles' heel, but he was still more powerful than any creature Nakano knew and, more than that, he was still in charge and he still expected his orders to be carried out without hesitation.

To prove that point, just as Nakano was leaving David's office he heard the headmaster mention that he would be greatly rewarded for his efforts. Sadly, Nakano already knew the kind of gift he'd receive in return for committing murder.

He took the long way to The Forest and walked around the back of St. Sebastian's, hoping he wouldn't run into anyone. The swimming competition and cheerleading seemed so far away now and so inconsequential; they seemed to have happened to someone else, not him. But it just wasn't his lucky day. A few yards away Michael and Ronan were stealing kisses behind a tree, wearing only their gym shorts, their bodies fused together as one. When they finally separated, Nakano saw that matching gold medals hung from their necks. Of course God would let them win gold since they didn't have enough already. They just had each other, the perfect relationship, the perfect bodies, the perfect lives, everything Nakano would never have. Running off into the bowels of The Forest, Nakano didn't hear Michael call out to him. He only heard the voice in his head telling him he was getting exactly what he deserved.

When the damp air poisoned his nostrils he cursed himself for returning to the cave, but what other choice did he have? Where else did he have to go? He had to talk to someone, and Brania was the only one he could confide in and the only one who might possibly be able to help. Kano knew she wasn't on the best terms with David, but she was still his daughter. Maybe she could intervene, get him to find someone else to carry out this horrendous deed. Or better yet, get him to reverse his decision and realize it was a mistake. He could talk to Saoirse; she had become a friend. But no, despite being surrounded by the supernatural she was still an innocent, and Nakano couldn't take that away from her. No, Brania was his only hope.

As usual Ghost Girl was lurking about, sulking because she was lonely or bored, and Brania was acting as if she actually enjoyed being in this hellhole. How could anyone enjoy living here? And how could anyone think killing Jean-Paul was a smart idea?

"Because it'll mean my father will forever be in your debt," Brania reasoned.

That would have made sense if Nakano had wanted a connection. The real problem was he didn't want to be tied to David; he wasn't sure he wanted to be tied to any of his race any longer. "But why me?" Nakano replied. "Your father's got an army of henchmen, bloodthirsty killers who love this sort of thing."

Brania wasn't surprised that her father was too much of a coward to kill Jean-Paul himself, but she was surprised that he had sealed his fate so quickly. He was obviously a desperate man. Desperate, yes, but also cunning, duplicitous, and quite possibly the most resourceful man she had ever known. "Because Jean-Paul would never suspect you to be his assassin," Brania replied. "It's quite a brilliant plan actually."

That was not what Nakano wanted to hear. Bowing his head, he tossed a few tiny rocks against the side of the coffin. "Stop that!" Imogene shouted. "I don't come to your home and throw rocks."

"This isn't a home. It's a cave!" Nakano shouted.

Staring at Imogene, Nakano thought he found the answer: The entire world had gone insane. A vampire's life was not supposed to be like this; it was supposed to be too good to be true! It wasn't supposed to be filled with questions and repercussions and guilt.

"You have nothing to feel guilty about," Brania said, reading Kano's mind. "You're only following your master's orders."

"Then why do I feel sick?" Nakano asked.

The question gave Brania pause. She wanted to tell Kano that he'd get used to the feeling just as she had, but there was no need to admit the things that crowded her own heart; those things were not meant to be shared. "My father must have a very good reason for asking you to do this," she said, trying to sound as if she didn't know exactly what that reason was. "Jean-Paul must have done something terrible. Perhaps he committed treason or betrayed our race. He must have done something unspeakable to have the mark of death placed on his head."

That could be true. Nakano had witnessed Jean-Paul's evil

side firsthand when he saw the vision of him killing Diego without mercy, compassion, or necessity. It was very possible that he had done something even worse that David had found out about, something that deserved the ultimate punishment. The more he thought about it, however, the more he realized his ambivalence had nothing to do with killing Jean-Paul and everything to do with saving himself. "It's just that... I've tried hard... really, bloody hard... to turn my life around," Kano cried. "I don't know if I can do this."

"Kano, you've already killed once before," Brania said gently. "Will it really make that much difference if you kill again?"

That's why he had come here, so he could hear someone speak the truth out loud, a truth he was too afraid to acknowledge. He was already damned. It wouldn't matter if he were damned twice.

Counting the pebbles he still held in his hand, Nakano replied, "I guess you're right."

His voice was so resigned, so defeated, Brania almost felt sorry for him. Almost. "I have something that will help you," she said.

She walked over to the coffin and pulled out the white rose that Rhoswen had given her. It was even more full-bodied than it had been before. "Put this in your pocket and keep it with you at all times," she instructed, handing Nakano the rose. "And you'll succeed in carrying out our leader's wishes."

Whatever powers this flower possessed, they were pretty remarkable. All Nakano had to do was think *Lead me to Jean-Paul,* and it was as if his legs were walking on their own. Until they picked up speed and began to run, then glide over the land until he wound up at the hideout in Eden.

The last time he had been here he had snuck away from school so he and Jean-Paul could make love. Turns out there really had been no love involved, not from Jean-Paul's point of view anyway. Today, Nakano would be the one with the cold heart. At least he was trying to keep it cold, and he had been doing a good job of it until he heard that unmistakable French accent.

Standing outside, he overheard Jean-Paul's breathy voice and remembered how mesmerized he had been by the sound, how important it had made him feel to know Jean-Paul was talking to him. When he got inside, however, Nakano understood that Jean-Paul's words were now meant for someone else.

"Alexei," Nakano said, startling the half-dressed couple. "Don't you have a race to swim?"

The Russian picked up his T-shirt from the floor and used it to wipe away some sweat bubbles that had formed above his upper lip. "I medaled already," he snickered. "Not due back until the team competition in a few hours."

"Gold?" Nakano asked.

After a pause, Alexei replied, "Bronze."

Before Kano could make a wisecrack, Jean-Paul spoke. "I 'ear zee only medal you can ween eez for shaking your pom-poms."

Nakano heard their laughter, but didn't respond to it. He didn't ignore it; he simply used it as fuel, motivation to push him closer toward his goal. "Hello, Jean-Paul," he said. "You blokes do remember there's a bedroom right upstairs?"

Jean-Paul's lips sloped into an arrogant smile. "We were so 'ungry, we couldn't wait."

"Well, don't let me stop you," Kano said, then impressed himself by coming up with a solution to his problem. "Unless you fancy some company."

What an interesting proposition. Jean-Paul turned to Alexei to see if the boy was just a boy and was pleasantly surprised that he wasn't. "Despite crossing over to Lady Academy, you showed some pretty smashing moves out there in the gym this morning," Alexei marveled. "Could be fun."

Nakano couldn't promise that. He couldn't promise anything except that it would be memorable. Fact was he didn't know what was going to happen next. He was no longer thinking, only saying the first thing that popped into his head, and he had no idea if he was in control or if the rose had taken over his mind as well as his body. "I can only promise that it'll be an afternoon you'll never forget."

"Then what are we waiting for," Jean-Paul said. "Let's go upstairs."

Jeremiah's old room was the same, except that it looked like it hadn't been cleaned in over a year. It had always resembled a flophouse, but without any upkeep it had slipped into a further state of decay. Other than the accumulation of dust, there was very little else in the room besides the bed, which was all they really needed anyway. Watching Jean-Paul kiss Alexei, Nakano waited to be gripped by jealousy, hate, something, but nothing came. He watched the passion behind their kisses escalate, but felt no emotion whatsoever. As he had climbed the narrow stairs to the room he had thought he would go ballistic seeing the two of them become intimate with each other, but he had been wrong. Might be for the best—he wouldn't be distracted by his feelings and could focus on carrying out David's orders.

His heart remained steady when he felt Jean-Paul's hand on the back of his neck push him toward Alexei. His heart rate didn't increase when he felt their lips touch, when their tongues flicked against each other. It was as if it was all happening to someone else. But it wasn't; it was happening to him, and he had to grab hold of his mind and his feelings before they floated away completely and weren't retrievable. If he was going to do this, he had to take responsibility for his actions. He might be a soldier, carrying out a direct order, but he also had a choice.

He could feel Alexei's hands on his body. He just didn't think about them; he thought about his options. Maybe he could defy David's command and run far from Double A, become a fugitive. But how realistic was that? David could track him down wherever he ran to or instruct one of his minions to hunt him down and kill him for his disobedience. No, Nakano wasn't thrilled with his life, but he wasn't suicidal. He only had one choice, the one David had given to him. The one he had given to him without explanation.

How could anyone who was able to kiss this well do something that would warrant a death penalty? It was ludicrous. Jean-Paul's lips tasted the same, sweet and soft, in stark contrast to his rough beard, and his long tongue had its own lazy rhythm. All the incredible times they had spent together rushed back, and Nakano remembered why he had fallen in love with Jean-Paul in the first place. The only thing that seemed off was his laugh. That didn't make sense. Why was he laughing?

"I'm sorry, Kano," Jean-Paul said as he clutched his stomach and rolled back onto the bed. His open shirt fell to the side and exposed his smooth, lean chest and the thin, vertical line of black hair that started just below his bellybutton. He looked beautiful, but his appearance was truly the only beautiful thing about him. "I can't do theese," Jean-Paul said, howling with laughter. "You are, 'ow do you say? Yes, making me seeck."

Nakano was the only one who didn't think it was a funny thing to say. Alexei cracked up and fell back onto the bed, his head resting next to Jean-Paul's. "You're like that leetle peeg," Jean-Paul continued. "That fat peeg Diego."

Finally the feelings that Nakano had been ignoring burst inside his heart like a balloon that was filled with too much air. He fell forward onto the bed, his head dangling, and heard something release from his lips, like a groan. There were no words, only sound. The mattress was dipping slightly from the sudden extra weight, and Nakano's forehead pressed against the sheets as he slowly started to punch the bed. Once, twice, so many times that he lost count. He had no idea how he looked, and he didn't care. Jean-Paul and Alexei, however, thought he was putting on one hilarious show.

Rolling onto his side, Alexei shouted, "Somebody toss the pig some pom-poms!"

Jean-Paul wailed and started banging the bed with his fist, mocking Nakano. When he caught his breath, he begged, "Now squeal for us, leetle peeg! We want to 'ear you squeal!"

"Sorry," Nakano replied. "This little piggy would rather kill."

Reaching inside his jacket Nakano whipped out a wooden stake that he had whittled from a thick branch he had found in The Forest. A second later, the laughter had stopped.

Kano's empty black eyes stared into Jean-Paul's frightened irises, and he watched them grow, aware that Jean-Paul believed his life was coming to an end. But Jean-Paul was not ready to give up. As Nakano raised his arm, Jean-Paul grabbed Alexei and used him as a human shield, and when Kano's arm slashed through the air he didn't have enough time to stop the movement. The stake that was meant for Jean-Paul rammed straight into Alexei's heart.

As the unlucky Russian burst into flames, Jean-Paul rolled to one side and Kano jumped to the other, both shielding their eyes from the sudden explosion. The only thing that separated the two were bright red, billowing wisps of flame, outlined in black, that crackled and licked the air. And then there was nothing but a pile of ash.

"Sacre bleu!" Jean-Paul screamed in his native tongue as he scrambled to his knees. "Murderer!"

"Now who's squealing like a leetle peeg?" Nakano asked.

Speechless, Jean-Paul reached for the edge of the bed so he could stand up, but only succeeded in grabbing the sheets. He lost his footing and fell backward as the sheets and

Alexei's disintegrated body fell on top of him. *"Merde!"* Jean-Paul shrieked, brushing the ash off of him wildly. "You weel burn in 'ell for theese. David weel see to eet!"

"And who do you think ordered your death?"

A wave of shock washed over Jean-Paul's face. "That ees a lie!" Jean-Paul spat, finally standing and facing Nakano. "My father would never send you to keel 'is only son."

His son? Jean-Paul is David's son! That can't be true. Brania would've said something. She must know Jean-Paul was her brother. Nakano stumbled back as Jean-Paul moved toward him. As twisted as it sounded, Nakano knew Jean-Paul spoke the truth. But how could a father order his own son's execution? Nakano's own father despised him, but Nakano could never imagine he would place a price on his head. How could David do such a thing? And why had he been put in the middle of it all?

"You're David's son?" Nakano asked.

"Yes," Jean-Paul replied. "And I weell see to eet that you suffer for what you 'ave done 'ere today!"

But Nakano wasn't finished. As Jean-Paul reached out to grab the stake from Kano's sweaty hand, the white rose vibrated in the boy's pocket. Before Kano could comprehend what was happening, Jean-Paul slipped on the fallen bedspread, his body lurching forward, and he clutched Kano's shoulders. They both looked down at the same time and saw that the stake had found a second target.

In an instant Jean-Paul's beautiful face was gone, replaced by a ball of fire. Then just black soot. As the ash smoldered at his feet, Nakano pulled the crumbled rose out from his pocket and watched it bloom to life. "Brania was right about you," he remarked, before tucking it back for safe keeping. Who knew when he'd need that kind of luck again?

When Nakano walked into David's office a few minutes before midnight, he didn't acknowledge the headmaster, but went directly for the geisha's ornate box. It really would make the perfect urn. He opened up the brown paper bag he was carrying and emptied the contents inside of it. Closing the lid, he presented it to David.

Outside, the cheers continued, the students still reveling in Double A's gold medal victory in the Team of the Year competition. Inside, the celebration was much more subdued.

"You have done well," he said, his voice thick, but too in shock to cry.

"I'll expect my reward shortly," Kano replied.

As he left the room he couldn't help but smile. David had no idea his treasured souvenir actually contained Alexei's ashes. The bag that had been filled with Jean-Paul's remains was floating somewhere in the polluted water of the Eden sewer system. Nakano couldn't think of a more perfect resting place for the bastard.

chapter 28

O feathered wings that soar above this land that we
    call home.
Immortal creatures filled with love protect us as we
    roam.
Throughout this earth and back again over land and
    sea, guide us so we may return where we were born
    to be.
This hallowed ground, our resting place, Archangel
    Academy.

When David finished singing the school's anthem he felt his shoulder blades twitch. His own wings were eager to present themselves, eager to come out of hiding and show the assembled crowd indisputable proof that David was and would always be their unrivaled leader. Looking at the sea of faces staring at him, the blank expressions of those who had gathered in his office, David thought they could use a jolt, a reminder that they existed only to carry out his bidding, but now wasn't the time for exhibitionism, now was the time for action.

"By the end of today's Tri-Centennial Celebration, I will have destroyed The Well!" David announced.

Morgandy's whooping cheer would have sounded more raucous if it had had company.

"Haven't we stumbled down this road before, David?" Vaughan's question lingered in the air for several seconds before David corralled his instinct to kill and decided to respond.

"This time . . . *Vaughan,*" he began, "I will use one of their own to help secure victory."

Lips pursed, Vaughan felt the air slowly exhale from his nostrils as his fingers gripped the side of the leather armchair. He desperately wanted to ask David who he was using, which water vamp was going to act as his unwitting accomplice, but as Michael's father he knew it was a question David expected him to ask. As much as Vaughan wanted to know, he didn't want to give David the satisfaction. Luckily, Morgandy was as inquisitive as he was enthusiastic.

"Is it Ciaran?" Morgandy asked. "Did one of his stupid experiments finally work?"

"Ciaran is human, you bloody fool!" David howled. "And an utter disappointment. Like all humans, he has proven he is useless. His mother, however, is a different story."

"Edwige?" Vaughan hoped his voice didn't sound as shocked as he thought it did.

"Do you disapprove Vaughan?" David asked.

Vaughan wasn't thrilled to know David was going to use his significant other, but at least David wasn't using his son. "It's an excellent choice," he said.

Satisfied, David turned his attention to the rest of the group. He needed to rally them, make them understand how important today was, how their lives were about to change forever. "Once that exquisite milestone is achieved, I will give the command for you to kill as many water vamps as you can," he said. "Spread out, seek, strike, and slay." He loved how his words sounded, the deep, strong tenor of his voice. "Then we will scour the world and give every water vamp we capture a choice: convert or be killed."

This time when Morgandy cheered, Oliver and several others joined him. David's fervor was starting to catch on like a restless flame, though there were still some less than enthusiastic dissenters in the room. "We seem to be missing an important member of our flock," Joubert said, then asked, "Where's Jean-Paul?"

Finally, Nakano heard something interesting. He stared at the geisha's gift-turned-urn perched on the desk behind David and wondered what strategy the headmaster would employ. Would he reveal the truth and present Nakano with his reward in front of this group of fools? Or would he offer up some cryptic response?

"Jean-Paul," David said, almost choking on his dead son's name, "is exactly where I need him to be."

Score one for the cryptic response. But wait, maybe not so cryptic. David's eyes betrayed him, and he stole a guilty glance at the urn. It was quick, but obvious, and it was enough to convince Joubert that his friend wasn't missing, that Jean-Paul was dead. Furious, Joubert wanted someone to pay; he wanted revenge. Brania simply wanted a response.

"Should I interpret your tardiness to mean you were not successful, Father?"

No one heard Brania's silent query, but everyone saw the sneer form on David's face. His daughter wasn't even in the room, yet she was still controlling the situation. Speaking for the group, Oliver asked, "Is something wrong, Headmaster?"

Flustered by so many questions, David barked, "I have another matter to attend to!" But just as he reached the door, he realized he had been too hasty in his exit, and Jean-Paul was not exactly where he needed him to be. Walking back to his desk, he grabbed Jean-Paul's final resting place and, ignoring the puzzled looks of everyone in the room, he left.

Cradling the urn in his arms like an infant, David walked from his office and through The Forest, into areas he had never ventured into before as he followed Brania's voice. Now that she had decided to reconnect, the barriers were broken, and David was being given access to her secret lair. It enraged David that he had become a plaything to his daughter's whims. He should know where all of his subjects resided. No one should keep secrets from him. But he kept reminding himself that even kings had to suffer hardships to solidify their power. Entering the cave, he took in the prehistoric dwelling, the child sitting in the coffin as if it were a rowboat, and thought that if he had to stay here for more than a few minutes it might prove to be one hardship that even a compromised king like himself would be unable to bear. "I hope utilities are included, my dear," David quipped. "There seems to be quite a draft in here."

Brania gnashed the loose gravel with her heel as she fought the urge to walk toward her father. She might have allowed him entry to her home, but he was not a guest who needed to be greeted formally. He was a courier. "While your sophomoric observation *is* amusing," she said, "I'd much prefer my gift."

Reluctantly, David presented the box to her. His hands shook as he realized he was offering one of his children to the other, and he felt his anger build. He prayed that she would come forward and take her prize before he lost control of his fury and smashed it on the ground at her feet. *You wanted your brother's ashes, well here they are!* No! No, he couldn't do that to Jean-Paul. He had already taken his son's life; he couldn't take his dignity as well. David raised the urn even higher. "Your brother's remains," he said solemnly. "Per your request."

As expected Nakano proved to have more guts than her father. So much was going through Brania's head when she walked toward David, she was surprised she didn't topple over. She was livid and wanted to call David out for his cowardice, for once again making a child do the work of a parent; she was remorseful and wanted to tell Nakano she was sorry for convincing him to do her father's dirty work; there was even a part of her that was ashamed that she had allowed her jealousy of Jean-Paul to lead her to orchestrate his death. But when she took the lid off of the box and the intoxicating odor of death enveloped her, she was proud. She had gotten what she deserved: she was an only child once more. "Bravo, Daddy," Brania cooed. "All is right with the world."

"Not quite," David snapped. "Not until you take me to The Well as you promised."

"Well, you see, that's really not up to me," Brania replied, placing the urn on a small flattened rock that jutted out from the wall. "It's up to Imogene."

"Who!?"

"She's talking about me."

Turning to face Imogene, who was lounging in the coffin, David could no longer conceal his fury. "I'm through playing games with you, Brania!" David spat, his fists clenched and shaking violently. "I held up my end of our bargain. It's time that you held up yours!!"

"You outsourced your chore!" Brania cried. "Proving once again that you are incapable of ruling our race!" Reveling in her father's flummoxed look, Brania slowly walked toward him again. This time her mind wasn't jumbled. Only one thought permeated her brain: how wonderful it was going to be to strip her father of every ounce of his power. "When our people realize you have failed *yet again* to destroy The Well and that this insane quest of yours for total supremacy is archaic and untenable, they will look for a new leader! They will look to me! They will expect and *beg* your only heir to take over and wear the crown that no longer fits your head!!"

It was an articulate speech and a persuasive argument, but Imogene wasn't listening. "Noooo!!!!"

Whipping around, Brania cried, "Not now!"

"It's Edwige," Imogene gasped. "She's feeding!"

Rushing to Imogene's side, David growled, "If you treasure your pitiful life, you'll take me to her now!"

On Imogene's other side, Brania seethed. "No, Imogene! Our plans have changed!"

Defiantly, Imogene grabbed them both, and then together, they all disappeared.

One by one the kids started to appear, forming clusters all around campus. Some were still chattering on about yesterday's major swim team win, which happened even though Alexei never showed up for the final relay, while others were excited about the Tri-Centennial Celebration and were bowled over when they realized Double A had been in existence for three centuries. Michael and Ronan met up with Ciaran and Saoirse outside St. Martha's and were hoping to enjoy themselves, but experience had taught them that if David organized an event, fun would not be on the schedule. But it was clear that Rhoswen's arrival had unnerved David. Maybe it had distracted him enough to just let the event unfold properly, as the drama-free festivity it was supposed to be.

Taking one long sip of her iced mocha, Saoirse did a pirouette and scoured the grounds. "Has anyone seen Kanosan?"

"Is he your new GBFF?" Ciaran replied.

Stopping abruptly and immediately bending into second position, clearly in the throes of a caffeine rush, Saoirse said, "Spell it out, Ciaran my boyo."

"Gay best friend forever," he explained.

Jumping up and down in a way that would shame even a beginner ballerina, Saoirse cried, "That's brill! Somebody write that down and mail it to the people who make up new words. No, no, no! E-mail it, 'cause e-mail's faster."

Ronan silenced his sister by grabbing her drink out of her hands. "Looks like someone needs to switch to decaf."

"Give it back, Roney!" she yelled. "The barista forgot to add a shot of blood, so you're not going to like it."

Shaking his head, Ronan handed Saoirse back her coffee. Maybe the day was just going to be filled with laughs and nonsense. The way Michael looked, it was clear he didn't share his boyfriend's opinion. "Try not to worry, love," Ronan said, rubbing the warm center of Michael's neck. "Until, you know, there's something to worry about." On cue, Vaughan emerged from behind the building. "Which," Ronan finished, "would be right about now."

"Dad!" Michael shouted. "What are you doing here?"

Looking over his shoulder, Vaughan realized it wouldn't be wise to carry on a conversation with his son and his son's friends out in the open. "Come with me," he said, leading the group to the Dumpsters behind St. Martha's.

"The smell is goppin'!" Saoirse said, getting a whiff of the odor of rotting food wafting from inside the metal containers. "All those in favor of reconvening elsewhere, raise your hand."

Before she could raise her arm, Ronan grabbed it. "Cut it out, Seersh," he ordered. "What's going on, Mr. Howard?"

"David is planning to destroy The Well," Vaughn said. "You have to get there to stop him."

"Oh, come on," Ronan scoffed. "He's tried it before and failed."

"That was my first thought too, but this time he's using one of your own," Vaughan replied, his heart starting to race a bit faster. "He's using Edwige."

Ronan didn't have to speak; Michael understood. Despite

the fact that he was estranged from his mother, she was still his mother, and if David was using her to get to The Well, then she was in danger. They had no choice but to try and protect her. The only doubt Michael had was what role Vaughan was playing. "Why are you helping us?" he asked.

"Because I'm your father." Vaughan's declaration surprised everyone, including Grace, who was never far from her son. His words, however, filled her with relief. Her ex-husband might be sinful and at best a complete jerk, but he still loved their son, and for that she was grateful. So grateful that she allowed Vaughan to see her smiling at him for a split second, just enough time so he knew she was watching him, time enough to make sure he kept his word. He understood.

"Hurry!" Vaughan ordered.

Michael didn't move. He remembered Phaedra's warning that wherever Rhoswen went, death would follow. He had no idea where Rhoswen was, but he could smell death as clearly as if its scent was floating on the wind. "You'll protect Ciaran and Saoirse," he said. "In case anything goes wrong."

Vaughan's renewed commitment to his son didn't waiver. "I promise."

The second after Michael and Ronan ran off to The Well, Saoirse informed Vaughan that she didn't need his help. "If things get all shambolic again, take care of Ciaran," she instructed. "I've got this Atlantium gene running through my veins that makes me sort of indestructible."

"Care to put that theory to the test?" Morgandy asked.

"Blimey!" Saoirse shouted. "Were you hiding in the bushes?"

"On the other side of the Dumpsters," he replied.

"Of course," Ciaran said. "With the rest of the rubbish."

Not used to bickering teenagers, Vaughan immediately regretted his promise, but true to his word, he positioned himself in front of Ciaran and Saoirse, making them back up against the metal bins. "What's going on?" he asked. "David hasn't called us to action."

Morgandy inched closer to Vaughan and his charges. "I'm tired of waiting!" he barked, his face beginning to transform. "So I'm taking matters into my own hands."

This was never supposed to be like this! Years ago when he had crossed over and become a vampire, Vaughan had thought it would bring him an eternity of luxury, wealth, untold adventure. He had never thought he'd have to be a bodyguard. "But that's against David's orders," Vaughan cried, his voice desperate.

Standing directly in front of Vaughan, Morgandy's face and body were no longer human. "He isn't capable of giving orders any longer," Morgandy seethed. "So I'm making up my own."

Taking a step back so his body was now flat against Ciaran and Saoirse, Vaughan reluctantly allowed his own form to change. He didn't want it to appear as if he was agreeing to do battle, but he had to be prepared; the two lives behind him were counting on it. "I . . . I hear there's a water vamp settlement in Cyprus!" he said, trying to reason with Morgandy. "Let's leave at sunset. They'll never suspect an attack!" But the boy was beyond reasoning.

"No," Morgandy said flatly. "I want to kill these two."

"But . . . but they're not even water vamps!" Vaughan cried.

Revolted, Morgandy had had enough of Vaughan's resistance. "You're a bigger faggot than your kid!"

Morgandy hit the ground before Vaughan even realized he had punched him. He hit the ground so hard that he didn't get back up for quite a while. If Grace had still been present, she would've applauded Vaughan for defending Michael's character. She wasn't, so Saoirse clapped instead. "That was brilliant, Mr. Howard!"

Brilliant, but not a permanent solution. Jumping to his feet, Morgandy was prepared to attack Vaughan for striking him. He wasn't prepared for Saoirse to attack first. Michael was her friend, she loved him like a brother, and no one was going to get away with talking about him like that. Grabbing the back of Morgandy's skull, Saoirse didn't even notice how soft his curls felt. She just hurled his body through the air with more power than she knew she possessed. Twenty seconds later they heard the shattering of glass and knew his body had finally landed. Dumbfounded, Vaughan turned to the girl. "What in bloody hell are you?!"

"Honestly," she replied, "I've given up trying to figure it out."

"Just be thankful she's on your side," Ciaran said, unable to conceal a smile.

So now Vaughan was on the side of his longtime enemy. Yes, it would seem that way. Well, if he wanted to keep peace, he couldn't just stand there. Peering into the distance he could see Morgandy almost a mile away, not moving, but chances were he wouldn't stay like that for long. Looking toward the left, he could see a group of kids filing into the gym. "Go to St. Sebastian's," he ordered. "I need to make sure Morgandy doesn't get himself into any more trouble."

David found his second journey of the day to be much more rewarding. "I've done it, Zachariel!" he exclaimed, his voice bellowing throughout the underground cave, startling Edwige, who had just finished her monthly offering of blood. Speechless, she ran to the other side of The Well to conceal her naked body. "Hello, Edwige," David said. "I hope you don't mind company."

"As long as the feeling's mutual, David," Michael added as he and Ronan entered the cave.

It was a historic moment. Never before had there been so many people gathered in front of The Well at one time.

Unfortunately, it was not a moment that made The Well happy.

chapter 29

The vibrations started slowly. The movement of the ground was almost imperceptible. In fact, David didn't even notice anything was happening. How could he when he was so elated that he was finally here? Finally standing in the presence of the godforsaken Well, the legendary being that had eluded him for so long. And look at it! It was nothing more than stone. It looked like something you'd find in a country field, used by an illiterate laborer to fetch water. This was their deity?! Watching Edwige cower and hide her hideous flesh from the others, David thought it was a fitting god.

"I must say how appropriate this foul-smelling place is," David remarked. "For such primitive, naked beasts, of course."

Ronan handed his mother a wet clump of yellow and black material. She let the fabric fall to the floor and stepped into it; it was the long dress that she had left on the shore of

Inishtrahull Island before making her way to The Well. "Thank you," she said.

"Oh no, thanks be to Zachariel," David corrected. "It's because of his guidance that I've accomplished what you never thought I could." Spreading his arms out wide in front of him, David shouted, "I have found The Well's elusive hiding place!"

This time when the ground shook, David felt it. He even teetered off balance a bit. The sensation didn't invoke fear, but rather joy. "You *should* be afraid!" he cried. "The day has come for your pitiful race to end!"

Even though David was addressing his tirade to The Well, Michael felt that every word was meant for him, and he felt his stomach fill with anger. He was the only one who was an outsider; he was the only who had been brought here, summoned to this part of the world. And he was the only one whose destiny was to be The Well's next guardian. "You'll never succeed!" he roared. "NEVER!"

Flying through the air and transforming at the same time, Michael didn't notice David had reacted even more quickly and had moved to the side until there was nothing before him but empty air. He dove onto the ground, and by the time he stood up and turned around, David was holding Ronan by the throat. A small piece of Michael's heart died as he watched Ronan's body flail and convulse uncontrollably a few feet from the ground and his hands clutch at David's fingers that were squeezing tighter and tighter around his neck. His boyfriend was being assaulted, and Michael was just staring at him. What the hell was wrong with this picture?

Once again David proved that his reflexes were just a bit more honed. Age and experience did sometimes triumph over youth and bravado. Just as Michael soared forward, David flicked his wrist and sent Ronan flying into The Well. He struck the wall so hard two stones were dislodged and fell off, one of them hitting Ronan on the side of his head, slicing off a bit of flesh before crashing onto the ground.

By the time Edwige and Michael ran toward Ronan, flanking him on either side, two new stones had grown in the empty space. The Well was rejuvenating itself. "You see!" Michael cried. "You can't destroy The Well, and you can't kill us!"

"Just like I could never find my way here?!" David replied. "Don't you remember, you stupid, little boy, that rules are made to be broken?"

"Just like truces?" Edwige asked. She was kneeling beside Ronan, holding him in her arms, but she was looking directly into David's eyes. "You swore before your goddamned Zachariel that you would uphold peace between our two races!"

"I lied," he said simply.

Edwige wanted to strike David herself for going back on his word, for wreaking havoc and endangering the lives of so many innocent people, but just then Ronan stirred in her arms and she forgot about global salvation and focused entirely on her son. "Ronan," she whispered. "Can you hear me?"

"Yes," he replied softly. After Michael helped him stand, Ronan whispered, "Thank you, love."

Enough sentiment! It was time for the animal to be released from its cage. After ripping off his shirt, David tossed it to the ground, and his massive chest began to heave. He felt his shoulder blades splitting apart, and even though the pain was less excruciating than it had been the first time the metamorphosis had taken place, the feeling was still bone-chilling. Clenching his fists, David raised his arms, his biceps bulging, his neck resembling the trunk of a tree, and he howled. "Ahhhhhhh!!!!!"

No one knew what to make of the scene. They were horrified and transfixed, and it looked as if David was going to explode. They never imagined he was going to sprout wings.

Slowly two feathered wings, the color of midnight, emerged

from David's back. They were majestic, about eight feet in length and several feet high, and took up more than half the entire length of the cave. When the transformation was complete, David's breathing returned to normal, and his wings fluttered lazily behind him. The only sound in the cave was The Well's vibrations that increased tenfold in response to David's incredible makeover. When Michael finally spoke, his words could hardly be heard. "Oh . . . my . . ."

"God," David said, finishing his thought.

"What the bloody hell is happening!" Blakeley shouted. England wasn't supposed to have earthquakes? Was she? Well, she must, because the ground was shaking. And it wasn't just because a stampede of students was rushing past him to get inside St. Sebastian's and hopefully to safety. All except those two. "Ciaran! Saoirse!" Blakeley cried out. "Don't just stand there! Get your arses into the gym!"

But when Blakeley got closer to them he couldn't move either. It wasn't every day he saw a colleague ripping open a student's neck with his teeth. "Joubert!" Blakeley gasped. "What the . . ." That's all he could say before Joubert let go of Talisa's convulsing body to lunge at Blakeley like some deformed animal and knock him to the ground. He heard some bones in his back break and, sadly, he knew they were the least of his worries.

Flat on his back, staring up into his colleague's now-unrecognizable face, Blakeley finally understood what was happening. Evil really was walking among the angels. Lochlan had been right all along! Not only was evil alive at Double A, it was living inside his colleagues. He didn't know if the thing on top of him was a monster, a zombie, or a vampire. It didn't matter. Whatever it was, there was still a chance that his friend was trapped inside. "Gwendal!" Blakeley cried. "Listen to me, please!" Frozen on the sidelines, Ciaran and Saoirse watched Joubert release his hold on Blakeley and look down at him with a quizzical expression. It was working; Blakeley was reaching him. "Let me help you, mate," Blakeley said. "You don't have to do this!"

Stupid mortal. Joubert already knew that. But he also knew that the leader he had once trusted was out of his mind, Jean-Paul had been senselessly murdered, and all his years teaching theology had brought him no closer to God. He was damned, and there was nothing Blakeley could say or do that could help him.

"I know I don't have to," Joubert finally replied. "But I want to."

At first Blakeley didn't feel a thing, then it was like a branding iron was being seared into his neck. His body was flooded with so much burning heat that Blakeley thought he was going to spontaneously combust. And when he saw the flames erupt in front of him, he was convinced that the fireball was him and not Joubert.

"Oh my God, it worked!" Ciaran said as he stared in amazement at the syringe he was still holding in his hand. When he had realized he had an extra one in his pants' pocket, he wasn't sure if it could substitute for a stake, but he jammed it into Joubert's back, piercing his heart from behind, just in case. Score one for the Science Boy! Seeing his coach turn paler by the second, he thought it might be a hollow victory. Then again, maybe not.

"Coach," Ciaran said, bending low and whispering in his ear. "Hold on! We can reverse this; we can make you live forever. You just have to say the word, and we'll find someone."

Saoirse was shocked. Even in the face of death, Ciaran was a scientist and looked for a way to prolong life. Taking in the extent of Blakeley's injuries, she wasn't sure any vampire would be able to help him become immortal. They would never know, however, because Blakeley had another wish. "Get me to Sister Mary," he said urgently. "Now."

Ciaran could try to cheat death; Saoirse wanted to respect

Blakeley's request. Scooping the coach up in her arms, she barely felt his weight. "Go to the gym, Ciar," she ordered.

"I'm not leaving you alone," her brother protested.

"Aren't you the one who's always telling me how special I am?" she asked. "Let me prove it."

Reluctantly, Ciaran was forced to admit that Saoirse could protect herself better than he could. "Be careful," he warned.

Following her instincts, Saoirse sprinted to Archangel Cathedral and wasn't surprised to find Sister Mary praying in a pew near the back of the church. She was surprised, however, to see Nakano kneeling next to her. Suddenly, her burden was too heavy, and Saoirse gently placed Blakeley on the cold, marble floor. He didn't feel the chill. Switching places, Sister Mary knelt next to Blakeley, and Saoirse sat next to Nakano. As Kano held his friend's hand, Blakeley reached up for Sister Mary's.

The nun cradled his head in her lap, not looking away from his fearful eyes, not flinching at his grotesque wounds. She crossed herself and then kissed the small, silver crucifix that always adorned her neck.

"Sister," Blakeley said, as the blood poured from his neck, staining her habit. "Please . . . teach me to pray before I die."

"Repeat after me," she said. "Our Father, who art in heaven, hallowed be thy name." She continued, pausing after each phrase so Blakeley could repeat her words, so he could finally speak out loud the prayer that had eluded him for almost his entire lifetime. Saying the words softly, slowly, he felt like a child learning how to speak, learning a language he had never known existed. He wanted to thank her for giving him such a beautiful gift, but the moment after he mouthed the word *Amen,* he was dead.

chapter 30

The Well wanted to be alone. It had had enough of intruders and uninvited guests and wanted them to leave. It was trying to be subtle, vibrate at a low frequency, shake the earth noticeably, but lightly, hoping its message would be received. Several minutes had passed, and still no one was taking the hint. All right then. The time had come for more drastic action.

Rumbling louder, The Well shook the earth more violently. Brania and Imogene fell to the ground on top of each other, and Ronan grabbed onto both Edwige and Michael for support so he wouldn't topple over. Only David stood tall, unfazed by the anger that was erupting around them. As the rocks in the walls started to grind against each other and shift position, the cave began to fill with dust. David smiled and raised his hands over his head, making his wings stretch out a few inches farther. "I pledge to you, Zachariel," David prayed, "that I will destroy this Well and wipe its existence from your earth!"

An earsplitting roar bellowed from The Well itself, and the stones in the ground and the ceiling started to split apart from one other. Michael didn't know who was in control—David or The Well—but it looked like the cave was starting to be demolished. He held on to Ronan tighter and was glad to see that his boyfriend was getting his strength back, that the fire was returning to his eyes, but Michael wondered if it was too late. What could they possibly do to stop David from carrying out his depraved plot? Sure, the man was demented, but he had been successful. He had found The Well's location just as he had threatened.

"Water connects life to death, bridging the gap to immortality," David said. "Once I sever your connection and destroy the source of your *abhorrent* race, you will wither and die as Zachariel and I have always wished it to be!"

"Will you shut up about Zachariel!" Michael cried. "He is nothing compared to The Well!"

David loved accepting a challenge from someone he considered a fool. "Let's see about that," he fumed.

Standing with his back to The Well, David tucked his wings in close to his body. Then he arched his back so they could unfurl at a rapid speed and slap against The Well's already shaking stones. Laughing wildly, David kept flapping his immense wings, and each time feather struck rock the entire cave shook. Soon it looked like The Well was being torn from its foundation. Michael couldn't believe it. David was doing it; he was actually destroying The Well. This had gone too far.

"Are you strong enough to fight?" Michael silently asked Ronan.

"I'll be right by your side, love."

Splitting apart, they each jumped up and grabbed onto a

wing, but David's unnatural appendages were so thick and powerful, they wouldn't bend. Michael and Ronan could only hang onto them, unable to touch the ground with their feet to gain leverage. As a result their added weight did nothing to slow down the wings' assault.

"Slide!" Michael heard Ronan silently yell, and they both slid down the wings in opposite directions until they were at the tips. There they could plant themselves firmly onto the ground and hold on to the uncooperative wings. As they dug their heels into the cave's vibrating floor, it took all their strength to prevent the wings from unfurling completely. But they were succeeding. They heard David's laugh die as his wings fluttered with even more intensity, like a fly's when it knows it has been captured. Only this time Michael and Ronan were the pests.

Even though the boys had interrupted David's assault on The Well, destruction had been set in motion, and all around them the hallowed ground was crumbling. Water was starting to pour into the cave from crevices between the rocks, crevices that were widening with each second. Brania felt the cold rush of water around her feet, and she realized that she was way out of her element. Not to mention her comfort zone.

"Just how far underwater are we?" she asked.

"A few hundred miles," Edwige replied. "Give or take."

Give or take?! Brania was suddenly gripped with an irrational fear of drowning. It was irrational because she was a vampire, and she should have the ability to swim a hundred or so miles while holding her breath. But this living and breathing underwater thing was an unknown concept to her. She had spent the past several centuries landlocked, and she preferred it that way. Plus, her feud with water vampires made her despise the sea, so perhaps her fear of the water wasn't so irrational after all. It was, however, going to pose a problem, since the water was now rising up to her knees. "How am I supposed to get out of here?!"

"The same way you got in," Imogene replied.

That's my girl, Brania thought, *always willing to serve your mother.*

"As long as you give me my freedom in return," the girl said.

The words stung Brania and created such a heat within her body that it threatened to boil the water around her. "What?"

Despite all the chaos, Imogene was calm when she spoke. "Whatever is going to happen to me, if I continue to live or die or remain in this limbo, I want to do it without being tied to anyone," she explained. "I want to be free."

As much as Brania wanted to get angry, as much as she wanted to throttle Imogene and hold her ungrateful head under the icy water to see what really would happen to the girl, she couldn't, because more than anything else, she was hurt. She had come to love her companion in a way that she had never loved any other being. The feeling, clearly, was not mutual. Brania wanted to tell Imogene that Imogene had been her salvation this past year, the only ray of light in an endless tunnel of darkness that had threatened to destroy her. But she was not used to pleading; she was not used to fighting for a relationship to survive. "Fine," Brania said, her voice much harsher than the feelings that lay in her heart. "If that's what you want, you can have your bloody freedom."

"Thank you," Imogene replied. Satisfied, she grabbed hold of both Brania and Edwige, and then there were no more women in the cave.

"That leaves this hellhole to just us boys!" David bellowed. He was frantic to make it look and sound as if he were still in control despite the counterattack Michael and Ronan were putting forth. *I promise you, Zachariel, I will not lose this time!* David gave his wings one powerful flap, and both boys were sent hurtling in different directions. It was a crushing move, but it wasn't enough to claim victory.

Wading in the frigid water that was now up to their waists, the boys saw that The Well had recovered, it had stopped shaking, even though the cave continued to tremble, and was back in full control. Enraged by The Well's fortitude and spirit, David let out a growl and flew to the top of the cave, seemingly intent on diving into the belly of The Well to see what treasures he could find and annihilate on the other side. The Well had other ideas.

Just as David dove, the stones on the top ledge of The Well multiplied and spread out to create a lid, a barrier to conceal its precious contents from sight and seal itself from trespassers trying to gain unwelcome entry. David was descending so quickly he was unable to decrease his speed or switch direction and smashed into The Well's new protective shell.

Dazed, but clinging to the top of the stone, David began to spin around as The Well burrowed itself lower and lower, plunging under water until it ultimately disappeared into the ground. "Nooooo!!" David shrieked,

"Looks like you've failed yet again," Ronan jeered as David rose from the water.

His jet-black wings were fully outstretched and dripping with water that made each feather glisten. But it was an illusion. His wings were actually starting to molt, and soon the water around him was sprinkled with feathers, making it look like he was standing in a pool of black rain. Noticing the change in his appearance, David fluttered his wings faster, which only made the shedding quicken. What was happening? Was Zachariel playing some cruel joke? No, the fallen angel was just tired of backing a loser.

"Once again you have failed!" Zachariel said, his voice booming throughout the decomposing cave. The voice was so thunderous and so hateful that Michael and Ronan had to cover their ears. David merely fell to his knees. "No!" he protested. "I've come so far. I beg you, Zachariel, do not abandon me now!"

"After all the power I've bestowed upon you, you are still nothing but a failure!" the livid angel roared. "David Zachary, you are on . . . your . . . OWN!!"

"Noooo!!" Wailing like a lost child, David rose as stones fell into the water with such frequency and fury that waves started to churn, and it was as if they were in the middle of the ocean. This couldn't be happening; this *shouldn't* be happening to him. No, there was still time to teach Zachariel a lesson. To teach them all a lesson that they should never underestimate David's power.

Diving underwater, David disappeared. The cave wasn't that large, but Michael and Ronan still couldn't find him. They craned their necks, peered close to the water's surface, and still no sign of him. They only saw David when he shot back up, one hand reaching out, not content until it wrapped itself around Ronan's neck.

Startled, Ronan tried to pry David's fingers from his flesh, but the man was determined to take him hostage. With one fist raised overhead David flew higher and faster, breaking through the rock, and into the sea above. He had turned his rage at Zachariel for deserting him into action. And not a moment too soon, because seconds after he broke through the rock ceiling, the cave was gone. It was no longer a safe haven, no longer The Well's sanctuary, just another part of the ocean.

Michael felt the current swirl around him, swift and encouraging, as if trying to get him to follow them, but he couldn't, he was frozen. It was as if he was locked in an iceberg, too frightened to move, just like in the vision he had had before school started where he was locked in a sea of ice and Ronan was just out of reach. Think, think! What had

Ronan said in his dream? What did he tell him he had to do? "You must protect me." Well, of course he would protect him. Michael didn't need to be told to do such a thing. Oh really? Then what was he doing in the middle of the ocean while Ronan was being taken God knows where by David? As Michael swam closer to the surface he was more determined than ever to make his dream come true.

This Tri-Centennial *Disaster* was not the stuff dreams were made of. All Fritz wanted to do was hang out with Ruby all day, maybe sneak in a little private time, advance their relationship, but the earth was not cooperating. Why did it have to wait until his one day off from studying and schoolwork to go all wonky? Instead of holding Ruby's hand as they strolled through The Forest on their way to St. Sebastian's, Fritz was constantly sidestepping rolling rocks or dodging falling trees. It was downright apocalyptic. If the world wanted to end, why the hell didn't it just do it already and stop pussyfooting around? Being greeted by Ciaran the second they set foot into the gym was further proof that the planet was against him. He wanted his end-of-the-world moment to be just him and Ruby. He didn't want it to turn into some sort of group hug.

"Ruby, are you all right?"

Nor did he want Ciaran to steal any of his thunder. He had ignored his friend's previous attempts to chummy up to his girlfriend, feeling rather confident, though not entirely certain, that if given the choice Ruby would choose him. But with the whole "sky is falling" fairy-tale thing coming true, he wasn't about to take any chances. "Hey, mate," Fritz said. "I think it's time you back off."

A deafening growl of thunder prevented Ciaran from hearing Fritz's demand and made Ruby more eager than ever to sit as far away from the windows as possible. The earth was revolting. Now the sky was going to join in too? "I saved a space for us in the middle of the gym," Ciaran said.

"Ain't that just hunky dory," Fritz groused. Another thunderclap, another missed opportunity to help Ruby lie down and rest her head on a rolled up sweatshirt.

"Sorry, I'm not used to so much running around," she said. "Since I lost my sight I haven't been able to be very active."

All that was about to change, because Rhoswen had decided it was time to part ways with her host.

Ciaran wasn't sure if the ghost rising from Ruby's body went unnoticed by everyone around them because there was so much commotion or if she only appeared to a chosen few. Fritz was not happy to be one of the selected.

Staring in fright at the apparition who had just stepped out of his girlfriend's body, Fritz's first thought was that the guest monster of issue seventeen of *Tales of the Double A* had come to life. That was the issue in which Parasitico, the alien from another planet who has to take over people's bodies to survive, first appeared. Fritz didn't actually have a second thought because he fainted.

A bit more used to witnessing unexplainable phenomena, Ciaran was entranced by Rhoswen's eerie beauty and not disturbed by the fact that she had been living inside Ruby's body. Rhoswen couldn't see Ciaran, but she could sense his presence. And his future. "Stay here, and you will all be safe," she said. "And don't worry, Ciaran. Before the summer ends, Ruby will be yours."

Beaming, despite the tragedy he had recently witnessed, Ciaran sat next to Ruby and held her hand as she slept. He was greatly relieved to know that they wouldn't need any help to survive the so-called celebration that was raging all around them.

* * *

Imogene didn't need any help either. She had gotten what she wanted—her freedom. Standing on the other side of the rocky dunes on Inishtrahull Island near an inlet about a mile from the shore, Imogene, with Brania and Edwige behind her, waited for it to come. When they saw the boy walking toward them, they knew Imogene's freedom had arrived.

"Penry!" Imogene squealed. She was so excited she jumped up and down in place and forgot that she could run, that she was free to do as she pleased. She didn't have to wait for instruction or fear to compel her to disappear. Or maybe she just wanted Penry to make the first move. She didn't have to wait long.

Penry didn't stop running until he had wrapped his arms around Imogene and lifted her up off the sand. "I've been waiting for you for so long!" he cried, his red hair shining in the sunlight.

All Imogene wanted to do was count the freckles on his cheeks. She couldn't remember how many there were, and a girlfriend should know those sorts of things. But there was time for that. "I'm sorry," Imogene replied, not letting go of his embrace, but tilting her head to indicate the other women on the beach. "I was kind of delayed."

Edwige looked away to give the couple some privacy. She knew that she should feel guilty for having killed Imogene, but she didn't. She wanted to look at life differently, so she accepted the fact that she was the one who had made it possible for Imogene to be reunited with her boyfriend. Truth was, she couldn't take all the credit.

"My plan worked!" Imogene cried.

"What plan?" Penry asked.

"To die."

That didn't make any sense. They all knew that she had fought harder than anyone else to stay alive. They just had no idea how hard she had fought to stay dead. "I didn't want to die, Pens," Imogene clarified. "I *wanted* to live to a ripe old age with you by my side, but there was no way I was going to hang out with either of them for eternity, so I decided to take some action."

Edwige couldn't help but smile. Imogene really was a spitfire. Brania felt her heart shrink. Imogene really was an ingrate.

"I'll fill you in later," Imogene said. "But once I realized I had some power over my situation, I took advantage of it."

Shaking his head, amazed as he always was by his girlfriend's moxie, Penry shrugged his shoulders. "All that matters is that we're together, and now I get to show you the world," he said. "You won't believe how magical everything looks from this side."

"I thought you said you were waiting for me?" Imogene cried. "Not traipsing all over the earth."

"Crikey, Ims! You were taking your sweet time. What did you expect me to do?" he laughed. "I did wait, but then I got bored so I started to explore a little."

She couldn't blame him. He had returned when she needed him, and she knew he would never leave her side again. "Well, what are you waiting for?" she asked. "Let's go explore."

Watching Penry and Imogene run down the beach, holding hands, on their way to start their journey together, Edwige blushed. The warmth in her cheeks was comforting, because it meant she understood what it was like to have known a love that was so innocent and pure. Brania had no such knowledge.

Edwige also knew that there was a man in her life who might be able to help her feel that kind of love again. He wasn't as good as Saxon, but in time and with her love as encouragement, he could be a worthy successor. Before she left the island to go find him, she hesitated and thought about her children. Her maternal connection was rusty, but it was still working. She knew that Ciaran and Saoirse were unharmed, and she knew that as long as Ronan was with Michael he would be safe and, most important, loved. It was time for Edwige to commit to finding those same joys with Vaughan.

The only thing Michael knew for certain was that if David didn't land soon, he was going to crash onto the beach with Ronan's lifeless body still clutched in his hand. His feathers were peeling off his wings and swirling in the wind as they floated onto the ocean's surface, polluting the water with their filth. Now that David had proven himself unworthy of Zachariel's unholy gift, the vile archangel was destroying his creation. Michael prayed he didn't destroy his boyfriend in the process.

Standing on the shore, Michael watched as David whirled about at a dizzying speed. Up, down, around, spinning, diving, flipping. Michael couldn't tell if David was showing off or if he was throwing a tantrum in the sky. He had never felt more frustrated, more helpless than he did watching Ronan hang like a rag doll in David's grip. But then all motion stopped, and David hung in the sky like a vulture that spies a bleeding lion. And just like a greedy vulture, David swooped down toward the beach zeroing in on yet more prey.

Michael was prepared to move at the last second. He would not become David's next victim. But David wasn't returning to land to seize Michael; he was after a different treasure. Rolling on the beach to avoid being whipped in the face by a rotting wing, Michael turned around just in time to see David grab Brania by the throat and soar back into the sky. What the hell was he doing?! Attacking Ronan was one thing; it was a vicious act, but it was understandable. Trying to kill his own daughter too? That was deplorable. Michael had always believed David was an immoral being, and now he had proof. A blight on an otherwise gorgeous blue sky, David hovered miles above ground, his wings unsightly, half-evaporated, holding Ronan and Brania like puppets in front of him.

A shiver of fear ran up Michael's spine. He did not have a good feeling about this. And he was right. A maniacal laugh spilled out of David's mouth, poisoning the air, the sea, and the earth below.

The laughter continued as David raised his arms and let his cargo fall.

chapter 31

Michael watched Ronan's body free fall through the air, and he couldn't believe that another one of his visions was coming true. He hadn't wanted to believe this one was a prophecy. He didn't want to believe Ronan's life could be in danger. All this time he had held onto the hope that he had remembered it wrong or that he had misinterpreted the true meaning of his dream. And now that the vision was coming to life before his very eyes, he realized that's exactly what had happened.

When he heard the words "You must protect me" spoken once again, he heard them as they truly sounded, not the way he had imagined hearing them. It wasn't Ronan's voice that called out to him; it was The Well's. He recognized the magnificent voice immediately as the same one that had spoken through Saoirse last year, and the moment he heard The Well call to him, he knew what he had to do. Just before he ran across the waves, his feet hardly touching the water, he begged Ronan for forgiveness.

Pushing fear from his mind and trusting his instinct like Rhoswen and Phaedra had previously instructed him to do, Michael leapt into the air and caught Brania in his arms. As The Well's guardian, his first priority was to protect it, and the only way to ensure its safety was to maintain peace with the enemy. If Brania died, she would never take the crown from her father, and there would never be hope for peace between their two races. When he carried Brania safely to shore and saw that she was in shock but still breathing, he knew hope had been salvaged. She was weak, but she was alive. And when she regained her strength she would take the reins from David and grow into a much more compassionate, beloved leader than her father could ever dream of becoming. One who understood that courage and devotion deserve mercy. A leader just like The Well.

Rising from the ocean's surface, Michael recognized the familiar circular structure made entirely of ancient stones. The Well had not abandoned them; it never would. It hadn't run away to secure a new hiding place; it didn't have to hide. It was simply waiting for the right time to return. As Michael watched Ronan plunge into the center of The Well, into its comforting, silvery water, he humbly realized the timing could not be more perfect. As David watched from above, he realized his time had come to an end.

"Damn you, Zachariel!!" he shouted as the last feather fell from his wings, and then he too plummeted to the earth. Falling, falling, falling, David cursed his duplicitous lord, he cursed his vengeful daughter, he cursed every one of his subjects who he felt were unworthy of his leadership. He even cursed the fates as he became acutely aware that immortality like life itself was fleeting.

Conscious when he hit the surface of the water, he imagined it was like crashing into concrete. But then his mind went blank as he continued to fall deeper into the ocean, and, when he floated into his sister's waiting arms, he had no idea if he was alive or dead. It didn't matter to Rhoswen. "I knew you'd come back to me, Dahey," she said, instinctively knowing it was her brother she was holding even though all she could see was darkness. "Now you can read to me for all eternity, the way you used to."

After more than three centuries, Rhoswen had finally gotten her revenge.

And after years of prayer, Ronan had finally gotten his wish. "Dad?" He didn't know where he was, in the past, the present, earth, heaven, he didn't care. He was looking at his father again, and it didn't matter if it was a dream or real or a gift from The Well.

"Hello, son," Saxon said.

His voice was exactly the same as Ronan remembered. It was strong and gentle and loving. Trembling, Ronan had so many questions. There were so many things he wanted to ask him, so many things that he wanted to know about his father, but his heart was so filled with emotion he couldn't speak a word. "I am so proud of the man you've become," his father said.

Tears came first and, finally, words followed. "Oh Dad . . . I've missed you so much," Ronan cried. "But how is this possible? Where am I?"

Smiling the same way he had when Ronan last saw him as he was engulfed by flames, Saxon explained, "You're on the other side of The Well. It's where our race began and where it will end."

Ronan had no idea what Saxon was saying; he couldn't comprehend a word. He just wanted to stare at his father's strong, kind face. He wanted to relish every moment because he knew that it wasn't going to last. This wasn't supposed to happen; he had just gotten lucky. As lucky as he had always been. "Michael is a wonderful partner and a noble Guardian," Saxon said. "The Well could not be in better hands."

"And neither could I," Ronan added.

Smiling, Saxon could feel the love his son shared for his soul mate, a love that should no longer be apart. "You should go now," Saxon said. "Your Michael's waiting for you."

Before Ronan could respond, before he could tell Saxon how much he loved him, how wonderful it was to see him again, how he hated being separated from him, he opened his eyes and he was staring at Michael's beautiful face. So everything he wanted to tell his father, he would just tell his boyfriend. "Hello, love."

Embracing Ronan and holding him tightly to his chest, Michael kissed his neck, his forehead, his mouth. Gratitude wasn't the emotion he was feeling at the moment; it was bigger than that. After everything that had happened, after everything that *could* have happened, Ronan was fine. And Michael was humbled because he knew that it was only partly due to divine intervention; it was mainly because he had trusted his instincts. Whatever the reason, the best part was that Ronan was still forever beautiful and still forever his.

When Michael looked up to offer proper thanks he saw that The Wall was gone and the sky had returned to normal. No matter. As The Well's newest Guardian such formal communication was unnecessary. The Well knew, as it always had, the truth that lay in Michael's heart. In many ways, so did Brania.

"*I am your leader now,*" she telepathically told her people. "*David has succumbed to hubris, to his own foolish quest. From here on in we shall live in peace with the water vampires. This war is over.*" Turning to Michael and Ronan she informed them that she had called a truce. "This is a new beginning for all of us," Brania declared. "I can't wait to see what the future brings."

Michael saw his image reflected in Ronan's beautiful, blue eyes, and he knew their connection had never been stronger. "Neither can we."

epilogue

Three Months Later

Archangel Academy was resilient. So were her students.

Only a few indications that carnage had ripped through the school during the Tri-Centennial Celebration remained. There was a small memorial site near the entrance to The Forest made up of a cross that was spray-painted in Talisa's favorite bright shade of pink and surrounded by notes from her heartbroken classmates, along with the most incredibly robust white roses that usually only grew outside St. Joshua's. The window that Morgandy had crashed through, near the front door of one of the smaller buildings next to the cathedral, had been replaced with a colorful stained glass rendering of an olive branch. And right above the entrance to the locker rooms was a portrait of Coach Peter Blakeley. Depicted wearing his navy blue and gold Double A tracksuit, he had his whistle draped around his neck, and his expression was more smirk than smile. But he looked as strong and as valiant as he had the moment he died.

The gym was alive and noisy as always. The windows had been cranked open, and the space was filled with a warm breeze that floated in from the outside bringing with it the smell of lavender mixed with pine. The pool was full of students splashing, dunking one another, and simply enjoying an impromptu end-of-summer party. Despite everything that had happened, despite the loss of life and the shift in power, Double A had survived. And probably would for another three hundred years.

"So I hear McLaren is going to be the new headmaster," Nakano said, sitting on the edge of the pool, his legs dangling in the cool water.

"Really?" Saoirse replied, holding onto Kano's ankles and treading water. "I was hoping they were going to give it to Sister Mary, show some girl power for once."

Cocking his head to the side, Kano thought for a moment. "Would've been a right fine choice," he remarked, then added a bit shyly, "But not nearly as hot a choice as Professor Brit Lit."

Splashing Nakano with a huge wave of water, Saoirse shouted, "Why do you have to be so gay all the time?!"

"Why do you have to be so loud all the time?" Nakano shouted back, jumping into the pool. Just before dunking Saoirse under water, he smiled very happily and whispered, "How else could I be your GBFF?"

When she popped back up, Ciaran and Ruby had joined them. "Have you heard from the other Ms. Glynn-Rowley?" Ciaran asked.

"Yes," she confirmed. "Mum's still on safari with Michael's dad and probably terrorizing natives as we speak."

"I can't believe they lasted this long," Ciaran said, more to

Ruby than to anyone else. "I thought they would've killed each other by now."

Ruby gazed at Ciaran's sweet face. Now that her sight had returned, spontaneously and, some rightfully declared, miraculously, she loved spending hours just looking at him. "Maybe true love prevails after all."

Before anyone could snicker, Fritz cannonballed into the pool and splattered his friends with a man-made tidal wave. When he broke the surface he was right in the center of their group, a bit too close to the girlfriend he wasn't completely ready to give up on, and asked, "So when's Nebraska getting back from Nebraska?"

"In a few days," Saoirse advised as she started to crawl on top of Nakano's shoulders. "How long can a tour of Weeping Water actually take?"

"Well, they better get back soon," Fritz barked. "Senior year's about to begin, and it won't be the same without those two."

And then Saoirse did a flawless backflip that was met with an enthusiastic round of applause. It was the perfect pool party, the perfect way to spend the last few days before the beginning of the new school year. Watching the action from outside, hidden behind some trees, Morgandy didn't agree. But it didn't matter what he thought, because he wasn't invited and, for the moment, he was outnumbered.

The number astounded Ronan. "Just how many churches does this town of yours have?"

"Two more than the number of bars," Michael said, smiling over at Ronan from the driver's seat of their rented Chevy. "And when I say bar, I mean bar and not quaint little fifteenth-century pub."

"Well, that makes sense then," Ronan replied, extending his hand outside the car window and letting the wind flitter through his fingers. "Where there's sin, there has to be redemption."

Slapping Ronan's leg, Michael teased, "Now don't you talk like a heathen."

"I'm no heathen, love," Ronan said, smiling devilishly. "I'm a vampire. Sin and redemption go with the territory."

A light on the dashboard turned red. "Well, this here is mortal territory," Michael said. "And we need to get some gas."

Pulling up next to the pump, Michael never expected to see R.J.'s face peering down at him. But it was exactly where R.J. was supposed to be. In Michael's dreams R.J. had always been manning the gas station. Why should reality be any different?

"Mike?" R.J. said, surprised but delighted to see his familiar face.

"Hi, R.J." Michael said. "How are you?"

If appearance meant anything, R.J. was just fine. His body was still lean and lanky, his long hair was still tucked behind his ears, and his face was still a golden bronze from spending so much time outside. Resting his arms on the window ledge, R.J. looked into the car and smiled. "I'm doin' all right," he replied. "For a hot August day."

"This is my boyfriend, Ronan," Michael announced. After he spoke Michael wasn't embarrassed; he didn't feel his cheeks grow warm. He had simply told the truth, and it felt good. What made it even better was that there was no awkward pause. R.J. just reached into the car to shake Ronan's hand and introduce himself.

Squatting next to the car, R.J. lifted his faded cowboy hat with his index finger to reveal some sweat on his brow. One drop, two drops, three drops, four slithered slowly down the sides of R.J.'s chiseled face, and Michael remembered how he had loved to stare at the young man. Boy, did that seem like such a long time ago. He would have laughed out loud at the memory, but R.J. interrupted him. "You know there's this club over in Omaha, Buddy's Place it's called, I've, uh, gone there a couple of times," he said, smiling just enough so Michael and Ronan would understand what type of club it was. "I think you two might like it. It's, um, filled with our kind of people."

Well, what do you know? All this time Michael had been wrong. He had never been different, he had never been unnatural, there were others like him, closer than he had ever imagined. He just had to travel halfway around the world to learn not to be scared or ashamed of the person he was always meant to be. And travel halfway back to learn that he had never really been alone.

Driving out of the gas station, the gravel crunching under the tires, Michael didn't see R.J. smile with admiration and pride at the young couple. He just reached out to hold Ronan's hand, the hand that still felt like cool water over rock-hard stone. Staring ahead at the long road ahead of them, Michael was happy. He felt safe and confident. He knew as well as Ronan did that no matter what future obstacles came their way, no matter what hardships they would have to endure, as long as they had each other—and they both knew that they always would—they would never, ever have to be afraid.

**Please turn the page for a special Q & A
with Michael Griffo.**

What's next for you as a writer?

First and foremost I'm thinking of some new characters and some new books to write. That's something that I'm constantly doing, even if I'm working on another project. Sometimes I get a vague idea; other times I get a character's name. Just the other day a girl's name came to me—Dominy Robineaux. So I've decided she'll be the heroine of my next book, *Moonglow*.

At the moment I'm preparing the syllabus for a playwriting class I hope to teach as an adjunct professor for the spring 2012 semester at a college in New Jersey. I've taught a few workshops and seminars in the past, but I've always wanted to teach my own writing class. I'm still awaiting the final word, but I'm optimistic that it'll happen.

In addition, I'm working on a new play after taking some time off to concentrate on novels, so that's exciting. To me, writing is writing, so I really enjoy jumping back and forth between genres. I'm looking forward to seeing how this play develops after working so exclusively in the world of fiction. It should be an interesting journey.

Do you think Michael and Ronan will live happily ever after?

Well . . . happily ever after can spell doom for a couple in the world of fiction, so I'm not sure if I'd say that. However, I know that they will continue to learn from each other and enjoy and experience life as a couple. The reason for that is because I stand by the words I've written in the three books thus far as well as the relationship that has developed between Michael and Ronan, and I believe that no matter what danger they may face they will face it together. These two are a team in every sense of the word and regardless of what the future holds for them, that's how they'll remain. I think it's much more interesting—and challenging to me as a writer—to have them work together against evil than to see them separated by extraneous forces just to further the plot. To me that kind of storytelling is boring because in my heart I know that Michael and Ronan are destined to stay together. If the series does continue, rest assured that it'll be an exciting and adventurous tale, but one that they confront together.

Is David really dead?

Hmmm . . . Yes, for the moment David is a member of the community of the dead. He is in Rhoswen's realm, and she, for the time being, is calling the shots. She's got her big brother back to read her stories for quite a long while. But (and I'm sure you knew a *but* was coming) David is a supernatural creature, and a very powerful one at that, so the normal definitions of life and death don't hold much weight where David's concerned. He sort of transcends those restrictions.

However, as we've learned, supernatural creatures aren't invulnerable, and they can be killed. I guess the real question to ask is, "How long will David stay dead?"

In terms of the storyline, were there things that caught you by surprise while you were writing? Were there plotlines or ideas that were unexpected developments?

There were actually many unexpected developments that arose during the course of writing these three books. As a writer, I'm rather organized, so I began each book with a very detailed outline, somewhere around fifty to sixty pages of specific plot points. So when I began writing I really didn't think that much would change from my outline or that I would be surprised by any major new ideas. Needless to say I was proven wrong on many occasions.

One of the first developments was the true history of Inishtrahull Island and Weeping Water, Nebraska. I chose those locations for specific reasons: I wanted Ronan to come from the northernmost point in Ireland, and I wanted Michael to come from the heartland of America. However, I had no idea that both locations were steeped in legends that had to do with water and bloody battles. These two seemingly random choices were perfect fits for the Archangel Academy series because water and blood are vital elements to the story. I'm not sure if it was luck or the storytelling gods pointing me in the right direction!

I also had no idea that the origin of the white roses was going to play such an important role in the overall story. When I first introduced this interesting, but minor plot point, I thought it was simply a bit of fun, just a nice addition to the Double A folklore. I truly had no idea that they would turn into the huge plot point they eventually became. It was a wonderful surprise to me and hopefully to you readers as well.

When I decided to have Phaedra leave in book two, I cried. Partially because it was so unexpected, but also because it made such perfect sense. Of course, I loved the character so much (especially her name! and I think you've figured out by now that I love really interesting and unique names) that I would have found a way to bring her back into book three even if it didn't make complete sense. Luckily for me (and you), her bonds to Fritz and Michael were still very strong, so it was totally fitting for her to return and play an important role in *Unafraid*.

And finally, I think one of the biggest surprises was the character of Ruby. Originally I had her in one scene in *Unnatural* when her family comes to bring Penry's body back home. She was Penry's older sister and named Cecily. After I submitted the first draft and while I was plotting out *Unwelcome,* the idea hit me that Cecily was really Penry's twin sister and that her name needed to be Ruby because she was going to be possessed by Rhoswen's spirit and Rhoswen means white rose and Ruby is red like the color of blood. Make sense? I also toyed with the idea that Ruby and Penry were born as conjoined twins, but realized that would be a bit of a stretch because conjoined twins are always the same gender. I know the Archangel Academy series is all about the supernatural, but some things just won't fly!

Why do you like writing for a YA audience?

I actually never knew how much I loved writing for the young adult audience until I started. Then for the longest time I just felt an emotional connection to the work and the audience and never questioned it until someone asked me during a book signing and I was forced to articulate my feelings. For me, it's because the YA audience is fearless and without restrictions. They're willing to join a writer for the journey and go wherever the next page may lead without cynicism or preconceived notions, and that is really liberating for a writer. As long as I maintain the architecture and the mythology of the story and don't start changing defined elements halfway through the novel, the audience will accept pretty much anything that's thrown at them. For instance, I can't establish Nakano as a regular vampire and then have him walk in the sunlight in Weeping Water, which is something I actually did in the first draft! I was writing so quickly that during a scene in *Unnatural* I had Michael and Nakano go to Weeping Water for the funeral of Michael's grandmother, and the scene was during the day. Of course when I reread it I had to change it so they traveled at night and Nakano had to stay inside during the day.

The other great thing is that the YA audience is not at all shy about telling you how much they love or hate a character or a particular element of your story. I've gotten such incredible (and, thankfully, mostly wonderful) feedback from young readers. The YA audience is really quite a smart, well-read group, and I thoroughly enjoy writing for them.

What are your favorite books?

Too many to mention or remember, for that matter! However, my absolute favorite book of all time is *Jane Eyre* by Charlotte Brontë. It's a beautifully written and timeless story of one resilient child's ability to overcome terrible adversity. It's also a terrific melding of gothic, supernatural, and romance. I just love it. *The Picture of Dorian Gray* is another favorite of mine that I only read a few months before starting the outline for *Unnatural*. It clearly made a huge impact with me because I made the novel and the author, Oscar Wilde, himself such an integral part of Michael and Ronan's relationship.

Other favorites include John Knowles's *A Separate Peace,* one of the best YA novels of all time, and Alice Sebold's *The Lovely Bones,* which is not generally categorized as a YA novel but is a beautifully told story with a teenage protagonist. I guess I've always loved YA novels and didn't realize it. If my books can be mentioned in the same breath as these wonderful pieces of literature, I will be one very happy writer.